They were settled on the bed amid all the roses. Darius held her hand and looked deeply in her eyes. "Cherish, I know I started taking you for granted. That was not my intention at all."

"I know, Darius." Cherish wondered where he was leading with all this.

Darius hugged and kissed her. His hands roamed over her body, hovering around her breasts. He deepened the kiss, bringing her body closer to his, letting her feel his arousal.

Cherish couldn't believe it. Finally. After four months and all the hints she'd dropped, were they finally going to make love?

Cherish broke from his embrace and sat on the bed. She ran her hands over the soft rose petals, inhaling their sweet floral scent. Darius sat beside her on the bed. He took off her sweater and kissed her neck. "Cherish, can we make love tonight?"

THE FOURSOME

CELYA BOWERS

Genesis Press, Inc.

Indigo Love Spectrum

An imprint of Genesis Press, Inc.
Publishing Company

Genesis Press, Inc.
P.O. Box 101
Columbus, MS 39703

Copyright © 2007 by Celya Bowers

ISBN: 13 DIGIT : 978-158571-256-4
ISBN: 10 DIGIT : 1-58571-256-6
Manufactured in the United States of America

First Edition

Visit us at www.genesis-press.com
or call at 1-888-Indigo-1-4-0

DEDICATION

This book is dedicated to the following people who helped shape me into the person I am and the person I will soon be:

My mother, Celia Mae Bowers Shaw Kenney, for showing me the light at the end of the dark tunnel. I miss you.

Mrs. Van Dora Washington who lost the fight to Alzheimer's in December 2003 and who inspired me to write this novel.

To a woman who had her own special light, Freddie Faye Johnson-Hill, who lost a valiant fight with cancer in October 2006.

To Mrs. Winnie Williams, a very special lady, who passed away in March 2007.

ACKNOWLEDGMENTS

Special thanks:

To my family: Darwyn Tilley, Jeri Murphy, William E. Kenney, Sheila Kenney, Kim Kenney, Shannon Murphy, Rod Kenney, Yolanda Tilley, and Celya Tilley, for keeping me grounded.

To my readers: Kenneth Portley, Judy Brown, Natasha Swindle, and Melody Alvarado, for your input.

To my crew: Cherry Elder, Erica Black, Eulanda Bailey, Sharon Hickman-Mahones, Lester Brown, Lisa-Lin Burke, Roslin William, Linda Hodges, Darlene Ramzy, De Andra Garrett, Brandye McCool, Huini Mwangi, Michella Chappell and Annette Freeman, for always having my back.

To my military connection: Lawrence Leonard (Navy), Brad Northcutt (Air Force), Tom Paine (Air Force), and Justin Thompkins (Navy) for protecting the country at all times.

To the members of Celya's Corner: Sherry Ramsey, Stacey Plummer, Gail Coleman-Surles, Janice Coleman, Winston Williams, Veta Holt, Jacoby Stennett, John Brown, Jessica Kenney, Janet Kenney, Sherry Kenney, Elliot Charles, Kimberly Williams, Marnese Elder, Kerry Elder, Lesley Paine, Paula Washington, Mary Thompkins, Mary Bell, and Paula W., thanks for being there for me.

To my critique group, The Sizzling Sisterhood: Diane O'Brien Kelly, Angela (Cinnamon) Cavener, and Shaunnette Smith, for all your insight.

If I've forgotten anyone, charge it to my head not my heart.

Peace and Sanity,

Celya

PROLOGUE

Darius Crawford walked into his childhood home expecting to see his newly retired father practicing his golf swing in the living room, as he had every day for the last two years.

His father had summoned him and his sister Darbi to have dinner. That could only mean bad news. His sister hadn't made it to the house yet. He heard his father rummaging through his desk in his office.

"Where did I put that list?" he heard his father say. "I just had it. I must have left it on the . . ." His father's sentence drifted into space as he noticed Darius standing in the doorway watching him.

"Hey, Dad. Can I help you find something?" Darius's usually calm father had been jittery lately. Another bad sign. Today, he was dressed in a polo shirt and slacks. At least that was normal, Darius thought.

"No," came his father's short reply. "Just wait in the other room."

Darius nodded, taking his six-foot-three-inch frame to the living room. Just as he sat down on the comfortable suede sofa, he heard the front door open and close. He smiled as his sister walked in and plopped down beside him.

"Hey, Darius. What's up with Dad?" Darbi Crawford asked her older brother. "You think he's mad because I found my own place?"

"No, Darbi. You've been back almost a year. It was time. I think it's something else. Besides, when have you known Dad not to speak his mind?"

She laughed. "True. I called him the other day and he nearly bit my head off. Then he asked me about something that made no sense whatsoever. He asked me about Amos, as if he were still alive."

Darius nodded, holding his breath at the mention of his dead brother-in-law. He had noticed his father's forgetfulness, but hadn't wanted to say anything. Something was wrong with the strongest man he knew.

Otis Crawford walked into the living room with a stack of papers in his hand. He sat across from Darius and Darbi in his favorite chair.

"I know you're wondering why I asked you here today. I went to the doctor a few days ago for a follow-up to some tests I took a few weeks ago," he explained.

"What is it, Dad?" Darius hoped it wasn't something terminal.

"Well, I've been having some problems remembering things lately. I was supposed to meet the guys for golf and I went to the wrong course. I missed an important luncheon at the senior center and the board meeting at the church. I mentioned this to the doctor at my yearly physical a few months ago and he thought of a few things that could cause it. Dementia, Alzheimer's, you know, all the things you don't want to hear. So he ran a few tests."

Darius choked the words out. "What is it?"

Otis looked at his children. "It's Alzheimer's," Otis whispered. "Doc said it's good that we caught it this early. He said most people don't realize something is wrong until it's almost too late to do anything. But with the progress they've made with the disease in the last few years, I could live up to twenty years with it. But lifestyle changes will have to be made."

Darius's heart sank at those words. "What kind of changes?"

Otis stared at his son with sympathetic eyes. "I know you just finished building your house last year and haven't really gotten used to it yourself, but the doctor suggested that I live with a family member. He also said that eventually I'd need a nurse. I know that house has been your dream for more years than I want to count, but your place is big enough for me and a nurse."

Darius nodded, too afraid to say anything. He knew if he opened his mouth the wrong words would come tumbling out. Being the oldest, he should have figured whatever it was would fall on his shoulders. He had just moved into his custom designed five-bedroom house less than a year ago and now his father and nurse would take up an entire wing. Just his rotten luck, he thought.

His father continued. "I'm selling this house. Between that, my retirement, stocks and bonds, I should have enough to pay for the nurse."

Finally, Darius found some courage. "Dad, money isn't an issue. However . . ." He let the sentence drop.

"What is it?" Otis asked impatiently.

"It's just that today I was named vice-president of marketing and my workload will increase. I worry about you being there alone with a stranger." Especially if his father would eventually lose his memory.

Otis smiled. "Congratulations, Son. I knew that job would one day be yours. Don't worry about the nurse. The doctor referred me to a reputable agency to find one. Since it's your house, you can interview her when the time comes. But I get final say-so."

Twenty years of hard work at Sloane, Hart, and Lagrone had finally paid off for Darius. He was vice-president. This should be the happiest time of his life. But the news of his father's illness took all the wind out of his sails. He would gladly trade that promotion for his father.

"Dad, I wouldn't have it any other way. What do you need from us?" He knew that his father would also have to sell his prized possession, his restored 1969 Corvette. His father loved driving it.

"Well, I have a few things I need to get in order. I appreciate this. I know this isn't what you envisioned, but I am grateful."

Again Darius nodded. He watched tears slide down his father's weathered, dark brown face. Darius wished he were strong enough in his manhood to cry.

"Dad, we can both help you," Darbi said, wiping her eyes. "I can keep you company during the day and we can do exercises to keep you active."

Otis shook his head at his daughter. "I thought we agreed that you were going to give college a try. You've been offered a second chance. Don't let it slip away."

"I'd rather stay with you," Darbi said softly.

"No. You're going to enjoy your life. I don't want you holding no bedside vigil. Is that understood?"

Darbi nodded. "All right. You win."

Darius smiled, albeit sadly. All their lives were about to take a serious change. But how would that fit in with his work schedule?

CHAPTER ONE

Six months later

"It's time, Cherish. You can do this," Cherish Murray chanted to herself, grasping the doorknob of her late mother's room.

Though her sweet mother had gone to her great reward over nine months ago, Cherish still lacked the courage to sort out her mother's belongings. The room held so many painful memories. But it was time. She opened the door, sneezing as the dust settled.

The corner where the hospital bed had stood for over five years was now empty. Slowly and carefully she began going through her mother's belongings. Each dress told a story of its own: Cherish had gotten the purple dress for her mother to wear on Mother's Day and the pink one for her 65th birthday, which would have been the coming week.

She picked up and gently caressed the gold-framed picture of her mother, wiping away the tears as they spilled against the glass. "I wish I could take all those years back, Mama, those years when I thought I didn't have time to visit. I wish we could have had more time." She took a deep breath and put the picture in a box of things she'd keep.

She looked toward the heavens and made a vow. "I will make this up to you, Mama. I know I wasn't there for you when you needed me, but somehow, someway, I will make this up to you." She retrieved more clothes from the closet.

Cherish continued to wipe away tears as she folded dresses and put them in the box marked *Shelter*. She folded bed jackets, robes, and other items. Soon the box was full. She was just leaving the room when the phone rang.

She ran to her room to answer it. Her lips curved upward in a smile as she recognized the caller.

"Hello, sweetie," said the familiar voice.

"Hello, Aunt Diane," Cherish said, sitting on her bed.

"Have you cleaned out your mother's room yet? It's been nine months. Cherish, you can't blame yourself for the past."

"I could have helped her more than I did in the beginning." Cherish paused. "But to answer your question, yes, I just finished." She grabbed a Kleenex and wiped her eyes. She heard her aunt talking, but it wasn't registering. Her mind had floated back to that dreadful day.

"Cherish, I have Alzheimer's," Margaret told her only daughter during her monthly visit.

"Mama, why didn't you tell me earlier?" Cherish faced her mother, determined not to shed a tear.

Margaret watched her daughter struggle for control. "When, Cherish? Before or after your report on your job successes?"

Cherish wanted to say that her job hadn't taken precedence, but it had. She had noticed her mother hadn't looked well the last few months, but had said nothing, fearing it might interfere with her life. "How long have you had it?"

Margaret handed her the latest report from the clinic. "The doctor suggested I either move in with a relative or into an Alzheimer's nursing home."

Cherish quickly scanned the paper, but the words were blurry. "Mama, according to this, you're in the second phase. How many phases are there?"

Margaret spoke softly. "There are three."

"And you're at phase two! You're more than half-way into this mess and now you tell me!" Cherish yelled. Then immediately she said, "I'm sorry, Mama. I wasn't yelling at you. How have you been getting to the doctor? Your medicines?"

"Diane."

"Aunt Diane took you to the doctor all this time without saying one word to me!"

Her mother nodded. "I didn't want to burden you," she added in a voice that broke Cherish's heart.

"Cherish?" Her aunt called her name again louder. "Cherish!"

She heard her name and realized she'd become lost in the past. "I'm sorry, Auntie, what were you saying?"

"You can't change the past. It's gone. That's why I called. You can do something about your future. A friend told me about a support class at the college, and I thought about you."

"I already have a degree," Cherish teased her aunt.

"I know that, smarty. This is a support group. It meets on Wednesday nights. So you have five days to get ready for it."

Cherish loved her only aunt dearly. Even though she knew that her aunt meant well, Diane Prudehome sometimes overstepped the boundaries of being an aunt. "Auntie, I'm fine. I've been working on my designs really hard. I have been thinking about other things besides Mama."

Cherish tried to speak confidently, so her aunt wouldn't worry about her so much. "It's a slow process for me. You know she was both mother and father to me. So it's like I lost both parents at once. She worked two jobs to put me through college."

"Cherish, she was my sister and I miss her too. This group is for the children of Alzheimer's patients. You spent the last five years of your life helping with your mother's care. Luckily, you were able to work from your home, but now you have to start living. It will be good for you to know other survivors. Call me and tell me how it goes."

Cherish looked at the receiver as it hummed at her. She knew she had to go to that class or her aunt would hound her until she did. At least she had a few days to get used to the idea. She walked into her large bathroom and looked at her face in the mirror. Her usually blemish-free honey brown skin was a little spotty. It had been a long nine months and her grief had taken the form of acne. As she stood there, she heard the annoying beep of her fax machine in the background, her cue to return to work. She walked briskly to her office down the hall.

~~~

"Hey, Mr. Vice-president. I got something for you." Curran Fitzgerald sauntered into his friend's office. He yawned as he put a folded piece of paper on the desk and sat in the chair, grunting like a man of eighty.

Darius smiled at his friend. He loved hearing the term vice-president. And because he was the first African-American to be promoted to executive status, he was very proud. His friend Curry was Irish-American, with curly dark blonde hair and hazel eyes women just went nuts for. "Rough night? I told you Tamara was too young for you." Darius spoke of the redhead who had been occupying Curry's nights lately.

Curry smiled tiredly, then yawned again. "I was the victim of a moshing." He expelled an exhausted breath.

"And that is what?"

"That is a group of young people who don't have a day job, jumping around like they are crazy." He yawned again, leaning back in the leather chair.

"Was it really worth it?" Darius already knew the answer, but wanted his free-spirited friend to finally admit chasing those young girls left him empty.

"No. I woke up this morning on my couch and had to crawl upstairs. I had to take some muscle relaxers just to get dressed for work."

"When are you going to date someone closer to your age? Those young girls see a guy with money and that's all. Curry, you deserve better."

That statement brought Curry erect in the chair. He let out a dramatic sigh and shoved a flier toward his friend so he would stop talking. "I know, Darius. I'm just having fun."

Darius nodded, knowing his friend did not like discussing the fact that he dated so many different young women, unlike Darius, who rarely dated. The outcome was still the same: loneliness. He turned his attention to the flier. "What's this, Curry? You know I've got a meeting this afternoon."

"I know you have a meeting, I do too. Remember, I'm the director of advertising. My friend Sean is hosting a class I thought you might want to attend." Curry ran his hands through his hair, a sure sign he was uncomfortable discussing the subject at hand. "It's called 'Children of Alzheimer's Patients: How to Cope with Your Parents and Not Feel Guilty.' Sean says it's an awesome class for adult children having to take care of a parent."

Darius opened the flier and read the information. Now it was his turn to let out a dramatic sigh. He didn't like discussing his father's illness. His father had been living with him for only three months, and he both resented it and felt guilty for resenting it. "Thanks for the concern, Curry, but I don't know about this." Darius hesitated. It would be nice to talk to others in his position, but he kept envisioning those Alcoholics Anonymous meetings that he had seen on TV. *My name is Darius*

Crawford. My father has Alzheimer's and I feel guilty about him living with me.

Curry smiled as Darius weakened. "Dare, you should go, it will help. It will kind of give you a heads up on the disease. I know ever since your father announced he has Alzheimer's you've been frightened because you don't know anything about it. This way you can learn right along with him. You probably should ask the rest of your family to go as well. Has the nurse moved in yet?"

"Not yet. She's supposed to move in this weekend," Darius said. The life he'd worked so hard for the last twenty years was fading away. "My sister would probably go, since she's helping with Dad as well."

~~~

Later that evening, Darius and Curry walked down the halls of Fort Worth University, a private college in Fort Worth, searching for the classroom with the meeting. Curry tried to ease Darius's fears.

"Darius, it will be fine." He stopped walking. "Here it is. Look, there are quite a few people in there already." He guided his friend into the room, and they took a seat.

Darius gazed around the classroom, taking inventory of the attendees. Though the other people looked as if they came from every walk of life, he saw very few African-Americans in the room. He thought that was strange since Alzheimer's knew no racial boundaries and was becoming more prevalent in the black community.

"I'm going to say hello to Sean. I'll be back," Curry said as he stood and walked toward his friend.

A tall African-American woman sat down beside Darius. "Sorry I'm late," Darbi said, patting her brother's knee. "How are things going?"

"Pretty good." Darius smiled at his sister with pride. She was definitely a survivor. She had endured who knew what during her marriage. Luckily, that jerk of a husband had died. "Did you register for college?"

"Yes, I registered. I even got a part-time job there," she said proudly.

"My offer for you to move in still stands."

Darbi smiled. With smooth, medium brown skin, wavy hair and a big smile that hid sorrow and heartache very well, she was the exact image of their mother. If only she could let go of her past and find the happiness she deserved, he thought.

"Darius, Dad lives with you. Soon the nurse will be there full-time. That's enough people living with you, especially when you weren't counting on any of this."

As Darius opened his mouth to reply, he noticed Curry walking back toward him. Curry's hazel eyes lit up with challenge as he noticed Darbi sitting next to Darius. Darius hated that look. Since a broken heart was often the end result, Darius would have to run interference. Reluctantly, he introduced them. "Curry Fitzgerald, this is my sister, Darbi." Darius watched as they exchanged pleasantries.

She leaned toward her brother and whispered, "You never mentioned that he wasn't black. I did think Curry was an odd name for a brother."

Curry coughed loudly, no doubt hearing Darbi's remark. "Darius tells me that you just returned to Fort Worth last year. How long were you away?"

"Almost fifteen years. My husband was from Philadelphia, and we moved back there after we married. He was killed in a car wreck last year, so I came home," Darbi said simply, as if those events hadn't saved her life.

Curry nodded. Another voice interrupted the conversation.

"Hello, I'm Sean Cummings. I'm a psychologist by day. This class or session is for people who have either lost their loved ones to Alzheimer's or have loved ones who have it now. First, why don't we introduce ourselves, and tell what stage your parent or loved one is in."

One by one, members of the class stood up. Darius noticed every one of the three stages seemed to be represented.

He gazed around the room. It was the turn of a beautiful African-American woman with light brown skin accented by dark shoulder length hair. That body-hugging suit didn't hurt either. He had watched the silent woman since the class started. She'd fidgeted in her chair, then tapped her stiletto clad feet. What was her story?

Wiping her eyes, the woman took a deep breath and looked toward the ceiling. Then she stood and began to speak in a shaky voice. "My name is Cherish Murray. My mother, Margaret, passed away nine months ago. She suffered with Alzheimer's for the last seven years of her life." She exhaled and took a seat.

Darius watched her as her breathing returned to normal. After a few more people spoke, it was his turn. He wiped his sweaty palms on his slacks and stood up. "My name is Darius Crawford. My father, Otis, is in phase one." He sat down.

Throughout the meeting, Cherish tried to let the guilt leave her body, one bad deed at a time. She even asked a few questions. Could she have prolonged her mother's life if she had known more about the disease? Would she have been more understanding? Would she have recognized the symptoms? Hot, moist tears trickled down her face as she relived the past.

She wiped her eyes with the back of her hand, glancing around the room. She could sympathize with so many people. Especially the tall, dark-skinned man and his sister. They had a very long road ahead of them.

After feeling cold during most of the class, Cherish was glad when they finally were able to take a break. She walked over to the coffee pot and poured a cup of warmth.

"I'm sorry to hear about your mother." The woman offered her condolescences.

"Thank you. She suffered a long time."

"I just can't imagine my dad not knowing me or my brother, though I know it'll happen. I think that's what scares me the most. Oh by the way, my name is Darbi Crawford." She extended her hand to Cherish.

Cherish nodded, taking her hand. "I'm Cherish Murray, nice to meet you. I know what you mean about them forgetting you. In the last year my mother thought I was some woman she knew as a teenager and hated. Sometimes she thought I was my aunt, her sister. At first it hurt, but in the end, I got used to it."

CHAPTER TWO

After next week's session, Cherish, Curry, Darbi, and Darius decided to go to Starbuck's, which was across the street from the college. After everyone settled at the table, Cherish found herself sitting next to Darius. Cherish discreetly examined his long, manicured fingers. She wondered what he did for a living to have such well-kept nails.

"How's your father?" Cherish asked.

Darius looked at Cherish and smiled. "He's doing pretty good. He hasn't killed the nurse yet." Darius, Darbi, and Curry laughed. Cherish felt left out of the private joke until Darius explained.

"My dad is very independent; he doesn't take kindly to orders. Especially from a woman."

"Oh." Cherish nodded. "My mom was the same. She was running off the nurses quicker than I could hire them. I ended up working from home to help with her care." She wiped her eyes at the memory of her mother throwing a vase at a retreating nurse.

"We didn't mean to upset you." Darius placed his hand on Cherish's in sympathy.

"You didn't. Really."

"How about we change the subject?" Darius handed Cherish a linen handkerchief.

Cherish nodded, afraid to let him know how much his gallant action melted her heart. "How's school, Darbi?" Cherish wiped her eyes.

"Frightening," Darbi admitted. "Everyone is so young, except in my history and English classes. There are actually people my age in those classes."

Curry looked up from his coffee cup and cleared his throat. "And how old is that?"

Three sets of eyes stared at Curry in disbelief.

"I was just curious," he explained to his audience.

Darbi smiled. "I'm 38, Curry."

"Wow, I thought you were younger."

Darius toyed with his coffee cup. Then he coughed, looked at his friend, and spoke. "Why don't we get this age thing over with? Curry, here, is 43. I'm 44. And you are?" Darius looked at Cherish.

"I'm 39. The girls are younger!" Cherish and Darbi high-fived each other in celebration.

~~~~~~

When Cherish arrived home later that evening, she began mentally replaying the scene at the coffee shop. Had Darius actually been staring at her as much as she thought? *Quit borrowing trouble.*

Darius had enough going on in his life without a guilt-ridden woman swooning over him. With a sigh, she prepared for bed. The phone rang, interrupting her nightly face cleansing routine.

"I know it's late," Darbi apologized, "but I was wondering if you'd like to go out for dinner or something."

Cherish hesitated, not quite knowing how to answer.

"I'm not asking for a date, Cherish," Darbi reassured her in her soft voice. "It's just that I really don't know anyone here anymore. I mean, Darius has been great, but he has a life, too. However boring," Darbi added.

Cherish smiled. She thought Darius was stiff as well. In fact, nerdy would be a more accurate term. "I'm pretty much in the same boat as you. I was taking care of my mom for so long, I lost touch with most of my friends. Dinner sounds great. How about tomorrow?"

"I can't tomorrow." Darbi paused. "I'm watching Dad. It's the nurse's evening off. Darius plays racquetball with Curry on Thursdays," she added unnecessarily.

"How about Friday night, then? We could go to Restaurant Row or something. You know, have a real girls night out." Although she genuinely liked Darbi, Cherish had an ulterior motive. She wanted some insight into Darius and this might be her only chance.

"That sounds great, Cherish," Darbi said cheerfully. "I'll meet you downtown, if that's okay. I live near there."

"Sure." Cherish was amazed at how chipper Darbi sounded. She must be a night person, Cherish reasoned. "How about eight at the Fountain? We could have a drink before dinner."

Darbi agreed, and the women ended their call.

Thursday evening, Darius was already dressed for the gym by the time Darbi arrived at his house. He looked at his sister with pride. At thirty-eight, she had a second chance for a fresh start. He was determined to make sure she reached her goal this time. During the course of her marriage she'd endured so much in the name of pride. It was a wonder she wasn't crying now.

Darbi thought she was overweight, no matter how many times he told her that she wasn't. Her tall, healthy frame had already attracted the attention of Darius's neighbor, John. But John was married with children. He'd immediately backed off, once Darius told him that she was his sister. Darius thought since she had gotten her hair cut short, she looked twenty-two. The fact that she was wearing shorts and a Fort Worth University t-shirt reinforced her youthful appearance. She smiled at him as she entered the house.

"Darius, you're going to be late. Your gym is at least twenty minutes away."

He smiled as his sister tried to shoo him out of his house. He shook his head. "Curry is coming to get me."

"Why?"

"He said he was going to be in the area. The gym is actually closer to him, since he lives in Arlington." Darius thought it was strange, but didn't question his friend's motives.

Darbi shrugged, dropping the case of Curry Fitzgerald. "I brought my homework with me. How's Dad?"

"He's fine. He was trying to write a letter or something earlier when I looked in on him. He said he might ask you to write it for him." Darius didn't know if it was guilt or hurt that he felt because his father hadn't asked him.

"Okay. I really do like the time we spend together."

Darius nodded as he searched his gym bag. "My ID. It must be upstairs." He made for the stairs. "If Curry comes, tell him I'll be right back."

~~~~~

Darius panted and leaned against the wall of the racquetball court for support. His favorite Nike t-shirt was now soaked with sweat. He knew he hadn't heard Curry correctly. "They're going where?"

Curry panted and fell to the floor in exhaustion. "Darbi . . . said . . . they . . . were . . . going . . . out . . . to dinner." He took a deep breath between each word.

Darius couldn't believe it. He was glad his sister had made a new friend, but he wanted to ask Cherish out. Eventually. Would he be competing with his sister for Cherish's attention? He reached out his hand to help his friend up. Darius thought about just showing up—if he only knew where they were going.

After Curry dropped him off, Darius walked into his house, deep in thought. He wondered if Darbi would tell him where they were going. He walked to his father's room in search of his sister. She wasn't there. His father sat up in bed scribbling in his journal. Darbi had suggested it to keep his mind active. Darius appreciated it for the small victory it was.

"Hey Dad, how's it going?"

"Pretty good. How was racquetball?" Otis put his journal away, smiling at his son.

"It was fine." Darius fidgeted with the doorknob, searching for something to keep the conversation going. "When is your next doctor's appointment?" Darius reached inside his bag for his computer organizer to check his schedule. Hopefully he wouldn't have to miss a meeting. His father's answer stopped him.

"Tomorrow afternoon. Darbi is taking me. You know, I'm so proud of the way you took me in without any reservations, and the way Darbi's helping out by taking me to the doctor. I know this was not in your plans when you had this house built."

Darius choked back his guilt. *If his father only knew.* "You're my dad. I know you would do the same." Darius walked out of the room to find his sister before he started apologizing to his father for feeling guilty. He finally located her outside by the pool. She was sitting on the edge with her feet in the water.

Darbi turned as she heard the door open. "How was racquetball?"

He pretended not to see his sister's tears, deciding not to pressure her into talking about the past. Since her return to Fort Worth last year, Darbi hadn't been very forthcoming about the details of her marriage or her husband's demise. She'll talk when she's ready, he kept telling himself. Darius sat by her. "Fine. How's Dad doing? He seems in pretty good spirits."

"He's actually doing well. He's been writing in his journal. He can remember some little things, like the way Mom looked the day he met her. He can remember the details, but not the date."

Darius, being a man, didn't see the importance. "So?"

Darbi looked at her brother. "How did you graduate top in your class at Princeton? You have the sensitivity of cardboard." She sighed. "Dad met our mother, Valentina, on Valentine's Day."

CHAPTER THREE

Darius sat in his home office reflecting on the last three months of his life. Going to the sessions had definitely helped him to kinda sorta come to grips with his father's illness. His sister had found a new friend in Cherish. That gave his heart a lift.

He'd also found Cherish easy to talk to as well. That is when he had enough courage to talk to her. Something about the way she looked at him with those sultry eyes did crazy things to his usually well-behaved hormones. He wanted to ask her out for a date, but didn't know how.

When the phone rang, Darius wondered who would dare interrupt his Saturday morning routine. He sat his oversized coffee cup down, lowered the volume on the Duke Ellington CD, and went to answer the summons. Shocked at the sound of Cherish's sexy voice at the other end, he dropped the cordless phone onto the carpeted floor. Not believing his luck, he hurriedly retrieved it and spoke again.

"I hope I didn't startle you?" Cherish cleared her throat, attempting to hold back her laughter.

"No, the phone slipped," Darius lied.

"I was wondering if you were free for lunch today. Nothing fancy, just lunch."

Could this really be his chance? "Yes, I'm free. I don't know about Darbi. I haven't heard from her today."

Cherish laughed. "I wasn't calling for you and Darbi, just for you."

Darius smiled. The gods were with him today. "I would be delighted to join you for lunch. Where?"

"How about Cleo's? It's in downtown Fort Worth. About one?"

He couldn't tell her that he worked downtown across the street from the home-style restaurant and ate there often. "Sounds great. I'll see you there." He smiled as he hung up.

Darius was already at the restaurant when Cherish arrived that afternoon. He watched as she gracefully exited her car and walked across the street. Her shoulder-length hair was pulled back in a ponytail and bounced as she walked. The short denim skirt showcased her smooth legs and her cotton sweater gave a hint of cleavage. He guessed her as four or five inches shy of his own six-three height. Dressed in business casual slacks, button-down shirt and a tie, Darius felt overdressed.

"Hi, Darius. Have you been waiting long?"

"No, I had just walked up to the entrance when I spotted you."

After they got their food, they settled down at the table. Darius nervously picked at his lasagna, wishing he had Curry's charisma.

"Darius, you can look at me," Cherish teased. She was nervous as well.

Darius breathed a little easier. "I'm glad you called. I've been wanting to ask you out for a long time."

"Darius, you stare at me all the time. I've been waiting for you to ask me out. After months went by and you didn't, I thought I'd ask you."

Darius smiled. He had wanted to ask her out for so long, but didn't know how. A woman asking him out would have normally turned him off instantly, but with Cherish, just like everything else about her, she did it with class. "Where do you work?"

"Actually, I work at home. Officially, for Hervé Zar," Cherish boasted.

"The designer?" Darius asked, instantly impressed.

"Yes. I started with him right after college. He was great while Mama was ill. He let me work from home and I sent my drawings in by messenger. I liked the arrangement so much that I decided to keep it after she passed away. However, I sometimes feel so out of touch with people." Cherish realized that she was rambling and changed the subject. "What do you do?"

Darius smiled. "I'm vice-president of marketing at Sloane, Hart, and Lagrone. I'm glad that you and Darbi have become friends."

"I am, too. She has so much energy. I know that she really enjoys the time she spends with your father."

"Yes. It seems since she came back home, she's a lot more laid back."

"She said she's been given a second chance. She wants to enjoy life." Cherish leaned across the table, giving him a bird's-eye view of her breasts, and whispered, "I'm not prying, Darius, but Darbi has talked about her marriage. It sounded horrible. Why didn't she come back sooner?"

"Pride," Darius said, failing to keep the regret out of his voice. "Stupid pride." Darius relaxed in Cherish's company. She didn't ask about his stock portfolio, assets, or what kind of car he drove. She asked about his family.

After they finished lunch, Darius walked Cherish to her Chevy Blazer. Feeling comfortable in her presence, he decided to just go for it. "How about dinner tonight?"

Surprise etched on her face, she answered, "You're on."

Darius opened his mouth, but nothing came out. She'd said yes. He coughed and cleared his throat. "How about Costa's Greek Restaurant? I could pick you up about seven."

Cherish agreed and gave him her address. With the briefest kiss on her cheek, he closed her door, and she drove away.

Darius walked to his Yukon with a smile plastered on his face.

⌐⌐⌐

Darbi browsed through the medical section at the local bookstore in downtown Fort Worth. She'd decided she wanted to learn more about her father's illness. She found five books that she wanted, but her budget would only allow for two.

She took them to the coffee shop area of the book-store. After ordering a café mocha, she sat at a vacant table and started leafing through them, quickly learning more about Alzheimer's than she wanted to know. She dreaded the years ahead. A voice interrupted her thoughts.

"Hi, Darbi."

"Hi, Curry. What are you doing here?"

He sat down with his coffee and a sports magazine. "Long story."

"It's Saturday. I have time to listen," Darbi suggested, looking directly at Curry. He and Darius seemed total opposites. Where Darius was staid, Curry seemed a free spirit. Today he was dressed in a sweatshirt and jeans. Darius would never dress that casually.

"Well, I was supposed to have a date later tonight. You know how it is, you make a date and then decide you and that person have very little or nothing in common. So I called her and told her that I didn't want to date her anymore. She made it into this huge scene and asked me to meet her here so we could talk. I didn't want to, but I did."

"Before you dumped her, huh?" Darbi interrupted him, remembering Darius's tales of Curry's dates.

"I just didn't see the point of going out on a date that I didn't want to go on. That's not enough for me any-more. Anyway, she finally got the message. So while I was here, I thought that I would browse around a little. Then I noticed that you were here and thought I would join you. I love coming here. It's always so peaceful. Why are you here?" Curry couldn't seem to keep his hands still. Nervously, he ran his fingers through his hair.

Darbi shifted her books. For some reason she needed to keep her hands busy as well. This was just Curry, she reminded herself. He was Darius's best friend, and was just being nice. "I thought I'd research Dad's illness."

"Good idea. How's school?"

"Better. It's almost time for midterms, though. I didn't realize how much studying college required."

"Yes. I remember that when I was at the University of Washington, I barely had time to party." Curry winked one of his hazel eyes at her.

Darbi laughed. She liked her brother's friend. He always made her laugh. "Well, I don't think I'll be attending any parties. Darius would kill me."

"Where is Darius?"

Darbi shrugged her shoulders as she played with her coffee cup, avoiding Curry's hazel eyes. "I don't know. I haven't talked to him today. I went to aerobics this morning."

"Oh." He smiled at Darbi, watching as she flipped aimlessly through the books. "How about something stronger?"

"I'm sorry?" Darbi was puzzled.

Curry laughed. "You know, a drink with alcohol in it. There's a pub right across the street."

"I don't know, Curry." Darbi hesitated, recalling Darius's tales of Curry's many escapades. A scene with a blonde throwing a glass of wine in his face quickly flashed through her mind.

Curry continued as if she had already said yes. "Come on, I promise, I'll be good."

Darbi weakened. What could one drink hurt? Besides, he was Darius's best friend and he was white, so she knew she definitely wasn't his type. "All right, Curry. One drink."

Curry smiled. "One drink."

One drink turned into dinner at a restaurant down the street from the pub. Darbi wasn't used to all the attention that she was getting from Curry. He pulled her chair out for her and asked her what she wanted to eat.

"What do you recommend?" Darbi asked Curry as he pretended to look at the menu.

"The surf and turf is good. So is the baked chicken with lemon. The shrimp and pasta is great, too."

"You must eat here a lot," Darbi reasoned as she studied the menu.

"Usually at least once a week," Curry said.

The waiter took their order. Darbi decided on the shrimp and pasta. The waiter kept looking at Darbi after she gave her order. Curry coughed discreetly.

The tall waiter smiled at Darbi. "I'm sorry for staring. Do you have English with Professor Thomkins at Fort Worth University?"

"Yes, I do. How did you do on the test?"

The waiter grinned. "Not as good as I had hoped. I made an 88. How did you do?"

Darbi smiled; with Cherish's help she'd done quite well. "I made a 94."

"So you're the one who wrecked the curve? A 94 is like making a 100 in any other teacher's class. Rumor has it no one makes above a 90 on any of his tests."

Darbi had thought that the class was hard for her because of her age and having been out of school so long. Thank goodness, it was that the professor was just a hard teacher. "Really?" She smiled with pride. "I studied hard enough."

The waiter cast a nervous glance in Curry's direction, then said, "Hey, maybe the next test we could study together?"

"That would be fun. It might help me." Darbi watched as the waiter wrote his name and phone number on a napkin, handing it to her. She did the same. The waiter smiled and left the table.

Curry said in a loud whisper, "You know, that guy didn't have studying in mind."

"I know," Darbi said, giggling.

"You know, he might be twenty," Curry commented. Jealousy might as well have been written in bright red letters onto his pale skin.

"I know. I'm not going to keep his number, Curry. It's just nice that someone asked for my phone number."

"You could always give it to me." He winked one of those sexy hazel eyes at her and smiled.

Costa's Restaurant was every bit as elegant as it had been described in the newspaper. Housed on the top floor of the Reunion Tower in downtown Dallas, the elegant Greek restaurant was everything Cherish could have wished from a date with Darius Crawford. After they were shown to their table, Cherish rose to enjoy the skyline view from the tower.

The bright lights and noises made her realize how much she'd missed the allure of downtown. While her mother was sick, Cherish seldom went anywhere. Standing there, she watched people milling around West End Market Place, a popular weekend spot for tourists as well as locals. She'd like to walk around after dinner, maybe even get some high calorie ice cream, but couldn't see Darius doing something that spontaneous. She walked back to her seat.

Darius smiled as Cherish returned to the table. "You look pretty tonight, Cherish." He choked out the words. Complimenting women didn't come as naturally to him as to Curry.

"Thank you, Darius." Cherish sipped her wine and looked at the menu. She couldn't decide between the salted fish, a Greek delicacy, or the steamed lobster. "Have you been here before?"

"Curry brought me here for my birthday last year. The lobster is excellent."

Cherish decided on the lobster and Darius chose the steak. The waiter took their order and left the table.

After dinner, Darius drove around the lake near his home, giving Cherish an informal tour of the area. Soft jazz music played in the background, melting Cherish's resolve. Looking at Darius's chiseled features, she longed to run her fingers over his face, touch his full lips and maybe even taste them. But as Darius turned onto her street, she realized that she wouldn't get the chance.

He parked, exited, and walked to her side of the truck to open the door and help her out. At her front door, he finally made eye contact with her.

"What are you doing tomorrow?" He unlocked the front door for her.

"Not much. I thought about calling Darbi," Cherish said as she walked into the entryway of her house.

"Well, how about coming over for brunch tomorrow? Darbi will be there and you could meet our dad."

Cherish didn't know if she was ready to face another Alzheimer's patient yet. "I don't know, Darius. When my mom was sick, she was real skittish around people." Cherish remembered her mother throwing a vase and other things at Cherish's aunt in those last dreadful months of her life.

"Dad likes the attention. Curry usually drops by. He and Dad always talk about political issues and the economy. Personally, those subjects bore me, so Dad really does enjoy talking to other people. I think it helps keep his mind active."

It would be nice to meet him before he gets really sick, she thought. "All right, Darius. I would like to talk to Darbi as well." She just didn't tell him that he would be the topic of discussion.

"Great! Brunch is at one. I live at 2461 Canal Street, by the lake. If you get lost, just call, and I'll walk you through the directions."

Cherish nodded, knowing that wouldn't be necessary. Darbi had already given her directions to Darius's house months ago. "Okay, Darius. I had a nice time. Thanks for dinner." She waited.

Darius nodded. He kissed her on the cheek and was gone by the time she turned on her living room lamp.

CHAPTER FOUR

Sunday morning, Darius rose early, needing to prepare a menu for brunch. To his surprise, when he walked into the kitchen to make some coffee, both coffee and breakfast were ready and waiting. It was barely after seven. He shook his head and laughed, knowing who the genie was. His father's nurse, Elisabeth Collins, had fixed breakfast even though he'd told her several times that it was unnecessary. Apparently, Mrs. Collins disagreed with him.

She walked into the kitchen as if on cue. Darius took the opportunity to plead his case again. "Mrs. Collins, you don't have to do this, as I have said before." Darius fixed himself a *fry-up* as she called the sausage, eggs, and potatoes.

"I know, Mr. Crawford. But your father is doing well and I really don't have to be here full-time. I feel better doing other chores as well," she said in her proper British accent. She sneaked a peek at the piece of paper he'd scribbled his notes on. "I can make brunch for you today as well."

"No, Mrs. Collins," Darius countered, using his executive voice that usually sent underlings at work running for the hills. "I appreciate you being here and your cooking for Dad. I'll fix brunch."

"No, Mr. Crawford," she said in a tone that matched his. "I've been in this country for twenty years, and I've never accepted anything I didn't earn. I am not about to start now. Coffee?"

Darius knew the discussion was closed. He nodded and held out his cup. He now knew why his crusty father got along so well with her. She didn't take any lip from anyone. "All right, Mrs. Collins. You can fix brunch. Can we have it about one? I have a lady friend coming over this time."

"That's wonderful, Mr. Crawford! You work much too hard." She smiled as she heard the front door opening. "That will be your sister. She called last night, while you were out. I'll make shepherd's pie if that's all right. Everyone loves that."

Darius nodded and enjoyed the rest of his breakfast. Originally, he'd had doubts about hiring the nurse, not knowing how his very black father would react to a white female nurse, who wasn't even American, but she had turned out to be a good choice. She had only been in the house a few months, and already Darius saw a change for the better in his father.

Soon Darbi walked into the kitchen and sat opposite her brother. She spied her brother's plate and smacked her lips, immediately heading for the stove. She fixed herself a plate, got some coffee, and sat down again.

"Hey, Darius. What's for brunch today, or should I say who?" Darbi winked at her brother.

Darius smiled. Women. He knew Cherish and Darbi had become close friends in the few months they'd known each other, but this might be too close. She had already told Darbi about lunch, before he had a chance. "Well, Miss Inquiring Mind, Mrs. Collins is making shepherd's pie and some other items. And yes, I invited Cherish. You don't mind, do you?"

Darbi smiled at her brother and took a sip of her coffee. "No, I don't mind," she answered honestly. "I think it's great. Have you asked her out on a real date yet?"

"Actually, yesterday," Darius said. "She asked me out for lunch. Then I asked her out for dinner. I tried to call you yesterday to share my good news. Where were you?"

Darbi buttered her toast. "I went to aerobics. Then later I ran into Curry at the bookstore. We had some drinks and then dinner."

Darius didn't want his sister getting tangled in Curry's web of charm. "You need to watch Curry. He chases anything in a skirt." Darius watched Mrs. Collins fix a breakfast tray for his father. He waited until the nurse left the kitchen to continue. "He's always dating those young girls. You know, early twenties. Personally, I never could see what they would have to talk about."

Darbi reached across the table and patted her brother's hand in reassurance. "Don't worry, big brother, he was a perfect gentleman. He never touched me. Not even a kiss goodnight. So now I can't even get a philandering playboy to touch me. Thanks, Darius!"

"I didn't mean anything, Darbi. Curry is my friend, but he has been married twice and has dated more women than I even want to know about. He doesn't take much seriously anymore. To him, life is just one big party. I think he's referred to as a major player." Darius paused as he noticed Darbi's crestfallen face. "I just want you to not get your hopes up."

"It wouldn't have anything to do with him being whiter than a sheet?"

"No, Darbi. If he were black, I would tell you the same thing. He's a good friend. I would do almost anything for him and I'm sure it's vice-versa. When he divorced wife number two, he stayed with me for a few months. The right guy will come along. He'll probably be right under your nose."

"I'm not looking for anybody right now, anyway. I have school and it's taking practically all my free time. Don't you worry, Darius."

"I'm not. I just don't want to lose you a second time. Oh, Curry might come by with a date later. Is that going to be a problem for you?"

Darbi rolled her eyes at her brother. She refilled her coffee cup and doctored it. "No. I think he was just bored last night. He probably felt guilty since I was sitting alone in the coffee shop. His eyes seemed empty to me."

"What?" He'd heard women comment on Curry's eyes, but never like that.

"You know, empty, hollow. It's like he's emotionally detached. Your eyes have a twinkle in them when you look at Cherish. I want a man to look at me like that." Darbi sighed wistfully. "I want a man to be nervous when I walk into a room."

"It'll happen, Darbi. I just don't want you settling for anything less than happiness." Darius hoped that

Cherish hadn't noticed his twinkle or he'd be in for a world of trouble.

⁓〜⁓

Otis Crawford lay in his bed watching the PGA tournament on TV. He turned his head toward the door as he heard it opening. He smiled as his daughter entered the room.

"Hey, Dad. How are you feeling?" Darbi sat in the chair nearest the bed. She actually looked happy. Tears weren't tugging at her eyelids, threatening to spill onto her cheeks.

"Fine, honey. You look good. You dating yet?"

"No, Dad. I had dinner with a friend last night. You know, there's a whole world outside you're missing by staying in bed."

"I know, baby. I'm just afraid. What if I forget something? I guess I'm worried I'll go outside and forget how to get back here."

The look on her face told him she worried about the same thing, but her voice wasn't in agreement. "That's why we're here. Are you writing in your journal?"

"Yes. I was just going to get dressed for lunch. Who's this woman Darius invited?"

Darbi laughed. "That's Cherish. We met her at the Alzheimer's meeting. Her mother passed away six months ago. She's a fashion designer. Personally, I think she and Darius would be perfect for each other."

"Good." Otis smiled as he spoke. "I was beginning to wonder if he even likes women anymore."

"Dad!" Darbi admonished her father.

"I know, he's focused on his career. He's always been like that. I guess we instilled too much work ethic in him when he was growing up. If he's not careful, life will pass him by. He'll wake up one morning, and he'll be an old man with nothing but regrets."

"What do you regret, Dad?" Darbi watched her father's mood. She'd read in her research about the sudden mood swings and was prepared for surly, but he was feeling melancholy that morning. His usually gravelly voice was soft and just above a whisper.

"Not much. I wish I'd listened to your mother more before she died. I regret this damn disease will rob me of my memory, especially now that you're home."

"You can't let it," Darbi said as she dabbed her eyes. "We're here today and you're doing very well. We could take a walk and you could see the neighborhood you live in. You can still play golf. I can make you cheat notes, so you don't get frustrated."

Otis nodded. "I miss my friends and playing golf. I know I can't hide forever. You're making sense. That crazy nurse has been telling me to start exercising, that I was letting my fears get the best of me."

"Great, Dad. You're ahead of so many sufferers who don't find out until it's too late to do anything about it. You found out early, thanks to your doctor." She wiped her eyes again. "You get dressed and we'll go for a walk before brunch." Darbi left the room before he could answer.

Darbi walked into Darius's study. She didn't knock, thus breaking the cardinal rule. Darius's eyes were closed and Duke Ellington played softly in the background. She didn't care about any of that. "Darius, do you talk to Dad?"

Darius opened his eyes and turned in the direction of his sister's voice. "Of course I do."

"I don't mean impersonal chit-chat. He's your father, not a client!"

"What do you mean, Darbi?" Darius stared at her for a long moment. "What's going on with you? You look like you're ready to kill someone."

She took a deep breath, trying to calm her nerves. Her brother didn't respond well to hostility. Making him defensive would solve nothing. "Darius, I've been talking to Dad. We talked about what he's feeling and what he's missing. Why are you distancing yourself from him?" Darbi almost didn't recognize her own voice as it rose. "You should encourage him to stay active, not hide in here, missing out on what he can still enjoy."

"Darbi, I'm not distancing myself from him. At first, yes, I was. But I realized the changes are subtle. I know that that's something that I have to deal with, and I'm trying."

Darbi studied her brother. They all were suffering with their father's illness, each in their own way. "Darius, all I'm asking is that you talk to him like a son."

Cherish parked behind Darbi's VW Beetle, in awe of the large two-story house in an exclusive subdivision on the lake. The house matched Darius, traditional and brimming with class. She walked the few steps to the front door, rang the doorbell, and waited.

A middle-aged white woman answered the door. Her brunette hair was in a very efficient bun. She smiled at Cherish, revealing metal braces on her teeth. "You must be Ms. Murray," the woman said in a British accent, smiling at her.

"Y-Yes, I am. Is Darius or Darbi around?" Cherish glanced at the woman's attire: slacks and a blouse with an apron over it. She didn't look like any of her mother's nurses.

"Yes. They are in Mr. Crawford's study. Follow me, please."

Cherish followed the woman to a wing of the large house. They stopped at a closed door. The nurse nodded to her and left Cherish on her own. She listened at the door for noise before she knocked. The door quickly opened.

"Cherish! You made it." Darbi hugged her friend. "You look great." She surveyed her friend's dress.

Cherish looked at Darbi's outfit. "You look great yourself. That's a cute dress. Don't you love being tall?"

Darbi laughed. "Sometimes. Dad and I are going for a walk while you and Darius get better acquainted." She walked down the hall.

Darius and Cherish exchanged nervous glances. He looked over her slender body with masculine approval.

"I'm glad you made it. Please, sit down." Darius watched as she took a seat and crossed her legs.

"This is a gorgeous house. Was it custom-built?"

Darius smiled. "Yes. I designed it myself. I've been in it about a year. Could I get you something to drink? The food is almost ready."

"Darius," Cherish started, "I'm fine." Cherish took in his outfit. Even though it was Sunday and everyone else was dressed casually, Darius was dressed in a button-down shirt, tie and slacks. "Do you ever just relax? You know, just let go?"

"No. That's never been an option for me. I guess being the oldest child I've always been one of those rigid people who follow all the rules at any cost."

Cherish thought so. He seemed to be dressed for work even when he wasn't at work. "Darius, you can relax and not lose your standing at work. One thing I have learned from this Alzheimer's is that you only have one day for sure—today. I used to be like you, always thinking about work. Then I watched my mother go from the strong woman I had known all my life to a person who didn't recognized her only daughter. That's when I started to relax. I missed the first stages of her illness, but we did have some good times before she got really sick."

"Cherish, I'm sorry. I know I can be stiff. Darbi told me almost the same thing earlier. I was letting this illness affect my relationship with my dad. I'm going to work on that."

Cherish smiled. Maybe he had potential after all. "If you ever need to talk, I'd be happy to listen. Remember, I've been there."

"I will. Do you like big band music?" he asked, changing the subject. "How about chamber music?"

"I like classical," Cherish admitted. "I have to be in the mood for big band. Usually if I'm designing something retro, I'll listen to some big band to put me in the mood."

Darius smiled as he digested the information. "The few women I've dated have hated anything big band or classical and called me old fashioned." Sounds of John Coltrane filled the large room, generating smiles from both.

"Sounds like you have been dating the wrong women, Darius."

He nodded. "Very true. Want a tour of the house?" Darius rose and walked toward the door.

Cherish nodded. "I would like that very much."

Darius led her around the house. She was amazed at his eye for detail, especially in his bedroom. It was a man's room, no doubt. A massive king-sized bed stood in the middle of the room. A dark armoire stood in the corner, as well as a dark bureau in the opposite corner. His bed was made, unlike her own. After a tour of his father's wing of the house, they headed to the patio. The water from the pool glistened in the afternoon sun, relaxing her. She also noticed the large gas grill at the other end of the patio.

"Darbi usually spends a lot of time out here in the pool," he said, attempting to fill the silence.

Cherish didn't doubt it for a minute. Darbi had lost quite a bit of weight since she met her, and now had muscle tone. "Yes, Darbi looks great. This is gorgeous."

Darius nodded shyly. "This house and my job have been my dream for a long time." He guided her back to the living room.

"I'm sure your father and his nurse didn't figure into that dream, did they? I know what you're going through, Darius. When my mom moved in with me, I felt just as you do now. Bordering on duty and guilt." She patted his hand. "It's still a beautiful house. Are Darbi and your Dad going to be okay outside alone?" Cherish peeked out of the front bay window watching them. "The street seems very quiet."

"Sure. Most of my neighbors have met Dad and Darbi. Darbi made him get out today. I've been selfish by not encouraging him, but not anymore."

Cherish and Darius watched Darbi and his dad as they talked to some of the neighbors. Cherish smiled as she watched the elder Crawford laughing as he and Darbi headed back toward the house.

"How was your walk, Dad?" Darius met his father at the door.

"Very good. I see they are still building more houses," the elder Crawford said, sitting down on the couch. Cherish walked to the couch and sat beside Darius's father. Before she could introduce herself, Darius did.

"Dad, this is Cherish Murray. Cherish, this is my dad, Otis Crawford." Darius nervously shoved his hands in his pockets as he made the official introductions.

"Hello, Mr. Crawford. It's nice to meet you." Cherish extended her hand to the mature gentleman, instantly realizing Darius had inherited his delicious shade of brown from his father.

Otis looked at his son and then smiled at Cherish. "You're a pretty thing. I see why my son is gawking at you like a teenager in heat."

"Dad!" Darius and Darbi said at the same time.

"It's fine, Darius," Cherish said as she tried to hide her laughter.

CHAPTER FIVE

After brunch, Cherish and Darius decided to take a walk to the park, especially after Darbi all but pushed them out the front door. Ten points for Darbi, Cherish mused.

The layout of the park impressed Cherish. The skaters' path was so inviting Cherish almost wished she had learned to inline skate. A little further, they came to the lake. Cherish grabbed Darius's hand. To her surprise, he squeezed hers in return. She smiled as she spotted a bench.

"Why don't we sit down, Darius?"

Once they were seated, Darius took a deep breath, then kissed her on the cheek.

"Darius!" Cherish was shocked. "You think you could maybe kiss me on the lips next time?" She smiled as she teased him.

They shared a laugh, easing some of the awkwardness of the moment. Then Darius kissed her again, on the mouth, his full lips soft against hers, just soft and long enough to get her blood simmering. "What are you doing after the session Wednesday night?" Darius kissed her again just as gently and scooted a little closer to her.

Cherish couldn't think at that moment. Her mind was still on the soft and gentle kiss that did nothing to curb her feelings for him. She leaned against his strong shoulders. "I told Darbi that I'd help her with her English paper."

Darius sighed audibly with regret. "Oh, I don't want to interrupt your plans with Darbi."

"Maybe another night?" Cherish held her breath. Ask me, she silently pleaded.

"How about Friday night? Dave Koz is playing at the Jazz Club in downtown Fort Worth." Darius intertwined his fingers with hers.

"Isn't it too late to get tickets?" She had wanted to go, but heard the jazz concert had been sold out for months.

Darius smiled as he held her closer. "There's always a way."

"I'd love to go with you Friday night."

"Great, I'll pick you up about six. We can have dinner at the Rooftop Garden before the concert."

"That sounds great." Cherish knew of the restaurant. It was one of the most romantic restaurants in the city, according to the local newspaper. It was also one of the most expensive.

They sealed their plans with a kiss.

Darbi sat at the desk in Darius's study, outlining her English project and hoping Darius was taking advantage of his time with Cherish. The ten-page research paper was due at the end of the semester, which was about eight weeks away. The chiming of the doorbell halted her studying. Answering the door, she expected to see Darius and Cherish, but Curry stood there.

"Where's your date?" Darbi looked at his button-down shirt, appreciating how it showcased his flat stomach and broad chest. And the fit of those jeans . . . Oh my, she thought.

"What date?" Curry looked at the cleavage of her dress.

"Darius said you were bringing a date. Why didn't you tell me you were a philandering playboy?" she teased him. "You could have told me I has was having dinner with the Don Juan of Texas."

"Because I'm not," he answered shortly. He stalked past her and sat on the couch. "Why don't you sit down?"

Darbi sat by him, then scooted away. She didn't want to give him the wrong impression. Somehow she knew Curry Fitzgerald with those hollow hazel eyes would be quite dangerous.

She had to do something to diffuse the tension forming between them. "Would you like something to drink? Darius should be back soon. He and Cherish went for a walk. Dad is taking a nap," Darbi reported. She took a deep breath.

Curry smiled. "I'm glad Darius is finally talking to Cherish. He's been drooling over her long enough."

Darbi stood. "Well, I have to get back to work on my English paper. If you need something, just let Mrs. Collins know."

Curry stood as well. "I can help you with your paper, if you like."

Darbi looked at those empty eyes. She could get to know him and find out why his eyes were so empty. Maybe hearing someone else's misery would distract her from hers. "Okay, Curry."

Curry silently followed her to Darius's study and sat opposite her when she handed him her notes. As he read, he made judgmental noises, reminding Darbi of her English professor. Curry looked from the paper to Darbi's face, then back to the paper, then back to her. "When is your paper due?"

"Six weeks." Darbi didn't like his tone or the expression. She was rethinking the topic of her research paper when Curry spoke.

"How about racquetball later?"

"I can't. I have a math test tomorrow, and I need to study." She took her notes out of his hand.

Curry chuckled. "Math is my favorite subject," he said innocently, planting the hint.

Trouble ahead. Darbi could feel it, but was helpless to stop it. "I didn't bring that book with me," she said quietly.

"Why don't I follow you to your place?" Curry suggested slyly. "I could help you study."

"Well, Cherish offered to come over later," Darbi lied. There was something about those eyes, she thought.

"I'm sure Darius would appreciate any extra time he could spend with Cherish." He winked at her.

He had her there. Darbi wanted her two favorite people to get together, however slowly. "I'll just leave him a note." Darbi scribbled her brother a note and said good-bye to her father. Then she and Curry were gone.

"Let's talk about you." Darbi returned from her tiny kitchen with two glasses of soda on a tray. "We've been studying for over two hours, and it's time for a break." She sat on the couch next to him.

Curry shrugged his shoulders. He didn't like talking about himself. Despite his professional successes he'd had two failed marriages. He was still lonely. "Not much to tell. Born in Seattle, went to the University of Washington. Got married, got divorced, moved to Texas about ten years ago. Got married, made director of advertising about five years ago, got divorced. What about you?" he asked, turning the tables on her.

"There's not much. Married Amos. Moved to Philly when I was 22. Amos died and I moved back here." A lone tear escaped her eyes.

Curry wiped her tear away as gently as he could. He wanted to hug her, but didn't know how she would react, not to mention that Darius would kill him for taking advantage of Darbi. "What's wrong?"

"Just the past." Darbi brushed his hand away. "I'm fine, Curry. Let's just get back to studying."

Curry watched her for a moment. Darius had mentioned that Darbi's marriage was shrouded in mystery. Darius suspected Amos had abused her, but wasn't sure as to what extent, since Darbi refused to talk about it. While he didn't know if it was physical or mental abuse, Curry knew something was very wrong.

She shivered and he scooted closer and put his arms around her. As if she had taken her finger out of the dike, her tears ran full force. She cried and sobbed all over his shirt. He comforted her through her crying spell, whispering soothing words, and the tears slowly subsided.

"I'm sorry, Curry. Thank you," she said, her voice muffled against his chest.

"That's okay, Darbi. Are you okay?" Curry rubbed her back in comfort. Usually women with any kind of issues scared him and he stayed at least a hundred miles away, but this was his best friend's sister and he wanted to help her.

Darbi sat up and looked at Curry. "Sometimes reminders of the past consume me and that's my only way to deal with them. Usually, I wake up with a wet nightshirt. Please don't mention this to Darius," she pleaded in a soft voice, breaking Curry's heart. "I'm just thankful that part of my life is over."

Curry nodded. "My shirt is always ready for a good cry. Remember that."

"I will."

"What are you doing tomorrow night?" Curry asked as he gently stroked her arm.

"No plans. Why?"

"How about a game of racquetball? Maybe dinner afterwards?"

"Curry," Darbi started, "I don't want to date you. You're Darius's friend and between us there are three marriages. Darius told me . . ."

"Darius told you what?" Curry stopped stroking her arm. "Darbi, can't you decide for yourself what kind of person I am?" He looked at her. "I'm so tired of my past preceding me. Yes, I have been married twice. I made two mistakes. Sometimes I feel like the word *failure* is stamped on my forehead."

Darbi watched Curry. In the few months she'd known him, he'd shown only a carefree and happy-go-lucky side. "Curry, I'm not judging you. I'm merely taking my brother's advice. I'll play racquetball with you tomorrow, because I love to play and for no other reason. Your past is your past. Just like my past is my past."

Curry nodded and was out of her door in record time.

Darbi breathed a sigh of relief. That was too close, she thought. Curry might have thought he was just comforting her, but she was having an entirely different reaction. She sat on her couch, her algebra test forgotten. When she looked at her clock, it was nearly eleven. Nevertheless, she called Cherish. After apologizing for calling so late, she asked Cherish for her thoughts on the hazards of Curry Fitzgerald.

Cherish laughed into the phone, not surprised at the subject matter. "I thought Curry had a crush on you. He always coughs whenever you casually touch his leg and he actually looks nervous when you smile at him. He watches you all the time. Several women at the meetings tried to start a conversation with him and he acted like he didn't even notice that they were trying to pick him up. You know, he still comes to the meetings even though no one in his family has Alzheimer's and he always manages to sit by you. Darbi, what are you feeling for Curry? Friendship? More than that? Does the fact that he's white alter your feelings for him?"

"I don't know what I'm feeling for him," Darbi admitted. "It's been a long time since any man paid any attention to me and I thought maybe that explained my feelings. I'm really enjoying myself right now, but I'm a little concerned as to what Darius will say. Speaking of?"

Cherish giggled. "We have lift off! He actually kissed me on the mouth today. With a little direction, of course. We're going out Friday. But if you want to hang out with Curry, don't worry about Darius. He'll come around. I know he wants you to be happy. Just make sure you explain to Curry what you want."

Darbi smiled into the phone. If Darius could get his act into high gear, Cherish would be perfect for him. "Thanks, Cherish. I'm glad my relationship-dense brother is making some progress."

The women shared a laugh as they hung up their phones.

Cherish paused, then called Darius. She knew she was treading on thin ice trying to run interference for Darbi, but she had to try. Waiting patiently as the phone rang, she rehearsed her questions. She grinned as Darius answered the phone on the third ring.

"Is everything all right, Cherish?" he asked, concerned as to why she was calling after just saying goodbye less than two hours prior.

"Yes, Darius. I was calling to see if you were busy tomorrow night. Maybe we could meet somewhere for dinner or something?"

"Well, usually I work late on Monday nights. You know, trying to get a head start on the week. I have a meeting with a potential client Tuesday evening and I want to be prepared."

That sounded just like the Darius Crawford Cherish knew. She doubted Darius showed up for anything unprepared.

"Darius, have you ever done anything just for the fun of it?"

"I didn't get to be vice-president by acting as cavalier as Curry," he said rather defensively. "That's probably why we get along so well. He's so laid back nothing bothers him. But he's been acting strange the last few days. I can't believe he didn't show today. That's really not like him."

Cherish realized Darius didn't know Curry had been at the house. "Didn't you see Darbi's note?"

"Yes. She went home to study. Come to think of it, Dad said he thought he heard a man's voice right before she left. I chalked it up to Dad hearing things, probably something to do with the disease."

Cherish knew she had to tell him Curry had been there or Darius would worry his father was getting worse. "Your father isn't hearing things. Curry was there, but just for a moment."

"Cherish, what are you not telling me?" Darius demanded in that cool matter-of-fact voice that told her he could read between the lines.

As Cherish pondered how to answer, he answered for her.

"He left with Darbi, didn't he? He probably convinced her he could help her study or something idiotic that would lead to her not studying."

"Darius, you should give both of them more credit than that. I know you feel you have to protect Darbi from Curry or something, but she's an adult, Darius. Don't criticize her or make light of what she's feeling. Just be there if something goes wrong."

Darius didn't say anything. Which meant he knew everything. She had said too much. Cherish mentally chastised herself for getting involved with Darbi's problem. All she had wanted to do was to keep Darius away from the gym and now he knew the entire story.

Monday evening, Darbi walked into Bodyworks Gym in Arlington, hoping that Darius wasn't there and that Curry was. After she gave her name to the attendant at the front desk, she was directed to the third racquetball court.

Darbi walked down the hall to the courts. There were two men still playing. She glanced at the clock on the wall. They had a few minutes left. Darbi stretched her muscles while she waited.

"I thought you might stand me up," Curry murmured. He was already dressed in loose fitting knit shorts and a t-shirt.

She couldn't help admiring his well-formed muscular legs and defined calves. "No, after my test today, I needed something to look forward to." Why was her heart beating so fast? She watched as the two men exited the court. This was just Curry, she reminded herself, as he held the door open for her, even if he did have the sexiest tanned legs she'd ever seen in her limited experience.

"After you." Curry motioned for her to precede him into the room.

Darbi walked ahead of him and unzipped her racket from its leather case. She took a deep breath and practiced a few serves and Curry did the same. She looked at Curry. He didn't seem the same happy-go-lucky Curry she'd met so many times before. She didn't like this Curry. He was being very short with her, almost clinical. As they decided who would serve first, Darbi wanted to apologize for last night. She opened her mouth, but realized she didn't have anything to apologize for.

Curry served first. He slammed the ball against the wall with all his strength. Darbi returned his serve with vigor. She'd thought he was going to go easy on her. The ball whizzed past Curry because he was watching her instead of the ball. He served again. This time when she hit it back to him, he returned the ball, starting the world's longest volley.

"Hey, you're pretty good." Curry readied to serve the ball again. Every time he served the ball, Darbi wondered if she would be able to return it. After sixty sweaty minutes, their time was up and were both drenched with sweat. He led her out of the court. "You played a good game, Darbi." His hand rested on the small of her back, guiding her to the changing area.

"Thanks, Curry. It was very stimulating." She wiped the sweat from her brow. "I need a shower." She was glad she had brought extra clothes with her.

Curry's eyes scanned her body, his gaze resting on her sweaty t-shirt outlining her sports bra. "Why don't we meet in the lobby after we shower? Say twenty minutes?"

Darbi nodded and walked to the women's locker room.

CHAPTER SIX

"How about dinner?" Curry escorted Darbi out of the gym. He didn't like the way all those guys were checking her out.

She shook her head. "I have class in the morning, Curry. Maybe another time?" She started walking to her car.

But Curry couldn't let her get away. Not tonight. He had tried to obey Darius's wishes and stay fifty feet away from her, but there was something about the way she'd cried in his arms the night before, something about the way she felt in his arms. He had to investigate what those feelings meant.

"We could order something," he offered. "I live probably ten minutes from here and you could be home by nine."

She opened her mouth to object, but instead she heard herself say, "Okay, Curry. I'll follow you. That way I can leave straight from your house."

He knew that was her way out. "Okay, but don't forget I know where you live. So don't think about trying to escape."

She flashed a toothy smile at him, melting his heart. "I know." She walked to her little Volkswagen.

Curry hurried to his BMW and unlocked the door. After he slid behind the wheel, he noticed Darbi's car was now near his. Smiling at the possibilities of the night ahead and ignoring the possible consequences of tomorrow, he put his car in gear and took off.

He pulled into his garage and Darbi parked in the driveway. He initially thought about making room in the garage for her car, just in case, but knew that would definitely scare her off.

She exited her car with her purse in hand. Curry escorted her inside the house before closing the garage door.

Darbi glanced around the large kitchen, then settled on one of the leather bar stools near the counter. "Okay, Curry, what are we eating?"

"Whatever you like." He opened the drawer next to the refrigerator. "I have all kinds of menus." He placed a handful of various take-out menus on the counter.

Darbi glanced at them. She picked one from a Chinese restaurant. "I'll have broccoli beef."

Curry nodded, immediately picking up his cordless phone and speed dialing the restaurant. After placing the order, he offered her a glass of wine.

"I have class in the morning." She glanced through the glass refrigerator door, spotting the bottle. "Maybe just one."

He breathed easier, got the wine and poured some into two glasses. "Why don't we go to the living room?"

Darbi slid off the bar stool and followed him. "Show me your house."

Though not used to showing his house to anyone, Curry obliged her. They started upstairs. "This is the master bedroom." He opened the door and closed it quickly, remembering he didn't make the bed that morning, and his maid wasn't due until the end of the week.

Darbi giggled, easing his discomfort. "I'm not as rigid as Darius. I don't make my bed every day either."

Curry relaxed and he continued showing her the rest of the four bedrooms, three of which held no furniture. "I keep meaning to furnish those rooms, but I just haven't had the time." Or the desire, he mused.

Darbi nodded. "You have nothing but time, Curry. When the mood strikes you, you'll finish."

Curry was thinking of something to say when the doorbell rang. "Looks like dinner is here. See, I told you." He grinned and grabbed her hand, leading her downstairs.

After they finished eating, Darbi grabbed her purse, ready to leave. "This has been fun, Curry. Thanks."

Curry walked her to the front door, trying to think of a reason for her to stay. He opened the door only to have Darbi close it.

He couldn't hide his confusion. "Darbi, what—"

She interrupted him with a gentle kiss on the lips. Then Darbi smiled at him. "I'm sorry, Curry." She stepped away from him and tried to open the door.

Curry's hands were on top of hers on the doorknob. "Darbi, what's going on?"

"Just let me leave. I'm sorry. I shouldn't have kissed you, okay?"

"Why did you?"

"Look, don't make me say it," she pleaded.

But he wanted to know if she felt what he had been feeling for the last few months. Or maybe he was just feeling incredibly horny. He looked down into teary brown eyes. She was embarrassed. He leaned down and kissed her.

Darbi moaned against his lips, dropping her purse on the hardwood floor with a thud. Her arms encircled his neck as she opened her mouth to give him access. Curry drew her body to his, giving in to the desire he'd been fighting for months. His hands breached her shirt and caressed her stomach intimately.

Finally, he found a miniscule scrap of control. He wanted her, but he wanted her to be sure. There was too much at stake. "Darbi, we need to talk."

She licked her lips and grabbed his hand, heading for the stairs. "We can talk some other time. Right now I want you."

This was what he had been wanting. He'd had dreams with this very scenario in it. So why was he scared to death?

He shook his head. "We have to talk. Please."

She paused dramatically, showing her frustration. "All right, Curry."

He took a deep breath. "Darbi, are you sure you know what you're doing? I mean, you know what Darius is going to say?"

"Curry, do you like me?"

"Yes."

"Do you find me attractive?"

"Yes."

"Do you want to make love to me?"

"Yes."

She grabbed his hand and led him to the stairs with confidence. "I think we've done enough talking." She led him to his bedroom.

As she opened the door, Curry wondered where this Darbi had been hiding all those emotions. There was no trace of the shy, emotionally fragile woman he had encountered and wanted desperately to help. This was a woman intent on making love and had the confidence to do it.

Once Darbi led Curry into his bedroom, she didn't know what to do with him. She sat on the bed waiting for him to make a move. Never in her life had she made the first move and once they entered the room, her confidence headed south. She sat on the bed looking at her hands.

Curry stood in front of her, smiling. He kneeled down so they were eye level. "Darbi, if you've changed your mind, I understand. I know things weren't exactly normal in your marriage, so we can move on your timetable." He straightened his tall body and sat beside her.

But she wanted him.

Slowly Darbi stood, took off her shirt, and dropped it to the floor. Curry watched her, his expression indescribable. When she reached to unzip her jeans, Curry's hands stopped her.

"No, Darbi. Let me." His arms encircled her waist, drawing her closer to him. He kissed her stomach as if it were the flattest, firmest, most beautiful stomach on earth. While he was melting away her worries with his tongue, he unzipped her jeans.

Darbi moaned, rubbing her hands through his curly blond hair, loving the feel of his firm lips on her bare skin. She stepped out of her jeans and stood before Curry in only her bra and panties. She took a deep breath as he slipped out of his shirt. His chest was magnificent. He patted the space beside him.

Gratefully, she sat down. Her knees weren't going to hold her up much longer. He kissed her gently, easing her down on the bed. Before she knew it, he had divested her of her bra and panties and he had taken off his jeans and boxer shorts. They lay naked in his unmade bed.

She watched him reach for the condom, knowing she should at least mention what hadn't happened in her marriage. But he was kissing her too thoroughly for her to stop and tell him.

He unwrapped the foil wrapper and remnants of latex floated out of the packet. A nervous laugh escaped her lips. "I hope you have another one."

He reached for another condom. He opened the packet, smiling. He pulled out the condom and eased it on. Just as he prepared to enter her body, he stopped.

"I can't believe this!" He moved away from her, walking into the bathroom, slamming the door.

Darbi didn't know what was wrong. Maybe he'd changed his mind and didn't know how to tell her? She covered her nude body with the sheet. "Curry, maybe I'd better leave," she said to the bathroom.

"No," he called from the bathroom. "It's just that the second one broke and I'm looking for some different ones."

Darbi breathed a sigh of relief. At least he hadn't told her to leave. At least not yet. Curry emerged from the bathroom with a large smile plastered on his face. He held a gold packet in his hand, waving it like the American flag.

"I found one." He strode toward the bed. "And I checked the date. It hasn't expired. How about one more try?"

She glanced at him. She had one option. "Okay." She plastered what she hoped was a seductive smile on her face.

He slid into bed beside her and eased his body on top of hers. "Now where were we?" He leaned down and kissed her.

Darbi wrapped her arms around him, ready to take every heart-stopping minute she knew only Curry could provide. "I think we were just about to step into paradise."

Curry nodded, trailing a string of hot kisses across her cheek, neck, shoulders and her breasts. Darbi's heated body was fast on its way to becoming a raging inferno.

"How did that happen?" Curry asked, stopping at a three- inch vertical scar, just above her most sensitive area.

She'd forgotten about the scar. "Amos stabbed me about five years ago. I really don't want to talk about it right now." She wanted him to continue his exploration of her body.

He nodded. "I'll wait until you're ready." He hesitated a moment before he resumed his actions. His tongue ran the length of the scar before he moved lower.

His fingers gently entered her body as he kissed her stomach. A moan escaped Darbi's lips, then a loud scream.

Immediately he stopped. "What's wrong?" He withdrew his hand.

Darbi sat up, wiping the tears from her eyes. "My marriage was awful. When I didn't get pregnant Amos found someone else for his pleasure. So it's been a while," she said evasively.

Curry kissed her gently on the lips. As Darbi got lost in the intensity of his kisses, he invaded her with his fingers again. She moaned against his lips. He increased the pressure of his kiss as his fingers copied the motions of his tongue.

Darbi couldn't focus on the pain she should have been feeling. She couldn't focus on the deep, mind altering kisses either. She focused on the climax washing over her body and over Curry's fingers.

"Oh, Curry," she gasped. "That was amazing."

Curry rolled over on his back. He guided Darbi's now pliant body on top of his as he quickly donned the condom. She gasped as he first entered her body, moaned as he pushed further inside her, but when he asked her if she wanted him to stop, she shook her head.

"No, Curry, it feels wonderful." She moved against him, enjoying her new seat of power.

He wrapped his arms around her waist, crushing her body to his, letting her feel the entire length of him. "I've been dreaming about this for months," he admitted.

She gazed at him, feeling the wonder of the moment. "I've been dreaming about this all my life."

The next morning, Darius walked into Curry's empty office. He was shocked that his friend wasn't at work. He did know that Curry and Darbi had played racquetball the night before, quite by accident. Cherish had let it slip during their phone conversation. Darius wasn't too concerned about that since both parties involved insisted that they didn't want any entanglements at the moment. He knew Darbi wasn't Curry's type. She was too old, too mature, and too smart to fall for any of his lines.

His thoughts were on Cherish. He needed some advice from the master of love about her. He also needed to get tickets to the sold out jazz concert. Sometimes, it seemed to Darius that the whole world must owe favors to Curry Fitzgerald. He could usually get tickets to anything, anytime. But Curry wasn't there. It didn't look like he'd even been in that morning. His computer screen was blank. Curry's supermodel secretary interrupted his exploration of his friend's office.

"Mr. Crawford, Mr. Fitzgerald won't be in today," Mica Diaz said in her quiet voice.

Darius couldn't help his reaction; Mica was tall and beautiful and every time she spoke in her seductive

Spanish accent, he thought she should be advertising something for Victoria's Secret. However, she was all business. As a native of the Dominican Republic she wanted to be taken seriously.

"Is something wrong?" Darius asked. It wasn't like Curry to miss work. He worked almost as much as Darius. He wondered if something had happened the previous night between Curry and Darbi.

"He didn't say. He said he had some personal business to take care of." Mica noted something in her planner notebook.

Darius thanked her and went back to his own office. He was preparing for his next meeting when his phone rang. Cherish's voice brought an instant smile to his face.

"Hey, Cherish! How are you?"

"Great! I was coming downtown and wondered if you were free for lunch."

"Lunch would be great. Where?"

"You can choose." Cherish giggled.

Darius mentioned an Italian restaurant in the downtown area. They agreed to meet at one. Smiling, he hung up the phone.

A few hours later, Darius entered the elevator with visions of Cherish in his head, but Tamara interrupted his thoughts. The five-foot, six-inch redhead was a copywriter on Curry's advertising team. He knew Curry had dated the 28-year-old a couple of times, against Darius's advice. Curry needed someone to settle him down, not rev up his engine.

"Darius, what is going on with Curry? He's broken several dates with me, including last night. He told me he had some important business meeting. I drove by his house this morning and there was a strange car in his driveway. You know, one of those small German cars, a fly, a bug, you know, something like that."

Darius's words stuck in his throat. He forced them out in a hollow breath. "A Beetle." That explained everything.

Tamara looked up at Darius in confusion. "Oh, I get it. Yeah, I guess it was a Beetle. I know you're his friend. Has he found someone and neglected to tell me?"

"Honestly, Tamara, I don't know." But he did know. "He has been acting weird lately."

A funny feeling settled in the pit of Darius's stomach. Curry had played racquetball with his sister last night, his vulnerable, widowed sister. He would have to warn Darbi about Curry again. Apparently she hadn't been listening the other day.

He walked the short distance to the restaurant. Cherish was already there waiting at the entrance door. He smiled appreciatively at the body-hugging denim dress and greeted her with a kiss on the mouth. "Hi, Cherish."

Cherish nodded, grabbing his hand as they walked to the table. After they were seated, Darius tried to keep his mind on Cherish, but couldn't. He felt responsible for his adult sister and now she was lost in the clutches of Curry. He didn't know what to do. He sighed.

"Okay, Darius," Cherish said, her soft voice full of concern. "What is it? Your father? Is something wrong with him? You can tell me. Remember, I've been through it."

Darius smiled at Cherish's concern for him and his father. "Darbi."

Cherish was quiet, the first sign of a guilty conscience. "What's wrong?"

Darius pretended to be interested in the menu. "I think she and Curry went out last night. You know, like a date."

Cherish choked on her wine. "Is that a problem for you?"

"No, not really. I know Curry isn't the settling down type. Or the monogamous type either. But he isn't at work today."

"I wouldn't worry, Darius. She'll tell you, when the time is right." Then Cherish added quickly, "If she did go out with him on a date."

"Of course. I'm sure you two have already discussed this in detail. I know Darbi is an adult. I just don't want Curry to hurt her in his quest for a good time. She's been through so much already." And he didn't know if Darbi would survive the heartbreak in her present emotional state.

"Well, Darius, you'll just have to be patient."

Darius took a swig of the tea. "I know." He took a deep breath, willing himself to calm down. "What brings you downtown?"

"Hervé wanted some last minute changes on a design. So I came in to work on them. He's leaving for Europe tomorrow."

The waiter appeared, took their order and left before Darius spoke again. "Have you ever been to Europe? You know, for the fashion shows."

"Once. I thought it was great. We went to Milan, Paris, and London. I really did like it."

"Why didn't you go this year?"

"Hervé usually takes one designer with him. I've been out of the loop so long at work, I'm kinda at the bottom of the list."

"Why don't you go out on your own? You know, start your own lines of clothes."

Cherish shrugged. As the waiter set the plate before her, she pondered his question. "I thought about it. Once. But now I don't know if I could do it. It would take so much planning. Plus, I would need to start locally. I have designed a lot of things since Mama passed away; it helps me with the grieving process, or so I'm told. Sometimes, it doesn't feel like it."

Darius nodded. He knew she was having a difficult time with her grief. Occasionally at the meetings he'd seen her wipe tears from her eyes. He wished he could help her with closure, but he had enough on his plate already with his family and their problems. Still, he wanted to be closer to Cherish. He also knew if she was a designer for Hervé she was better than good.

Cherish broke into his thoughts. "I asked if you wanted to see my sketches sometime? Sounds like a come on line, doesn't it?" She winked at him and began to laugh.

Darius hoped so. "I'd be delighted to see your designs, anytime." He winked at her in return.

A few hours later, Cherish sat at Darbi's kitchen table, wiping tears of laughter from her eyes as she listened to Darbi's recounting of her previous night's escapade with Curry. Her stomach muscles were hurting from laughing so hard. "I can just imagine Curry's face when the second condom refused to cooperate." She watched as Darbi poured her a glass of wine.

"I really hadn't planned on it going that far. But he was so attentive, and it had been ages since I'd been intimate with a man. After I didn't get pregnant during the early years of our marriage, we...you know. I felt like a virgin last night." Darbi smiled at the memories of the previous night. She put some salad on Cherish's plate as well as her own. "I know Darius will be upset when he finds out Curry and I have been intimate. But I feel so different now."

"He knows you guys played racquetball last night," Cherish informed her friend. "What do you feel for Curry now?" Cherish put some spaghetti on her plate as she watched Darbi.

Darbi reflected as she took a bite of salad. "I think he's practice. I know he doesn't have a serious bone in his body. I don't think he's serious relationship material. Besides, I just got out of a horrible marriage. I would like to enjoy life for a while."

As Darius drove to session on Wednesday evening, he had to remind himself to remain calm. He had successfully avoided Curry all day at work, which wasn't too hard, considering Curry was doing the same with him.

He would have to make Darbi understand that Curry would only end up hurting her. He wasn't what she needed. She needed someone stable, responsible and caring. Those words didn't describe Curry Fitzgerald.

He would also have to broach the issue of birth control with Darbi. The last thing his emotionally fragile sister needed was to get pregnant.

He walked into the room, immediately spotting Cherish and Darbi. After he kissed Cherish, he sat by her, but quizzed his sister. Even though Darbi gave him her pissed off face, she still answered his questions.

"Did you at least make it to your classes yesterday?"

"Yes, Darius. I went to work as well."

He nodded, but continued his interrogation. "Protection?"

Both Cherish and Darbi laughed. He really didn't like that. Darbi glanced at Cherish before she spoke. "Yes, Darius. Would you like to know what kind?"

He held up his hand. "All I want to know is that you guys used something and didn't play pregnancy roulette." Darius watched as Curry walked into the crowded room. He had noticed before that the chair next to Darbi was always vacant. It was almost as if the world knew that seat belonged to Curry.

Darius observed his best friend and sister pretend there was nothing between them. They sat side by side, barely acknowledging each other, barely touching, though they both fidgeted in their chairs. He liked seeing them sweat for a bit. Each time Darius tried to have a conversation with Curry, he wouldn't make eye contact. At that point, Darius knew he would have to talk to Curry later.

After the session was over, the foursome chatted outside in the parking lot. Curry stared at Darbi, but she wouldn't look at him. Darius almost felt sorry for Curry. Almost.

Since the women were going to study, Curry seized the opportunity and invited Darius for coffee.

After getting their coffee and finding a table, Curry finally looked Darius in the eye. "Okay, Darius, you got me. I know you know. I know you're disappointed in us for giving in to our lust."

"I understand things happen in the heat of the moment, Curry. But you know what I've told you about her previous marriage and how emotionally vulnerable she is. There wasn't any other black woman you could have picked on besides my sister?"

"Darius, I hope you're not saying what I think you're saying. I like Darbi; she's fun to be around. And for the record, I've slept with a black woman before. Why can't I be attracted to your sister? I'm not good enough, is that it? Have I been married too many times? Or is it that my skin is too white?"

The quiet stretched between them. Darius stirred his coffee, feeling like a racist and hating himself for even thinking such horrid things about his friend. He took a deep breath. "I'll mention this once, and we'll drop the subject." Darius took a sip of coffee and cleared his throat. "Curry, Darbi hasn't had the amount of experience you've had. Your marriages were at least part of the time happy. Darbi didn't have anything but pain. I just don't to see her get hurt. I don't want to see her as unhappy as she was when she got here last year. If I have to choose between our friendship . . ." Darius paused. "Just don't make me have to make that choice."

"Dare, I don't regret Monday night. I don't plan on hurting her. Neither of us knows what we want. Yes, she was the reason I didn't come to work Tuesday."

Darius held his hand up to stop Curry. "Curry, please, no details. The less I know the better. And the healthier you'll be."

Curry cleared his throat, his signal that he was about to say something that Darius wasn't going to like. "I have to say this, or our friendship would mean nothing. Did you know Amos stabbed her? She has a three-inch vertical scar on her stomach. She also cries at night. I'm not talking about a few sniffles from a bad dream. I'm talking about gut-wrenching tears. It's like she's reliving the nightmare every night."

"I didn't. Damn bastard!" Darius hated Amos for all the pain he'd caused Darbi, both mentally and physically. If he weren't already dead, he would have killed him. "You see, Curry, that's what I mean. I don't want her too afraid to tell me what's going on in her life. That's what kept us apart for the last fifteen years."

CHAPTER SEVEN

Friday night, Cherish fussed with her hair, waiting for Darius to arrive. It had been two days since she'd seen him last and she was acting as if it had been several weeks. The ringing of her doorbell brought an end to her preparations.

She checked herself in her mirror. The peach-colored dress showed off both her cleavage and her family lineage of trim, almost boyish hips. *Very nice, Cherish,* she smiled to herself and wondered if Darius would even notice. After putting on her peach-colored stilettos, she grabbed her purse and headed downstairs.

She opened the door and hello tumbled out of her mouth at the beautiful sight of Darius Crawford. He stood before her dressed in a black suit, a white silk shirt, and a coordinating tie. Cherish sucked in a breath. That man was some kind of eye candy. She inhaled his cologne. Sexy. His short hair was freshly cut and his smile melted her heart.

"Hello, Cherish. You look lovely." He leaned down and kissed her.

"Thank you, Darius. You look very handsome as well. Shall we?" As Cherish pulled the front door closed behind her, Darius held out his hand for her keys. He locked her door and handed the keys back to her.

Showing his Southern manners, he bent his elbow so she'd take his arm, allowing him to escort her to his truck. After she took her seat, he planted a soft kiss on her lips before closing the door. Cherish watched him as he walked around to his side of the truck, licking her lips as she did.

As he drove through the busy downtown Fort Worth area, Cherish admired the scene. When they passed the Jazz Club, the line was quite long.

Fortunately Darius had made reservations at the restaurant. He held her hand as they were led to their table. Cherish marveled at the romantic atmosphere of the restaurant. Soft jazz music played in the background, and candle lights lent ambience. As Cherish opened her menu, she noted that it had no prices; she smiled.

"Would you like an appetizer?"

"Sure, if you would."

"How about calamari?"

Squid! Yuck! Cherish turned her nose up in disgust. She didn't want to be sick on their first official date. "How about crab cakes?"

The waiter appeared, as if on cue, to take their order. Darius also ordered a bottle of Dom Perignon. "1978, if you have it."

Cherish looked at Darius in shock. Darbi had already informed her that he didn't date much, so he might go overboard and she obviously hadn't been kidding. He'd just ordered a three hundred dollar bottle of champagne. Cherish sighed, wondering how Curry and Darbi were making out. She smiled at her own pun.

Darius smiled at her expression. "What's so funny?"

"Nothing, just thinking."

⁓

Once at the jazz club, they walked up to the *Will Call* desk and Darius gave Curry's name. An usher immediately appeared and escorted them to their seats. Darius was always amazed at the connections Curry had. Tonight was no exception. They had front row seats. Any closer and they would have been on stage.

His mind floated to his sister. He knew she and Curry had a date tonight as well. He worried if the two people he cared for the most were making a horrible mistake.

Curry was such a free spirit, and Darbi was still trying to find herself after a disastrous marriage. Darius hoped the oil and water cliché didn't apply. Or did he?

"Darius, what are you thinking about?" Cherish asked as the waiter repeated his question to Darius.

"Nothing," he lied.

After their drink order was taken, Darius watched Cherish. She was the prettiest woman in there and he felt like the luckiest man in the world. He hoped this date would be a springboard to many more. "Well, what do you think?"

Cherish glanced around the crowded room. "How did you get front row seats at the last minute? I happen to know this concert has been sold out for months."

"Curry." Darius smiled. "He always knows somebody who has front row tickets to something. I think it's that whole luck of the Irish saying. He can usually get anything he sets his mind to." Darius hoped that didn't include his sister.

⌒

Saturday morning, Darius knocked on his father's bedroom door and waited for him to answer. After hearing his father's greeting, he entered the room. His father was sitting in bed, reading *Golf Digest*. He smiled at his son.

"Darius, I didn't think I'd ever see you relax." Otis looked at Darius's attire of beltless blue jeans and a t-shirt. "Something is very different here." Darius sat in the chair nearest the bed.

"Yes, it is. I was thinking of having a cookout later this evening. There won't be any strangers. It'll just be Darbi, Cherish, Curry, you, Mrs. Collins, and me. How's that sound to you?"

Otis sighed. "Darius, this your house. You don't have to consult with me if you want to have people over. I appreciate it, though. It makes me feel that you still respect me as the man who gave you life. I'm glad to see you're enjoying yourself."

Darius smiled at his father. He hoped he would have his strength when he got older. "Dad, I will always respect you. You're very important to my life and me. I don't want you feeling uncomfortable here. This is your home, too."

"You need to start taking things easy."

"I'm trying, Dad. Old habits die hard." Darius stood and walked toward the door. "I'll let you know about what time we'll eat." After his father nodded, Darius walked out of the room.

~~~~~

Darbi looked around Omar's dining area for Cherish. They were meeting for their weekly lunch. The popular sidewalk café was always crowded. Finally she saw her wave; Cherish was already seated at a table. Darbi quickly walked over to her.

"Hey, sorry I'm late." Darbi bubbled with excitement.

Cherish looked at Darbi's flushed face. "What happened to you?"

Darbi sat down and began talking immediately. "I was leaving the gym this morning and this guy asked for my phone number!"

Both women yelled in excitement at the same time. "Ahhh!"

"That's great, Darbi. What about Curry?"

Darbi waited until the waiter left the table before she answered. "He said he just wanted a casual friendship," Darbi said matter-of-factly. "You know, something with no strings attached. What happened on your date with Darius?"

"It was very romantic. We even had Dom Perignon with dinner," Cherish said. "He can be charming."

"Any action?"

Cherish took a deep breath and hoped this would not return to haunt her later. "He seems overly cautious."

Darbi nodded. "Cherish, if you're ready for the next step, you may have to give Darius a little nudge. He hasn't had a lot of practice."

"Unlike Curry," Cherish guessed. "What has Darius been doing for the last twenty-five or so years?"

"Working his way up to vice-president. He's always been work focused. Personal life is secondary to him."

Cherish was beginning to believe that. "How did your date with Curry go?"

"Well, it wasn't anything like yours. We went to Putt-Putt Golf and then to Vino's Pizzeria. After that we went back to my place to talk about Monday. We decided to be friends, just friends. Then we started making out and I sent him home."

"Are you going to Darius's tonight?"

"Yes, after a nap. I'll go over early to see if he needs any help."

When Cherish arrived at Darius's house, Curry's black BMW was already parked in front. In North Texas, a November day like this was cool enough for a sweater, but not too cool for a cookout. North Texas was known for its unusually warm winters.

Mrs. Collins led Cherish through the house to the pool, where Darius and Curry were sitting and drinking beer. Mr. Crawford was outside as well, but no Darbi.

"Hi, Cherish." Darius walked to her and greeted her with a kiss in front of Curry and Otis. "Want something to drink?"

"Hi, Darius, Mr. Crawford, Curry. I'll pass on the drink for now." Suddenly, she noticed Darius was dressed in t-shirt and blue jeans. Darius Crawford had on blue jeans. Curry was his usual casually dressed self in a Dallas Stars hockey sweatshirt and jeans. Even Mr. Crawford was wearing jeans. Cherish was glad she'd taken Darbi's advice and dressed casually. "Where's Darbi?"

Darius looked Cherish over as he answered her question. He admired the way her jeans molded her hips. "I guess she's running late. I thought she was coming earlier to help." He stopped talking as he heard Mrs. Collins greet someone.

Darius looked at his sister as she arrived poolside and plopped down in the patio chair. She let out an exhausted breath.

"Sorry I'm late," she finally managed. "I had an unexpected phone call just as I getting ready to leave and we stayed on the phone for hours."

Darius feared it was someone from Amos's family who had finally tracked her down. He braced himself for the worst. "Who was it?"

"DeMarcus Jameson. We met at aerobics. He seemed nice."

The name sounded familiar. Darius remembered hearing it somewhere. But where? All at once it hit him. Darius exhaled sharply and stared at his sister in amazement. "The linebacker for the Dallas Cowboys?"

Darbi shrugged. "Maybe. He said he was in sports and worked in Irving. I thought he meant he taught high school athletics or something. Come to think of it, when we were chatting at the gym this morning, there were a lot of people who kept coming around. One woman even had the nerve to give him her phone number with me standing right there." She shook her head. "Some women."

Darius and Curry exchanged glances. He saw the disappointment in Curry's eyes as he chugged his beer, staring at Darbi. He looked like a broken man. But this was Curry. Nothing like Darbi having a date with another man should have rattled him. Darius listened as his sister continued talking.

"I have a date with him tomorrow," Darbi said as casually as she could.

Cherish gasped. "You're kidding."

"No, we're going to dinner." The women laughed excitedly.

Darius smiled. Curry frowned. Otis laughed out loud.

"Cherish, could you come over tomorrow and help me pick out something to wear? I'd like to make a good impression," Darbi said, not looking in Curry's direction.

"Sure, Darbi. No problem." Cherish darted a glance in Curry's direction.

Darbi finally faced her brother. "Darius, do you need me to do anything?"

"Why don't you start the salad? I'll show you what to use." Darius started toward the inside of the house.

Astutely, Darbi followed, knowing Darius wanted to speak with her privately. She waited until Mrs. Collins vacated the kitchen before she spoke. "Okay, Darius, what's wrong?" She reached for the large salad bowl.

"Darbi, what about this thing with you and Curry?" Darius leaned against the counter, staring at his sister. He watched as she averted his stare and pretended great concentration in making the salad.

"Darius, he said he just wanted to be friends. You know, hang out. Aren't you always saying that I should have a back-up plan?"

Darius continued watching Darbi as she worked on the salad. "Did you see the expression on his face when you mentioned you had a date?"

"No, I didn't. But Darius, weren't you the same person telling me what a philanderer he was and to watch my step? I thought you'd be happy that DeMarcus asked me out."

Darius stared at his sister. Yes, he was happy someone else found his sister attractive, but he also felt Curry's pain. "This isn't about me. This is about you. What makes Darbi Ariane Crawford happy? I don't want to see anyone get hurt, but I think it's already too late for that." Darius walked out of the kitchen.

Darbi sighed and started chopping up tomatoes, lettuce, onions, cucumbers, and peppers. She looked into the refrigerator for salad dressing as she heard the door open again. Why was the kitchen so busy today?

"Got a minute?" Curry's deep baritone voice penetrated her thoughts.

Darbi turned and faced him, determined not to run into his arms and start kissing him. "Sure, what's up?"

"What happened to us?" Curry walked around the table and stood next to her. "What about what happened between us the other night?"

Darbi gently placed the knife on the table, trying not to remember how good she'd felt in his arms. "Curry, I believe you said we should be just friends. DeMarcus and I are just friends as well." She resumed cutting the vegetables for the salad.

"Will you be having sex with him as well?"

Darbi stared at him, not dignifying his comment with an answer.

"When can I see you?" He moved closer to her.

Darbi reached for the salad bowls on the shelf in the oak cabinet.

After she set the bowls on the counter, from behind he slowly wrapped her in a bear hug and kissed her on the neck.

"H-How about Tuesday night?" She tipped her neck to give him better access. Curry took full advantage and nibbled on her neck as his hands traveled to her waist and stopped. He turned her around to face him and kissed her longingly. Darbi could hardly breathe when the kiss finally ended.

"Okay, Tuesday night," he said, his lips just centimeters from hers. "I'll pick you up around seven. Call me after your date with Mr. Football." He was out of the kitchen in a flash.

During the course of the meal, Mr. Crawford quizzed his daughter about her upcoming date. Cherish had the feeling the elder Crawford knew of his daughter's fling with Curry. Each time he asked Darbi something about DeMarcus, he looked in Curry's direction for a reaction. Nothing. After he laughed at Curry, he tried to give his daughter some tips.

"Now you need to know some football terms. You know, honey, like quarterback, linebacker. Who carries the ball? How old is this boy anyway?"

"He's 28, Dad."

Curry coughed loudly. "He's ten years younger than you. What could you possibly have in common with a 28-year-old?"

Darbi stared at Curry. "Aerobics," she said defensively.

Darius and Cherish both laughed.

Cherish noticed the hurt look in Curry's eyes. He'd made the rules, Cherish thought, and now he was paying the price. Served him right! She tried to redirect the conversation. "Darbi, do you still need me to help you with your paper this week?"

Darbi cut her steak as she discreetly watched Curry. "No, since next week is Thanksgiving, I don't have class Wednesday. I'm taking a breather until after the holidays."

Cherish looked at Darius, who was watching Curry as well. Except for that one outburst, Curry had been otherwise quiet. "Darius, what are your plans for Monday night?"

Darius set his bottle of beer down, gazing at Cherish. "No plans."

"How about dinner? You could look at my drawings." Cherish had never asked a man out on a date in front of his entire family before. She hoped he didn't think she was too forward.

Otis laughed. "Is that anything like come and see my etchings?"

CHAPTER EIGHT

Sunday afternoon, Cherish went over to Darbi's condo as promised and helped her chose a dress for her date. The sleeveless lavender body-hugging dress showed off her new slender frame and toned arms. "You look great, Darbi. Where are you guys going?" She watched Darbi twirl around in front of the mirror, like a debutante going to her first dance.

"DeMarcus called earlier and said we were going to the La Plaza de Sol." Darbi walked to her vanity table to put on some makeup. "I can't believe he's taking me to such an expensive place on our first date."

"Wow! Now that's a ritzy place."

Darbi walked over to where Cherish sat on the bed and sat beside her. "I do wonder what I'll have in common with a twenty-eight-year-old. What will we talk about?"

"Pretend you like football," Cherish advised. "Men love attention. Just pretend to hang on his every word, no matter how stupid it sounds," Cherish quipped.

Soon Darbi's phone rang, interrupting their talk. DeMarcus was at the entrance gate. After she buzzed him in, she touched up her makeup and fussed with her hair, waiting for the doorbell to ring.

Cherish picked up her things to leave also. "I can't wait to see him in person. He'll be my first celebrity sighting."

"You should come to aerobics. He's there every Saturday," Darbi teased as the doorbell rang.

Darbi opened her door. DeMarcus filled her doorway, all six-foot-seven of him. He was dressed very smartly in a dark suit, but she thought the sunglasses were a bit much, considering it was evening. She noticed the large bouquet of red roses that he attempted to hide behind his back.

When DeMarcus presented the flowers to Darbi, he bowed. "Beautiful flowers for a beautiful lady."

Darbi took the flowers and inhaled their aroma. No man had ever brought her flowers!

"Thank you, DeMarcus. They're beautiful." She nodded toward Cherish. "This is my friend, Cherish Murray. Cherish, this is DeMarcus Jameson." Darbi watched Cherish go from the classy woman she had known for the last few months to the babbling football groupie.

"Wow! This is great. I watch you all the time. You are the best thing to happen to the Cowboys in a long time." Cherish finally got hold of herself and returned to her usual demeanor. She took a deep breath and said, "Hello, DeMarcus. It's very nice to meet you."

DeMarcus smiled. "Hey, sweetie. How you doing?" He looked down at Cherish.

Cherish giggled, came to herself, said her good-byes and left. Now Darbi was alone in her condo with the football player. She watched as he gave his approval of her dress.

"Baby, that dress is tight."

Darbi ran her hand over her dress. "No, it just looks tight. See?" She pulled at the fabric, demonstrating for him.

DeMarcus shook his head. "No, no. I mean it looks great. Hugs your fine body in all the right places. Ready to jet?"

Darbi looked confused. "DeMarcus, I'm not really up on hip-hop lingo. You'll have to speak properly if you want me to answer you."

"Sorry. Ready to leave?"

Darbi smiled. Better. "Yes, I'm ready."

She followed DeMarcus to his Range Rover. He didn't hold her hand or open her door for her. He slid behind the driver's seat and waited for her to get in before starting the truck.

I sure miss Curry, Darbi mused as they arrived at the restaurant. Her ears were still ringing from the gangsta rap DeMarcus played on his Bose stereo enroute. After he handed his keys to the valet, they were escorted inside the restaurant. They followed their hostess to the cozy table in silence. Again, DeMarcus didn't help her with her chair; the waiter did.

"What would you like to drink, sir, madam?"

DeMarcus looked at Darbi as she glanced around the room. "Darbi, would you like some wine or something?"

"A glass of merlot." Darbi looked around at the elegant atmosphere. The lighted candles gave it a romantic touch. She heard DeMarcus order a Crown and Coke.

"This is a gorgeous restaurant," Darbi commented. "You come here a lot?"

"Every now and then."

The waiter reappeared. "What would you like to start off with?" He looked at Darbi for a reaction.

"I'd like the lobster taco."

"I'll have the Texas crab cakes," DeMarcus added.

The waiter left, then returned quickly with their order. DeMarcus ordered another round of drinks. Although it was an elegant restaurant, with romance oozing everywhere, she wasn't having as much fun as she'd had with Curry. Maybe I'm prejudging him because he's an athlete, she thought. He could be interesting. DeMarcus's deep voice shocked her back to their meal.

"Darbi, I asked you what you were doing for Thanksgiving."

Darbi shrugged her shoulders. "Probably have dinner at my brother's."

"Why don't you come watch me play football? I can show off my skillz," he said with hip-hop inflection. "You know, the reason they call me DeMarcus Da Man." He finished his drink.

She shook her head. "I can't. My father's sick and I like to spend my spare time with him." Darbi took a small sip of her wine and glanced around the room again.

"Okay, I understand. How about you, your dad and your brother come see me sport my skillz?"

Darbi immediately added Cherish to the equation. "There would be four of us."

"Four! Woman, I'm not trying to pay for your entire family, just a select few."

The waiter interrupted Darbi's retort. "Ready to order your entrée?"

They both nodded. Darbi ordered prime rib and he ordered grilled salmon. She also asked for another glass of wine, somehow needing courage from a bottle. The waiter nodded and left the table.

Darbi resumed the conversation. "DeMarcus, I wasn't insinuating you had to buy tickets for my entire family—"

"He can't even pay me child support. He better not be trying to buy nobody nothin'." A very loud female voice interrupted their conversation.

Darbi looked at the owner of the voice. She was a medium height brown-skinned woman, with enough hair extensions for two people. "DeMarcus?" Darbi glanced around the room to see if they had any spectators.

But DeMarcus didn't speak and the woman continued her tirade. "Yeah, he's always frontin' like he gots money. He doesn't want to even pay for our baby." Pouting, she stood with her hands on her small hips, daring DeMarcus to contradict her.

Finally, DeMarcus spoke. "Keisha Monroe, what are you doing here? Does the phrase 'restraining order' not mean anything to you?"

"I followed you, fool. I would have confronted you at Miss Thang's," she pointed at Darbi, "but the security gate almost closed on my Geo Metro. I didn't think you liked women with short hair. You were always telling me to go get some hair."

A weight-challenged African-American woman soon joined the trio at the table. Darbi couldn't quit staring at the large colorful tattoo adorning her bountiful bosom. Her blonde extensions looked almost as matted as her friend's. The woman spoke, ending Darbi's observation of the two women.

"Keisha, don't let this sucka try to talk that smack about Jordan not being his son. He owes you, girl."

"I know, girl." Keisha nodded to her friend before turning her attention back to her victim. "DeMarcus, why you trippin'. Just write my check and I'll be gone."

Darbi wanted to cry. Twice married, white, carefree Curry looked excellent right now. She wanted to leave the restaurant as quickly and quietly as possible. She made eye contact with DeMarcus. He placed two one hundred dollar bills on the table to pay for the meal they didn't eat.

The waiter appeared and DeMarcus gave him the money. He and Darbi almost ran out the restaurant in embarrassment. His Range Rover was parked out front with the motor running.

"What was that about?" Darbi asked as soon as they were safely away from the restaurant.

DeMarcus glared at the road as they headed back to Fort Worth. "Well, a few years back, I was going through a rough time. I was on the injured list most of the year. There were rumors of them trading me to an inferior team. I met Keisha at a nightclub. She was wearing next to nothing and was in awe of me."

"Why don't you just pay her child support?" He reminded Darbi of Amos, who was always ready to blame someone else for his foibles.

"I would pay her, if the kid were mine. I have good reason to believe that it's not mine." DeMarcus turned down a dark road lined with trees. The area looked oddly familiar to Darbi. It reminded her of the park near Darius's house.

DeMarcus reached for his visor and pushed a button. Soon the gate they approached opened and closed behind them.

"Where are we?" Darbi reached into her purse to make sure she had her mace with her. She relaxed as she found the metal canister.

"Fort Worth, by the lake. I still owe you dinner. I can cook something for us to eat. I'm really sorry about those women showing up and ruining our date. The last thing I need is bad press." As they reached the large two-story house, he pushed another button and the garage door opened. He parked the truck and got out.

Darbi followed him into the house. "Why don't you think it's your baby?"

"Because," DeMarcus paused, looking in his fridge, "I'm sterile."

Darbi peered at the giant man as he hid behind the large refrigerator door. "How do you know that?"

"Because when I was married, we tried for two years to have a baby. I thought it was her, and she thought it was me. She was right. After thousands of dollars in fertility tests, we discovered I had a low sperm count.

Almost non-existent. I can never father a child." He finally faced her after he found some steaks to grill. "After Keisha found out she was pregnant, she tried to get money out of me. My lawyer thinks I should pay her off."

Darbi did, too. "Why don't you?"

"Because I will not give in to that mentality. She thinks I'll be her meal ticket. She'd probably sell me out to the papers anyway."

"Have you told her you're sterile?"

DeMarcus stared at her. "Of course not, it's a man-thang. I can't let the nation know that De-Man can't father a child."

"So you'd rather allow this *girl* and her friends to follow you all over town and harass you and your dates." Darbi didn't know whose situation was the worst: hers or his.

"You sound like my mother," he said accusingly, but he still smiled.

"DeMarcus, you could take the test, take her to court and it would be over." Darbi thought she heard a noise outside. "You could be rid of her, once and for all."

Suddenly, they heard DeMarcus's name being called and a few choice expletives.

Recognizing the words, DeMarcus cursed. "I can't believe this!" He walked to the nearby wall phone.

"Who is it?" Darbi had an idea of who it was, but she hoped it wasn't so.

"Those stupid women from the restaurant. I'm going to call the police. I'm afraid I'm going to have to give you a rain check for dinner. I can take you home after I finish with the cops." He punched a number on the wall phone with short, angry strokes.

Darbi just wanted to get out of the situation before it got any worse. "That's okay. I can call my brother. He lives near the lake. What's the address here? I'm sure he can't be that far."

DeMarcus gave her the address and Darbi realized he was about half a mile from her brother. She would have walked if she'd thought she could get past those women.

Darbi called her brother and after answering a few embarrassing questions, was told he was on his way. Darbi thanked him and hung up the phone. She stared at DeMarcus.

"Please don't let this evening be our last evening together," he pleaded.

"Of course not, DeMarcus," Darbi said in a soft voice, but her brain had another thought: *If I see this man again, it will be too soon!*

Darius's eyes darted from the road as he looked at his sister in disbelief. She sat in the passenger seat of his truck calmly reciting the events of the evening leading up to her having to call him to pick her up on a deserted road near his house.

"They came into the restaurant and caused that big a scene?" He tried to gauge his sister's reaction as he continued driving.

"Yes, it was horrible. They were yelling and shaking their hands at us, like we were criminals or something. It's a wonder we weren't on the news. Why can't I find one good man?"

Darius felt guilty for pushing her away from Curry. Maybe his friend wasn't so bad for his sister. "Curry was quite upset you went out with DeMarcus," Darius said.

Darbi shook her head as she looked out the window. "Curry isn't my worry right now. He said he only wanted friendship, anyway. You know, tonight reminded me of Amos and his family."

Darius guessed those were painful memories. That was the first time she had mentioned her dead husband or his family in some time. "I'm sorry, Darbi."

"That's okay, Darius. Actually, it was funny now that I look back on it." She started a small giggle that soon grew into a boisterous laugh.

Darius laughed as he drove. "Your date sounds like some of Curry's past dates. What did the cops say?"

"They hadn't got to his house yet. Have you talked to Cherish tonight?"

"Don't start." He didn't tell her he was on the phone with Curry when she called.

~~~~~

A few days later, Cherish hummed a melodic tune as she fixed dinner for Darius. She wondered what he would do if she asked him to spend the night. Talk about being a perfect gentleman. Darius was a true Southern gentleman and he was driving her right up the wall. She laughed as she imagined his shocked face.

Darbi had reminded her she would have to make the first move if she wanted Darius and their relationship to move forward. Cherish didn't know if she could, knowing he would turn her down. However polite his answer, it would still mean that they would not be making love anytime soon.

Darius had a lot going on in his life at the moment, and the last thing he needed was a woman forcing him to sleep with her. Cherish laughed at the role-reversal. Wasn't the man supposed to be desperate for it and the woman supposed to put him off?

She turned her thoughts to her task, trying to rid herself of every erotic thought she'd had of Darius, which seemed impossible, since he was coming over for dinner.

Cherish prepared salad, steak, baked potatoes, and cheesecake. Thanks to Darbi, she also had his favorite beer, Samuel Adams, and another item she was sure she would not use that night. Earlier that afternoon, she and Darbi had gone shopping. In a moment of *girl power*, they'd both bought a box of condoms. As she turned the steak over on the indoor electric grill, Cherish mused that Darbi would probably use hers way before she did!

Why was Darius so slow in the relationship department? she wondered. Was he afraid of something? Did someone hurt him badly? Her doorbell chimed, bringing her back to the evening at hand. She took off her apron, straightened her suede skirt and went to answer the door.

"Hi, Cherish. You look beautiful." Darius kissed her, then handed her a dozen yellow roses.

Cherish smiled. "You look very handsome. Thank you for the flowers." She took the roses from his outstretched hand and inhaled deeply. "Come in."

Cherish led him to her couch, and nodded approvingly at his corduroy green trousers and green cashmere sweater, knowing that both Curry and Darbi had given him fashion advice. "Would you like something to drink? I have some Sam Adams." She headed for the kitchen.

"I didn't think you liked beer," he yelled so that she could hear him in the kitchen.

Soon Cherish returned with a tray. The tray held a bottle of beer, a frosted mug, a bottle of wine and a gold trimmed wine glass. Darius took the bottle of beer and the frosted mug. "Thank you, Cherish."

"You're welcome. How was your day?" Cherish asked as she sat by him. That really sounded lame, she thought.

"Pretty good," Darius said as he opened the bottle of beer. "What are you doing Thanksgiving?" He poured the ale into the mug and waited for her answer.

Cherish poured a glass of wine, took a sip, letting the liquid soothe her nerves. Had it been a year already? "I really haven't thought about it."

"I want to invite you over for Thanksgiving dinner. Darbi will be over and Curry will be out of town, so I bet she could use the company."

"Does Darbi know that Curry is going out of town?"

"I don't think so. He's going to tell her tomorrow night. He's taking her to a hockey game." Darius took a deep breath. "Since his last divorce, he goes home to Seattle for the major holidays. He says being around family makes the holidays hurt less."

"The hockey game sounds like fun." Cherish stood. "Shall we eat?"

He followed her to the dining room. The lighted candles and the flowers complemented the table. After he pulled out her chair for her, he sat down across from her. "This smells delicious, Cherish. I hope your culinary skills rub off on Darbi. Honestly, I don't see how she made it in a marriage without cooking."

Cherish nodded her thanks and began eating. Anything so she wouldn't start blubbering like a schoolgirl at his compliment. No one ever praised her food before.

"Ready for dessert?" Cherish asked a little later.

"Why don't you show me your sketches?"

Knowing it wasn't man code for sex, Cherish got up and retrieved her leather portfolio case and joined him on the sofa. Cherish proudly showed Darius her portfolio, but she had a hard time concentrating. His cologne invaded her senses and penetrated her good judgment. She moved a little closer, hoping he would take the hint.

Cherish took the large leather portfolio case of out of his hands, and kissed him. "I thought we'd...talk." She gave him her best seductive glance. She did everything but stand naked in front of him.

Darius breathed a sigh of relief. "Good. I thought you were trying to get fresh with me," he joked. He resumed looking at the sketches.

Frustrated, Cherish stomped off to the kitchen to get dessert. Before she returned to the living room, she opened the freezer compartment of the refrigerator and stood there several minutes. Feeling cool, calm and in charge of her world again, she grabbed the cheesecake and returned to Darius.

After they finished dessert, Cherish gave him a tour of her house. Though it wasn't on the same scale as Darius's, he seemed impressed with the two-story house. He held her hand as they walked from room to room. When they came to a closed door, Cherish didn't offer an explanation or open it.

"What's this room?" Darius grasped the doorknob, slightly opening the door.

Cherish took a deep breath. "It was my mother's room. I can't bear to go in there. I had to a few months ago, to finally clear her things out. It just still hurts so bad. I can still see her sitting up in bed in her favorite bed jacket, staring at me with that blank stare because she didn't know who I was," Cherish whispered.

Darius closed the door and stood directly in front of her and wrapped her in a tight hug. His strong body cradled her smaller one. "Cherish, if you want to talk, I understand. I've lost a parent. I know how that feels."

Cherish stepped out of his embrace. "Thank you, Darius. That hug was what I needed." That and a little more, she thought.

"How about Thanksgiving? Come over for dinner. Dad likes you." Darius led her back downstairs.

Cherish nodded. Although she didn't really remember the beginning stages with her mother, she could actually see that Otis Crawford was in his beginning stages. She cringed at the memories of the times when she was too busy to spend time with her mother. *You can't change the past, Cherish.* She forced happy thoughts. Mr. Crawford appeared to be doing well. Between Darbi and the nurse, he exercised every day. It took that concerted effort, according to Darius, to keep his father active.

"I'd love to come over Thursday," Cherish said. Perhaps this was her chance to make up for her mother.

CHAPTER NINE

"Darius, you can't be serious!" Curry exclaimed to his friend as Darius recounted his most recent date with Cherish. Curry leaned back in his chair listening carefully, shaking his head in disbelief. "What are you waiting on? I've heard of women holding out, but come on!"

Darius looked at his friend. Curry looked different; his hazel eyes sparkled at him. Darius smiled. If it had been any other man, Darius would have thought Curry was in love. Not Curry. He was responsible for more broken hearts than Brad Pitt when he married Jennifer Aniston.

"Curry, now is just not a good time. I have a big project I'm working on and I don't want to fail. I like to concentrate on one thing at a time. I don't want something happening in the heat of the moment and we both regret not waiting."

"As opposed to me?"

"Curry, you're different from me. You're a free spirit. I'm more..."

"Anal?" Curry smiled. Darius liked the rigidiness of a schedule. "Dare, there are some things you can't plan." Mica, Curry's assistant, interrupted the conversation.

"Mr. Fitzgerald, here are the tickets for tonight's game. You're right behind the glass. Also, your reservations for Pierre's have been confirmed for ten-thirty," she said in her seductive accent, and placed the envelope on Curry's desk.

"Thank you, Mica."

She nodded and left the office.

Darius looked at the envelope. "Pierre's? Well, I'm impressed. I hear there's a two-month wait for a week-night reservation." Darius smiled; it seemed Curry was going to a lot of trouble for just a friendly date with Darbi. Pierre's was a swanky restaurant by the new hockey arena in Dallas. "How do you know so many people with great tickets and connections?"

"It's my personality." Curry smiled confidently.

"Bull!" Darius laughed and left Curry's office.

～～～

The next evening, Curry glanced at Darbi as he drove into Dallas from Arlington. She had been quiet almost the entire trip. He wondered if she regretted their date. Would she rather be out with DeMarcus? "Anything wrong?" He patted her leg.

"No, I'm fine," came her soft reply. "Where are we going?"

"It's a surprise." He hoped it would be. He'd called in some pretty big favors to get last minute reservations at the restaurant. He hoped it would soften what he had to say. He chuckled softly. When had he cared if a woman objected to his holiday plans? "I'm going to Seattle tomorrow for Thanksgiving." For the first time in three years, he wanted to stay in Texas for the holiday, but he knew his mother would disown him if he did. "I'll be back Sunday," Curry told her as he negotiated through the arena traffic.

"That's good, Curry," she whispered. "You should be with family during the holidays."

"Will you be at Darius's?" He gently caressed her hand, hating the thought of being away from her for even a few days.

"Yes. He's going to have dinner there. So I'll probably just stay with him Wednesday night."

"Good." Curry wanted to know where to call. At least she wouldn't be with DeMarcus, he thought. A point for me!

Curry parked the BMW in underground parking at the American Airlines Sports Center in Dallas. Then he opened the car door for her and offered his hand. DeMarcus could take some tips from Curry, Darbi thought. She took his hand and eased out of the seat. They walked toward the arena hand in hand. "Curry, what's this?"

"It's a hockey game. Do you like hockey?"

"Now is a fine time to ask me, isn't it? Yes, I do like hockey. Actually, I love hockey. In Philly, I worked at this video store and most of the guys who worked there loved hockey. So I started going to the games with them, less Amos, of course."

"I'm glad to hear that you have some good memories of Philly." He listened to her rave about her favorite team, the Detroit Redwings. "Unfortunately, the Dallas Stars aren't playing them tonight."

Darbi felt apprehensive as they neared the entrance door. She looked around and saw very few African-Americans, which was different from Philly. However, the ticket taker made her welcome with a big smile and a hello. Darbi laughed as she heard him say: "You go, girl!"

"What was that?" Curry looked for their section of seats.

Darbi smiled. "In case you haven't noticed, there aren't a whole lot of African-Americans here. I guess hockey hasn't caught on down here yet. In Philly, there were many more, though not like a football game."

Curry shrugged, dismissing the subject. "I guess I really hadn't noticed. Does it bother you being with me?"

"No, Curry, not in the least," she said with confidence.

After the game while they waited for traffic to die down, Curry bought an authentic hockey jersey for her. Where, she wondered, did that fit into their 'just friends' relationship?

Pierre's, one of Dallas's most elegant restaurants, was close to the arena. When they pulled into the parking lot, Darbi expected it to be crowded, but it wasn't. Considering they were both dressed in blue jeans and sweaters, Darbi expected them to be turned away from such an elegant restaurant. A tuxedo-clad gentleman greeted them with a large smile plastered on his chubby face. "Can I help you, sir?"

"Reservation for Fitzgerald," Curry stated with confidence.

To Darbi's surprise, the maitre d' smiled and summoned the waiter.

Once they were seated, the waiter placed a linen napkin in her lap and poured the wine. After the waiter departed, Darbi spoke. "This is a beautiful place, Curry." She glanced at him across the table.

Curry was about to answer her when someone broke into the conversation. He almost dropped his wine glass.

"Curry, what are you doing here?"

Curry looked at the five-foot-seven-inch blonde. Not here, not now! "Ava! How are you? This is my friend, Darbi Crawford." He nervously nodded to Darbi. "We just left the hockey game," he added for no reason.

The blonde woman shook Darbi's hand. "I'm Ava Bradley. I'm the second ex." She emphasized the word *second.* "Curry, you never brought me here," she chastised him. Her tone was teasing, but Darbi could tell she was not.

"Because you don't like hockey. Darbi does. How's Jason?" Jason was the man she had left him for.

"We're divorcing. I just can't seem to find the right man at the right time. I'm moving as well. That's why I was here. Farewell party."

"That's nice, Ava." Curry stared into Darbi's eyes, silently apologizing.

"Yes, Texas holds a lot of painful memories for me. I thought I'd start fresh somewhere else. It was nice to meet you, Darbi." Ava left the table.

As the woman retreated from their table, Darbi saw the look of relief on Curry's face.

"Sorry," he said apologetically. He took a sip of his drink to calm his nerves. He hoped Ava's impromptu visit hadn't spoiled the evening.

"That's okay. I could tell you were really uncomfortable. I'd probably react the same way if some of Amos's family showed up."

"Is that a possibility?" He wondered about her past with Amos, but didn't know how to ask. She always had an unhappy look on her face when she spoke of him.

"No, I think they disliked me as much as I disliked them." Darbi picked up the menu, closing the subject.

Curry watched her over his menu. They both had so many cobwebs in their closets. "They obviously don't know the Darbi I know," Curry joked, trying to lighten the mood. "Ava divorced me to marry Jason. She was ready for the family thing. I wasn't. Don't know if I'll ever be."

～⌒

Later that night, Curry stared at the ceiling of Darbi's condo as she slept next to him. After making love to her two earth-shattering times, he was spent. As tired as his body was, though, sleep eluded him. He was not supposed to be feeling these kinds of emotions with Darbi.

It was supposed to be a bit of fun, he reminded himself. But each time he was with her, he felt even more drawn to her. Though she never asked about his past, he was getting curious about hers. He watched as she tossed and turned in her sleep and wondered what could have such a hold on her.

Darbi's hand ended up on his stomach and slowly descended lower. Slowly she began to caress him, hardening him instantly. When her hand wrapped around him like a vise grip, he couldn't hold back his excitement. Curry held his breath, anticipating her hand's next move. He gritted his teeth against the growing erection, but it was useless. She massaged him for a few heart stopping strokes, then opened her eyes.

"I must have been dreaming." She smiled shyly at him as she removed her hand. "Sorry." She was obviously embarrassed.

Curry moved on top of her. "Don't be. Now I'm dreaming." He kissed her as he took her for another ride on the Fitzgerald Express.

A few hours later, Curry was startled awake by sudden pain in his chest area. When he opened his eyes, he realized Darbi was hitting him in the chest and crying. Her eyes were open and unfocused. Curry sat up and grabbed her hands. She jumped and blinked.

"Curry, what are you doing?" Darbi snatched her hands away and covered her nudity with the sheet. "Why is your chest so red?"

"Because you've been pelting me and crying." He slowly rubbed her back. "Darbi, I won't hurt you and

Amos can't hurt you anymore. He's dead." He drew her to his chest and eased down against the pillows. He listened as her sobs slowed down and faded into the night.

The next morning, Curry woke and decided to fix breakfast for her. After he showered and dressed, he walked into the kitchen. He winced in pain as he reached for the coffee cups. His chest muscles were tender.

After fixing breakfast and placing it on the tray, he walked into the bedroom. Darbi was just walking out of the bathroom, dressed in tight jeans and a sweater. He motioned for her to sit on the bed. "How do you feel?" While he wanted to ease her fears before he left for Seattle, he knew it was something that couldn't be accomplished over breakfast.

Looking at him, she found a comfortable position on the bed. "I'm really sorry about hitting on you like that. I wish I could just let go. Does it hurt?" A tear escaped her eyes.

Curry sat next to her on the bed and placed the tray in front of her. Suddenly it mattered a great deal to him that she understood it wasn't her fault.

"Darbi, if hitting me helps you get over your past, then no, it didn't hurt." He watched as she touched the red and purple bruises on his chest.

"Curry, I know you must be hurting. I wish I hadn't done that to you of all people. You've helped me so much. Why can't I just get over it?" She wiped the falling tears with the back of her hand.

Curry caught her hand, then dried her eyes with a paper napkin. "You will. It will just take time. You have fifteen years of hurt to get rid of. I can't even imagine what you must have gone through. Eat."

Darbi drew in a deep breath and grabbed a piece of bacon. As she chewed the meat, the tears finally went away. Curry felt his heart overflow with love.

~ ⌒ ~

The ringing of her doorbell awakened Darbi a few hours later. She opened her door to find a deliveryman holding a gorgeous array of flowers. They were from DeMarcus. She tipped the deliveryman and read the card as she walked to the kitchen: *I can't express sufficient regret for Sunday night. Please accept this as an apology. DeMarcus.*

She sniffed the aromatic bouquet. It was a grand gesture for that debacle of an evening. She noticed another envelope; it held four tickets on the 50-yard line for the Thanksgiving Day game. After she invited Cherish to the game, she called her brother. "I hope you don't mind, I invited Cherish," she said, knowing that he didn't.

"No, that will be great." Darius hesitated, then said in his brotherly tone, "I know you said that Curry only wanted friendship, but are you sure about DeMarcus? Especially after all that mess the other night. You deserve so much more."

"Darius, it's just a football game," Darbi explained. She should have known he'd worry about her. He had ever since she returned home over a year ago. "He's apologizing for Sunday, that's all. What about you?"

"What?" Darius played innocent.

"You're frustrating Cherish. Darius, she thinks something is wrong with her, since you still haven't, you know. Don't you like her?"

"Of course, I do," Darius reassured his sister. "She's interesting, beautiful, smart and independent. I just want it to be right. She's still grieving for her mother. I don't want to add to her hurt."

Darbi smiled through the phone at the concern in her brother's voice. "Darius, I know you wouldn't hurt Cherish. Not on purpose anyway. I know Cherish really enjoys your company, but brother, you are stressing her unnecessarily."

"Darbi, you're going to have to trust me," he said in his boardroom voice. "I do care for her. Dinner will be at noon, so we'll have time to eat before the game. Please thank DeMarcus for me."

CHAPTER TEN

Darbi glanced around Darius's large dining room. At Thanksgiving dinner Cherish sat next to Darius and relished in his overly-attentive manner.

Darbi knew Darius and Cherish were meant for each other. Now if he would only put out. . . . She giggled at the thought. Darius would die of embarrassment if he knew that Darbi knew the intimate details of his relationship with Cherish.

After they feasted on turkey, dressing, mashed potatoes and corn, they prepared to leave. They were getting into Darius's Yukon to head to the game, but before they could, a long, black stretch limo pulled up. The driver got out and introduced himself to the astonished foursome, and informed them the car was courtesy of DeMarcus.

Settling in the car, Darius took Cherish's hand. He smiled at his sister who was sitting by their father. "Tell DeMarcus I said thanks."

Darbi smiled. "I will."

After they arrived at the stadium, they were shown to their seats, which were almost on the field. Darbi gazed at her father, who looked happy. That brought joy to her troubled heart. "How are you doing, Dad?"

"Great, honey. I've never been to a live professional football game. I always meant to, but you know how life is. There was always something that came up. This is amazing. All those years I wasted watching the game on TV. I don't think I want to know what DeMarcus is apologizing for. I might have to have a little talk with him," Otis commented in his fatherly tone. "I still remember how to shoot a gun." He winked at her.

"It was nothing, Dad." She smiled at her father's concern and didn't want him to worry needlessly.

"You just enjoy yourself this time 'round, okay?" Otis grabbed Darbi's hand. "Promise me."

"I will. Promise," Darbi said. She hoped she could keep that promise to her father.

Darbi was seated next to Cherish. The women shared a knowing look. "Again!" Cherish exclaimed. "Man, this is really unfair!"

Darbi giggled. "It was much better this time. I thought he would have called today, but . . . We're still just friends." She didn't mention her latest emotional episode, because Darbi didn't want her new friend to know she was teetering on the brink of a nervous breakdown.

Cherish nodded at Darius. "Why can't he be like Curry just a little bit?"

"Ms. Darbi Crawford?" A baritone voice boomed to the foursome, interrupting Darbi's answer.

"I'm Darbi Crawford." She looked at the man in wonder. Dressed in an Armani suit, he didn't look like an usher. He handed her an envelope.

Darbi quickly realized he was waiting for her reply. She opened the sealed envelope, scanned the note and smiled. "That will be fine," she said, folding the white paper and stuffing it in her purse.

The man nodded and left the group. Cherish, Darius, and Otis stared at Darbi in question.

"DeMarcus asked me out for tomorrow night," she explained.

"Oh!" said the group in unison.

Luckily, the Cowboys won, so the men were happy, Otis more than Darius since Darius didn't watch football. The women chatted all the way back to Darius's house.

"Want to go shopping tomorrow?" Cherish asked Darbi.

Darbi nodded. Given the fact that she wouldn't be working for a month, because of the semester break, she needed to hit the sales. "Sounds great. What time?"

Cherish hesitated. "Well, my mom and I used to go at six, when the stores open." Cherish took a deep breath. "If you don't want to go that early, I understand."

"No, it sounds great. I've never been shopping that early. Why don't you spend the night, so we can head to the mall sooner?" She knew Cherish was having a hard time with the holidays. Darbi watched her struggle for emotional control, then she looked at her brother for a reaction. Nothing.

Would Darius ever let his guard down and get it right?

~~~~~

Friday morning, Cherish and Darbi woke early and joined the Christmas shoppers, scoping out the bargains. Darbi soon began to enjoy the early morning atmosphere. After getting most of the gifts they needed, the women decided on breakfast.

"Let's put the packages in the car and then get some food," Cherish suggested.

Darbi nodded in agreement as her stomach rumbled.

As they ate, Darbi toyed with her silverware. The curiosity was killing her. "Cherish," she started, "did I do anything in my sleep last night?" She couldn't bear the thought of Cherish seeing her out of control and crying.

Cherish watched Darbi closely. "Yes, you did scream. I thought someone had broken into the house, but then I found you crying. I comforted you for a few minutes, then you went back to sleep as if nothing had happened."

"Was that the only time?"

"Yes, Darbi." Cherish took a deep breath. "You can tell me what's bothering you; it could help. I'm your friend and I won't judge you. You should know that."

"Someday." Darbi picked at her food. The ham and cheese omelet didn't look so appetizing anymore.

"Do you do that every night? I didn't want to mention this, but I have noticed over the months that we've known each other that you cry at commercials. Actually you cry at TV shows, the news, or just about anything."

"When I first came back home, I would usually have crying spells in the evening. You know, I could be studying, then all of a sudden I would start crying uncontrollably. Then after I told Curry about them, they stopped. I didn't know I cried during the night until I made love with Curry. He found me in the shower, soaked to the bone and crying like a baby. I don't know how I got there. I would like to talk to someone about it. I hit Curry in the chest the last time we were together, in my sleep, of course."

Cherish felt sympathy for all the pain Darbi had endured. "Just be happy that part of your life is over."

"I am." Darbi felt better already and her appetite had returned.

❧

After they returned from shopping, Darbi left to get ready for her date with DeMarcus. She didn't feel too excited about the date, viewing it more as an obligation for DeMarcus giving her the football tickets than a date.

Cherish sat on her living room sofa thinking about the Crawfords. This time she was preoccupied with Darbi more than Darius. She realized that she was getting closer to Darbi than she had expected. Initially she'd viewed Darbi as a way to Darius, but now she saw Darbi as a true friend. A friend who desperately needed help.

Cherish wanted to know what could have such an emotional hold on her. Why couldn't Darbi just let her dead husband go and move on with her life? Finding her crying like that in the middle of the night had frightened Cherish. She was tempted to call Darius and tell him, but that would be betraying Darbi's trust. She wanted to help her friend, but how? And if she did, would she betray Darius in the process? She shook her head at the maze she was getting herself into. Then her phone rang. The male voice sounded oddly familiar.

"Vincent?" Cherish said in disbelief, hearing her ex-boyfriend's voice.

"Yes, Cherish. It's Vince."

"How are you doing? What's it been? Like five years?" She hadn't seen him since their breakup.

"Yeah, it's been a long time. I heard about your mom last year, but I was in Rome at the time."

"So what's up, Vince?" Cherish cut to the chase.

He laughed. "Yeah, you know me like a book, don't you? I'm doing my first solo fashion show in a few weeks. I wanted you to be there, but it's in Toronto."

Cherish had always known Vince would make it. He'd chosen New York over her and her ailing mother when they ended their relationship five years earlier. "That's wonderful. I'm very proud."

"So you can come?" he asked.

Silence. A long pause of silence. "I would love to come, Vince, but I don't know." For once, she wanted a man to say, *I need you, Cherish.*

"If you can, let me know. It's December 8–10, at the Victorian Hotel. In scenic Toronto," he added in the voice of a hyper travel agent.

"I'll let you know. It was so nice to hear your voice." The ex-lovers rang off.

Cherish hung up the phone and pondered Vince's invitation. The fashion show was two weeks away. If she wanted to get back into the fashion game, she would need some exposure. Maybe Vince could help in that aspect. As she thought about it, she realized she was tired from getting up so early that morning, and decided a nap was in order.

When she opened her eyes again, it was past seven in the evening. She pondered what to do with her future. As she walked through her house, she noticed her sketchpad on the desk. Walking to her sketch table, she turned on the stereo and began to sketch. Cherish sketched for two hours without interruption, until Darius called her.

"How was shopping?" Darius wondered why Cherish hadn't called him. He had grown accustomed to her daily calls, but this time he'd had to call her.

"It was great. Darbi went crazy shopping. How's your dad?"

"He's fine." Darius had the feeling that for once he didn't have Cherish's undivided attention. "Are you busy?"

"Actually, I was in the middle of a sketch. Can I call you tomorrow? I don't want to lose my momentum."

"Sure." Darius hung up the phone without even saying bye. Just as he began to feel guilty about his bad phone manners, the phone startled him as it rang. *Probably Cherish*, he thought. To his surprise, he heard Curry's deep voice when he answered the phone.

"Dare, could I speak to Darbi?"

"Sorry, Curry, she's not here." Darius waited an eternity for Curry to speak.

"Oh?" he paused. "Did she and Cherish go out for the night? I thought you and Cherish would be somewhere trying to break a bed." Curry's rich laughter carried over the phone line. "I tried her condo, but I didn't get an answer. I tried yesterday, too. Did you guys go out for dinner? I thought you were cooking?"

"I did cook. Actually, DeMarcus sent Darbi four tickets for yesterday's game. We were on the 50-yard line. It was awesome!" Darius tried to soften the blow of the bad news. "You should have seen Dad's face. He was like a kid in a candy store." Even if Curry wouldn't admit it, Darius knew Curry was feeling more than friendship for Darbi.

"W-where is Darbi?" The words tumbled out of Curry's mouth.

"She went out with DeMarcus tonight." Darius waited for Curry's reply. Nothing.

"I gotta go. Bye." Curry cut the connection.

In the eight years he had known Curry, he'd never known him to act so childishly. Darius dialed his friend back. After the fifth ring, Curry finally answered. "Curry, I know you would never hang up on me. There must be a fault in your phone line." Darius waited for an answer, knowing there wasn't.

"Sure. Yeah. I'm sorry, Dare."

"Curry, is there something troubling you?"

"No," came Curry's short reply.

"Curry?" Darius prodded, knowing this time it was Curry who needed a push instead of him.

"Darius, there is nothing wrong."

"Curry, I've known you eight years. I know when you're upset. You're pissed because Darbi went out with DeMarcus. But I believe you spouted something about a casual friendship."

"I know what I said. I don't need to be reminded of it at every turn, do I?" Curry yelled into the phone.

"Curry, don't get miffed at me because you told my sister you only wanted friendship and now you're mad because she took you at your word."

"What should I do now?"

Darius laughed out loud. "This is too funny. Is this the same man who has dated half the women in the office, under thirty, I might add? And now you're asking me what you should do about my sister. I'll have to note this auspicious occasion on my calendar!" Darius couldn't stop laughing.

"Darius?" Curry persisted. "You're really not helping."

"Okay, Mr. Lover Man," Darius calmed his laughter, "I'd say honesty is the best policy. I know that may be a new concept for you concerning a woman." Darius paused. His friend had become awfully quiet at the other end of the phone.

"What do you want, Curry? Do you want a relationship? Why are you back so early? How are your parents?" Darius knew but wanted his best friend to admit that he was in love with Darbi.

Curry took a deep breath. "I wanted to see her. I couldn't get her on the phone yesterday, so I came back early."

"I'll tell her you called." Darius thought about his earlier conversation with Cherish. He had acted as childishly as Curry, and hated himself for it. He had to rectify this. "I'll talk to you later. Why don't you try and calm down before you talk to her?"

After Darius ended the call with Curry, he decided it was time to eat some major crow. He dialed Cherish's number. She picked up immediately.

Darius spoke before she could get a word in. "Cherish, I would like to apologize for my behavior earlier. I was being childish and inconsiderate."

"Well, Darius, at least you were expelling some kind of emotion. At least you seemed a little more human."

"What does that mean?"

Cherish sighed, regretting bringing up the subject. "Darius, you need to let go every once in a while."

No one understood what was at stake in his life; why should she be any different? "Cherish, my father is sick. My sister has a mysterious past she doesn't want to talk about it. I think she's about two feet from a total breakdown. How am I supposed to act?"

"I didn't mean to upset you, Darius. I would just like for you to enjoy the life you've worked so hard for."

"I want to. I just want a semblance of normalcy in my life. I want Darbi to at least be happy and if that is with Curry, I'm dealing with that."

"I didn't want to mention this, but I feel that I have to."

"What is it?" Darius's heart raced.

"Well," Cherish started, "you know Darbi spent the night with me last night, so we could go shopping today."

"Yes, Cherish."

"In the middle of the night, I heard her crying. You would have thought someone was actually hurting her. I comforted her and she went back to sleep. Darius, I think something's wrong with Darbi."

He thought so too, but like dealing with the onset of his father's illness, he'd ignored the signs. "Yes, I have noticed her crying and Curry told me about another crying episode. I'm working on an idea, but I need to make sure she doesn't think I think she's crazy. Thank you, Cherish."

"For what?" she said, surprised. "For telling you that you are too stoic?"

"No. For being a good friend to both me and Darbi. Curry confessed the same thing to me. If you guys hadn't cared enough to mention it, this could have gone on for the rest of her life."

～～♪

Darbi breathed a sigh of relief after she said goodnight to DeMarcus. Ending the relationship had gone much easier than she had expected. Besides being African-American and liking to work out, they just didn't have anything in common.

She opened her history book and began to study for her upcoming test. A knock stopped her before she read the first page. *Why does everyone show up when I'm studying?* She walked to the front door and opened it.

"We need to talk." Curry stomped inside her condo, heading for the couch.

"Curry, I'm studying." Darbi closed the door. "Why don't you come in?" she asked sarcastically.

He sat on her couch. "I'm not leaving until we talk."

"Okay, Curry, what is it? I have a test coming up and I need to study. Finals are next week." Darbi didn't mean to sound short with him, but she needed to finish her extra-credit assignment for her history class. She sat beside him on the couch.

Curry rubbed his face with his large hands. "I know, Darbi." He stood and took a deep breath. "Remember when I said I just wanted friendship?" He paced the small room.

Darbi nodded.

"I think we went past that the first time we made love. Hell, I think we went past it the first time we kissed." He scooted closer to her. "I guess what I am saying is, I want us to be together."

"Curry, is that why you were sitting in the parking lot when DeMarcus brought me home?" She thought he looked incredibly cute as he tried to hide his jealousy.

"You saw me?"

"I wasn't sure it was you, until five minutes ago. Why were you waiting for me?"

"I told you why. You didn't answer me."

"Curry, I like my freedom. Let's keep it as it is." Darbi averted her eyes. She wanted to keep the independence she had fought so hard for the last two years.

"I'm not proposing, Darbi. I just want to date a little more seriously than the occasional hockey game."

"No demands?"

"No demands. Except you gotta dump Mr. Football."

"That sounds like a demand to me." She smiled, not wanting him to think he had the upper hand and could dictate orders to her. "DeMarcus and I are just friends, just like we are. You cannot invade my life, Curry Fitzgerald."

"Okay." Curry backed off. "I just want us to date."

"Why? Why do you want to date me?"

"You're driving me crazy, Darbi!" Curry kissed her impatiently, his mouth hard on hers, forcing her lips apart. His kiss started out hard, but suddenly it was gentle, making her want more. Finally he broke the kiss and whispered against her kiss-swollen lips, "I know I have a less than great track record when it comes to relationships, but I want to give this an honest shot."

"Give what a shot? I might agree to a few extra dates, but not a relationship." She put some distance between them, just for her own peace of mind, or she would have to kiss him again. "Curry, I don't think you're ready for that. I know I'm not ready for that. So how about just a few extra dates."

Curry looked at her as she spoke. "Okay, Darbi. You make the rules. How about dinner tomorrow?"

"I need to study, Curry. How about Friday night?"

"That's a week away. Nothing sooner?"

"Curry," Darbi spoke slowly, as though to a child seconds from a tantrum. "I have to finish my report that's due Wednesday morning. I have group Wednesday night, and Thursday I'm with Dad. So yes, it's Friday. Take it or leave it."

CHAPTER ELEVEN

A week later, Cherish sat in her office sketching her latest inspiration. She drew the almost transparent dress and smiled as she played with the neckline. Darius's eyes would pop out of his head if she sketched the neckline any lower, she thought. With a mischievous smile on her lips, she plunged the neckline and created a vision of seduction. *Darius be damned!*

Almost everyone around Cherish seemed to be heading in the right direction. Darbi and Curry were officially dating, although Darbi didn't see it as such. She saw it as just a few extra dates, not a real commitment. Otis was doing well and in good spirits.

Then there was Darius. He still seemed to be operating in neutral. She wondered what it would take for him to do more than kiss her. As she was thinking these thoughts on a Thursday afternoon, her phone rang. Vincent's excited voice immediately alarmed her.

"Cherish, I need a huge favor!" Vincent's voice was at least an octave higher than his usual baritone.

"Anything, Vince. What is it?"

"My flighty assistant decided to get sick. I need you bad. Can you come to Toronto? ASAP? My show is tomorrow night. I need to do some major alterations. Please, please, Cherish!"

Cherish laughed at his anxious tone. "Sure, Vince. I can take the next flight out. Where are you staying?"

He rattled off the necessary information and Cherish hung up the phone. She searched the Internet for the next available flight to Canada. With all the new security regulations, the first available flight was leaving Dallas International Airport at nine that night.

She called Darius's office and his assistant politely told her he was in a meeting for the rest of the afternoon. Cherish thanked her and then called Darbi. Luckily, she knew Darbi had taken the afternoon off to study for her upcoming finals.

"Cherish, that's awesome! What did my stiff brother say?"

"He was in a meeting." Cherish reached into her closet for her Eddie Bauer luggage, the cordless phone nestled between her neck and chin. "I'll tell him later tonight. I wish you could go with me."

"Me, too. But I've got to study for my finals. I will tell him tonight, when I go sit with Dad."

Darius watched Darbi park her VW in front of his house. He marveled at the changes in her since returning to college, even if it was his idea. Darbi was more confident, and she was crying less, but he didn't know if he could attribute that to school or Curry. Probably the latter.

She was dressed in jeans that Darius thought were too tight, and a light sweater. With her backpack slung over her shoulder, she looked the part of a college student. Darius let her inside the house before she could use her key.

"Hey, I thought you weren't coming tonight?" Darius prepared to leave for the gym. "Don't you have a final tomorrow? Have you studied? How are your grades?"

Darbi laughed and raised her backpack to show him. "Yes, Darius. My history final is tomorrow. I've been studying all week for it. My grades are pretty good for a 38-year-old freshman, I think." She paused, not meeting Darius's eyes. "Cherish called me earlier."

Darius stopped fiddling with his gym bag. "Really?"

"She's leaving for Toronto tonight to help a friend with his fashion show." She spoke slowly and carefully, choosing words that wouldn't send him over the edge.

"Oh," came Darius bland response. He couldn't believe he sounded so calm when his heart was about to pop out of his chest. "One of her designer friends?"

Darbi nodded. "Yes, Vincent. His assistant got sick and his fashion show is in a couple of days. He really needed her help," Darbi explained.

Darius sat down with a thud in a nearby leather chair. Had he lost her to an ex-lover?

"Yes, Darius," Darbi said, reading his mind, "he's straight. From the pictures that I've seen of him, he's a hunk." Darbi coughed. "You're taking this quite well. I'd be going nuts if it was me."

Darius said nothing as he contemplated his next move. "Why would she leave like that? Not even a good-bye, nothin'."

"She tried to call you, but you were in a meeting. Besides, you don't display a lot of affection, Darius. A few kisses here and there aren't going to cement your relationship. You're going to have to shift into high gear or you may be dateless again."

The doorbell silenced his retort. Darius went to the door and let Curry inside. The friends exchanged glances.

Immediately Curry sensed something was amiss. "What is it, Darius? Is it Otis?"

"No, it's Cherish." Darius quickly filled his friend in on the recent chain of events.

"You have to go to her," Curry said.

Darius shook his head. "I can't just show up. She didn't ask me to come to Canada."

Curry shook his head. "Darius, if you don't go, you'll kick yourself forever."

"I haven't packed or anything," Darius mumbled, hating that he was even thinking the same harebrained thing as Curry.

"You can buy clothes when you get there. You need the element of surprise," Curry stated, his eyes on Darbi.

"I don't even know where she's going to be staying," Darius whined. "How am I supposed to find her and show her how much she means to me if I don't know where she is?"

Curry nodded in Darbi's direction as she studied. Both Curry and Darius looked to the one person who held the information that they needed. Slowly, they both walked toward the sofa. Darius sat next to his sister.

Maybe she would take pity on her dimwitted brother. "Where is Cherish staying?"

"The Victorian Gables, room 1224. Vincent reserved the adjoining suite to his, since they would be working late." Darbi smiled as Darius absorbed the information.

Darbi's one very informative sentence decided his fate for him. Tonight, Cherish Murray would know exactly how Darius Crawford felt about her. "I'm going to her."

"I'll take you to the airport," Curry volunteered. "That way I know you will get on the plane. Don't worry about work. I can cover for you. You've certainly done it for me enough times."

Darius called and made arrangements for the next flight to Toronto. Ten-thirty was his best option. He'd arrive at three in morning with the time change. Satisfied for the moment, he hurried upstairs to pack. He started downstairs in time to see Curry kiss his sister. Darius smiled. They really thought they were being secretive. If they only knew.

He made loud noises as he walked downstairs, laughing as they jumped apart so he wouldn't catch them. An hour later, Curry ushered him out of the door and they were headed for the airport. A new and a spontaneous Darius Crawford would surprise Cherish Murray that night!

When he arrived at the Victorian Hotel, it occurred to him that he didn't know what to say to her. Would she welcome him with open arms or would Vincent tell him to get lost? An idea sprang into Darius's mind as he checked into the hotel.

The desk clerk was more than obliging after Darius placed two one hundred dollar bills in his hands. "Miss Murray is out, but it can be arranged, Mr. Crawford. You're in room 1421."

Darius looked at his watch. "It's after two in the morning and she's still out!"

"Yes, sir. There's a lot of preparation for a fashion show."

Darius nodded and left the desk. Once settled in his hotel suite, he ordered room service, and checked in with his sister.

"Would you mind checking in on Dad until I get back?" Darius asked as he prepared for his shower.

"No, Darius, I don't mind. Have you talked to Cherish yet?"

"No, she's out. But I have a great idea, even you would be proud. Tell Curry thanks." Darius looked at the bed and smiled.

Darbi wouldn't let him forget why he was in Canada in the first place. "Yes, Darius. Go find Cherish."

When Cherish arrived in Canada and settled in her room, she thought she would have time for a nap. But Vincent was anxious about his show and wanted to get started on the changes as soon as possible. She watched

Vincent as he checked and rechecked the garment for flaws. Cherish glanced at her watch and stifled yet another yawn. It was now past three o'clock in the morning and she was tired.

"Okay, Cherish," Vince said on a tired exhale. "Let's call it a night." He patted her on the back. "I really appreciate you coming on such short notice. Why don't you sleep in tomorrow and I'll call you about noon?"

Cherish gratefully nodded. She was exhausted and right now a paper bag would look good. "I'm sorry, Vince. I know I'll be fresher in the morning, after a little sleep. I'll see you tomorrow." Cherish walked out of the dressing room and through the lobby. She was thinking only of a hot bath and sleep as she passed the desk. The front desk clerk called her name.

"Ms. Murray, there was a problem with your room."

"What happened?" Thoughts of her hot bath floated away.

"Well," the desk clerk started, "the floor above yours had a water leak, so we moved you to another room. We hope you don't mind. For your inconvenience, we gave you a suite at no extra charge."

"I normally don't like strangers handling my personal items, but in this case, thank you." Cherish was so tired, she just wanted to lie down. She wasn't even particular as to where.

The desk clerk nodded. "You're in room 1421." He handed her the room card and watched as she walked toward the elevators, breathing a sigh of relief.

After Cherish exited the elevator on the fourteenth floor, she looked for the room. It was a corner room, assuring her of a peaceful night. Cherish walked in and instantly decided they'd given her the wrong room. This room was for lovers. Fresh rose petals covered the bed and made a path on the floor. A bottle of champagne was beside the bed in a silver ice bucket and two glasses sat on the nightstand. Candles lighted the room, and soft jazz music played. Cherish sighed. "I could get used to this," she muttered to herself.

"I hope so." Darius walked up behind her.

"Darius!" Cherish spun around and faced him. "What are you doing here?"

"I wanted to see you." He held her in a tight embrace and kissed her with a hunger that she would never have attributed to Darius Crawford.

Cherish rested her head on his chest. He had kissed her like a man intent on making love in the very near future. She had to be dreaming. Darius wouldn't do such a wacky thing. He would never do something this romantic. This was entirely too spontaneous, not to mention self-indulgent. She gazed around the room. "How on earth did you set this up?"

"You'd be surprised what a couple of Benjamin Franklins will do. Well, what do you think?"

"That you're amazing!" She couldn't contain her excitement, and didn't even try.

"The best is yet to come," he promised.

"One day you will have to tell me how you did all this," Cherish said.

They were settled on the bed amid all the roses. Darius held her hand and looked deeply into her eyes. "Cherish, I know I started taking you for granted. That was not my intention at all."

"I know, Darius." Cherish wondered where he was leading with all this.

Darius hugged and kissed her. His hands roamed over her body, hovering around her breasts. He deepened the kiss, bringing her body closer to his, letting her feel his arousal.

Cherish couldn't believe it. Finally. After four months and all those hints she dropped were they finally going to make love?

Cherish broke from his embrace and sat on the bed. She ran her hands over the soft rose petals, inhaling their sweet floral scent. Darius sat beside her on the bed. He took off her sweater and kissed her neck. "Cherish, can we make love tonight?"

Cherish nodded, taking off his sweater by way of answering. She pushed him down on the bed and she took in the sight before her. Darius was quite a beautiful man. His rock hard abdomen and chiseled chest that had just a scant amount of matted hair were lovely sights. "You're beautiful," breathed Cherish. Her small hands eased over his chest and down to his waist. Her full lips followed her hands, igniting a fire in his loins.

"No, Cherish. You're a vision. Why did we wait so long for this moment?" Darius ran his fingers through her hair, bringing her closer to him.

"I was waiting for you," Cherish murmured against the planes of his flat stomach.

He sat up and reached for her. She willingly went into his arms. He pressed his lips against her for a breathtaking kiss before he spoke. "And I was waiting for you." Darius's shaky hand caressed her face. He leaned down for another kiss. As their tongues danced together, she felt him unfastening her jeans and sliding them down her long legs. She helped him free her from her denim prison.

Cherish sat up and unbuttoned his pants, ready to get the show on the road. She eased them down his legs, revealing silk boxers. She quickly disposed of them as well. He was some kind of man, and Cherish was very happy about that.

He divested her of her bra and underwear, pulling Cherish to him, body to body. He kissed her again as he embraced her and eased her under him.

Cherish's head was spinning. She and Darius were making love. Barely thinking straight, she muttered, "P-protection."

Darius was already reaching for the packet. "Yes, right here. But I have some work to do first."

Cherish looked at him with her 'please don't make me wait any longer' face. Darius lay next to her, kissing her with burning lips. His long strong hands glided over her naked body, squeezing, probing, memorizing every inch, as if he were going to lose his sight. When he reached her most sensitive area, he gently fanned her womanly curls with his hand. His tongue played with hers as his fingers entered her body.

Cherish knew she was out of control. She didn't want to stop the feeling erupting from places she'd thought forgotten. As his fingers stroked her lower body to the point of no return, she moaned his name, giving over to the sensations.

"Darius," she purred. "What about you?"

What about him? He wanted to love her all night and forever. He slipped the condom on his erection and entered her body in one full stroke. "Oh, Cherish, baby, you feel so good. I knew you would." He kissed her in rhythm with his strokes. His heart almost stopped when she wrapped her legs and arms around him. As he increased the tempo of his strokes, Cherish purred in his ear, urging him on.

"Don't stop," she commanded. Her hands eased down his sweaty body, and she rubbed her smoothly shaven leg against the smooth skin of his butt, spiriting him along.

He clasped her tightly in his strong arms, determined to give her what she was asking for, wanting her to ride the wave of pleasure with him.

Passion-filled moans pierced the quiet of the night as they went over the edge. Gasping and spent, Darius moved so that he snuggled Cherish's exhausted body. They lay spoon fashion, her back to his front. Both panting, they silently thanked the gods of destiny for making this a reality.

"Cherish, you are amazing." He kissed her neck, moving closer to her sated body, laughing as his body made him aware that he was in fact lying next to a beautiful and most desirable woman.

Cherish yawned. "What's so funny?" She spoke into the soft pillow. She yawned again, her eyes closing.

Darius watched her, realizing she was tired. "Nothing that can't wait until morning." He reached for the comforter and pulled it over them. As he did, some of the rose petals fell onto their naked bodies, making the night seem even more magical.

CHAPTER TWELVE

Cherish awoke to the sound of the ringing phone. She was having the most beautiful dream about Darius making love to her. But it wasn't a dream. Darius *had* made love to her. He'd made mind-bending love to her. In her wildest dreams she would have never expected to feel so satisfied.

Darius moaned beside her and shifted his position, snuggling closer to her, as the phone rang again. She smiled and reached for the phone as Darius's hands grazed her breasts and began to feel her up. She contemplated not answering the phone, but another ring made her respond. After mumbling hello, she recognized Vincent's voice.

"Vincent! Oh, my gosh! What time is it?" Cherish looked at the window and daylight slapped her in the face. Her body felt as if she'd just gone to sleep.

"Cherish, calm down. It's about eleven. The front desk told me you switched rooms last night. What gives? You didn't like being next to me?"

"No, that wasn't it." Cherish hesitated. "A friend surprised me last night." She glanced at said friend as his hands still continued to drive her out of her mind.

"Oh, that's good." Vincent's voice dripped with innuendo. "Listen, why don't you come about two? That will

...ned up their mess. Cherish watched him as she
...ght sleep, but she lost the battle and closed her eyes.
...After a good night's sleep, they decided to take in
...of the sights of Toronto on Sunday. As they walked
...ghout Market Square, a collection of small shops
...d between some international chain stores, a chord
...lment struck her as she saw a condom store. She
...Darius inside.

...erish, we shouldn't be in here," Darius protested
...ked around.

...us, it's just a condom store. No one is looking at
...ably too much spontaneity for him, she thought,
...gining him having a panic attack. "Okay,
...e led him out of the brightly colored store.
...lked a few feet and he stopped cold. "Hey,
...record store." He pointed across the square
...hop.

...lled her eyes toward the sky. "Darius, why
...rst, then go to the record store?" She knew
...the record store, she would never get him
...arius looked at her with those dark brown
...r into the store, immediately heading to

...ter, they finally left the record store.
...n of satisfaction of his face. He'd found
...gs of jazz great Charlie Parker and he
...to be shipped to Texas. They headed
...nt.

...was taken, they decided how to spend
...Canada. "How about let's stay in?"
...ne. "We could chat or something

give you and your friend a little recovery time." Vincent
laughed as he ended the call.

Cherish laughed as she hung up the phone. "Darius
Crawford! I know you are not asleep! So you just open
those beautiful eyes."

Darius opened his eyes, smiling at her. He kissed her
softly, easily sliding his tongue inside her hot mouth as
she returned his morning kiss. His hand gently stroked
her naked thigh.

"Good morning, Cherish," Darius said, kissing her
on the neck, hugging her even tighter.

"Good morning, Darius." Cherish straddled his
body, reveling in their morning romp. "Last night was
indescribable, Darius. I've never been loved like that
before." She kissed him again. "You made me feel very
special last night."

Darius rubbed her backside as she spoke. "Cherish,
you just bring something out in me. When Darbi told
me you were in Canada, I couldn't think about anything
except how to get to you. I didn't want to lose you."

"Why did you wait so long, Darius? I know I made
my feelings for you quite clear, but you held back. Not
that you weren't totally worth the wait. Is it the fear of
intimacy thing that I hear so many men claim?"

He continued stroking her butt, their bodies slowly
grinding to the ease of the conversation. "No, all my
adult life I've been career focused. Relationships seemed
to always be on the back burner," he answered.

Cherish, needing all her senses to understand what
he was saying, slid off his body and snuggled next to

him, not wanting to lose all the body contact. "I don't understand."

He took a deep breath. "It's always been career first. Everything else second."

Cherish nodded. "So you don't want to be in any kind of relationship?"

"No. I want a relationship with you. Since my dad has taken ill, I see what living only for my career deprives me of. I want to share my successes with someone special. Someone like you."

She inhaled, digesting the words. Darius Crawford had just rocked her world again. She needed space to think. She slid from the bed, reaching for her bathrobe.

"Where are you going?" He pulled her into his arms, kissing her neck, ears, cheek, and whatever else he came into contact with.

"I was going to take a shower," she giggled.

His lips found hers. He kissed her. "What time do you have to be downstairs?"

Cherish laughed, not believing the range of their conversations. "I don't have to be there until two."

"That means we have three whole hours." Darius reached for the box of condoms and shook them at her. He took one out and slipped it on his erection and eased himself on top of her. He leaned down and kissed her. Cherish moaned as he entered her, driving his passion into high gear. He caressed her breasts before kissing each one gently. His kisses slowly moved toward her mouth. "Easy, Cherish," Darius whispered against her lips. Their moans of passion again filled the quiet room.

Later that evening Cherish finally re[...] room after helping Vincent; it was well af[...] was exhausted. Vincent had had he[...] minute she arrived until she left sever[...] declined his invitation to the after p[...] was a hot bath and to relax in Dari[...]

As she opened the door to[...] breathed a sigh of relief. There [...] and it didn't look as seductive [...] She hoped he was as tired as [...]

Darius walked out of th[...] sat on the bed. "You look[...] Darius kissed her. "We do[...] thinking maybe we coul[...] What do you think? [...] you are through helpi[...]

"Sounds great. [...] be able to take ove[...] take a shower."

When Cheri[...] nightgown an[...] most sensitiv[...] service. A r[...] and a pot [...]

"Than[...] want a [...] dinner[...]

"I'm all for the 'or something.' " Darius stared at Cherish as she giggled. "I guess that makes it unanimous," he joked.

Food became less important to them as time went by. They barely finished their meal before running back to their hotel for their last night in Canada.

Monday afternoon, on their flight back to Texas, Cherish and Darius discussed the monumental step they had just taken in their relationship.

"This is new territory for me," Darius admitted. "I usually don't date much." He looked at her as she pretended to flip through the in-flight magazine. Seeing her hands shake a little, he smiled. She was as nervous as he was. "I really like you, Cherish. I think you are smart and beautiful. I want us to remain honest with each other. For instance, Dad will take precedent over anything if he becomes sick. You need to know that up front. I also know that you and Darbi are close and I'll try not to intrude on your relationship with her. I know I'm overprotective of her. I just want her to have some happiness in her life."

"Darius, I understand. This is kind of new for me, too. Vince was my last boyfriend and that was over five years ago. How do you feel about Curry dating your sister?"

Darius gently caressed her face. "At first, I thought he was just trying to sleep with her. But even if he won't admit it, I can tell he's feeling more than friendship for her. I don't know what she's feeling for him. I think her previous marriage with Amos is clouding her feelings right now. I'll just have to wait and see where it's going and be there for both of them if the need arises. Sometimes I feel like I'm walking a tightrope between her and Curry."

"How?"

"Curry and I always talk about dating and other matters. He talked me into coming here. I'm really glad that he did. He's always been there to give me that little push I sometimes need. Like going to group session. Curry's idea. But I think he's a little hesitant to tell me things about Darbi because she's my sister and I'm so protective of her."

"Darius, how do you feel?"

"Ambivalent, I guess. I know their relationship is going to cost me something, I just don't know what. But if it makes the two people I care a lot about happy, then the price won't be too high." He hoped he wouldn't have to pick between his sister's happiness and the job he'd fought so hard to get.

Cherish caressed his hand and kissed it. "This weekend was delectable. I would never have thought it would have turned out like this. But I'm glad it did." She leaned against his chest and sighed.

Darius stroked her hair as he remembered the last few days. He'd done something completely out of character for him. He was glad he'd followed his friend's advice; he hoped Curry had taken his. "How about dinner tonight?" Darius kissed her cheek.

"I can't tonight. How about tomorrow?"

"Okay, I'll pick you up at seven." Darius kissed her forehead. Perfect. For once in his life, he was where he should be. Perfect.

After he got home and checked on his father, Darius went to his own bedroom to take a much-needed nap.

A while later a timid knock woke him. "Come in." Darius sat up as Darbi walked into his bedroom. He liked the relaxed look on his sister's face.

"Hi, Darius. How did everything go?" She smiled as she said it. "Aren't you glad you acted spontaneously for once?"

"Yes, Darbi. Everything is fine. How are your exams going?" He hoped Curry had respected the fact that Darbi had finals and let her study.

Darbi sat on the edge of his bed. "Fine, I had my last one today. I came by to check on Dad and noticed your bags downstairs."

Apprehensively, Darius watched as she almost bit a hole in her lip. "What is it, Darbi?" He knew something was bothering her.

"I'm not sure what to get Curry or Cherish for Christmas. Any ideas or suggestions?"

Darius laughed. Perhaps his sister did feel something for his friend after all. "I'm sure whatever you get will be fine. You're very creative. As long as it's from your heart, it will be fine." He noticed a sad look on her face. Just one day, he would like to see her happy and not concerned about the past. "Darbi, you can talk to me about your past. I won't judge you. I know something is haunting you about Amos. If you feel you can't tell me, please talk to someone or it will keep you from being happy." He'd been toying with the idea of suggesting she get some counseling, but didn't know how to broach the subject without hurting her feelings.

"I know. I'm trying to let go. Some days are harder than others. Thanks." She rose from the bed and left her brother's room.

A few days later, Darius had a great idea for Christmas. First, he had to clear it with his father. After Otis gave him the green light, he needed to ask Cherish. He felt he could help both Cherish and Darbi with their closure.

He needed to ask Darbi as well. He knew Darbi was out with Curry, since it was a Friday night. In keeping with Darbi's rules of dating, she went out with Curry each Friday and Saturday night.

Darius smiled as he thought of his sister and his best friend. He couldn't believe Curry had gone along with the Friday and Saturday night only business. Another sign that his friend was in love, whether Curry liked it or not.

Cherish arrived for dinner at eight. Otis let her into the house. She thought he looked great dressed in jeans and a sweatshirt. When she first met him, Darbi had had to drag him out of his bedroom to get him to interact with people, but now he was answering the door and offering Cherish some wine while she waited for Darius. She couldn't contain her surprise any longer.

"You look terrific, Otis. I'm very happy for you."

Otis grinned at Cherish. "I blame Darbi and the nurse, always making me walk. Darbi makes me read," he whispered to Cherish. "Don't tell them I like it."

Cherish nodded and sipped her wine.

"Darius should be down in a minute. He's getting dressed. You'll be okay until he comes down?"

"Yes, Otis, I'll be fine."

Otis nodded. "I'll say goodnight, then." He stood, walking toward the door. "Maybe I'll see you at breakfast." He winked at her and started down the hall to his room.

Hours later, Cherish snuggled against Darius's chest. She yawned and stretched. They had just finished making love for the second time. "Are you sure your dad can't hear us?"

"Yes, he's downstairs, in another wing of the house. What are you doing for Christmas?" His hands lingered around her waist.

"I don't know. My aunt is going to my cousins' in Denver. I had thought about joining them, why?" Cherish closed her eyes, attempting to shut out the past.

"Why don't you come over here? You could spend Christmas Eve and Christmas with us. I want all the future holidays to be special for Dad."

"Christmas sounds great. Maybe it'll help me too. My aunt has been great since Mama died, but I want to move on with my life."

"I was hoping maybe between the two of us, Darbi would talk about her past."

"I would like to help her, too. So yes, I'll come."

Darius kissed Cherish and turned out the light. "Good, I think I'll ask Curry, too." He kissed her again.

~~~~~~~~~~~~~~~~~~~~

As Darbi unlocked the front door to Darius's house, she instantly knew something was different. It was just a little after eight on a Saturday morning and the house was quiet. Her father was usually up by now arguing with the nurse about what he wanted to eat.

She made coffee while she waited for someone to get up. She sat at the kitchen table sipping her coffee, thinking of her previous night's date with Curry. He had taken her to see the musical version of *A Christmas Carol*. She smiled as she drank her coffee. She heard someone walking into the kitchen. *Finally*, she thought, *someone in the house is up!*

"Good morning, Cherish!" Darbi said with a sly smile. She enjoyed the sight of her friend in her brother's bathrobe.

Cherish giggled. "Good morning, Darbi. What are you doing here so early?" Cherish sat at the table and poured some coffee in a cup.

"I'm taking Dad Christmas shopping. It seems no one is awake at this hour. I'm glad to see you here." She smiled broadly at her friend. She hoped she would one day feel the love for Curry that Cherish and Darius had for each other.

Cherish nodded. "Me, too. You know, I thought this would be awkward between us, but it isn't. Darius and I had dinner last night. How was your date with Curry?"

"We went to a musical. He was very romantic last night. He was almost like a relaxed Darius. We're supposed to go to a Christmas musical at the college tonight, *The Nutcracker Suite*."

"Wow, Curry, seems to be slowing down. Your idea?"

Darbi shook her head. "No, I thought maybe Darius had said something to him. I miss the old, fun Curry. You know, the putt-putt golf, the hockey games, that kind of stuff. Any ideas of what to get him for Christmas?" Darbi sipped her coffee.

Darbi looked wistful and was agonizing over what to get Curry. "Think with your heart, Darbi. The right gift will jump out at you."

Mrs. Collins interrupted their conversation. "I'm sorry, Ms. Crawford, Ms. Murray, I guess I overslept." She tied the apron around her waist over her usual uniform of a blouse and slacks. "I can't believe your father didn't buzz my room. I think he's excited about going shopping." She began fixing breakfast.

Cherish rose from the table and headed back upstairs. Darbi chatted with Mrs. Collins until the phone rang.

"Hey, what are you doing there?" Curry asked. "I tried your place and when you didn't answer figured you were at Dare's."

Darbi smiled. Was he checking up on her? "I told you last night that I was taking Dad shopping today."

"Oh, I remember. I thought we could have lunch today, but I guess not, huh?"

"No, I'm afraid not." Darbi saw her brother walk into the kitchen. "I'll talk to you, later." She hung up the phone, wanting to tease. "Good morning, Darius," Darbi crooned, like a first grader to the teacher.

He smiled at his sister. "Stop smiling so smugly!" Darius was so happy at that moment even his sister couldn't ruin his mood.

"I'm just glad to see you . . . um . . . relaxing," Darbi said honestly.

"Thanks, me too. Are you coming over Christmas Eve? You can spend the night."

"Yes. I'm helping Dad wrap his gifts."

CHAPTER THIRTEEN

After her father got up and had his breakfast, Darbi took him to the mall. At first she was a little hesitant about him going shopping with all the insane last minute shoppers, but as he had every day since announcing he had Alzheimer's, her father surprised her. He joked around with perfect strangers, loving the feel of Christmas. Then he shocked his daughter.

"What do you think I should get Curry for Christmas?"

Darbi stared at her father, trying her best not to let her emotions show. She shrugged carelessly. "What do you usually get him?"

Otis winked at his daughter, winking at her. "Darbi Ariane, don't you try to put one over on your daddy. You know why I'm getting that boy a gift." He walked toward the men's store. "I think he might need cologne. No man can have too much cologne. I'm sure you can pick him out a good brand."

"Dad," Darbi said, trying not to smile, "I have no idea what you're talking about."

Otis grinned, walked inside the store and headed for the counter with Darbi on his heels. "Okay, while you're denying that, what do you think Cherish would like?"

Later that evening, Darbi wrapped his gifts as he wrote out the nametags himself. She wondered what he had got her and how he got it without her knowing. When she noticed him yawning, she smiled. "Just one more gift to go, Dad." Darbi wrapped his gift for Darius.

"Thank you, baby girl. This day has really tired me out." Otis finished writing the nametag and handed it to Darbi. "I'm going to change for bed."

Darbi knew that was code for 'get out of the room.' She smiled at her father, feeling that their relationship was moving right along. Quietly, she let herself out of the room, closing the door.

Seeing Darius and Cherish cuddling on the couch in front of the fireplace, Darbi felt like a third wheel. She knew they wanted to be alone. "Well, guys, goodnight."

"No, stay. Curry was supposed to come over. I don't know what happened to him..." The doorbell inter-rupted Darius. Darbi sat down. Darius walked to the front door and smiled as he opened it. "I wondered what had happened to you."

Curry walked inside the house, shaking his head. "You try telling my mother that you're not coming home for the holidays." He walked into the living room, heading for Darbi. Smiling, he sat beside her. "I've been on the phone with her for the last three hours. Hi, Cherish. Hey you." He smiled at Darbi.

"You look tired," Curry observed. He caressed Darbi's hand, tentatively looking in Darius's direction.

"Exhausted. Dad ran me ragged today." She stood, releasing his hand. "I'm going to bed. Goodnight."

Cherish was awakened by a noise. In the darkness of Darius's bedroom, she listened as the noise continued. It sounded as if someone was crying. The house was otherwise quiet. Remembering Darbi's crying spells, she decided to check on her, just in case. She eased out of bed and put on her bathrobe.

"Where are you going?" Darius called out to her in the dark, startling her.

"I'm just going to go check on Darbi." Cherish tied the sash on her silk bathrobe and walked out of the room, closing the door, not giving him a chance to reply.

As Cherish walked down the hall, the sobbing became louder as she neared Darbi's room at the top of the stairs. She opened the door and turned on the light. Her heart skipped a beat. Darbi was crying uncontrollably, fighting an invisible force.

"Amos, please don't hit me! I promise I won't do it again!" Darbi cried and held her hands in front of her face as if she were fending off her attacker.

Cherish stood rooted at the foot of the queen-sized bed. Darbi was still asleep, yet her nightshirt was drenched in tears. Slowly, Cherish sat down next to her on the bed. Gently, she caressed Darbi's arm. "Darbi, it's okay," she whispered.

Slowly, Darbi awoke. "Cherish, how long have you been here?" She dried her eyes, noticing her nightshirt was damp. She tried to compose herself.

"Not long. Darbi," she paused, "why did you let Amos abuse you so?"

Darbi sniffed. "He filled my head with horrible lies and I believed him. He told me my family didn't love me. Over the years he hid my mail from them. I began to believe him. Then the year before he died, I found out he had been lying to me. All that time, he lied to me. One day, I decided to call Dad and found out the truth. Actually, I had started putting a little money back to leave Amos. But I guess fate had a better plan." She tried to dry her eyes but the tears were coming too fast.

Now Cherish had tears as well. "Darbi, Amos is gone. He can't hurt you anymore. How did Amos die?"

"In a car wreck, like I told the family."

Something in her voice told Cherish that a little prodding was in order. "Darbi, I mean, what were the chain of events that led to his death?" She held Darbi's shaky hand.

Darbi sat up and dried her eyes with her bed sheet. She took a deep breath. "If I tell you, you won't think less of me, will you?"

Cherish's heart melted at the sight of Darbi's brown eyes filling with more tears. She was as vulnerable as a child asking if Santa was real. "Of course not. I could never think less of you. You're my friend." Cherish moved closer to her friend, giving her the support she needed.

Darbi took a deep breath and began speaking quietly. "Well, it was a Friday night. We had been out to eat, since it was my payday. That was probably the only thing we did together. We stopped at a convenience store before going home. He sent me in to get some liquor." Darbi took another breath. "I could see my car from inside the store. I saw two black cars drive up on each side. The drivers never got out. I could see Amos talking to them, like he knew them. I figured he probably owed them money. Usually that was the only time anyone came to see him. Anyway, I went to the cash machine to get some money out to pay them. Usually it was a couple of hundred dollars. I paid for the liquor and walked out of the store. But Amos was gone, my car was gone, and those other two cars were gone. I waited for almost an hour to see if he would come back for me. When he didn't, I decided to walk home."

"Why didn't you call a cab?"

"We lived in a bad part of town. Cabs seldom came to our neighborhood, especially not after dark. I waited up for him for a couple of hours before I fell asleep. He never came home that night."

"What happened next?" Cherish felt like someone was telling her the plot of a good suspense novel or a movie. Except Darbi was real and her scars were deep.

"The next morning, I was getting ready to go to work at the video store. The only time I was truly happy was when I was at work away from Amos. The police showed up as I was leaving the apartment. They asked me the usual kinds of questions: Did I own a 1990 Toyota Tercel? Was Amos my husband? Was he missing? Did he use drugs? Yes to all. They found my car, but the car was burned and Amos was in it, shot in the head. They found my car in a small town over a 100 miles away in Plumdale, near Amish country."

"Oh dear! Did the police suspect you?"

"Yes. They asked me where I was the previous night, and how I got home. When I could produce a receipt from the ATM at the time of his death, it cleared me. You know, Cherish, through all that I never shed one tear because I was so happy to finally be out of that hell. I think the police were suspicious when I didn't break down and cry, but after they pulled his police record, they offered me some advice."

Cherish held her breath. "What was on his record? What did they say?"

"There were arrests I never knew about. He had been arrested over twenty times over the course of our marriage and I knew nothing about it. The police told me to go back where I came from, because Amos's death was drug related. I didn't know he was selling drugs. He apparently owed some big time dealer thousands of dollars. He worked at a freight company for about the last year of his life, but that turned out to be a cover for his sideline business of drug selling."

"Where did the insurance money come from?" Cherish knew Darbi had paid cash for her tiny condo and her Volkswagen Beetle.

"Well, Shaw and Stone provided good benefits for their employees. He had a $100,000 life insurance policy. I also had him insured. So after his funeral, I gave away all his possessions to his greedy family. His mother befriended me, once she found out about the insurance policy. I decided how to sneak out of town without them knowing. I knew if they found out I was leaving they might try to hurt me. The only thing they knew about me was that I was from Texas. They didn't even know my maiden name. I gave away the furniture and never replaced the car. I left with no forwarding address and resumed using my maiden name. I felt like a secret agent sneaking out like that. I had made some really good friends at the video store, but I couldn't tell anyone where I was going. When I came back home Dad took me in and asked me no questions. He seemed happy to have me home and I was grateful. Cherish, I know Amos was not the best husband or lover, but I still feel guilty about moving on. After Curry and I made love the first time, he found me in the shower, crying. I dreamed Amos had found me and was trying to kill me." Darbi exhaled.

It was a long time before Cherish spoke. "My mother died in my arms," Cherish started. "Those last few months she was in another world. She spoke in gibberish when she spoke at all. I pretended I could understand what she said. My aunt had even stopped coming over because Mom would throw things at her." Tears fell down Cherish's face. "If I had to do it all over again, I would still take care of her, but I wish I could have been more caring in the beginning stages. Back then I was only concerned with my career. Nothing else mattered. Meeting you and Darius, I feel like I have a second chance to help someone. Darbi, you have to let Amos go. Yes, he died an awful death. But maybe he died like he lived. Darbi, it wasn't your fault, you can't blame your-self." Cherish dried her eyes with part of the sheet.

"I know. Sometimes I just think of all I lost. The last fifteen years of my life are gone. I always wanted chil-dren, now it's too late. I'm thankful God has given me a second chance at life. I want to enjoy every single minute of it. Even if Darius and Dad did talk me into going to college."

"Just don't think about the past. It's gone. Concentrate on the now," Cherish said.

Darbi exhaled. "I am. I'm grateful that I'm able to go to school full-time and work part-time. Thank you, Cherish." Darbi leaned against Cherish.

"Thank you, Darbi. I've never told anyone about my mother's last months." Cherish sighed, remembering those final nights and feelings of guilt when she couldn't help her mother. It was over.

～～～

Christmas morning, Darius woke up early. Cherish had never returned to his bed the previous night. Earlier, in the wee hours of the morning, he'd tiptoed down the hall and heard Cherish and Darbi crying, so he'd returned to his bed, knowing he couldn't help either of them.

Now he wanted to see if the women were awake. He slowly opened the door and saw them sleeping peacefully. Hoping they had helped each other last night, he closed the door and decided to wake Curry, so he would have some company until Cherish woke up.

As he opened the door to where Curry slept, he saw his friend was already up and dressed. Darius smiled. "Hey, I'm glad you're up. The women are still asleep."

Curry walked to the door. "Feels good sleeping next to someone, doesn't it?" He winked at his friend.

Darius shrugged his shoulders as they headed downstairs. "She ended up sleeping with Darbi. She had a crying spell."

Curry nodded in understanding. "If she would just talk about the past, she'd feel so much better, I just know it."

"I think they talked last night. Let's go fix breakfast." They continued walking downstairs after listening at Darbi's door and not hearing a sound.

Darius fixed breakfast, hoping that Darbi and Cherish both had found closure the previous night. It would be nice, he thought, for tears to be a thing of the past. He rummaged through the cabinet for the waffle maker.

"How about waffles, Curry? Where could Mrs. Collins have put that thing?" He finally located the small appliance, and also located the mix in the large pantry. When Curry didn't answer any of his questions, Darius turned around to face his friend and smiled. Curry had the look of a man in love. He was staring into space with a silly grin on his face! Darius started to comment, but Cherish walked into the kitchen, fully dressed in a V-neck cashmere sweater and jeans, and smiling as well.

"Everything okay?" Darius poured her a cup of coffee before she could sit at the table. Cherish picked up the cup before she answered.

Cherish sipped the hot liquid. "Yes, it's fine. Darbi has endured a lot; she's still sleeping. Be gentle." She cast a knowing glance at Curry.

Darius just wanted his baby sister to be happy. "Yes, I thought so. I just want her to be happy and put that jerk behind her," he said grimly. "I just want her to know no one is judging her."

Cherish played with her cup. "I think last night was a start. How did she tell you Amos died?"

"Car accident." Darius knew there was more, but that day was not the day to find out. There would be a day when Darbi would confess and he could wait for it. "Let's just try to keep this day happy. I don't want Dad or Darbi upset today. Only happy faces!" Darius blew Cherish a kiss. *How could I have coped without her?*

Otis walked into the kitchen dressed in a jeans and a 'My daughter attends Fort Worth University' sweatshirt. "When is Darbi gettin' up? I'm ready to open presents!"

Darius, Curry, and Cherish laughed as Otis sat at the breakfast table. Darius nodded at Cherish, and she rose to check on Darbi for him. But Curry stopped her, surprising everyone at the table.

"I'll go," he said.

Darius nodded. He didn't need any other signs that Curry was in love with Darbi. He hoped his sister felt the same way.

Curry quietly walked into the room. Darbi was sprawled across the bed. She was also snoring lightly and looked as if she could sleep for hours. He sat beside her on the bed; she never moved. He lightly stroked her face and sighed. *Curran Fitzgerald, what have you gotten yourself into?* Quietly, he rose and left the room, heading downstairs. When Curry returned, the others had moved to the living room. Darius's eyes met his.

"Well? Is she awake yet?" He whispered so Otis did not hear.

Curry shook his head. "No, she's knocked out, even snoring. Last night probably wiped her out." And I'm love with your sister, he wanted to add.

Darius glanced at his gold watch. "I'll give her another hour. It'll be almost noon. I don't think Dad will wait much longer." He smiled at his father.

Curry helped Darius build an unneeded fire in the fireplace and watched as Cherish sat next to Otis; they began chatting like old friends. Curry felt like a part of the family.

Darbi awoke to an empty bed. It was the best sleep she had in two years. Amos hadn't been in her dreams threatening to kill her. She inhaled deeply; Curry had been in the room. His cologne permeated the air. Hurriedly, she took a shower and dressed in jeans and a sweatshirt. Since her confession to Cherish, she felt better and smiled at herself in the mirror before leaving the room. She was ready to face the day and her family. She walked downstairs to where the others were waiting.

"Dad's ready to open presents," Darius said in lieu of good morning.

"Okay." Darbi headed to the large, flocked Christmas tree. Everyone gathered around the tree and passed out their gifts. Darbi watched her father open his gifts first. Darius had given him a chess set and a laptop computer. Otis looked at his son, surprised.

"You can check your stocks whenever you want. I'm going to beat you at chess yet," Darius told his father, his voice full of pride.

Darbi thought the gift was an excellent idea. Along with her father checking his stocks he was using his brain, fighting off the Alzheimer's and postponing the inevitable.

Curry gave Darbi a Red Wings hockey jersey and tickets to a Stars/Redwings game. Overwhelmed, she kissed him in front of the family, surprising Curry. He fell backwards, taking her with him.

"It's about time," Otis chimed as he watched his daughter stretched out on top of Curry. "I was wondering if you were ever going to notice that boy."

Immediately, she sat up and scooted off Curry's lean body, realizing everyone was watching them. "Dad! You knew?" Darbi was shocked. She should have known: Those eyes didn't miss much.

He handed Darbi a box. "Honey, my memory is fading. Not my eyesight!"

Darbi, embarrassed, opened her gift from her father. She held the tiny tape recorder in her hand. "Thanks, Dad." She noticed something at the bottom of the box.

It was a gift certificate to a ritzy spa in Arlington. "Dad, this is great! When did you do this?" Although he had a serious illness, her father still surprised her.

Otis smiled at his baby girl. "Your brother picked it up for me. You've been looking so happy lately, I wanted to preserve the moment."

It was Cherish's turn to open her gifts. She opened Darius's gift to her. "Darius, this too much!" She held the envelope in her hand. It was two tickets to the spring fashion show in Paris, France, in March. There were also plane tickets to Paris. "You're coming with me, of course." She kissed him.

Darbi couldn't contain her joy watching her new best friend and her brother kiss. She wiped invisible tears and handed Curry his gift of silk pajamas and a matching robe. Cherish gave Darius the entire John Coltrane collection.

After they finished with the gifts, they cleared away the wrapping papers and boxes and headed to the dining room. The doorbell rang. Darius walked to the door, determined to give whoever it was on the other side of the door a piece of his mind.

"Is Darbi here?" DeMarcus's deep baritone voice resonated through the entryway.

Darius looked up to the tall man. "Y-yes she is. Just a minute. Please, come in."

"What are you doing here?" Darbi walked toward him, looking back at Curry. She noticed a large gift-wrapped box in DeMarcus's hand.

DeMarcus looked around the room. His brown eyes rested on Curry's pale form. "I just wanted to wish you a

Merry Christmas and to tell you I took the paternity test and the baby isn't mine." He held out the large box. "Just a little something to say thanks." He kissed Darbi on the cheek and left the house without a backwards glance.

Darbi set the box down on the table without opening it.

After they ate dinner, Darbi and Cherish cleared the table as the men relaxed in the living room. Darbi loaded the dishwasher and started it. Then she took a deep breath and faced her confidant.

"Cherish, I want to thank you for helping me last night. I think you might have saved me. Those nightmares were getting the best of me." She wiped her eyes with a paper towel.

"You helped me too, Darbi. Hey, let's go to the movies tonight."

"What about Darius and Curry? They might want to do something else."

Cherish winked at her friend. "They can go to their own movie. This is our night." The women laughed.

Darbi and Cherish exited the kitchen, giggling like schoolgirls. Darbi watched Curry as he sat on the couch talking to her father and Darius. Her heart swelled as his gaze met hers and he winked at her. The phrase 'girl power' suddenly sprang to mind. "Dad, Cherish and I are going to the movies. We'll be back soon."

Otis laughed. "All right, baby girl. The guys look a little put out, but you enjoy yourselves."

Both Cherish and Darbi laughed as they retrieved their coats and left, leaving the guys to pout.

⌐⌐⌐⌐⌐ᔧ

Days later, Darius sat in his office toying with an idea for his New Year's celebration with Cherish. He walked into Curry's office and sat down. Curry was busy concentrating on some proofs for the latest ad campaign.

"Hey, Dare. What's up?" He placed the grease pencil he used to circle the pictures he wanted on the desk.

Darius couldn't help noticing the content look on his friend's face. Everyone in the office had noticed the difference in Curry immediately, especially the women. His flirting had become nonexistent. Except for talking to his assistant, Curry didn't talk to any of the women in the office unless necessary. "I was wondering if I could use your beach house for New Year's?"

Curry smiled. "Sure. Doesn't seem like a stupid purchase now, does it?"

Darius nodded. "It seemed crazy for something you hardly use."

"I know. I've already put it up for sale."

Darius couldn't believe it. Curry had bought that beach house five years ago for $50,000 on a whim. He'd probably used it five times. It was beautiful, but in California. "Will you make your money back?"

"Yep. I'll actually triple my original investment. It's already sold. I have to go to California at the end of January to sign the papers."

"That's great, Curry. I really appreciate this. What are you doing for New Year's?" He already knew that Curry would be with Darbi.

Funny, Darius thought, a few months ago those same thoughts would have driven him nuts, but now he didn't mind the fact that his white best friend was in love with his sister.

Curry leaned back in his leather chair. "Nothing. Probably just stay at the house," he answered vaguely.

"You know, I don't mind you dating Darbi. I know I wasn't in favor of it initially, but you guys are good for each other. You can admit that you'll be with her. I'm okay with it. Don't worry about Dad. Mrs. Collins will be with him while I'm gone."

Curry relaxed. "I know you don't mind us dating, Darius. But I also know she's still your sister and she has been through a lot emotionally. You're protective of her, naturally. I understand. Darbi won't be satisfied unless she can see for herself that Otis is okay." His intercom buzzed, interrupting the conversation. "Yes, Mica."

"Your mother is on line one, Mr. Fitzgerald."

"Please tell her I will call her back."

"Yes, Mr. Fitzgerald."

Darius laughed at his friend. Yes, Curry was in love. Darius didn't think this day would ever come. Now if Curry would just admit it to Darbi.

～✦

New Year's Eve, Cherish thought the beach house was excellent. She could easily see Curry and his string of very young women coming here for a romantic weekend or a bit of fun, as he called it. But that was the old Curry. Not the Curry who was in love with Darbi. She smiled at the thought. "I can't believe Curry sold this." She watched as Darius poured her a glass of champagne, then sat next to her.

"Yes, he really doesn't use it much." Darius's large hand stroked her face as she leaned against him. "I think he was going through a phase or something."

Cherish exhaled. She entwined her hand with his. "What are he and Darbi doing for the holiday?" Casually, she placed his hand over her breast.

Darius looked where Cherish had placed his hand and smiled. "Nothing, I think. This is the first time in years he's spent this much time in Texas during the holiday season. Everyone at the office is freaking out. It's like he became me and I him." He kissed her neck as his hands squeezed her breasts gently.

Cherish knew about the change in Curry. He was trying to show Darbi he could settle down. Darius had become more extroverted. "I think the changes are great. I'm proud of you both."

"Thank you." Darius kissed her again. This time he took off her sweater and eased her down on the couch. He kissed her closed eyes and stood. "Let's finish this discussion upstairs."

Darbi spent New Year's Eve day with her father. After they watched a couple of Christmas movies, Otis was ready for a nap before dinner. As he slept, Darbi went to the kitchen to talk with Mrs. Collins about his diet.

"Could you make sure he has at least two green vegetables at lunch and dinner, Mrs. Collins?"

"Yes, Ms. Crawford. I started giving him more veggies like you suggested and he threw such a fit. He reminded me of a little boy."

"I figured he would," Darbi laughed. "I explained to him that the antioxidants would retard the growth of the disease. I also suggested he start taking B-12 shots. You can only guess what he said."

Mrs. Collins nodded. "I hope he didn't use that foul language at you." She continued fixing his lunch. "I did hear something about a new drug that could slow the progression of Alzheimer's. Have you checked into it yet?"

"Yes, I did. His doctor says Dad isn't far enough advanced to take it. He has to be in the middle phase to be tested for it." Darbi decided she would spend that night with her father, instead of Curry. As she fixed a snack, she wondered how Curry would take the news.

A few hours later, Otis walked into the kitchen and sat at the table. "Baby girl, what are you doing here?"

"I'm spending time with you." Darbi sat by her father.

"No." Otis shook his head defiantly. "You go spend some time with that boy. He likes you. Go have some fun."

Darbi looked at her father as he winked at her. "What will you do?" She felt a twinge of guilt for even thinking about leaving her ailing father for a night of unbridled passion.

Mrs. Collins placed a plate of baked chicken, broccoli, green beans, spinach and mashed potatoes in front of him, along with a salad.

Otis frowned at Mrs. Collins, then looked in his daughter's direction. "I know this is your doing. All these green things on my plate staring back at me. Where's my dessert?" He focused his eyes on the nurse just as she placed a small piece of chocolate cake in front of him. "I'm watching football. Go ahead, I'll be fine. Mrs. Collins knows she's to call you if something goes wrong."

"All right, Dad. I'll go later."

CHAPTER FOURTEEN

Sarah Fitzgerald walked through her son's house early New Year's Day. An empty wine glass sat on the coffee table, a DVD movie cover on top of the TV. She walked into the kitchen. Two plates of half-eaten lasagna were on the counter.

Her eyebrows knitted together. This was not like her Curran. He hadn't come home for Christmas and had not been returning any of her phone calls. Something was definitely not right with her son.

"I told you he was fine, honey. He's just in love," Thomas Fitzgerald told his sweetheart of fifty years. "See, now we can still make our Disney World Cruise."

Sarah smiled at Thomas. They were married at sixteen, and now, fifty years later, they were going to Disney World for the honeymoon they'd never had. "We still have a few days before we have to be in Florida. I am not stepping one foot on that boat until I know my son is okay."

"Okay, Sarah," said Thomas. As usual, he gave in to his determined wife. "But it seems like he's okay. The house looks like it's been inhabited lately."

"I'll just check upstairs. Be quiet, I don't want to scare him if he's asleep."

Thomas nodded and followed his wife upstairs. "I just hope he's alone and we don't embarrass him."

Sarah opened the door to Curry's bedroom. "Oh, my!" She hurriedly closed the door, slamming her eyes shut, attempting to block out the horrible picture she'd just witnessed.

"What?" Thomas whispered. "Is he hurt? Should we call the police?"

"No. He appears to be fine. There's a black woman in bed with my son and they don't have on any clothes!"

"Oh, is that all?" Thomas was relieved.

"Thomas?"

"So what. Big deal. At least it wasn't a black man. This is why he didn't want to talk about it at Thanksgiving when you were quizzing him as if he were a common criminal. He knew how you'd react. So we're going downstairs and you're not going to say anything." Thomas led his wife downstairs without giving her a chance to reply. They sat on the couch in silence and waited.

Curry knew he'd heard voices outside his bedroom door. He carefully eased out of bed, so as not to wake Darbi, put on his pajama bottoms and went downstairs. His heart almost stopped as his foot touched the bottom stair.

"Mom, Dad! What on earth are you doing here?" Curry studied his parents as they sat on his couch in silence.

With her eyes on her son, Sarah began explaining why they were there in Arlington, Texas, instead of Orlando, Florida, where they would be getting on a cruise ship bound for the Bahamas, an anniversary present from Curry. "When you skipped the holidays and didn't return any of my phone calls, we decided to come check on you on our way to Florida."

"I tried to call you yesterday," Curry pointed out to his mother.

"Why didn't you tell us about your *friend?*" His mother emphasized the word.

"Because I knew you'd over-react and I didn't want you prejudging her," Curry said. Darbi had been through enough without his mother giving her 'the stick with your own kind' speech. Curry walked toward the stairs, then turned to his parents and said, "I'm going to take a shower and *we'll* be right down."

After a very quiet breakfast, Curry took Darbi home. On his way back to his house, he sighed, realizing the day was only going to get worse. He was already emotionally drained from trying to reassure Darbi that everything would be just fine and now he had to face his parents.

He walked inside his house with apprehension. He knew he should have told his parents at Thanksgiving he was seeing Darbi, but he had not been sure himself of Darbi's feelings toward him. He still wasn't sure. He walked into his kitchen as his mother was cleaning up the breakfast dishes.

Curry sat at the breakfast table with his father. He waited.

Thomas spoke first. "Son, why didn't you tell us? We could have been prepared for this morning," he said in a voice tinted with disappointment.

Curry shrugged. "I don't know. I wasn't really sure of her feelings for me. I probably should have mentioned it, but this is new territory for me, too. I also know the color issue is a lot for you guys to take in."

"Well, as long as you're happy, and I can tell that you are, we'll adjust. We're open to change," his father offered.

Sarah offered her thoughts. "Yes, it was a shock. What does her family think of you?"

"She's Darius's sister," Curry explained. He knew they liked Darius. "I have been helping her with her school-work and we've been spending a lot of time together, playing racquetball." He smiled, remembering what had happened after the first time they played racquetball. "She's very vulnerable right now. Her marriage was hor-rible, so at dinner the subject of her husband and her marriage are off limits." Curry realized he'd made his dec-laration of love for Darbi without actually saying it.

~~~

"His mother saw you in bed with him?" Cherish asked Darbi. She and Darius had returned a few days ear-lier and Cherish and Darbi were having dinner and a little 'girl talk.'

"Yes, he kept acting like it was no big deal. Like it was every day a small white woman walked into his bedroom. I was freaking out!" Darbi watched Cherish as she grilled steaks for them on her indoor grill. "That was the last thing I was expecting."

"How did she react?" Cherish asked cautiously, hoping Darbi's feelings hadn't been hurt.

"Shocked at first. Then at dinner she asked me about Dad, Darius, and school. I could tell Curry had talked to her because she never asked me about Amos or my marriage or why I am just now attending college."

"That's good, isn't it?" Cherish hoped it was. The last thing Darbi needed was another emotional roadblock on her road to happiness.

"Yeah, I guess." Darbi abruptly changed the subject. "Darius won't talk about your time in California. Every time I ask him anything about the trip, he starts stammering and changes the subject. How was your holiday?"

Cherish smiled. She pulled down her turtleneck collar and revealed a red mark on the side of her neck. "He was out of control. He was so embarrassed. I wasn't supposed to tell you, but I couldn't resist."

Darbi shared a secret smile with her friend. She stood and slowly lifted her sweatshirt. She revealed several red marks on her flat stomach, then lowered her shirt.

"You should see Curry's stomach." Darbi laughed. "He got a little carried away. I was returning the favor." Darbi stretched her body. "He really did get carried away. I'm a little sore today. I had never been savored before. He made me feel like the most beautiful woman on the planet." Darbi stepped closer to Cherish. "I want to thank you for going to registration with me tomorrow. I don't know how I got through the first one, except that was late registration and someone was there to walk me through every step."

"No problem. I'm thinking about taking a class toward my master's," said Cherish.

"That's great. Oh, my! I'm sounding like Darius, aren't I? But it would really be great if you went. Thankfully, Curry has an important meeting he can't postpone or he would have gone with me."

"Why don't you want him to go to registration with you?"

"Because he keeps hinting I should major in advertising and he acts like I can't do anything for myself."

Cherish nodded, taking the steaks off the grill. She had noticed the change in Curry. He just wanted to make Darbi's life easier, but she obviously didn't see it that way. "I was thinking about being able to teach a class or something. Have you decided on a major?"

"Not really. I'm thinking about marketing. Don't tell Curry. I just don't know what I'm good at yet."

"I think Curry knows." Cherish teased her friend. Darbi looked very happy. Her smile was wide and honest. Cherish felt that Darbi had started to reclaim her life.

⌒

A ringing from inside Darbi's purse startled her. "I still can't believe Darius got me a cell phone for Christmas." She picked up the small phone, smiling as she noticed Darius's number in the small display screen. After he asked her the customary questions about her love life, he asked where she was. When he found out she was with Cherish and spending the night, he ended the call. Darbi laughed as she put the phone back in her purse. "He wanted to know where I was before he called

Curry. I think he's afraid he's going to call and I'll answer the phone one morning."

"I couldn't believe he got you that cell phone either. He said he worries about you driving at night. I thought it was sweet. Does Curry call you on it?"

"Yes, unfortunately," Darbi said, pouting. "He calls me at least twice a day. He even calls on my way to aerobics. I keep expecting him to walk in the gym one day. Sometimes he is too much, literally."

~~~~~

The next morning, the women headed to Fort Worth University for Darbi's registration. After joining the long lines of students, Cherish felt that she was back at college. Although some things had changed about registration, there were still long lines and crabby students.

Cherish studied the computer printout of the classes Darbi wanted to take. "Darbi, are you sure about this English class? It's at eight." Cherish remembered how she'd hated those early morning classes.

"Sure," Darbi answered, moving a few steps farther ahead in line. "I had an eight o'clock class last semester. I need to be done with classes by noon so I can go to work at one."

"Hello, Miss Crawford," a masculine voice called from behind Cherish.

Cherish turned around at the sound of the deep baritone voice and gazed up at a very handsome ebony

Adonis who was smiling at Darbi. It looked as if Curry had some competition, she thought.

"Hello, Professor Thomkins. This is my friend Cherish Murray. I was just going to sign up for your eight o'clock class."

"That's good. I'll look forward to seeing your smiling face in class." The professor walked away.

Cherish looked over the professor as he left. He oozed distinguished charm. "Girl, I think he was checking you out. I see why you take his class."

Darbi shook her head. "He's good. The first day of class he was reciting some of the works of Langston Hughes. I am embarrassed to say I didn't know who he was. After that I went out and buy a lot of reference books for his class. He reminds me of Dad." Darbi walked up to the cashier's booth.

After Darbi paid for her classes with Darius's credit card, she and Cherish walked across the campus to the bookstore. "I can't believe he still insists on paying for my classes and books. I can afford it," Darbi said.

Cherish smiled. Darius had a special place in his heart when it came to his sister, which only made him sexier to Cherish. "That's just Darius. He wants you to be happy."

CHAPTER FIFTEEN

Cherish watched Darius as he pretended to be involved in the movie they were not watching. His eyes were focused on the screen, but since settling on Cherish's sofa, he hadn't said one word.

"Darius, is something wrong?"

Finally, he glanced in her direction. "No, why?" He turned back to stare at the screen.

Cherish couldn't stand it any longer. She picked up the remote and turned off the TV. "Darius, something is bothering you. Is this about the cost of Darbi's tuition?" She was just about to remind him that Fort Worth University was a private college when he answered.

"No, don't be silly," he answered. "I was thinking about her and Curry."

"Are they giving you trouble at work about Curry dating your sister?"

Darius leaned back in the sofa. "No, not really. I don't fear any racial repercussions, if that's what you mean. I fear the women."

Okay, that made no sense whatsoever. "Darius, what are you talking about? Why would you be afraid of a bunch of young women?"

"Because this is Curry we're talking about. He's dated probably every woman at Sloane under the age of thirty.

I'm afraid when they find out that he's dating someone and it's serious, and it's my sister, they will blame me. You don't know these women when they get jealous. I've seen them almost come to blows over him."

"Oh, my." Darbi had told Cherish of the strange looks she received from some of the women the one and only time she met Curry at his office for lunch.

"Yeah. I guess I'm really afraid for Darbi. Curry's my friend and all, but Darbi is still reeling from that excuse of a marriage she was in. I think something like that might send her over the emotional edge. I don't want that. I know Curry doesn't."

"Darius, the truth will come out sooner or later," Cherish added softly. She didn't want anything to affect Darbi adversely either.

"I'm hoping for later. She's been so happy lately. I've somewhat come to terms with the fact that they're dating. All I can do is be there for her when it's over."

"Darius, that's awful. I know he's pretty serious about her."

Darius nodded. "Yeah, I know he loves her, but I don't know if she's able to return his love. So I guess I'll have to be there for both of them."

Cherish nodded. She felt Darius's burden. She knew she wanted Darbi and Curry to be happy, but the cost of that might be beyond Darius's reach.

A few weeks into the spring semester, Darbi felt good about school. Her classes interested her more, and she was becoming more at ease in class. She was taking English, sociology, philosophy and history, a full class load.

People around her also seemed good.

Cherish was spending more time at Darius's than at her own house. Curry was being his usual self: a major interruption in Darbi's life because he wanted to do everything for her. Her father didn't grumble as much about eating vegetables or exercising and had surprised Darbi by relenting on taking the B-12 shots she had suggested months before. Darbi smiled as she got busy at her afternoon job as office helper at Fort Worth University. Her life was good, finally. She sighed in contentment. She was busy sorting late registration forms when her supervisor approached her.

"Darbi, I'm having a happy hour this Friday, in celebration of my divorce. I would really like it if you could come. You could even bring a friend. No men, this is ladies night."

"Sure, it sounds like fun." Darbi liked her supervisor and had heard the rumors of her divorce. She could empathize with her on so many levels.

"Great! We'll meet at Zorro's Pipe Shop. It's on the square in downtown Fort Worth. At six." She walked back to her desk.

Darbi nodded. She knew what kind of place Zorro's was. Whether or not to tell Cherish was the question. She smiled as she pictured Cherish's stoic face as they walked into a male strip club. Cherish would kill her!

After Darbi left her study session, she sat in her VW Beetle and called Cherish.

"Sure, Darbi, it sounds like fun. I think I've heard of that place. Isn't it a male strip club?"

"Yes, it is. I'll pick you up at five-thirty." Darbi placed her cell phone back in her purse, started her car and relaxed as Brian McKnight sang to her. Her cell phone rang again. *Who could this be now? Can't I have one evening without someone calling to check on me!* Exasperated, she answered it and smiled instantly, her earlier frustration forgotten.

"What are you doing out so late?" a deep masculine voice asked.

"Curry, I'm an adult," Darbi quipped. "I think I can drive at night by myself."

"I know, Darbi," he said softly. "but I would prefer to drive you at night. You shouldn't be on the road by yourself. When is your next study session?"

"Same time next week, Tuesday. Curry, you really don't have to drive me. That's a lot of unnecessary driving for you."

"If it's for you, it's not unnecessary. I'll talk to you later." He ended the call.

Darbi hung up the phone. Curry was becoming as bad as Darius. Neither wanted her out alone at night. Darius had asked her to sell her condo and move into his house several times. Each time, she'd told him no. She was trying to build her independence, but it was hard with two pig-headed men watching her every move. Three, counting her father.

The next evening, Cherish watched Darius pace her living room like a caged tiger. He had called his sister twice. Each time he rang her condo, he didn't get an answer. Even her cell phone was turned off. "Darius, she's fine," she said. "Maybe she's at school. Whatever, I'm sure she's fine."

Darius sat beside Cherish and kissed her. "Curry!" Darius snapped his fingers. "I didn't check with Curry."

Cherish was confused. "I thought they didn't see each other on school nights?"

Darius smiled, then quickly called his friend. Relieved, he hung up the phone.

"Well?" Cherish asked as she tried to suppress her laughter.

"He talked to her earlier. She had an extra study session this week, her sociology class. Curry keeps telling her he'll drive her, but she's fighting him on that." Darius picked up Cherish's sketchbook. "How are your sketches coming along?" He opened the book and began looking at them.

Cherish scooted closer to him, so that now they were touching. "Pretty good. I showed them to Hervé and he liked them. He suggested a few changes. You know, like to use silk instead of linen, pleats versus gathers, short versus long. He suggested I should put some designs in his next show."

"That's great, Cherish!" He leaned over and kissed her.

She shrugged her shoulders. "I don't know. That's a lot of pressure. I like doing things on my own time."

"Cherish, we have all the time in the world." He pulled her closer and kissed her softly.

She didn't have time to revel in Darius's statement. The phone rang, breaking into their quiet moment.

"Cherish, could I speak to Darius?"

"Sure, Darbi." Cherish whispered into the phone, "Have you told you know who about Friday night?"

Darbi laughed. "Yes, I told him earlier. He wasn't pleased, but he didn't yell or anything. I kept expecting him to demand that I not go. I was all ready to read him the riot act for trying to tell me what to do."

Cherish handed Darius the phone. After a few minutes he ended the call, placing the cordless phone on the table. He stared absently at the sketchbook and said nothing. She waited an eternity.

Finally Darius spoke. "I hear you and Darbi are going to a strip club bar and watch strange men take off their clothes," he stated. He looked straight ahead. "Were you going to tell me at some point? Was I supposed to hear it from Curry? At least my sister had the decency to tell the man she's dating . . ."

"Wait just a minute, Darius Crawford! You haven't asked me for a date or if I was busy Friday night. I don't see what the problem is. Darbi and I are going out with her boss. You have no right to sit there with this male superiority thing going on. I will not have this, Darius Crawford!" Cherish stood and walked toward the kitchen.

"You get back here, now!" Darius yelled. He softened his request. "Please. You're right. I've no right to be mad. I'm sorry. I've no right to demand all your time." Cherish sat beside him again and he picked up her hand. "I guess this is what I get for laughing at him for getting upset. I know you and Darbi need some girl time."

Cherish relaxed. "Thanks, Darius. I was waiting for the right time to tell you. Thanks for understanding." She snuggled against him. "Maybe once in a while we need to have a girls'/boys' night out. I don't want you to get bored with me."

Darius looked at her, then took a deep breath, as if he were pondering a world crisis. "Cherish, I love you."

"W-what?" Cherish sat up straight. "Darius, what did you say?" She was flabbergasted.

"You heard me, woman. I said I love you. You're the reason I'm not fretting over the fact that my emotionally fragile sister is dating my white best friend and they have three marriages between them. You're the reason I haven't let Dad's illness get the best of me. I love that you and Darbi are friends, though sometimes a little too close for my comfort. But I'm still glad she has you to talk to when she thinks she can't talk to me." He kissed her forehead and hugged her.

She couldn't believe he'd said it. It took him forever to display any emotion and yet he'd said it. She couldn't stop the flow of tears. "I love you too, Darius, but I'm still going to the strip club."

"I know. I just wanted to get that off my chest." Darius placed his hand under her chin, bringing her face closer to his. He kissed her gently and then he kissed her tears away. Then his lips met hers in a deep kiss. He found himself lying on the couch with Cherish stretched out on top of him. As the kiss deepened, he unbuttoned her blouse. He smiled as she sat up, straddling him, letting him take off her sweater. He threw the unwanted garment on the floor.

Cherish stood and picked up the sweater, then grabbed his hand, making him stand up as well. "Come on, let's go upstairs." She led him to her bedroom. "You know, if I had known you would be this frisky, I'd have gone to Canada months ago." She giggled as they entered her bedroom.

"I feel like I've waited a lifetime, but I think we were worth the wait." Darius pushed her jeans down her long legs, and then took off his shirt. He pushed his jeans off and they fell onto the bed.

"Darius," Cherish said, stretched out on top of him. "I want to please you."

"You already have." He kissed her and rolled her over so that she was under him. "Nothing can compare to the feelings I'm experiencing at this moment."

Cherish caressed his face before she kissed him deeply. "No stripper could ever compare to you, Darius Crawford."

"Are you ready to see some good looking men, Cherish?" Darbi asked as Cherish settled at their table.

Her boss and other co-workers were already there and the champagne was flowing freely.

Cherish was too shocked to drink at the moment. She had heard what happens at male strip clubs, but to see it all firsthand was something else. The waiters walked around in nothing but the briefest things, which left little to the imagination. They were tanned, buff and Cherish couldn't seem to quit staring at their exposed butts. She decided maybe a drink would calm her nerves. She watched as the women stuffed dollar bills down one of the dancer's G-string. Cherish sipped her champagne and giggled.

Darbi tried to calm her usually composed friend down several drinks and a lap dance later. "Cherish, you're going to have to sit down."

"No way. This is too much fun. When is Zorro coming on stage?" Cherish stood on her chair. "These people are blocking my view!"

Darbi sat in her chair, laughing. "Man, you're a lot of fun once you get some liquor in you."

The scantily clad waiter approached the table. "Another round, ladies?"

"Yes. Two margaritas," Darbi paused, "make it four." She winked at the waiter.

The waiter laughed and walked away. Cherish finally sat down. "I'm thirsty. Where's the waiter?" She wiped her forehead. "Is it hot or is it just me?"

"I'm hot, too," Darbi drawled. "I think it was the last round of drinks. But I feel fine." The waiter returned depositing the drinks, quickly leaving the table before Cherish pinched him again.

"To feeling good," Cherish said as she lifted her glass to her friend.

"Yes." Darbi clinked her glass with her friend. "This is fun. Hey look! Zorro is coming out on stage." Darbi stood on her chair to see over the crowd. "Wow, Cherish, he's a hottie. You should see. Come on." She held her hand out to Cherish.

As Cherish watched the women throw money, napkins, and underwear on stage, the margaritas began to take their toll on her. The room started spinning counter-clockwise. She sat down and rested her throbbing head on the table, suddenly remembering why she didn't drink much.

Instantly Darbi sat down beside her. "Are you okay?"

Cherish held her head up. "Yes, the room is spinning. How many drinks have we had anyway?"

"I don't know. Probably seven, eight, eleven." Darbi wiped her forehead. "You know, my head has started to hurt, too." They both stared at the margaritas on the table before them and smiled. Darbi spoke as she lifted a glass, "We might as well enjoy tonight, because we're going to pay for this tomorrow." Darbi picked up her glass and drank the margarita in one gulp. Cherish did the same. They looked at each other and laughed uncontrollably.

Before they realized it, the club was getting ready to close for the night. "Last call for alcohol, ladies," a voice announced over the loudspeaker.

"Oh, no. We don't need anymore," Darbi said as she watched Cherish. "I'll have to call a cab as it is."

"Call Curry, instead. I spent my last twenty on that table dance," Cherish said, trying to stand up. "I love Darius, but he can be stiff as a board." Cherish laughed as the image appeared in her mind.

Darbi laughed as well. "Yeah, I think Curry would be an easier sell than Darius. At least he won't lecture us." Darbi stood slowly and then sat back down. She tried again, this time successfully. She helped Cherish up and they weaved through the crowd to the restroom. Darbi grabbed Cherish's hand to look at her watch.

"It's only twelve. Curry should still be up, huh?" She leaned away from the phone to see the numbers clearer; leaning closer, she listened as the phone rang.

"I wonder if he went out," Darbi said, just before Curry finally answered the phone. "Hey, Curry," Darbi yelled into the phone.

"Darbi, why are you yelling?" Curry laughed.

"I'm not yelling. You can't hear. Hey, is there any way you can come and get us without Darius knowing?"

Cherish watched Darbi's face as she nodded and hung up the phone. The look on her face told her instantly that Darius knew.

"Bad news, Cherish. Darius is coming, too. So get ready for some kind of lecture. You know, the basic ills of your actions or something like that." Darbi helped her friend up and they started out of the club. By the time they made it outside, Darius was getting out of his truck.

Darius and Curry watched as the women walked toward them, almost tripping over each other several times before finally making it to the men. Darius shook his head in disappointment. He scooped up Cherish in his arms and deposited her on the back seat of his Yukon. Curry did the same with Darbi.

The women sat in the backseat, leaning against each other for support.

"I sure hope they don't blow chunks in my car." Darius glanced around at the cars. He didn't see the tiny car anywhere in sight. "Darbi, where is your car?"

Darbi pointed behind her. "In one of those parking lots." She offered no suggestions.

Darius looked down the street. They were at least six or seven lots scattered along the street. "Do you have the ticket stub?" Darius asked his intoxicated sister. He realized it would be like finding a needle in a haystack if she didn't. He watched her move her mouth, but nothing came out. This was just wonderful, he thought. Finally she made a coherent sound.

"Pocket," was her only reply. Her eyes were closed and sweat poured down her face.

Darius shook his head and walked around the truck to where she was sitting. He went through her pockets until he finally found the ticket and used his cell phone to call a wrecker. After he arranged to have Darbi's car taken to his house, he turned his attention to the women.

After they buckled the women in their seats, they headed to Darius's house. Curry glanced back at the sleeping women as Darius drove. "Boy, they're going to pay for this tomorrow. I wonder how much they drank?"

Darius kept his eyes on the road. "I don't know. They smell like a brewery!"

"They were just having fun. I think they went way overboard, but just in fun."

"I know." Darius smiled. "Kind of funny, isn't it?"

The next afternoon, Cherish woke first. Slowly, she eased her tired body to an upright position. Even the small amount of light filtering in through the wooden blinds just about robbed her of her vision. Gazing around the room, she noticed clothes neatly laid out for her, and realized Darius was responsible.

After a shower, she dressed and headed downstairs. She didn't see the guys or Otis, so she headed into the kitchen. Mrs. Collins smiled as Cherish took a seat across from Darius.

"Mr. Crawford said you might not be feeling well. I made some potato soup for you and Ms. Crawford." Mrs. Collins left the kitchen with Otis's dinner tray.

Cherish rose and walked to the stove. Her stomach threatened to betray her as she inhaled the aroma. She filled a bowl with soup and sat back down. She noticed Darius and Curry had big, thick, juicy steaks and baked potatoes. Her stomach objected to the noxious fumes.

"Darbi is still asleep," she announced. "Looks like she'll be asleep for a long time." She inspected the soup before she took a spoonful to her lips. After she had a little of the delicious soup in her body her stomach settled and forgave her for getting skunked the night before.

"How do you feel?" Darius cut his tender steak. "You guys smelled like a brewery last night," he commented dryly.

"I know. I couldn't even begin to tell you how much we drank. But it was fun. I don't think I'll be doing it again for a long time though." She could only imagine how disappointed Darius was in both her and Darbi, for doing something so irresponsible. But it sure felt great while it was happening.

Darius smiled. "I hope so. I also hope you girls learned your lesson."

Cherish nodded.

A few hours later, Darius took Cherish home. Curry elected to stay, just in case Darbi finally woke up. But as Curry watched the highlights of the PGA tournament with Otis, he wondered if he should check on Darbi. She had been asleep all day.

Otis cleared his throat and smiled at Curry. "Maybe you should go check on baby girl. I'm going to bed."

Curry smiled at Otis as he stood. Disease or no, he was very sharp and knew what was going on around him. Curry nodded and headed upstairs.

He entered Darbi's room and smiled. In her sleep she had kicked off all of the covers, and was down to her underwear. She was beautiful. He walked over to the bed and sat down. His hands glided over her body with ease. She opened her eyes.

"What are you doing?"

"Watching you sleep off your alcoholic binge." He grinned as she placed her hand on top of his.

"I wasn't drunk. I maybe had a drink or two." She held his hand, lacing her fingers with his. She also made no effort to cover up her near nudity. "It seems quiet. Where's everybody?"

"Well, Darius took Cherish home a while ago. Otis is downstairs. He said he was going to bed."

"Bed?"

"It's eleven at night."

"On, no! I slept the whole day." She sat up. "Why didn't someone wake me?" She lay back down. "My head hurts," she said quietly. "Turn out that light." She pulled the covers over her head.

Curry shook his head. "I'll get you some aspirin." He got up, turned out the lights, and left the room.

CHAPTER SIXTEEN

"Dad, are you sure you feel okay?" Since arriving for her weekly visit, Darbi had noticed Otis sneezing constantly. "I can heat you some soup or something." She knew something as simple as a common cold could be very costly to an Alzheimer's patient.

"No, baby girl, I'm fine," he tried to reassure his daughter. He sat on the couch reading the paper and sneezed again. He muttered a curse.

"Dad," Darbi began, "the other day when you played golf with Curry, did you get cold?" Curry had mentioned Otis started sneezing while they were out on the course. Darbi walked over to her father and placed the back of her hand against his forehead. "I'm going to take your temperature," she told him.

Before he could voice his objections, Darbi was already down the hall.

She returned with the digital thermometer and took her father's temperature. "Okay, Dad. Go to bed."

Otis stood and walked down the hall to his room, with Darbi following silently behind him. After Otis settled in bed, she went to the living room and waited for Darius to return from racquetball.

A while later, Darius walked into the living room. "Hey, Darbi. How did everything go?" Darius set his bag down in the hall closet.

Darbi looked up from her studies and closed her book. She stood and walked over to her brother. "I think Dad is coming down with a cold or something. I was thinking of taking him to the doctor if he's not better by Tuesday." She took their father's health seriously no matter how slight Darius thought the problem might be.

Darius nodded. "Okay, whatever you think is best."

"If he's not better by next weekend, I'm not going to California." Darbi waited for her practical brother to agree with her. His answer surprised her.

"Darbi, I know when it comes to Dad, you like to be in charge. But this time I'm taking over. I can watch Dad. Plus, the nurse is here. That's her job," he reminded his sister. Darius tried to console her. "Just wait and see how he's doing by Monday. I'm sure he's fine."

Darbi walked back to the sofa and gathered her books to leave. "I'll come over tomorrow after I get off work."

"No, don't. I'm working at the house tomorrow; I'll be here. You have a date. I happen to know Curry's put a lot of thought into this date, so you have to go."

She looked at her brother and wondered what he and Curry were up to. "All right, Darius. I won't break my date. I'll come over Saturday morning after aerobics."

Darius nodded. That smug grin he wore didn't sit well with Darbi, but she'd wait until the bottom dropped out of her life, as it always did.

Friday night, Darbi watched as Curry drove them to the airport and parked. "What kind of date is this, Curry?" He'd only hinted it was a surprise.

"Just trust me," Curry said with a hint of mischief, helping her out of the car.

Darbi was skeptical. "I've seen the airport before." She held his hand. "Curry Fitzgerald, where are you taking me?"

"Just follow me." Curry led her through the Dallas/Fort Worth International Airport. They walked through a door marked *Charter*. "You just follow me." He kissed her.

Stunned, Darbi followed him onto the small plane. "Where are we going?"

"San Antonio."

"We can't. I told Darius I'd be over to check on Dad."

"Darius said he would be fine. You can even call and check on him if you'd like." Curry watched as dismay filled her eyes. "Would you rather not go?"

"Yes."

"Okay, we can go back." He muttered a curse and unfastened her seatbelt, then his own. "This is the last time I try to be romantic," he huffed. "Let's go."

"I'm sorry, Curry."

He didn't reply.

Cherish greeted them when they returned to Darius's house with a puzzled look on her face. "What are you guys doing back?" She looked from Darbi to Curry. Neither spoke.

Darbi reached for Curry's arm, but he stepped out of her grasp.

"I'd better go." Curry walked to the door and left the house without so much as a goodbye.

Darbi felt her heart had been ripped into two pieces and Curry had just carried one of those pieces away with him. She sat on the floor and held her head in her hands. Curry was one of the bright spots in her new life and she'd ruined it.

Cherish kneeled by her friend. Carefully, she placed her arms around Darbi's shoulder as she felt her tremble. "Darbi, I thought he was flying you to the coast for a romantic weekend."

Darbi took a deep breath. "He was. But Dad is sick. I didn't want to leave him alone." Tears began to trickle down her face.

"Darbi," Cherish began in her soothing voice, "Otis just has the sniffles. Mrs. Collins is a qualified nurse. I hate to say this, but he got along for fifteen years without you being here. He can surely make one lousy weekend without you."

"I want to be with my father," Darbi snapped. "I know I've been absent for fifteen years and that was my fault. Why does everyone take it upon themselves to remind me!"

"Calm down." Cherish wiped away some of Darbi's tears. "I'm just saying he'll be fine for one weekend, honey. Darius asked me to come over as well. I know you want Otis well, so does Darius. If he thought Otis was seriously sick, he would have told you."

Darbi wiped her eyes. "Cherish, I'm sorry for snapping at you. It's just I've missed so much of Dad's and Darius's lives, I don't want to miss any more. Now Curry's pissed at me. He didn't say one word the entire way back here. I cost him more money than I want to think about." Fresh tears appeared as she stood.

Cherish stood as well and wiped Darbi's face. "You love him, don't you?" She wasn't accusing Darbi, just simply stating what she already knew.

"Yes." Darbi didn't deny it. She couldn't if she wanted to anyway. "But don't tell him that. I know he doesn't love me. How did you know?" Darbi hoped that Curry didn't.

Cherish smiled, knowing what a turmoil this was for Darbi, especially after her marriage and its horrible end. "You're a mess of tears because you think he's mad at you. When he didn't touch you, I thought you were going to cry then. Tomorrow you guys will be laughing about this." Cherish hugged her friend in sympathy. "Darius is in with your dad. Why don't you go to bed?"

An hour later, Darius knocked and then walked into the room he had begun to think of as Darbi's. She was lying in bed in the dimly lit room. The room was eerily quiet. Even the TV was off. As he neared the bed, he noticed that though her eyes were closed, tears flowed freely down her cheeks. "Darbi," he sat on the bed, "I'm capable of taking care of Dad. Mrs. Collins is here and so is Cherish."

"I know, Darius." She sat up and faced him.

"Besides, it's just the sniffles."

"I know, Darius, but—"

"What are you going to do next weekend? I know Curry has already gotten your ticket, so you're going to California, if I have to go with you to the airport and personally place you on the plane." He narrowed his eyes at her to emphasize his point.

"I just worry about Dad."

"What about you and Curry? Do you know how much tonight cost him? Not just monetarily, but emotionally. Darbi, all I'm saying is there has to be a happy medium somewhere. You can go away for a weekend and Dad will be fine. You don't have to spend every minute of your free time here looking after Dad."

"I know. I guess I know in another fifteen years he may be gone." She wiped her face.

Darius realized she was acting the way he had just a few months before. "You could be too. Live for now. You have been through so much, and you deserve some happiness. Don't let a little sunshine pass you by while you are waiting for the hurricane." He stood and left her room.

～～⌒

Darius walked into his bedroom and smiled as he caught sight of Cherish dressed in a silk spaghetti strap short nightgown barely covering those hips he loved so. She sat on the bed, returning his smile, inviting him to bed.

"Well?" She settled the pillows behind her, looking very seductive.

"Yes, I talked to her. Hopefully, she'll go to California next weekend. I threatened to take her to the airport myself." He walked into the bathroom and changed into his pajamas, then sat by Cherish on the bed. "We're going to let them make up on their own. Agreed, Miss Murray?"

"Yes, Darius."

Darius slid into bed beside her, drawing her into his arms. He kissed her deeply as his body came to life. "Besides, if I know Curry, and I know I do, I'd say he's in love with my sister, but he'll probably never tell her that."

"Yes, and Darbi loves him. She doesn't think he loves her."

"I know. He's never really been in love before. He's dealing with unfamiliar emotions." *Much like me*, Darius thought.

"But he's been married twice!" Cherish gasped. "I understand why you guys are such good friends," she said as the light in her brain finally clicked on.

Women. "That doesn't mean he was in love." Darius offered no explanation. He kissed Cherish. "We'll let them take care of this on their own, remember?" Darius caressed her lips with his, hoping no further conversation of Curry and Darbi was needed. The kiss soon exploded into full-blown passion. Cherish suddenly pulled away.

Cherish looked at him with a hint of seduction in her brown eyes. She unbuttoned his silk pajama top. "You know, if I weren't so preoccupied with Curry and Darbi,

I could really concentrate on more important details." Her hand slowly glided over his muscular chest, flat stomach, and inched lower until he moaned in pleasure. She wrapped her hand around him, stroking him gently.

Darius was halfway to paradise when she stopped. "Cherish?"

"Call Curry." She sat up and looked at him with innocent eyes. "If you want me to continue my journey," she whispered against his lips.

Darius shook his head, reaching for the phone. *Only a few months and I'm already whipped!* He half-hoped Curry wouldn't answer his phone, but he answered on the sixth ring.

"Hey, Dare." Curry's usually upbeat voice was deflated and low.

"What happened?" Since they had been friends for so long, Darius dispensed with the idle chitchat.

Curry filled his friend in on the situation. "It's not the money, you know that. Is she going to always put Otis before everything? I mean, I could see her hesitation if there was no one there to watch him but you're there, the nurse is there and Cherish is there, too. Otis is not a child. He's sharper than many people half his age."

"I know, Curry," Darius agreed. "I've talked to her. I'm sure she's going out to California next weekend. I threatened to put her on the plane myself. I'll speak to Dad in the morning. He'll convince her that he's all right."

"Okay."

The friends ended their call.

Darius looked at Cherish. She was lying on her side with her back to him. "Satisfied?" he asked, snuggling closer to her still form.

A soft snore was his answer.

Darius awoke the next morning to an empty bed. He heard the shower running and smiled. He wanted to join Cherish but two things stopped him. One, he needed to talk to his father and two, he loved a solitary shower. With a sigh he stood, found his favorite black silk robe, and headed down the hall. He knocked on Darbi's door, but didn't get an answer. He continued downstairs to his father's room.

As he spoke to his father, Darius didn't think the elder Crawford looked well, but he didn't say anything. It was hard for Darius to differentiate between the disease and a simple cold. He left his father's room and headed for the kitchen. Mrs. Collins was busy making breakfast and the large breakfast table was already set. "Good morning, Mrs. Collins. Dad didn't look too well this morning. Could you check on him?"

She nodded, always one step ahead of him. "He's got a little bit of a cold. He's a little warm this morning so he's going to stay in bed."

Darius nodded, sat at the table and began to eat, savoring the eggs and bacon. Darbi came in and took the seat next to him. Her puffy brown eyes told him that she'd cried all night. "How did you sleep?"

"Very little." Darbi looked at the plate the nurse had placed in front of her and for once she pushed it away.

Cherish joined them a few minutes later and sat across from Darius. She was dressed in a red cashmere sweater and blue jeans. Darius knew what lay beneath those sensible clothes. "How's Otis?"

"Mrs. Collins says he's resting."

Darbi played with her breakfast. Food had lost its appeal. She wanted Curry. Not only that, but Darius and Cherish were playing footsies under the table and giggling like school kids. Darbi wanted to go back to her room to nurse her broken heart in private. As Mrs. Collins entered the kitchen, her eyes met Darbi's. "Ms. Crawford, your father would like to speak with you."

Darbi thanked the nurse and left the kitchen. She entered her father's room and sat down in the chair nearest the bed. "You wanted to see me, Dad?"

Otis looked at his baby girl. "You're the spitting image of your mother, right down to the stubborn streak. Baby girl, what is this nonsense about you not letting that boy take you on a trip?"

Darbi knew Darius had spilled the beans to their father. "I just wanted to be here in case you got sick."

"What do you think I pay that damned nurse for? This is just a cold. I don't want to be the reason you aren't enjoying life, understood?"

"Yes, Dad. I just worry about you. I want you to be around as long as possible."

Otis grabbed his daughter's hand. "Baby, if it is time for me to join your mother, than it's time for me to join your mother. We can't control our destiny. You of all people should know that. It will happen whether you are here, there, or wherever. You let that boy take you places."

Darbi noticed her father never called Curry by his name. "Do you like Curry? I mean, the fact that I am dating him?"

"Yes, I like him for the smile he's put on your face. I'd like him more if he were black, but we can't have everything, can we? Love doesn't always come in the package we think it should. He's good to you. He's good to Darius. I like the way he respects me. He always says sir. So you go to California next weekend. You hear me, girl?"

Darbi knew she'd been issued an order. There would be no discussion. "Okay, Dad, but only if you are better."

"You go. Have you talked to him this morning?"

"No, I called earlier, but he hung up on me." A lone tear escaped her eye.

"Sometimes you have to swallow your silly pride. Take your butt over to his house and make up with him. I'm sure your brother would let you use his truck."

"Dad, are you saying this is my fault?"

"Yes. Now, baby girl, you know I love you. Get out of my room, now!"

Darbi stood, dried her eyes, and kissed her father on his cheek. As she left his room, she laughed for the first time that morning. Darius stood in the hall with his keys in his outstretched hand. She smiled at her brother and hugged him. "Thank you, Darius. I'll be back in one hour."

Darius laughed, dismissing her last statement. "I'll come get it later. Somehow, I don't think you guys will be finished . . . um . . . talking in an hour."

"Darius, Darbi has been gone a long time. Aren't you worried?" Cherish asked as Darius was leading her upstairs. Pulling her up the stairs would be a more accurate description.

Darius had been trying to get Cherish upstairs with little luck for the last hour. He was taking advantage of the fact that his father was taking a nap and the nurse was in her room. Darius wanted to spend some quiet time with Cherish.

"They're fine. It's been over an hour. She'd be back by now, if they were still fighting."

They entered his bedroom. Cherish looked at Darius, folded her arms across her chest and sat on his bed. "Call."

"Women." Darius knew he was getting nowhere. "All right." Darius dialed Curry's number. The phone rang at least six times before Curry finally answered. He laughed as he placed the phone back in its cradle. "They were sleeping. See?"

Darius walked over and sat by her on the bed, enjoying the peace and quiet of a Saturday afternoon. He slowly began to undress her.

"Darius, do you think Curry will ever tell Darbi he loves her or vice versa?"

"Who knows? We won't tell. Okay?" He threw her sweater on the floor, along with his shirt.

"Okay, Darius. Let me do that for you." Cherish stood, got out of her jeans and undies. She then unbuckled his belt and took off his pants and boxers. "Now that we have each other's undivided attention, I say no more talking." Cherish straddled him and began their trek to the wild side.

The next week, Curry leaned back in the seat in satisfaction. Darbi was seated next to him in first class on a Thursday evening flight bound for California. They'd both jumped hurdles to make it happen. Darbi had taken her father to the doctor and he was fine. She'd also turned in her English paper early since she would miss class the next day. Curry had finished up the preliminary details for an impending ad campaign.

"We can have dinner when we get there." Curry sipped his cranberry juice.

"Sounds good. I'm so tired." She leaned against his shoulder and yawned.

Curry had guessed so. He simply kissed her forehead. When he heard Darbi's soft snore, he smiled in contentment. So this was what being in love was. He hadn't felt this way in either of his marriages. What was so different about Darbi Crawford?

CHAPTER SEVENTEEN

Saturday afternoon, Darius walked into his father's room, ready to have a serious talk about the illness. With Curry's urging, Darius had done some research on the disease and wanted to discuss some of the findings with Otis.

He cleared his throat as he took his customary seat by the bed. "How was exercise today?"

Otis grunted. "The same as it is every day. Awful. Of all the nurses you could have found, you got an exercise maniac. That woman runs me like I'm twenty or something. Doesn't she know that I'm suffering?"

Darius knew that 'pity me' routine well. He had heard it ever since Mrs. Collins came to work for them. He also knew that his father had been feeling much better lately. "Now, Dad, we're not going to start that again, are we? You know the doctor told Darbi that you're doing so much better than so many other Alzheimer's patients, due mostly to your exercise regimen and your diet."

Otis laughed. "You saw right through it? Just like your sister. She's become tougher than a marine sergeant since she's been learning all this stuff."

Darius nodded. "That's why I wanted to talk to you while she's in California with Curry."

"Go ahead, Son."

Darius didn't know if his father sometimes forgot his name or it was a term of endearment. Did it really matter? "Well, Dad, I know you're still in the first stage of it, and you've been doing very well. I wanted to see how you were dealing with all the other things."

Otis took a deep breath. "What do you mean?"

"I mean that along with discovering you have Alzheimer's, you also discovered that your widowed daughter is dating my white best friend, and then there's Cherish. How are you dealing with a stranger being in the house on occasion?"

"Oh, that. I'm happy that baby girl is with that boy for the most part. He makes her happy and I know he loves her."

"How do you know that?"

Otis stood and stretched. "You should watch him when he comes over and she's here. His whole demeanor changes; he becomes a gentler person. Christmas Eve when she had her crying spell and Cherish was with her, we had a chat in the kitchen. He wanted to go in there with her, but I talked him out of it."

Darius shook his head in amazement. He'd had no earthly idea Curry was up that night, let alone having a chat with his father. "Dad, you're incredible. How did you know Darbi had crying spells?"

"Because I'm her father. It doesn't take a degree from Princeton University to see that something is wrong with her. I figured that she just needed to tell another woman."

Again, Darius shook his head in utter amazement. Otis might not remember his wife's name, but he could remember where his son went to college. "It does seem she was better after finally confessing about Amos's horrible death. But how about Cherish?"

"What? Are you asking my permission to have your woman in your own house? I like her. She's not snooty and she spends time with baby girl. I like that. If I were a betting man, I'd say she's the one for you. But that's just an old man talking," his father said smugly.

Darius leaned back in the chair, smiling. This wasn't the conversation he'd come in to have with his father. It was much better.

⌒

Monday morning, Darius strolled into Curry's office, smiling at his friend. Curry looked the picture of contentment, something not synonymous with Curry Fitzgerald. "I hear you had a good time this weekend." Darius couldn't wait any longer to tease his friend.

Curry smiled. "It's not even noon yet! Yes, we had a good weekend. How did you know already? The plane from Malibu was delayed; we got back pretty late."

"For one, Darbi called Cherish last night, and two, I see fading hickey marks on your neck." Darius laughed as his friend's tanned skin turned red.

"Oh, no! I thought my shirt covered it up."

"It does, up to a point. It's barely noticeable to someone who doesn't know you're in love." He winked at his friend. "So did you get everything taken care of?"

"Yes, *we* did."

Darius raised an eyebrow at Curry's statement. For as long as he could remember Curry had only been worried about Curry. "Can I assume this relationship has taken on a new meaning?"

"Yes, it has. Which direction, only time will tell."

Darius looked at his friend's expression. It was one he had not seen before. Curry looked as if he had a touch of fear in his heart. Twice-married, Curry was dealing with an emotion he hadn't dealt with before: love. Curry Fitzgerald was in love and he was scared. "Curry, just because Darbi is my sister and was in a horrible marriage doesn't mean I can't listen with an uninvolved ear. You are still my best friend." Darius paused. "Unless you do something stupid to my sister."

～⌒〜

A few days later, Darius looked across the table at Cherish. The restaurant was crowded with lunch patrons, but Darius tuned out the noise. His mind was on his sister. Cherish's soft voice finally registered.

"Darius, what is it?"

"Darbi." As beautiful as Cherish looked, his sister occupied his thoughts. Darbi had been acting strange since her return from California.

"What is it? Is everything okay? I know she's been busy this week," Cherish commented.

"That's just it. She called me today and asked me if I could take Dad to the doctor tomorrow. That's not like her; she must really be sick. I know she's been playing catch up since she got back from California. I know she hasn't talked to Curry in a few days either and he's worried about that. When I talked to her this morning, she rushed me off the phone and she never does that."

"How did she sound? I haven't heard from Darbi since Sunday night, either. I just assumed she was busy," Cherish added.

"Hoarse. I know she's probably just tired from their weekend. With them both finally admitting they love each other it might have been too much. Maybe she's worried about that. I'll check on her after I take Dad to the doctor. Thank you." He smiled at Cherish.

"For what?"

"For being concerned about my family."

~~~

The next afternoon Darius followed his instincts and went to his sister's to see if she was all right. One look at her when she opened the door and he was so glad he had.

"D-darius what are you doing here? Did you take Dad to the doctor? What's wrong?" Darbi sneezed as she let him inside the condo.

Darius watched her as she tried to recover from sneezing. She was almost doubled over and had to lean against him for support. Slowly, she righted herself, looking at him blankly. He inspected his younger sister's face. Her usually clear skin was blotchy and her cheeks were flushed. "I came by to check on you. You look awful. What's wrong with you?"

Darbi slowly walked back to the couch. She lay back down, clutching her blanket. "Darius, I'm just a little tired. That's all. I'll be fine tomorrow."

Darius cast a stern glance at his sister, knowing her stubborn streak. "I'll tell you what," he started, "why don't you stay at the house until tomorrow?"

"I'm an adult, Darius." Darbi tried to sit up, but she didn't have enough strength. "I can't stay with you. How am I supposed to get to school or work?"

He watched her. She simply lay on the couch and closed her eyes. She was obviously sick, but tried to fight him anyway. He admired her spirit, but enough was enough. "Don't make me pick you up and carry you out of here. You know I can and I will." He watched as she snuggled under the covers.

She didn't answer him, but expelled a horrible amount of something he didn't want to clean up. Finally, she opened her eyes and spoke in a labored breath, "You win. Can you pack me some clothes for a few days?"

Darius nodded and walked into the small bedroom. He could see Curry's stamp all over it. A business suit still in the plastic provided by the local cleaners hung in the closet. His aftershave sat on the dresser, along with his cologne. Darius took a deep breath, trying not to focus on those items. His friend spent more time at Darbi's condo than Darius had realized. When he opened her undergarment drawer, the box of condoms, flavored ones at that, was almost too much. At least they're using protection, he thought. An unplanned pregnancy would not fit into anyone's schedule.

He found her overnight bag and stuffed the clothes in it. With bag in hand, he walked back into the living room. Darbi was sound asleep. He took the clothes to the truck and then carried Darbi, wrapped in a blanket, to the truck. She never woke up. After he made sure her condo was locked, he took her home.

As he drove, he watched the lump in the backseat. She never moved, which only told him she was sicker than she let on. He settled her in the room he thought of as hers and checked on his father.

Otis sat in the living room, reading a book. Darius smiled at that. Otis fought anything remotely related to exercise. Little did he know reading gave his brain a mental workout, thus postponing the advancement of the disease.

"How's Darbi?" Otis put the book down.

"I think she's a lot sicker than she thinks. She slept all the way here. I'm going to ask Mrs. Collins to check on her later."

His father nodded. "What about that boy?"

"I don't think he knows she's sick. I'll tell him tomorrow. He's been worried since she hasn't talked to him since they got back. It's weird seeing him this insecure about a woman."

Otis laughed. "That's what being in love is all about. Insecurity. You never know anything anymore. You second-guess yourself all the time. You should know that. You're in love with Cherish."

The next day, Darius sat in his office, preparing his notes for the afternoon meeting. Cherish had just phoned, letting him know that she had checked on both Darbi and Otis. Cherish's feelings mirrored those of Darius. His sister was very sick.

"Do you still want to go to San Francisco next weekend? I know it's Valentine's Day weekend," Cherish reminded him.

"Of course. She'll be fine by then." He sighed as he hung up the phone. He'd feel awful leaving with her being sick. He resumed preparing his notes until a familiar voice interrupted him.

"Dare, you got a minute?" Curry stood at the office door.

Darius looked up from his papers and watched Curry nervously shove his hands in his pockets. "What is it, Curry?" Darius thought Curry looked upset.

Curry walked inside his office and sat down. He rubbed his hands through his curly blond hair, a sure sign he was nervous. "I've been wondering what to do for over an hour. I have to know where I stand with Darbi. It's driving me crazy. I can't concentrate on anything." He took a deep breath. "I've tried to call Darbi several times, but she hasn't called me back. I know she's been busy and I'm trying to give her space, so I don't smother her. But it's been a few days since we talked last, so I called the university and they said she wasn't at work today. I know Darbi's work ethic is like yours. She wouldn't miss work unless it was absolutely necessary. Is she trying to dump me? You're right, I don't like it when the shoe is on the other foot."

Darius laughed. He couldn't believe Curry, the breaker of hearts, was feeling insecure. "This is my fault. I should have called you last night, but I got sidetracked. She's at my house. She's sick. I went and got her yesterday. I think she's just got a bad cold." He hoped that was all that was wrong with Darbi, but her fever and chills told him otherwise.

"Whew!" Curry wiped his brow in relief. "I didn't know what to think. I panicked." He laughed. "I'm really losing it. How's she's feeling?"

Darius didn't want to alarm his friend. "She's resting. Why don't you come over tonight?"

~~~~

A week later, on Valentine's Day, Darbi was still at Darius's. Her cold had turned into a full-blown flu. Darius had taken her to the doctor despite her pleas that she was fine. But that was a few days ago, and Darbi still wasn't feeling her best. She took all her meals in her room, when she was up to eating. Even when Curry came by to see her, which was every night, she stayed in bed.

Darius packed his bag for his weekend with Cherish. After playing nursemaid to both Darbi and Otis, he felt he needed a break. After he finished packing his bag, he went to check on his sister. As he walked into the darkened room, he heard her labored breathing. She still sounded very stuffy to him, even with the vaporizer going twenty-four hours a day. He had half a mind to cancel the trip, but then he envisioned Cherish sprawled out on a bed wearing next to nothing and changed his mind. Quietly, he left the room. He went back to his room, got his bag, and headed downstairs.

"You're worried about Darbi?" Cherish asked as she drove to the airport. "I thought about canceling the trip, since she's still sick. It seems strange she's still in bed after two weeks. Are you sure about the trip?"

Darius nodded. "Yes, I am. I'm sure she'll be fine. I just wish she were well or something remotely close to it. But Curry's there, and things should be fine." Darius cast a worried glance at Cherish. "Still . . ." he started.

"You'd rather stay." She leaned across the console of the Blazer and patted his hand. "Me, too. I don't think I could have a good time knowing she's so sick." Cherish turned her car around and headed back to Darius's house.

A month later, Darius packed for his trip to Paris with Cherish. He couldn't wait to step on that plane. Darbi walked into his room, shaking her head. He still couldn't believe how sick she'd been just a few weeks before. Now she was back to normal. "Are you sure you don't mind spending your spring break here with Dad?"

"Yes, Darius. Curry's coming over a few days to keep me company. Plus, I'm going to work on my degree plan."

Darius smiled. At last his sister's life was headed in the right direction. She had decided on a major, finally. To both his and Curry's dismay she'd decided on information systems. "Is he spending the night?"

"Not if you don't want him to, Darius. He did say he'd take a few days off from work, so he could spend some time with me." She smiled at her brother's worried face.

"I don't mind if he spends the night here." Darius paused. "You're still using protection, right?"

~~~~~

Curry was a mess and he needed help with the two women in his life. He went to the one person who could help him out of this trouble, Darius. Since his trouble included Darbi, Curry would have to be careful how he broached the subject. Food was always good. He invited Darius to lunch at his favorite restaurant.

Lunchtime at any restaurant was busy. Considering it was downtown, Cleo's was overcrowded. Curry needed advice about Darbi and he'd put his mother off for the third time. There would not be a fourth. So he offered to buy Darius's lunch to get some much-needed advice. "How was Paris?" Curry sat in front of his friend, nervously playing with his glass.

Darius smiled at the memories. "Paris was great! It was very romantic. However, I think I might need a few days to rest up from my vacation. We got back Saturday and I slept all day Sunday. I'm still tired," he grinned. "You know, we missed most of the fashion shows, but we caught the important ones. Once we arrived in Paris, those fashion shows were the last thing on our minds!"

Curry laughed as he picked at his crab salad. He coughed and took a swig of tea, wishing he had something stronger.

"Curry, what's on your mind? You've been edgy all morning. Is everything okay with you and Darbi? I told her I didn't mind you staying at the house while I was away. I really didn't."

"Well," Curry began, "next month is my parents' fifty-first wedding anniversary. My mom has informed me that she wants Darbi to attend. I'm just not sure how Darbi will react. You know, the first time they met was under some sticky circumstances. Any suggestions?" He gazed at Darius, hoping for some insight.

Darius leaned back in his chair, trying to hide his laughter. "I know about your parents catching you guys in bed together. Cherish told me. That was one way to break the news to your very Irish mother that you're dating a black woman." He laughed. "Curry, you're going to have to ask her. Explain to her how important this is to you for her to attend." Darius smiled at his friend.

Curry nodded and continued picking at his salad. He was starving and still he picked at his food. He hoped Darbi was as sensible as her brother.

Darbi drove up to Darius's house with apprehension. She wondered why her father had to see her tonight. She walked into the house and noticed Mrs. Collins, the nurse, setting the table for dinner. She smiled at Darbi.

"I'll tell Mr. Crawford you're here. He's been waiting." She walked down the hall, leaving Darbi in the foyer. She returned and informed Darbi that Otis was waiting for her.

Darbi nodded, thanked Mrs. Collins and walked down the hall to her father's bedroom. Darius was also there, sitting in a chair in the corner. Darbi's heart started beating harder. Whatever her father wanted to discuss with her was very important if he needed Darius for backup. Had he gotten bad news from the doctor? Otis sat on the corner of his made-up bed and offered her the chair that was nearest the bed. Darbi sat down and returned her father's stare.

Otis took a deep breath and began to speak. "Baby girl, I had a talk with your brother. You car is just too damned small. Now I went to the bank and withdrew some money. I want you to get something bigger."

"Dad, that car is just fine," Darbi argued.

"Baby, you need a bigger car. I'm too tall for that little car. I feel like I have to be pried out of it. Since you're the one who takes me to the doctor, you need a bigger car."

"Dad, I really like my Beetle. Buying it marked my first step toward sanity."

"Honey, I know. But think of this as a gift from me."

"Isn't this your retirement money? I can't take it. I do have some money if I really need a bigger car. I happened to think my car has plenty of room."

Otis watched Darbi. Then he glanced at his son. "Darbi Ariane, I am going to say this once. I drew out $15,000. I figure between your car and that money, you should be able to get a decent-sized car. Saturday morning, Darius will go with you to get something." He dared her to object.

"Okay, Dad." It was useless arguing with him. Illness or not, he saw a problem, he saw the solution. End of discussion. She took a deep breath. "Okay, I'll look for something bigger."

Otis smiled. "That's my baby girl."

Darbi kissed her father on the cheek. Then she noticed his smug look. He'd known she would give in! "What's for dinner?"

"Mrs. Collins said she would make shepherd's pie for you. She knows how you like it," Darius said.

Darbi yawned. "Do I have time for a quick nap?"

Darius looked at her, not hiding his worry. "Are you okay? You're not getting sick again, are you?"

"I'm just tired. I've been studying a lot lately."

Saturday morning, Darbi drove away from the car dealership in her brand new Ford Explorer XLT. She was glad Darius had gone with her. He'd helped her get a better deal.

Darbi drove back to Darius's house and showed her father her new car. Otis approved instantly.

"I like it, baby. This blue is a pretty color." He looked at the leather seats. "Your brother must have done some tall talkin' to get them to come down on the price."

"Yes, he did. I see why he's in marketing." She fished a check out of her purse. "This is your change." She handed the check to her father.

Otis looked at the check. "Wow, he is a talker." He handed the check back to his daughter. "You keep it."

"Dad, I can't keep this!"

"Your birthday is next week. Buy yourself something extravagant. You deserve it. It's a small price to pay to see you smile like that, baby girl."

Darbi couldn't stop the flood of tears as she hugged her father. He remembered her birthday.

CHAPTER EIGHTEEN

Cherish looked at the man sleeping beside her and lightly ran her fingers over Darius's full lips. He moaned and shifted closer to her. She hadn't seen him in almost a week; it felt more like a year to her. They'd dispensed with dinner, heading straight for his bedroom.

Slowly, Darius's hand began to roam freely over Cherish's naked body. He opened his eyes. "Who was that wild woman who made love to me?" Darius whispered in her ear, creating all kinds of delicious naughty sensations throughout her body. "I like it."

"I just missed you this week," she purred. Cherish snuggled closer to him. "You know, you never fed me tonight. I'm hungry. My man really gave me quite an appetite!" She giggled as she caressed his face.

"Later." Darius kissed her. "Later." He eased himself on top of her. "Would you rather have dinner now or later?"

Now it was her turn to say *later*. Thoughts of food fluttered out of her mind as Darius became the center of her universe. She wrapped her arms around him.

As his large hands roamed her body, Cherish wiggled underneath him. Darius laughed. "Will you be quiet? I thought I heard the doorbell." He kissed her on the mouth and wrapped his arms around her.

"Make me be quiet," Cherish challenged.

He did.

Hours later, Cherish waited for Darius to finish his shower. For some reason the bathroom was the one place they couldn't share their intimacy. They were so much alike, both believing in the privacy of a solitary shower. Cherish fussed with her hair as Darius walked out of his bathroom.

"Do you want to go out for something to eat? I know it's late, maybe an all-night restaurant?" He buttoned his jeans and put on a t-shirt.

"No, we can raid your fridge." Cherish tucked her blouse into her jeans.

"You just happen to be in luck. Mrs. Collins went shopping a few days ago." Darius walked over to her and kissed her.

Hand in hand, they walked downstairs and headed for the kitchen. Darius opened the refrigerator and took out the fixings for sandwiches. "Some Saturday night date, huh?" he asked, placing the items on the table.

"Darius, you've been busy," Cherish acknowledged. "This feels like heaven to me. Does Darbi like her car?" She poured wine into two glasses.

"Yes, even if Dad had to convince her to get it. I talked the salesman down on his price." Darius smiled in satisfaction. "He was putty in my hands," he said smugly.

"That's good. Where is she tonight?"

"Probably with Curry." Darius smiled. The thought of his sister and best friend was getting easier to accept each time he said it.

~~~

The next morning, Darbi snuggled closer to Curry in his king-sized bed as the phone rang. He loved the times when her body was awake, but her brain wasn't, when her subconscious took over and revealed her true feelings. Her slender hands traveled his body slowly, massaging his chest, lingering around his flat stomach and venturing lower. But the phone rang again, halting her actions. Curry answered the passion-robbing instrument thinking it was Darius. He was wrong. Very wrong.

"Curran, have you talked her into coming next week?" his mother asked.

"Mom," Curry whispered, "she's sleeping. She's still thinking about it."

"Let me talk to her," his mother commanded.

Curry knew that tone. His mother had given him too many opportunities to get an answer from Darbi and was ready to take matters into her own hands. She had the Irish gift of blarney. She could talk an Irishman out of his last drop of Guinness. "Mom!"

"Curran, will you let me handle this?"

He regretfully woke Darbi. After a few minutes of whispers, Darbi took the phone. He watched her take a deep breath before she spoke into the phone.

"Hello, Mrs. Fitzgerald." She sat up and pulled the sheet over her nude body as if his mother could tell what they were doing. She hit Curry as he laughed.

"Darbi, Curran tells me you are still undecided about coming. Seattle is beautiful in the springtime. I'm sure you would like to meet the rest of the family. We always have a celebration party for our anniversary. You see, Thomas has a heart condition and we never know which year will be our last together." Sarah let the hint float freely through the phone lines, reaching Darbi.

Darbi could relate to her last statement. "Yes, I'll come Mrs. Fitzgerald. I don't want to be the reason Curry doesn't attend." She would hate if they didn't go and something happened to his father.

"Great. We look forward to seeing you next Friday. It was nice chatting with you." Sarah ended the call.

Darbi stared at Curry as he lay beside her. "Why didn't you tell me that your dad was sick?"

"Because he doesn't like to talk about it. He doesn't want pity. Treat him like a person, not a heart condition. Besides, he exercises all the time. My dad is probably the same age as Otis. I'm glad you decided to go. The flight is Friday morning at eight. Get ready for a lot of Irish food."

Darbi gazed at him. "What's so different about Irish food?"

Curry kissed her lovingly on the mouth. "There's just more of it. How about breakfast?"

As Darbi entered her brother's house at lunchtime, her heart swelled with joy as she watched Cherish and Darius walking downstairs together, holding hands. *I made that happen*, she thought smugly. Mrs. Collins was setting the table for lunch as Otis made his way to the table. Darbi sat next to her father. She didn't miss her father's inspection of her features.

"How you doing, baby girl?"

"Fine, Dad." Darbi pretended to be involved in unfolding her napkin and avoided her father's eyes.

"What's wrong?"

Those magic words. They made Darbi felt better already. "I talked to Curry's mother this morning about their anniversary party. I was all set to say no, that I wasn't coming with him. Once she started talking about Mr. Fitzgerald's heart condition, I weakened and agreed to go. So now I have to go to Seattle next weekend. I don't know why that woman would ever want me in her house."

"Now, baby, she obviously wants you to be there. Apparently it's important to that boy. So go and have a good time."

Sometimes Darbi forgot that her father was ill. He could still make any problem seem small. "I will, Dad. Thanks." She kissed his cheek.

Over lunch the Crawfords and Cherish discussed Darbi's upcoming trip. Darius attempted to relieve her fears. "Darbi, I've met some of Curry's relatives, they seem nice," Darius told his sister.

"Yes, but you aren't sleeping with Curry! You know that woman hates me because I'm black. I can't see why she would want me at her house." During her tirade, Darbi realized that Curry hadn't use a condom the night before. "Oh, no!" She slapped her hand over her mouth.

"What is it?" Darius and Cherish exchanged glances.

"Oh, nothing. I didn't brush my teeth this morning," Darbi lied to her audience.

After lunch, Darbi and Cherish cleaned off the dining table. Cherish walked over to Darbi as she stacked the dishes. Trying to hide her nervousness, Darbi concentrated on putting the plate up without letting the dish slip out of her hand.

"Darbi, did you guys forget last night?" Cherish whispered.

Darbi nodded, avoiding Cherish's observant eyes.

"I thought you couldn't get pregnant anyway?"

Darbi whispered, "I think I'm right. For the last five years I didn't have a period. But the last few months, I've started having them again."

"After you and Curry became sexually active," Cherish guessed. "That's still odd. I've heard of skipping a few months if you're under stress or something, but that's weird. But I'm sure everything is just fine."

Darbi nodded, knowing that more than likely her fate was probably already sealed. She forced a smile. "I'm just worried for nothing." She hugged Cherish. "I'm so glad we met at group session."

The next day, Cherish sat at her drawing table. As she worked on her sketches, her mind floated to Darius. He wasn't the stiff board she had met months before; still, he wasn't as carefree as Curry. Darius would probably never be like that. She thought about Darbi as well. Their conversation at Darius's had her concerned for Darbi's health. She quickly called a doctor friend to see if that was normal.

Dr. Shelby Allen listened as Cherish described her friend's condition, inserting the appropriate words when needed. "Cherish, I don't think it's anything to worry about. From what you've told me, her mental state was probably retarding her cycles. Now that she's overcome some of her mental obstacles, her cycle has returned. I would caution her to use something in addition to condoms. Accidents do happen, you know."

"Thanks, Shelby. How have you been?" Cherish and Shelby had been friends since junior high and had attended had Fort Worth University together. Shelby with her tall, willowy frame had been in Cherish's first fashion show.

"Fine, girl," Shelby said. "Still searching for Mr. Right or even Mr. Will Do. It seems me being a doctor intimidates so many brothers. So dates have been few and far between. I refuse to date outside the brother network. I just go home to Jordan and be happy."

"Jordan?"

"That's my corgi. He's a cute dog, and he's four years old. Tyrell, the last casualty, gave him to me as a consolation prize for catching him cheating on me. How about you?"

"Well, I'm dating. Darbi is Darius's sister. He's great, a little reserved, but workable. Yes, he's a brother," Cherish laughed, beating Shelby to the punch line.

After the friends ended the conversation, Cherish relaxed and returned to her work thinking about Shelby. Shelby was educated, polished and intimidated men to no end, no matter what color they were.

CHAPTER NINETEEN

Darius wrapped his arm around Cherish's waist as they entered Balla's Italian Cuisine for dinner. They were quickly escorted to a candlelit table, just as he had reserved for them. He had wanted a quiet, romantic evening, so they could talk. With them both being so busy lately, it seemed almost impossible to find time just to have an intimate conversation. But instead of talking, he mostly stared at her, drinking in her beauty. Her shoulder length hair was in a French roll, calling attention to her delicate ears. The candles on the table added depth to her brown eyes. He was enchanted and tongued-tied. Nothing that came out of his mouth seemed coherent.

They enjoyed their meal of cabo san Italia, which translated into a grilled boneless skinless chicken breast wrapped in Italian bacon, topped with provolone cheese and marinara sauce, accompanied by angel hair pasta.

Cherish sipped her wine, watching her companion. "Is Darbi more at ease about going to visit Curry's parents this weekend?"

Darius laughed, coming out of his trance. "I don't know who's more anxious, her or Curry. He's been walking around more nervous than a bridegroom on his wedding day." He knew the trip meant a lot to Curry. It was almost as if Darbi was meeting her future in-laws.

After their meal, Darius drove Cherish home. He wanted to spend the night, but he knew he had an early meeting the next day. "I've got an early meeting." He looked down into Cherish's brown eyes, wishing that he could stay and fulfill the fantasies he'd been having all night. "You know I would otherwise." He kissed her goodnight and was gone, before he changed his mind.

Darius pulled into his garage and turned off the engine. Looking at his cell phone, he cursed himself for being weak, picked it up, and punched in Cherish's phone number. He smiled when he heard her sultry voice. "I wish I were there with you, now."

"Me, too. Goodnight, Darius," she purred.

~~~

Friday afternoon, his assistant, Bea, announced to Darius he had a phone call on line four. He sighed, knowing it was Curry calling from Seattle, again. He had already called twice about Darbi. She was a bundle of nerves and had lost her breakfast as soon as the plane landed. It would have been comical if it hadn't meant so much to Curry.

Darius picked up the phone and took a deep breath. "What's wrong now, Curry?"

Curry gave a shaky laugh, which only meant trouble. "I know I sound like a nervous wife or something, but she's been hovering over the toilet for about forty-five minutes. I'm just worried about all this throwing up."

Darius was too. He wanted Darbi to enjoy herself on the trip, not live in the bathroom. "Let me talk to her."

Curry breathed a sigh of relief. "Okay."

Darius heard a door open and Darbi moaning. Finally she spoke into the phone.

"Hello," she croaked.

"Darbi," Darius started, knowing that it was time for some tough love or Darbi would be sitting in the emergency room. "I want you to sit on the edge of the tub and put your head between your legs. It will help the nausea pass."

"But," Darbi countered weakly.

"Do it," he commanded. "Or you'll be blowing chunks until you make yourself sick. Curry's already called me three times worrying about you. So do it," he commanded with no room for discussion.

He heard her struggling into the position.

"Okay. Now what? I still feel sick to my stomach," Darbi reported, taking a deep breath between each word.

"I know, just be patient. You should feel better in about thirty minutes. Don't worry about Curry's mom, her bark is worse than her bite."

"It's not her." Another deep breath.

Darius knew immediately what it was. Not only was his best friend afraid of being in love, so was his sister.

"How was Seattle?" Cherish asked Darbi a few days after her return from Washington. She was dying to know what had happened and Darius had not been forthcoming. She knew Curry had called Darius several times for advice during the weekend.

"Pretty good. Those first few hours, I was violently ill. Then my nerves calmed down and it was okay. The party was fun. Of course, I was the subject of most of the discussions. No one believed I was 39. I had to show my driver's license. His brothers are a riot; they made me feel welcome instantly. Those people can sure eat." She took a deep breath, thankful that trip was over. "What's going on with you and Darius?"

Cherish breathed a long dramatic pause. "I don't know. We're going, I guess. He was so romantic in Paris, but once we returned here, it's like he turned the romance off. He's attentive, but not like Paris. I want some excitement."

Darbi laughed at her friend. "I told you. That's just Darius. He's always going to act differently away from home. At home he's always worried about his corporate image. One day something will happen and he's not going to care about what the higher ups at Sloane think, but until then, you'll just have to plan lots of trips."

"I just wish he could incorporate some of his away enthusiasm into everyday life. But that's asking too much, huh?"

"For Darius, yes."

~~~

Wednesday night, Darius sat across from Cherish at a candlelight supper for his birthday. All his favorites were included: steak, pasta, salad, and Italian cream cake.

After he consumed most of his meal, he said, "This was an excellent birthday, Cherish. Thank you." Darius held her hand across the table. "You're so special. I'm a very lucky man."

"You're my special man, Darius," Cherish said, feeling a slow tingle in her body. All Darius Crawford had to do was look at her with those chocolate brown eyes and she was liquid, or at least certain parts of her were. "Come to the living room for part two of your birthday." Cherish stood and walked into the living room. Darius followed her to the couch and sat down beside her.

"Close your eyes," Cherish ordered.

He did as he was told.

Cherish rose from the couch and walked to the hall closet to retrieve his gift. She dragged it across the floor to stand a few feet in front of him. "Okay, open your eyes," came her quiet command.

Darius opened his eyes and immediately smiled. "This is wonderful, Cherish. Thank you. Amazing." Darius looked in amazement at the forty x fifty oil painting of jazz great Dizzy Gillespie leading his band. "I'll hang it in the living room." He walked to Cherish and kissed her in celebration.

"We're not finished, Darius." She grabbed his hand and led him upstairs to her bedroom. "Wait here." She walked hurriedly to her bathroom.

As she entered her bathroom, she quickly undressed and put on the special nightgown she'd bought for the occasion. It was sheer and mauve, Darius's favorite color.

She wondered if he would notice she had nothing else on underneath. Probably not. Not her rigid Darius. She laughed at her own pun. She opened the door and almost lost her nerve at Darius's expression. Apparently, the gown was totally transparent. He was speechless!

Darius cleared his throat as Cherish walked toward him. "Cherish?"

She tried to walk seductively toward him, but her knees were giving her away.

Darius spoke softly. "I like what I see. Or what I don't see," he clarified.

Cherish led him into the bathroom. "This is for you, Darius." She pointed to the bubble bath, candles, champagne, and the jazz music playing softly in the background. She started to unbutton his shirt. After she took his shirt off, she noticed his hesitation. "What is it, Darius? I know we're never intimate in the bathroom, but I want to for you. I want to show you how much I love you." Cherish looked up at him, hoping he didn't object.

Darius nodded and unbuttoned his slacks.

Minutes later, Cherish and Darius sat in her oversized bathtub sipping champagne and giggling like hormone driven teen-agers. Cherish leaned against his chest and sighed. He wrapped her in a tight embrace, bringing her even closer to his body. She'd taken a big chance that he would like the surprise and he did.

"Why didn't we do this sooner?" Darius kissed her neck and caressed her full breasts gently. He let his hands glide over her flat stomach, enjoying the feel of silk beneath his hands.

"Because," Cherish whispered, "you said something about the bathroom being for one person at a time."

"You agreed with me," Darius countered as he drained the last of his champagne. "I may have been wrong about that."

Cherish smiled as she snuggled closer to his naked body. This was exciting to her as well.

CHAPTER TWENTY

A few weeks later, Darbi was having a bad reaction to the previous night's dinner. Early Saturday morning, she bent over Cherish's toilet throwing up. After her stomach finally settled, she brushed her teeth. Mistake. She stood over the toilet again.

"Darbi?" Cherish called to her friend. "Are you okay?" She opened the door. Darbi sat on the edge of the bathtub, panting. Cherish, dressed in her silk bathrobe, stood in the doorway watching Darbi.

"I didn't mean to wake you, Cherish," Darbi apologized. "Must have been something I ate last night." Darbi closed her eyes; her stomach had begun turning flips again. "Never brush your teeth after throwing up. Big mistake," she joked.

Cherish grinned, but concern was etched on her face. "If you don't feel up to going to the outlet mall, that's okay. Hillsboro would probably be a long ride for you since you're not feeling well."

Darbi smiled feebly at her friend. "No, I want to. Besides, in two weeks I'll be studying for finals." Darbi took a deep breath. "I don't know what's been wrong with me lately. The other night Curry and I were messing around in bed and I threw up all over him."

"That's odd." Cherish's lips formed a thin line of confusion.

"I think I'm just stressed about finals. I did so well my first semester. Dad and Darius were so proud, I don't want to disappoint them." Darbi put her hand against her stomach, silently willing it to calm down.

"How are your grades?"

"I'm holding steady at a B average, but Curry's birthday is right in the middle of finals. I don't know if he's willing to celebrate after the fact. He already says that I'm neglecting him."

"I'm sure he only wants your happiness," Cherish said. "Just remind him about finals and how important this is to you. What are you going to do this summer?"

"I'm not taking any classes. My boss asked me if I wanted to work full-time this summer. I told her I would." Darbi stood and attempted to brush her teeth again without throwing up. She was successful.

Cherish watched her friend, silently moving closer until she stood next to Darbi. "When was the last time you were intimate with Curry?"

"Right before I threw up on him. Before that a week ago. Why?" Darbi stared at her, not wanting to say her fear out loud.

"No reason. How do you feel now?"

"Better," she lied.

"Good. Why don't we eat breakfast, then go to the mall?"

The room shifted again, and Darbi had to sit down. She tried to focus on Cherish's face, but she wouldn't stand still. Now Darbi's stomach was fighting for control of her mouth.

Cherish sat by Darbi, putting her arm around her. She spoke in a quiet voice, which alarmed Darbi instantly. "Darbi, have you noticed any changes in your body lately? You know, like your breasts being tender, being tired?"

Darbi nodded. "Now that you mention it, this last week I've been taking naps after work. My appetite has suddenly gone finicky in the morning. I used to stop at the school cafeteria for breakfast, but the smells have started to make me sick. Last Saturday, after aerobics, I did notice my breast being especially sensitive. I thought it was because I was breaking in a new sports bra. Why?" *Oh no.* Darbi finally connected the dots and it wasn't the picture she wanted to see.

Cherish inhaled and exhaled deeply. "Darbi, I think you're pregnant. Why don't we go buy a pregnancy test later, just to be sure? I have a friend who's an OB/GYN. We could call her and maybe she could see you," Cherish said in her most reassuring voice.

Teardrops fell from Darbi's eyes. "Cherish, I can't be pregnant! We use protection!" Almost every time, she thought.

"Honey, it doesn't work all the time."

"Not now! Not Curry's! Darius will kill me! Dad will be so disappointed in me! I just can not be pregnant." Darbi cried uncontrollably.

"Darbi, we don't know for sure yet. Calm down. Let's just wait and see if you actually are first. Then we'll talk to my friend Shelby."

Darbi dried her eyes. "Okay, I'll wait to freak out. Don't mention this to Darius or Curry, please."

"I won't. If you are, though, you'll have to tell them both."

"I know. I'm going to take a nap. Oh, no, another symptom." Darbi left the bathroom and went back to bed.

~~~

"I feel better now," Darbi announced, walking into the living room where Cherish was sitting and reading the paper.

Cherish smiled, instantly relaxing Darbi. "Good. I called Shelby while you were napping and she said if we do the test today, she could see you Monday at five-thirty."

Darbi nodded. If she was pregnant, life as she knew it was over. Curry would definitely blame her. Amos always had anytime something in his life went wrong. So would Darius.

Cherish continued talking in that soft comforting voice. "She won't charge you as a favor to me. That's why your appointment is so late." Cherish tried to make her friend feel better.

Darbi nodded, her mind already on the evening ahead. "Well, we might as well get this over with. Let's go buy that test."

As Cherish and Darbi searched the drug aisle in the store, they were faced with a dilemma. There were all kinds of tests, from the easy to not so easy. Some required a pharmacist to interpret the instructions. Others used a variety of methods: a circle, a plus sign, a minus sign, and different colors. The women studied the boxes. Finally they found one they could actually do themselves.

"I have a college degree and I still don't get some of these instructions." Cherish watched Darbi's nervous face. "My treat. Don't worry, all things happen for a reason." She patted Darbi's shaky hand.

"All reasons aren't good, Cherish!"

After they purchased the test, they returned to Cherish's. The women went into the large bathroom to prepare for the test. Cherish watched Darbi's shaky hand as she attempted to open the box. After several failed attempts, Cherish finally opened the box for her and placed it on the marble counter. She walked toward the bathroom door. "This will be hard enough without an audience. I'll be outside the door." Cherish closed the door behind her. She stood outside the door for what felt like an hour, but it was just a few minutes before Darbi called her name.

Cherish walked back in the bathroom, watching Darbi's face for a reaction. Darbi sat on the edge of the bathtub concentrating on the test as it sat on the counter, willing the blue circle not to appear. Cherish sat by her and held her hand. Darbi exhaled. Just as she began to relax, Cherish screamed, "Look Darbi!"

Darbi watched in horror as the blue circle appeared and her dreams disappeared. "Oh, no! I can't believe this. Amos and I tried for years and nothing. I meet Curry Fitzgerald and a few months later, I'm pregnant!"

"I can't understand why you didn't get pregnant before."

Darbi lowered her head. "Amos said it was my fault." A teardrop splattered on her hands. "Why did I listen to that man?"

Cherish wiped away her tears. "Apparently he was the one with the problem." She took a deep breath. "Who are you going to tell first?"

"For one brief second, I thought about an abortion. But even if this is the most monumental mistake I ever made next to marrying Amos, I couldn't do that. I'll wait until the doctor confirms it before I tell anyone. I guess I should discuss it with Curry first. I'll have to pick the time to tell Darius and Dad. I know Darius isn't going to be pleased at all. Please don't mention this to anyone yet."

"What about tomorrow? You'll have to face both of them for Sunday dinner," Cherish reminded her friend.

"I know. I'll just wait until Monday."

"I'll go with you on Monday. I'll meet you at Shelby's office. It's attached to Briarwood hospital in Arlington." Cherish hugged her friend. "Hey, let's go out to eat. A pseudo-celebration."

~~~~

Monday afternoon, Darbi sat in Dr. Shelby Allen's waiting room, anxiously awaiting Cherish's arrival. She nervously looked around the room, hoping she didn't spot a familiar face. After she relaxed, she noticed the couple sitting across from her.

The man rubbed his pregnant wife's stomach as she tried to read an article in a magazine. She slapped her husband's hand away. As she did, Darbi noticed her very large diamond wedding ring. The gold band mocked Darbi as she watched the couple.

"Daniel, stop it. You're breaking my concentration."

"You break mine all the time." He kissed his wife's forehead.

A slender woman in a white lab coat approached the couple and interrupted their conversation. "Daniel, Keandra. Why don't we go to my office? I have the results of yesterday's sonogram."

Darbi noticed her nametag. So that was Shelby. Darbi watched as Daniel helped his wife to stand. His wife was beautiful and very tall. Darbi watched the muscular man put his arms around his wife as they followed Shelby. No one even gave the couple a second glance, she noted. She smiled. Daniel was white and his wife was not.

～～～

Twenty minutes later, Darbi heard her name. She felt a surge of relief as Cherish sat down beside her and began gently rubbing Darbi's shoulder. The rest of the day would only get tougher. Somehow Cherish had a calming effect on Darbi's out of control emotions. Otherwise she would be huddled somewhere in a corner crying her eyes out. After a few minutes of welcome silence, Cherish spoke.

"How are you doing?"

"Better. I just saw a couple go in a while ago. They looked so happy together. So it is possible." Just not with Curry Fitzgerald, the carefree, single man.

"Anything is possible if your heart is in the right place. Darius called. That's why I'm so late. He thinks you were acting strange yesterday. So does Curry."

"I know. I shouldn't have cried when he told me he didn't have any cheesecake!" Darbi laughed as she remembered both Darius and Curry offering to go get her some, just so she would stop crying.

"Yes. Good thing they're men or they would have figured it out!"

"Darbi Crawford, Dr. Allen will see you now," a monotone voice announced minutes later.

Both Darbi and Cherish stood and walked down the hallway to Shelby's office. As they entered the doctor's waiting area, Darbi saw the couple from the waiting room leaving, holding hands. The man now had a manila folder in his free hand. They both had enormous smiles plastered on their faces.

"I can't wait to tell Mom and Dad. Let's call them from the car," he told his wife as he kissed her.

Darbi watched them as they exited the doors. "I want a love like that. This time around I'm not settling for anything less than true love. I know Curry isn't ready." Darbi took a deep breath and walked into the doctor's office.

Dr. Shelby Allen greeted them as they entered the examination room. The doctor wasn't dressed like any doctor Darbi had ever seen in her limited experience. She wore a short lavender dress and matching lavender stilettos. The only familiar thing she had on was the lab jacket covering most of the dress.

"Hi, Cherish. It's great to see you! Darbi, just relax. The first thing I need for you to do is change into this gown." The doctor pointed to a screen in the corner of the examination room. "You can change in here, or there's an adjoining changing room. Which one makes you more comfortable?"

Darbi needed the mindless chatter of the two childhood friends to take her mind off her impending doom. "I'll change in here." She headed to the corner.

Shelby smiled at her. "Most women like to hear noises, it helps take their mind off the situation." Shelby and Cherish began chatting about other things in an attempt to ease Darbi's nerves.

Darbi emerged from the corner and sat on the edge of the examination table.

Shelby watched her. "Darbi, you're going to need to relax or we'll be here all night. Go into the bathroom. I need a sample. There's a cup on the sink."

Darbi nodded and did as she was told. Soon she returned and sat on the table again. Shelby went to conduct the official test. Darbi inhaled deeply. Maybe she'd done the test wrong. She hoped. Shelby returned twenty minutes later with a piece of paper in her hand.

"Yes, Darbi, you were correct. Usually those tests are wrong, but you are pregnant. Last cycle?"

"What?"

"When was your last cycle? Not specific, just ballpark."

Darbi shrugged her shoulders. "I think about three weeks, maybe four." She didn't want to admit that she didn't remember having one the previous month.

"Since you aren't certain, I'd like to run a sonogram to be sure."

Darbi nodded.

"Lie back on the table. I'm going to lift the top part of your gown and rub some gel on your stomach. It will be cold."

Darbi nodded.

Cherish focused a worried gaze on Shelby. "Is she all right?"

"Yes. I'm trying to pinpoint the date, that's all. If I can see the size of the embryo, I can tell how far along she is." She looked at Darbi as she rubbed the gel on her stomach. Shelby smiled as if she hadn't just changed Darbi's life forever, or at least for the next eighteen years. "I'll tell you if anything is wrong. I'm very straightforward." She looked back down at Darbi's stomach. "When did *this* happen?"

Darbi knew exactly what she meant. "My late husband stabbed me five years ago. I went to the county hospital and they stitched me up and sent me home."

"It looks like that's exactly what they did. This closure was shabbily done. Do you remember how many stitches?"

"I think it was about ten."

"There should have been at least thirty stitches, top and bottom." Shelby gently caressed the scar. "That will cause a problem later."

"What do you mean, a problem?" Darbi raised up to get a better look at Shelby's face.

Shelby continued moving the wand over Darbi's flat stomach. "It really depends on how you carry your baby. Since this is your first pregnancy and you're almost forty, we'll have to wait and see."

Darbi nodded. *First problem.*

Cherish stood next to Darbi to get a better look on the screen. "Look, Darbi! I see a little spot!"

Darbi turned her head to look toward the screen. "That tiny dot on the screen is my baby? Where's the body? The head?"

Shelby pointed to the screen. "At first it looks like a little pea. Then it will grow and look like a baby. You'll see. Why don't you get dressed, Darbi? There a few things I need to discuss with you. I'll be right back." Shelby left the room.

Cherish helped Darbi off the table. "Well, what are you going to do?"

Darbi walked behind the screen, and began changing her clothes. "I'll guess I'll tell Curry this Friday night. Then I'll have to tell Darius and Dad soon."

"Will you marry Curry?"

"Cherish, he's not ready for a third marriage. I don't think he could handle a wife and a child."

"I won't tell Darius. It'll be hard not to. But I will respect your wish."

"Thanks, Cherish."

Shelby re-entered the room. "Okay, Darbi, there are a few ground rules for this pregnancy. To put your mind at ease, I only handle high-risk pregnancies. I haven't had a fatality in over five years."

Darbi nodded. "Cherish said you were good. I'll do whatever you tell me." Darbi patted the new life in her tummy.

Shelby smiled. "Good, I love an obedient patient. The first thing is you're about four weeks along. I want to see you every week for the next few weeks to get a handle on your pregnancy. You'll probably need a C-section when you do give birth, because of that wound. So far it looks good, Darbi. You will need to take some vitamins and take it easy."

"Thank you, Shelby." Darbi and Cherish readied to leave.

Shelby looked over her appointment roster. "I can fit you in on Mondays about this time. Is that okay?"

"Yes, that's fine."

"Your due date is January 20, but in all likelihood you will probably deliver around Christmas, depending on that wound. If you notice any bleeding from that wound, please call me at once. Then come immediately to the hospital."

"Okay."

"Well, that's it. I'll see you next Monday." Shelby extended her slender hand to Darbi.

Darbi shook her hand. "Thank you, Shelby." As she walked out of the examination room, she wondered how disappointed her family would be in her this time.

Friday night, Darbi sat across from Curry at the restaurant. As he told her about his latest project, she felt she was drowning in his hazel eyes. He made her feel like she was the only woman in the restaurant.

She inhaled the aroma of the food and hoped dinner would stay down this time. Instead of her nausea coming just in the mornings, it sometimes came in the evening. It hadn't decided on a pattern yet, and she hadn't been sick at all that day.

"This account is worth about ten mill—Darbi, is everything okay? You've seemed somewhere else all evening."

"I'm fine, Curry." Darbi had tried to tell him several times about the pregnancy over the past few days, but each time, she'd lost her nerve. Would he jump for joy or blame her? Amos blamed her for any and everything. "I'm just stressed about finals and stuff."

"Oh." Curry studied her as he drank some wine. "You can tell me what's wrong, Darbi. I won't judge you, you know that."

Darbi leaned across the table and watched him as she asked, "Curry, what about your first wife?"

"Julie? What about her?" Curry watched her fidget in her chair.

"I know about Ava. Why did you and your first wife divorce?"

Curry finished his wine before he spoke. "Julie and I got married fairly young. I had just graduated from college. We were married six months."

"Why did you marry her?" Darbi didn't think she would like his answer, but she had to start somewhere.

"She trapped me," he said simply. "The night before our college graduation, she told me she was pregnant. Since we were both Catholic, I did my duty." He scowled at those memories. "After we got married, a few weeks later, we got a apartment in Seattle. About two months later, she miscarried and told me that she didn't love me anyway. That was fine with me; the feeling was mutual. We quickly divorced a month or so later. I haven't seen her in years."

Darbi knew at that moment she couldn't tell him. She'd wait until she had to tell him, like when she was being wheeled in for delivery. She didn't want to be referred to the way he was referring to Julie. She was doomed.

"Why did you want to know about Julie?"

"Just curious. You never spoke of her." Darbi sipped her tea.

"Are you sure you wouldn't like a glass of wine? You always have some with dinner. You said it relaxes you."

"No, the tea is fine."

"Are you sure you're okay?" He persisted.

"Yes, Curry." Darbi felt her stomach muscles clench and took a deep breath to relax.

Curry rose out of his seat. "We'd better leave. You look beat. We can go to bed early. How about racquetball in the morning?" He walked over to her chair to help her up.

"No, Curry. I need to study for finals. I have one on Monday. Why don't you take me home? I probably wouldn't be good company anyway."

"I have a presentation due next week, so I have something to work on as well."

Darbi nodded as they headed to the parking lot. She hoped her fragile stomach would not give away her secret.

* * *

Cherish sat patiently by the phone waiting for Darbi's call. She wasn't very good at keeping family secrets. Especially when the family wasn't hers.

Darbi was supposed to tell Curry that she was pregnant. Cherish could almost imagine the look of shock on Curry's face. But since she'd had a week to get used to it, she was happy for her friend.

Darius would be furious of course. The one thing he'd feared had actually happened and now there would be hell to pay. She could easily understand Darbi's hesitation about telling her family.

Finally her phone rang. "Darbi?"

"Yes, Cherish. I'm at Curry's. He's in the bathroom," Darbi said in a quiet voice.

From the tone of her voice, Cherish knew Darbi hadn't discussed the pregnancy yet. "You didn't tell him, did you?"

Darbi sniffed. "I wanted to, but I just couldn't." She paused and muttered something under her breath. "He's coming. Talk to you later." She ended the call.

Cherish replaced the phone in the cradle. Drat! She was really in the soup now.

After her history final the following Monday, Darbi went home to take a much-needed nap. The phone woke her a few hours later. She smiled, recognizing the caller.

"How'd your test go?"

"Fine. I have an A in that class. Where are you?" Darbi struggled to look at her bedside clock. It was five p.m.

"I was thinking about coming over to your place and taking a certain college student out to dinner."

"Oh, no, Curry, not tonight. I have an appointment and if I don't leave right now, I'm going to be late. I'll talk to you later. Bye." Darbi slammed down the phone and headed out of her condo. She was going to be late for her appointment with Shelby.

As Darbi sat in Shelby's office, she chatted with Cherish on her cell phone, telling her friend of her decision.

"I'm not going to tell Curry. He'll think I tried to trap him." Darbi didn't think she could recover from that kind of hurt. Certainly she didn't want to expose an innocent child to that kind of hatred. "He'll be one more person mad at me for getting pregnant. You know, it's always the woman's fault."

"Darbi, what will you tell your family?"

"I don't know. But I don't want to be with someone who doesn't want to be with me. I've done that, and it was horrible. Curry would just grow to hate the baby and me later. I don't want that. I don't think I could take it if he resented me."

"Okay, Darbi, I understand. I'm here for you," Cherish said. "If you want to hide out at my house to study for your finals, I don't mind. Darius is swamped at work, so I won't see him until Friday."

"Oh great! I may come over Wednesday night. My hardest exam is Thursday. My English test. I really need some quiet and Curry-free time." Curry called her every night asking her what was wrong. "I'll talk to you later." The friends ended their call.

Darbi watched a pregnant African-American woman waddle into the waiting room area and sit down. She was alone. Darbi breathed a sigh of relief. *At least I'm not the only unwed mother in town.*

"Peri!" A little voice called.

A blue-eyed, brown-haired little girl ran over to the pregnant woman and leaned close to the pregnant woman's expanded stomach to listen to the baby. She giggled.

"Hey, Chel. Where's your dad?" Peri ran her fingers through the little girl's curly mane and hugged her as best she could.

"He's talking to Dr. Allen." The little girl sat next to Peri.

As Peri rubbed her stomach, Darbi noticed her left hand. A large, sparkling diamond adorned her hand. Perhaps Darbi was the only unwed mother in town. *It'll be fine, Darbi. Don't settle,* she reminded herself.

A white man sat beside Peri and kissed her softly. As he spoke to his wife, Darbi noticed his sexy Irish accent.

"Why were you so late? We've been here thirty minutes. I was about to call the police to find you." He casually rubbed his wife's stomach. "How's my son doing in there?"

"Brendan, there was a wreck on the freeway and I forgot my cell phone. I'm glad you took the day off and could get Chel from school. I'm tired." She leaned against her husband.

"How about a massage later?" He kissed her again.

Darbi watched the couple and the little girl with jealousy. Was she doing the right thing? Was she denying Curry the chance to be a good parent and/or husband? *Remember, no more settling.* She knew she had made the right decision.

When she returned from her daydreaming, the family was gone. Soon she heard her name and walked down the hall to the examination room.

This visit was not as earth shattering as the first one. Darbi relaxed as she lay on the table and watched the computer screen.

Shelby looked at Darbi's flat stomach and ran her slim fingers across the scar. "Have you been having any problems?"

"Just throwing up," Darbi reported.

"That's just the beginning, I'm afraid. Has the scar been giving you any problems? It feels different."

"No. Other than throwing up, I've been fine." Except she too afraid to tell her family that she had failed at life once again, and this time an innocent child would be the victim.

"Okay, you can get dressed. I'm going to give you a prescription for some iron pills and some vitamins. Remember to stay away from greasy foods. Your appetite will start to increase, so don't be alarmed if you want to eat more than usual. But in moderation."

"Can I still go to aerobics?"

"No. I'm concerned about that scar. I can probably clean it up so that you are able to carry the baby closer to term, but I need to do a little research on that."

"What do you mean, Shelby?"

"As your stomach grows in size, the skin around that wound will stretch. But it can only stretch so far before snapping. Imagine a rubber band being stretched. There's a procedure to make the wound stronger, so that you can carry the baby, but I haven't done it in years, so I need to check on a few things. Also, start drinking at least two glasses of milk a day. Before you say no, it will be good for the baby."

Darbi nodded. Although the life growing inside her was an accident, Darbi wanted only the best. So if a little cow juice would help, no sacrifice would be too great. She only wanted the best for her baby.

CHAPTER TWENTY-ONE

Wednesday night, Cherish gazed in amazement as Darbi stuffed slice after slice of pepperoni pizza into her mouth. After she ate over half of it, she guzzled down two glasses of milk before burping and sounding like a drunk.

"Would you like some dessert?" Cherish laughed.

Darbi patted her flat stomach. "For some reason, I've been feeling hungry lately."

"Are you eating properly?" Cherish thought Darbi had lost weight instead of gaining it, and she always had a sick look about her.

"When it stays down. I had dinner at Darius's yesterday. I had to be careful how much I ate, so he wouldn't ask questions. I was starving by the time I got home."

"I can't even tell that you're pregnant, except by your increasing appetite. Has Curry said anything yet?" Cherish didn't want to mention that Darius was growing more concerned about his sister's behavior. He was ready to suggest she seek counseling. Cherish knew Darbi was stressed about finals as well as the pregnancy. She didn't want to add to that stress.

"No, luckily he's letting me study this week. We don't have a date until I'm finished with finals."

Thursday afternoon, after her last final, Darbi felt the knot in her stomach loosen. Her English grade held steady at B. She had been worried about her last essay on Langston Hughes, but her professor had enjoyed it and given her a B.

After a quick bite to eat in the cafeteria, she headed to work in the administration building. It was very busy since it was the last official day of finals. The lobby was full of students picking up their cap and gown for graduation. *In four years that will be me,* Darbi dreamed.

Her stomach picked that moment to let its presence be known. Darbi hurried down the hall to the bathroom, barely making it to the toilet in time. After she tossed her cookies, her stomach felt strange, almost clammy. Further investigation revealed the reason. Her wound had started bleeding. She went back to work and called Shelby. After that, she called Cherish.

The room suddenly grew dark, and voices around her seemed muffled. Darbi shook her head to clear it. When she did, things only got worse. She hit the floor with a thud as darkness consumed her.

Darbi's eyes fluttered open. She looked at the familiar surroundings. How did she get to the lounge area of the administration building? Students filed by watching her as she struggled to sit up on the uncomfortable couch.

"Darbi, you should just lie still. Why are you bleeding so badly?" Her supervisor questioned her.

Darbi could barely speak. She whispered the information to her supervisor. "I'm pregnant. It's complicated."

She didn't want to explain the horrific events to her supervisor, but felt she owed her some kind of reason. "The blood is coming from a wound I received over five years ago, but it didn't heal properly and now it's causing problems."

"I'm sure the ambulance will be here quickly." Soon the familiar sound of a siren filled the air. "Good. I'll go meet the paramedics at the door. We don't want to waste any time getting you to the hospital." She left Darbi to get the paramedics.

Darbi didn't know which pain hurt more: the pain in her stomach or the pain of anticipating what Darius would say when he found out the news. She wondered if she had already miscarried. *Please be okay*, she prayed silently to the love growing inside her stomach.

Soon the paramedics arrived and began tending to her. After they stopped the bleeding they started asking all the questions she wished she didn't have to answer. She glanced around the room and everything began to look blurred again. She let the darkness surround her in a cocoon of unknowing. Perhaps, she hoped, all this was just a bad dream.

~~~

Darius grabbed his notepad and pen and walked out of his office. He had a very important meeting concerning the new ad campaign for the senate race. Bernard Handley wanted to hire the firm to head up his campaign.

At first, Darius had been the only executive on board with the idea, but slowly the partners agreed, especially after accounting came back with the ten million dollar price tag and Handley agreed to the price. This was the first meeting.

Darius knew this would take up the rest of his free time. He sighed. He hadn't seen Cherish in almost a week. He was looking forward to their upcoming weekend together. They were going to the coast for some relaxation. His daydreaming ceased when he noticed his administrative assistant's nervous expression. "What is it, Beatrice?"

Beatrice forced the words out of her mouth. "It's Fort Worth University. They had to take Darbi to the hospital by ambulance," she said in a shaky voice.

"What?" Darius roared. He now had the attention of the entire lobby of Sloane, Hart, and Lagrone, but he didn't care. His sister was sick. He just hoped it wasn't life threatening.

"They're on line three." Beatrice handed him the phone.

Darius took the phone and punched the third button sharply. "Darius Crawford. What's the problem?"

"Mr. Crawford, I'm Darbi's supervisor. She was talking on the phone and passed out. When I got to her, she had blood on the front of her shirt; I couldn't tell what had happened. The woman on the phone told me to call the ambulance and have her taken to Briarwood Hospital in Arlington. So we did."

"Thank you." He ended the call and made eye contact with his assistant. "Beatrice, tell Mr. Sloane I had to leave." He hurriedly walked into his office, picked up his briefcase and jacked, and left.

~~~~~~

Curry wondered what had happened to Darius. It wasn't like him to miss a meeting, especially with so much riding on it. The Senate campaign involved both their departments and most of their resources. After the meeting, Curry walked into Darius's office and found Beatrice shutting down the computer and straightening Darius's usually tidy desk.

"Beatrice, where's Darius?"

"Mr. Crawford had a family emergency," Beatrice reported nervously. She continued her task, not making eye contact with him.

Curry's heart sank. Otis. But he had been doing so well lately. "Is it his dad?"

"No, it's his sister. I didn't realize she went to college. I think that's great."

Curry nodded. "What about his sister?" An uneasy feeling spread over his body, heading straight for his heart.

"The school called and said the ambulance took her to Briarwood Hospital in Arlington. I don't know why they took her there, seems odd. There are good hospitals right here in Fort Worth. Why take her to the most expensive hospital in the county? They probably have some deal with the school."

Ignoring Beatrice's ramblings, Curry walked back to his office in a daze. He sat at his desk, staring into space. What could be wrong with Darbi? She had been acting strange these last few weeks. His hand shook with fear as he reached for the phone. He dialed information and asked for the number for the hospital.

"Briarwood Hospital, Arlington. Can I help you?" a monotone voice answered.

"You have just admitted a patient there. Her name is Darbi Crawford. Can you tell me why she's there?" Curry loosened his tie as he tried to relax in his chair.

"Just a moment, sir. I will need to check the information."

Debussy's 'Claire de Lune' played on the phone while he was on hold. The soft music made him realize how much he had missed Darbi these last few days. The music abruptly stopped.

"Sir, she has just been admitted and is in room 325. That's all the information we have at this time." The call ended.

Curry looked at the phone and made his decision. Whatever had happened had happened to both of them, not just her. He grabbed his briefcase and left his office.

❧

Getting to Arlington in record time, Darius was directed to the third floor. He took a deep breath and walked into room 325 and stopped cold. Darbi lay in the hospital bed, motionless. She was asleep or unconscious; he didn't know which.

He watched the computer monitors as they recorded her every breath and heartbeat. One monitor piqued his curiosity. This monitor's wires ran to her stomach and were covered with a large oval bandage. Maybe her appendix ruptured, he reasoned. He saw tubes running in and out of her body. What took his breath away was the tube that ran into a plastic bag of blood. The antiseptic smell infiltrated his nostrils, reminding him that the last time he'd been at the hospital, his mother had died.

He swiped at his eyes, knowing he had to be strong for his sister. "Oh, Darbi," he whispered.

His sister didn't answer him. Instead, a different voice grabbed his attention. "Mr. Crawford?" The voice was soft, feminine.

Darius turned and faced a tall African-American woman. She was probably an inch or two shorter than Cherish or Darbi. Her dress, what he could see of it, was shorter than the lab jacket and she wore stilettos. Not normal doctor attire, he thought. "Yes, I'm Darius Crawford. I'm her brother. What's wrong with my sister?"

The woman extended her hand. "Mr. Crawford, I'm Dr. Shelby Allen." She paused, looking him up and down. "You had better sit down. I have good news and bad news."

Darius's heart sank as he took a seat. Would he lose his sister a second time?

"First, even though your sister is only about five weeks pregnant, there are some serious choices to be made."

"What?" Darius felt his heart break in two pieces.

"Yes, she came to see me last week. Cherish, who came with her, is a friend of mine. Now, back to what I was saying."

"What?" Darius felt betrayed. How could she be pregnant and not tell him? Why hadn't Curry mentioned it?

A look of realization cascaded over Shelby's face. "You didn't know, did you?" She caressed his hand in sympathy.

"No, I didn't. Please continue." He knew the worst was coming.

"She has a wound from five years ago. It was shabbily repaired and it will cause some pain for her if something is not done quickly. I knew it would cause a problem, but had hoped not right away. The wound started bleeding because as the baby grows, the stomach stretches. Because it wasn't properly stitched the first time, the wound can't stretch like it needs to. That's why it started bleeding today and that's why she passed out. She's lost a great deal of blood. The next three weeks will be the deciding factor. She'll need to be in bed as much as possible. Is that possible?"

"Yes." Darius didn't even have to think twice. "She'll be living with me." Like it or not, Darbi just sold her condo, he thought. Curry. *I'm going to kill Curry.* He could have told him.

Frustrated, he absentmindedly smacked his right fist against the flat palm of his left hand. The loud noise in the otherwise quiet room made Shelby jump in surprise.

"She'll be here at least a few days. There is a procedure I can use to clean up the wound. It's safe for both her and the baby. As I told her on Monday, I still need to do some research on the best way to proceed. But she will need to lie absolutely flat for the first week, so there'll be no pressure on the wound. That means no pillows." Shelby watched Darbi as she slept.

Darius nodded, taking in all the elements of doom before him. "I have some questions for you, Dr. Allen."

"Please. Call me Shelby."

"Shelby, what is your area of expertise? This looks like a very expensive hospital, and my sister doesn't have health insurance. I told her to get some, but she never got around to it. I can pay for her."

Shelby inhaled and exhaled, trying to calm her voice before she spoke. "Mr. Crawford, this is my area of expertise. I am a reproductive endocrinologist, meaning I specialize in high-risk pregnancies only. I'm sorry to say that this is what this pregnancy will be for your sister. Cherish and I have been friends since junior high. She really does care about your sister. I'm doing this as a favor to my friend who has had more than her own share of pain and loss. I'm glad she's reaching out to someone. When I first saw Darbi, I was treating her in my office for free. But this is a hospital and it takes money to run it. I pulled a few strings and have been able to find someone to insure her. All she has to do is to pay the premium. So it's all been taken care of." Shelby stood.

"I'm sorry, Shelby. This is kind of blindsiding me right now. I can pay whatever needs to be paid." He took out his wallet and handed her his credit card. "It has no limit."

Shelby handed the card back to him. "Keep it. Cherish already took care of it. Don't tell your sister." She extended her hand to Darius. "I'll see you in the morning, Mr. Crawford." She left the room.

Darius looked at Darbi's limp form. How could the three people he trusted the most betray him like this? Darius watched the tiny blip on the screen. At least he'd lived his dream in his dream house for a while. Now it would be filled with baby paraphernalia and a little one! With a sigh of regret, he reached for the phone to inform his father of the news. He wondered how his very traditional father would take the news of a bi-racial grandchild.

His father continued to surprise Darius constantly. That day was no different.

"I thought baby girl had been looking different lately. And those crying spells she's been having . . . she's been crying at everything! Where's that boy? I thought he would be telling the world she was pregnant with his child."

"I don't know, Dad. I wish somebody had told me. I'm going to stay at the hospital tonight. Will you be okay?"

"Yes, take care of your sister." Otis hung up the phone.

Later, Darius sat in the room willing himself to calm down. His mind buzzed with many thoughts. First, he'd sell her condo and move her things into his house. As both Cherish and Curry rushed into the room, he realized his long day wasn't going to get any better.

"Is she okay, Darius?" Cherish placed her purse on a nearby table and walked to the bed to check Darbi for herself.

"Why didn't you tell me?" Darius's eyes searched Cherish's.

"She asked me not to. She wanted to tell you herself."

"You knew the state of her health and still you said nothing. I can't believe you were so selfish!"

A lone tear ran down Cherish's face. "Yes, Darius. I guess I was. I was respecting her wish, as her friend. Don't stand there acting a typical man about this. She's sick and you're pouting because no one told you."

"Guys," Curry interrupted the shouting match, "what's wrong with Darbi?"

"You!" Darius walked toward Curry. "This is all your fault. You got my sister pregnant and didn't bother to tell anyone. I'd shoot you if I had a gun. What? Now you're ashamed that you got a black woman pregnant? You weren't ashamed to sleep with her, but now the tables have turned and you want out." Darius yelled at Curry, his fury pushing him to the edge emotionally.

"How dare you screw up her life after she worked so hard to get it together! I knew something like this was going to happen. But you just had to have her. The one woman I told you not to touch, you just had to have." He stepped closer to Curry with each word.

"Darius!" Cherish yelled, stepping between Darius and Curry, knowing Darius was about two seconds from knocking Curry out. She spoke in a softer voice, "Calm down."

Curry was bewildered. "What are you talking about?"

"This." Darius shoved Cherish out of the way and let his emotions speak for him. His fist connected with Curry's face. The crack of bone hitting bone filled the air.

It almost looked like an instant replay. After Darius hit him, Curry fell in slow motion. His head hit each of the three rows of metal bed rails before he landed on the hard floor, out cold.

"Darius, how could you?" Cherish kneeled beside Curry, lightly patting his face. He moaned, but didn't come to. She stood and faced Darius. "You freakin' idiot. He didn't know she was pregnant either. She didn't think he was ready for fatherhood. Now look what you've done!"

She walked to Darbi's bed and buzzed the nurses' station. Turning to face Darius, she said, "You were so worried about yourself and your precious corporate reputation. You didn't think about anyone else!" She slapped him and walked out of the room as the attendants walked in.

Darius stood dumbfounded and watched as the attendants took care of Curry, his best friend, who he'd just knocked out before he had all the facts. Thankfully, Darbi had slept through all the commotion and hadn't witnessed her brother behaving so foolishly.

The doctor walked in and assessed the situation. "What happened here?" He bent down to attend to Curry.

"It was a misunderstanding. That's all." The small man searched Curry's jacket pocket, finding his wallet.

The doctor read the identification card. His eyes squinted up at Darius. "Do you know Darius Crawford?"

Darius nodded, lowering his head in shame. "I'm Darius Crawford." He realized his ID badge emblazoned with his last name was still hanging from his belt.

"I was afraid of that. You're his emergency contact number. He's out cold. Care to tell me how he got this knot on the back of his head?"

"He bumped it on the bed on his way down to the floor." Darius felt horrible for the pain he had inflicted on his friend. *How am I going to make this right?* He watched silently as the hospital transporters picked Curry's limp body off the floor and loaded him onto a gurney. "Is he going to be okay?"

"We'll need to run a MRI and a CT scan to check his brain activity, since we're having trouble keeping him conscious. I'll keep you posted."

Darius nodded, watching the transporters wheel his best friend away. In one afternoon, Darius had jeopardized three relationships. He had jumped to all the wrong conclusions. He needed to relax and calm down before he did any more damage. Maybe it would look better tomorrow, he thought. He'd never seen Cherish so upset. That would definitely take some time to sort out. He would talk to Curry as soon as he was conscious. Darbi was an entirely different situation. When she woke he would be the one to tell her that her life was about to change drastically.

~❦~

Hours later, Darbi had still not awakened. The bleeding had finally stopped, but she hadn't moved or made any noises. From the sound of the machines, she was okay. Silently, Darius left his sister's bedside to check on his best friend.

After he found out that Curry had been admitted because of his concussion, Darius headed for his room. Quietly, he walked into the dimly lit room. Curry was sleeping peacefully. Darius noticed the bandage across his forehead, along with the purple bruise under his right eye. He took a seat by the bed. Darius wondered how he was going to fix all that he'd screwed up. He bowed his head in despair.

"Darius, why did you bean me like that?" Curry spoke just above a whisper.

"Because I thought you knew something that you didn't. I'm sorry, Curry. I blew my top."

"Dare, did you say Darbi's pregnant? I only remember bits and pieces of the conversation."

"Yes, she is. I'm sorry, Curry. I shouldn't have hit you."

"Why didn't she tell me?"

"I think you'd better ask her yourself, when she's awake. She's still sleeping. I don't think she's woken once." Darius watched as his friend struggled with the information. He didn't quite know how to handle this situation. He wished he could talk to Cherish, for guidance. But now that wasn't possible.

"Why, Dare?"

"Curry, I've hurt you enough for one night." He couldn't look at Curry knowing he'd caused him unnecessary harm.

"Why?" Curry persisted.

He knew Curry could be just as stubborn as his sister. "She probably thinks you're not ready for fatherhood.

She probably thinks you prefer your carefree lifestyle and doesn't want to be the reason you have to give that up." Darius had always thought Darbi would be the one to get hurt, but as he watched Curry struggle for control of his emotions, Darius knew how deeply Curry loved her.

Curry closed his eyes. "I would get up and go talk some sense into her stubborn head if mine wasn't pounding. So she took it upon herself to be judge and jury about the situation. I guess it doesn't matter to her that we spend all our time together."

Darius watched his friend's pale face. Beads of sweat dotted his forehead. He looked as if he were about to pass out. "Do you want me to ring for the nurse?"

"No, there's not any medicine for this pain. I can't believe Darbi." Curry wiped his eyes, not attempting to hide his tears.

Not used to seeing his best friend pale and vulnerable, Darius leaned closer to the bed and whispered, "Look, Curry, I've already talked to her doctor and Darbi's got to have some kind of procedure done. But don't worry about anything. I know it will work out. You get some rest. I'll see you in the morning." Darius walked out of the room.

~~~

The next morning, Darius woke feeling water on his face. Maybe by some miracle he had gone with Cherish and they were in Corpus Christi, enjoying the beach. But then he heard Darbi's voice. It was faint, but it was hers.

He opened his eyes and smiled instantly. Darbi had flung water with her fingers to get his attention.

"How do you feel?" Darius asked as he stood and stretched his body.

"My stomach hurts. Darius, I need to tell you something," Darbi began in a quiet voice.

"I know, Darbi. You could have told me. I do understand accidents happen." Darius felt awful for trying to inflict his rigid values on his sister.

"I didn't want you to be disappointed in me again. You were so excited when I started college. I never meant to let you down like this and surely I don't mean for it to affect your friendship with Curry or your job. I want you to know that I didn't get pregnant on purpose. But now that I'm pregnant, I have every intention of having this baby. I'll understand if you don't want to have anything to do with it." Darbi's eyes watered as she stared at Darius.

He walked to the hospital bed and held his sister's hand. "Darbi, nothing you could do could make me disappointed in you. I wish you had told me. You don't have to be with Curry if you don't want to. I understand your reasoning. But the Curry I know will be in your life, regardless."

"Thank you, Darius. I know this is a lot for you to comprehend right now. I appreciate you being here."

Darius smiled. "Darbi, I wish I could take yesterday back. Then I wouldn't have hit Curry and knocked him out. Or had that awful fight with Cherish." He took a deep breath.

"Oh, no! Darius, I'm so sorry. I never meant for all that to happen. I was just waiting for the right time to tell you."

"What's done is done. I've already apologized to Curry but Cherish is a different story. My only concern right now is you. Shelby says a decision needs to be made about your scar. She explained about the procedure and sounds very positive."

"I know. I just wish I hadn't lost so much blood. That was weird." She paused. "Darius, can you call the nurse?"

Darius watched a very funny color cross his sister's face. He called the nurse, but was too late. Darbi threw up all over the bed. He hated seeing his sister so helpless, but he didn't have the stomach to help her. Luckily two nurses rushed in and surveyed the situation. Darius was asked to step out of the room, so they could clean her up. He did, thankful he didn't have to watch. He went to check on his friend.

After getting released, Curry dressed in the clothes Darius had brought for him to change into. He slipped into the jeans and knit shirt and headed straight for Darbi's room, determined to get some answers.

He walked into the quiet room, surprised that she was awake. She stared at him as he made his way to the bed, as if he were a stranger, not the father of the life that was inside her. Her fragile condition made her look weaker, breaking his heart. The hospital gown was much too large and made her look even more helpless. Wires ran to and from her body, melting his resolve. He had practiced his speech for the last hour. Darius had discreetly gone home to change clothes to give them some privacy.

Curry took a seat next to the bed, watching the computers keep track of Darbi's every breath. "Hey, how are you?" he asked, for lack of anything else to say.

"Better than you. Sorry Darius hit you." She casually ran her hand over her belly. Her gaze went to the bandage on his forehead and his black eye.

"Marry me."

"No," Darbi said sharply, turning away from his gaze. Those monitors had suddenly become very interesting to her.

"Why not?" Curry felt a strong headache approaching. He rubbed his head, trying to relieve some of the pain of her rejection.

She faced him, her eyes full of fresh tears. "Curry, you don't have to worry. I won't force you to marry me. I would never trap you. You can see the baby whenever you want. You can be as involved as you want to be. I understand if you don't want to be."

Giving him the coward's way out only infuriated him. "I will be in my child's life one hundred percent. I will also be in your life one hundred percent, Darbi Crawford. Whether we are married or not! I still can't see why you won't marry me. I love you."

Darbi faced him. "I love you, too, but you aren't ready for this big of a commitment."

"Yes, I am, Darbi."

"No, you're not. Curry, being married would be a strain on both of us. You would grow to hate me because I messed up your carefree lifestyle."

Curry's teary eyes watched her, not believing she'd said no. He also noticed one of those computer readouts had speeded up. She was upset. "Okay, Darbi. No marriage, but what about us? Can I still see you?" Curry rubbed his forehead in pain.

"If you still want to. When I'm better. No marriage." Darbi closed her eyes and turned her head away from him, dismissing him.

Curry felt his heart had been torn into two pieces. One part was growing inside Darbi and the other piece had just gotten crushed.

CHAPTER TWENTY-TWO

Cherish was going to see Darbi. She hadn't seen her friend in two weeks. Had it really been only two weeks since her fight with Darius when she'd stormed out of the hospital? It felt like years. Darbi had told her, in one of the few times they had communicated by cell phone in the last two weeks, that she was living at Darius's. Cherish had call-blocked Darius's home and cell phone number.

Darbi had also told her that Curry had proposed several times, and each time she'd refused.

Cherish parked in front of the house, preparing to face Otis. She wasn't worried about running into Darius. His schedule was as predictable as snow in north Texas. Cherish knew he had already left for work. She took a deep breath, exited her car, and walked to the front door. She rang the doorbell and smiled when it opened. Mrs. Collins returned her smile and ushered her inside.

"Ms. Murray, it's nice to see you," she said in her British accent. "Ms. Crawford is expecting you. She's in her room." Mrs. Collins led her to the stairs. "Let me know if you need anything. Remember, Ms. Crawford is to remain flat. She's going to try to sit up, but don't let her. If she needs to go to the bathroom, please let me know. I will be in straight away." She left, heading toward the kitchen.

Cherish walked up the stairs and into Darbi's room. In the two weeks since Cherish had seen her, Darbi looked like she had actually gained weight.

She could see Darius's handiwork in the room. Because Darbi had to remain on her back, a flat-screen plasma TV was now mounted from the ceiling. An intercom system had been installed. A small refrigerator sat on the night-stand next to the bed. Everything Darbi could possibly need was just within arm's reach. Cherish sat beside the bed. "How's it going? I hear your condo has sold."

"Yes, Darius said if I wasn't going to marry Curry, I had to live here. He apologized for selling it while I was in the hospital, but he did get double what I paid for it just a year ago. These last two weeks have shown me a different side to my stiff brother. I think now that the shock has worn off, he's looking forward to a baby. He's already talking about private school." A few teardrops fell from Darbi's eyes. "Cherish, I'm sorry I put you in the middle of this. I should never have asked you to do such a thing."

Cherish patted Darbi's leg in sympathy. "Darbi, don't worry. You're my friend. You would have done the same for me. It's been two weeks, I've calmed down and maybe he has, too. I unblocked this number so you don't have to use your cell phone to call me." She glanced around the room looking for the phone and noticed there was none. Darius took Darbi's bed rest rules very seriously.

"I know Darius still loves you; this was just too much for him. Since I was unconscious, he lashed out at you. I'm sorry. I'll fix this, I promise."

"Darbi, don't worry." Cherish's eyes became misty at Darbi's committment. Although on bed rest, Darbi was still vowing to fix the rift between Cherish and Darius.

"You know, I've been home a week and Curry hasn't called me or anything. I know he talks to Mrs. Collins about my progress every day."

"You did say no, Darbi, several times," Cherish reminded her gently.

"I know, it's for the best. He's used to picking up and going wherever at a moment's notice. He's never had to care for someone else and stuff like that. I just can't visualize Curry married and changing diapers. I can't picture him walking behind a stroller. Can you?"

Cherish had also talked to Curry. He had called her one night in desperation, then again. Each time he had seemed more depressed. He wanted Darbi to marry him, but Cherish knew Darbi wanted what was best for the baby.

"Darbi, I think you should talk to Curry. I mean honestly, with all the cards on the table. You may find that he's more ready than you think." Noticing Darbi's swollen eyes welling up with tears, Cherish switched to another topic. "Hey, how's my godchild?"

Darbi patted her flat stomach. "Still making me throw up every morning. And my appetite, oh my gosh! I feel like I'm always hungry. I'm going to gain so much weight." She gently caressed her stomach.

Cherish smiled. "You're supposed to eat more. Remember, you're eating for two. Shelby says that's normal."

"I drink apple juice like crazy. I don't even like apple juice!" Darbi laughed. "I've missed talking to you like this." She held Cherish's hand and rubbed it gently.

"Me, too." Although she had known Darbi for less than a year, their friendship had a tight bond and nothing, thank goodness, could break it.

Before long, Darbi fell asleep. Cherish quietly walked out of the room and went downstairs. She headed to the kitchen, literally running into Otis as he walked to the kitchen for lunch. After they exchanged hellos, Otis invited her to join him. Cherish couldn't refuse and followed him into the kitchen.

"When are you and Darius going to make up over this silly mess?" Otis took a bite of meatloaf.

"I don't know, Otis," Cherish answered honestly. "We both said and did a lot of things we shouldn't have. It will be hard to get past the events of the last two weeks."

"You will. You'll see. I'm glad you're keeping baby girl company. I know that boy wants to marry her, but I just want her to be happy. If she feels like he's not the one to marry, then she doesn't have to marry him. That baby will have more than enough love." Otis exhaled. "I know everything will work out, Lord's will. That boy will do what's right for everybody concerned."

Cherish knew this wise old man was always right. "Otis, how did you get to be so smart?"

"Life, baby, life."

So far Darius's day had been awful. He was still playing catch up at work since he had been out the previous week with his sister. Now Curry sat in his office looking as if he had lost his best friend and his dog.

"Curry, how long are you going to mope around like this? You're moping around here and Darbi is at home, crying at everything in sight. Dad's afraid to talk to her. He asked her about the baseball game on TV the other night and she started blubbering." Darius opened his briefcase to fill it with more work he would have to do that night. He wondered if he would ever catch up.

Curry sighed. "I don't know. I still can't get over the fact that I'll be a dad in seven and a half months or sooner. I'll be responsible for a life or rather two lives." He ran his fingers through his curly hair.

Darius grinned; his friend had matured a great deal in the last few months. Something he'd thought would never happen. "You know Darbi's stomach is still flat. If it weren't for the fact that I hear her throwing up every morning, I wouldn't think she was pregnant. Why don't you come over and talk to her?" He hoped his sister and best friend could make up.

"Dare, I've proposed to her at least five times over the last few weeks. Each time she said no. What else can I say to her?"

"Curry, Darbi isn't going to marry you until she thinks you're ready for marriage and a family. Are you?"

"I think so. I know I want to be with her and only her."

Darius's eyes met two blood-shot hazel ones. "Curry, it's not just her. There's an unborn baby to consider. Since she's been pregnant, her mother hormones have kicked in. She only wants what's good for the baby. That means you're going to be there for other people. Your free spirit days will be over."

Curry smiled at his friend. "They're already over. Have been for the last few months."

"Well, you'll just have to show her. Slowly. Very slowly. If you rush her, she'll think it's just because she's pregnant. You do love her, don't you?"

"Yes, Dare. I love her."

"Okay." Darius felt satisfied that Curry was ready for a third marriage and fatherhood, but was his sister ready for her second marriage and motherhood?

"I have to tell my parents," Curry said quietly.

Darius winced. He'd forgotten about the other set of grandparents. "I forgot about Thomas and Sarah." He didn't envy Curry for one second.

"I wish I could. I can hear Mom's voice already. Want to make the call for me?"

~~~

Cherish sat at her drawing board, trying a new idea. Actually, she hoped that if she designed a wedding dress, Darbi would somehow need it. She hoped Curry could convince Darbi he had changed and was ready for marriage and a family. She would need a wedding dress. Cherish doodled on her sketchpad, designing a dress that she thought Darbi would approve of. The neckline showed off her cleavage blossoming with pregnancy. She even left a little room around the stomach area, just in case she would be showing. The doorbell rang, ending her creative flow.

She set her sketchpad down, walked downstairs to her door. Her heart started beating twice its normal speed. Curry Fitzgerald stood at her front door, dressed in a dark suit, looking like a depressed fashion model. Cherish let him in. "I didn't realize you knew where I lived."

Curry looked at her with a sly grin. "One night I followed Darbi here. I was jealous and I wanted to make sure she wasn't meeting that football player. I need to talk."

"What about?" Cherish led him to the couch.

"What else? Darbi. I need some help in convincing her to marry me. Any ideas?"

Cherish didn't want to be in the middle of their mess again, but she had no choice. "Curry, if you truly love Darbi, it will be easy. Just show her you're ready for fatherhood and marriage. She'll do what's right."

"What about you and Darius? Will you guys ever patch this up?"

Cherish gazed into Curry's eyes. She could understand why Darbi loved him. Those eyes. Anything seemed possible looking into those hazel eyes. "Darius has had a lot of adjustments to make. Once everything settles, we'll see."

One morning later in that same week, Otis opened the front door and ushered Cherish inside. He had such a serious look on his weathered face, she was almost afraid to ask. "How's Darbi?"

"She's waiting for you upstairs. She didn't want to eat until you got here. So you get on upstairs so my grand-baby can eat."

Cherish nodded and rushed to Darbi's room. Darbi sat propped up in bed, reading a baby book. "Darbi, you shouldn't have waited. You need your nourishment."

"I haven't been waiting that long. Daddy is just nervous about the baby." She rubbed her stomach gin-gerly. "You usually arrive soon after Darius leaves, but he's been gone an hour. Why are you so late?"

"I had to pick up something," said Cherish, mysteri-ously. She sat on the bed. Mrs. Collins arrived with a tray.

"Mr. Crawford said you'd arrived, Ms. Murray." She placed the tray on the bedside table, uncovering the platter of food. "If you need more, just let me know." She left as quickly as she came.

Cherish inspected the large amount of food and fig-ured it was enough for at least four people. Darbi didn't utter another word until she finished a second helping of Mrs. Collins's breakfast. Cherish wondered where Darbi put it all.

Cherished excused herself and retrieved her gift from the hallway. After Darbi settled in bed for her morning nap, Cherish produced the gift-wrapped box.

"I got you a present. In honor of your getting out of the hospital."

Darbi glanced at Cherish as she opened the box. It was a throwback. It had a Detroit Redwings symbol emblazoned on it. Darbi held it next to her face to feel the soft-ness of it. "Thanks, Cherish. Why?"

"Well, I know you have to take it easy. So this might make it easier for you to rest."

Darbi gingerly got out of bed, stood and hugged Cherish, which was not an easy task for her. It took all her energy. She carefully sat back down. "What would I do without you?"

"I don't want to find out." Cherish wondered how different her life would have been had she not followed her aunt's advice, and Darius not followed Curry's.

~~~~~~

That afternoon, when Darius walked into his house, he thought something was very wrong. He'd seen Cherish's Chevy Blazer out front. He had noticed there was an extra plate in the kitchen most days, and had won-dered about it. Maybe Cherish had just left her car there and he wouldn't have to actually face her. The thought of her being so upset with him made his heart ache.

As he walked inside his house a plan quickly formed in his mind: He would first fix himself a snack, and then try to escape upstairs. Darius hadn't slept a whole night in over two weeks; Cherish's face invaded his dreams, thus wrecking sleep. Not that he could easily close his eyes. He was too worried about his sister. He had to figure a way to get Curry and Darbi back together. In Curry's opinion they hadn't broken up; they were just on hiatus. Somebody should emerge from this fiasco happy, he thought. Walking into his kitchen, the thought of food, along with his heart, crashed to the floor.

He couldn't remember why he had walked in there. Otis, Cherish, and Mrs. Collins stared at him, waiting for him to do something. He had to do something or he'd look like an idiot. Opening and closing the refrigerator, he pretended to look for something. "Hello, Cherish," said Darius.

"Darius," she replied softly.

His father mumbled something incoherent. Then the loud scrape of his chair against the tile floor, signaled he was making his getaway. Mrs. Collins also made a hasty exit. Darius sat down in front of Cherish, still not meeting her gaze. He mumbled, "How have you been?"

"Fine," came her short reply.

"I'm sorry, Cherish." He winced at the inadequate words, trying to make an impossible moment better. "I'm sorry about everything," he confessed. "My only excuse is that I was in total shock. I had no right to accuse you, especially without knowing any of the facts. I understand loyalty. I'm glad that if Darbi thinks she can't confide in me, she can in you."

Cherish took a deep breath, relief evident all over her face. "I'm sorry for hitting you and calling the police on you when you came to my house. I was upset. We were all on edge, concerned about Darbi's health. But if I had to do it again, I would." Shyly, she stretched her arm across the table to his hand and caressed it gently.

Darius reveled in the assurance Cherish's small hand provided. "You know, I'd never been slapped before. My face still burns where you hit me," he teased.

"Would you like me to kiss it and make it better?" She seduced him with her eyes.

"Please."

Cherish stood and walked around the table to Darius. He grabbed her and she landed in his lap. He hugged her and kissed her hungrily. "Do you forgive me?"

"Of course. Do you forgive me?"

"There's nothing to forgive. You did what you thought was right. In hindsight I can say I probably would have killed Curry if you hadn't been there. So thank you for saving me from me." He sighed and inhaled her scent. If he squeezed her any tighter, she might scream in pain. She didn't.

Cherish nodded. "I understand you only want the best for Darbi." She kissed him quickly on the lips. "What are you doing home in the middle of the day?"

"Curry was driving me and everybody else crazy, moping around the office. You'd think he was sixteen or something and Darbi was the last woman on this earth." He smiled at the thought. "So I took the rest of the day off. I'm glad I did."

Later that evening, Curry stared mesmerized at the cordless phone on his coffee table, wishing it would give him some advice. It didn't. He had to tell his parents the latest development. Putting off making the call any longer would only make matters worse. How did one tell a traditional Irish mother that he'd fathered a child out of wedlock? And that the mother of that child was black. But he knew what he had to do. Darbi was at seven weeks. He wiped his palms on his pants. *Come on, Curry. Suck it up.* He took a deep breath and dialed the number.

His mother answered the phone and didn't sound surprised when he dropped the bomb. "Curran, you proposed, of course." It was not a question, more like a statement or a command.

"Of course," Curry said, "but she said I wasn't ready. She turned me down." He waited for his mother's outburst, but there was none.

"Curran, things would change in your life. This would be your third marriage, Darbi is already pregnant and she's black." Sarah paused. "I like Darbi. As much as I hate to admit this, when I first met her all I saw was skin color. But she's nice, and she makes you happy. So if this makes you happy, that's enough for me. I know she's not after your money like Ava was. I do like her, Curry."

Curry smiled. His mother seldom called him Curry. She always said she hadn't named him after a cooking spice, but had given him a sound Irish name. He listened as his mother continued. She was relentless.

"Do you love her? I mean, not the fact that she's having your baby, but her as person."

"Yes, I love her," he said without hesitation. "Why does everyone think I can't change?"

"Because," his mother started, "you have been single for some time now. Maybe you're just lonely. I know accidents happen. Don't harm two other lives in the process of doing your duty, if you're not sure."

"I'm sure. Both Darbi and Darius gave me an out. I don't want it. I do love her. Okay, maybe I wasn't originally thinking in terms of marriage, but I can't think of being without her. I don't run from anything or anyone. I'll convince her to marry me."

"That's my stubborn Irish son," his mother laughed. "Where's she? I'd like to talk to her."

Curry knew that meant trouble, something neither he nor Darbi needed at the moment. "She's been living with Darius since she got out of the hospital. She has to take it easy right now and can't move around a lot."

"Why? If she's only seven weeks, this sounds critical."

Curry didn't want to betray Darbi's past, but knew his mother wouldn't let up until she knew the truth. "She had a previous injury and it's affecting the way she carries the baby." Hopefully, his mother would not ask for too many details.

For once in his adult life, his mother didn't pry. "Well, Son, if you're sure of your feelings, and I think you are, show her that you can settle down."

"How can I do that?"

"Only you know the answer to that. I'll wait to hear when my unborn grandchild is a Fitzgerald." She ended the call.

Curry pushed the end button on his phone and rubbed his head in frustration. It had been over three weeks since Darius belted him and he was still having headaches. Or were they caused by extreme stress? Why didn't anyone think he could settle down for marriage? He knew without Darbi, he felt empty. These last few

weeks had been pure torture for him and only one thing
would help.

Darbi snuggled deeper under the covers in the bed as
Cherish answered the ringing phone down the hall. She
could tell exactly who it was by Cherish's tone and conversation. Darbi's hands immediately went to her hair.
She hadn't combed it in days and it probably looked a
mess. Darbi had a funny feeling she would be seeing
Curry soon.

Cherish walked back into the bedroom and smirked
at Darbi as she reclaimed her seat near the bed. She
waited a heartbeat before saying, "Curry may drop by a
little later."

"Oh, really." Darbi tried valiantly to sound uninter-
ested. She failed.

Cherish didn't get to tease her friend very long
because the doorbell rang, interrupting the conversation.
"I wonder who that could be at this hour?" She smiled,
rising to answer the bell.

After Cherish let Curry inside the house, she led him to
Darbi's bedroom, and then she went to Darius's bedroom.
He was supposed to be doing some work on the campaign.
Cherish entered his bedroom expecting to see him hun-
kered over some report, diligently studying. Instead, he was
lying on his back across the bed clad only in silk boxers and
deep in thought. She hurriedly slipped into something
more comfortable and snuggled next to him.

"What are you doing in here, Cherish?" He wrapped his arms around her, kissing her forehead. "I thought you were talking to Darbi." He kissed her on the neck and cheek before finally meeting her lips with his.

"I was," Cherish breathed. "Curry came over and I didn't want to be a third wheel. They have so much to talk about, I wanted to give them space. So I thought I would keep you company," Cherish said.

Darius smiled, looking very pleased. "He finally decided to talk to her. Good. Maybe he'll stop moping around the office. There's nothing sadder than a former player walking around with a broken heart." He grinned at Cherish. "I'm glad you wanted to keep me company. I was thinking about Darbi."

Cherish knew that Darbi's present condition made her everyone's priority. "What about her? She's doing very well, considering."

He reached for his organizer. "Oh, no!"

Cherish sat up. "What is it?"

"I have an appointment with the Senator tomorrow morning, and Darbi has a doctor's appointment tomorrow at eleven. I wonder if she could switch it?"

"I can take her. I'm sure Curry wouldn't mind, either." Cherish smiled, realizing that she had gotten involved again with Darbi's pregnancy and the Crawford family.

Darius shook his head. "No, don't ask Curry. I don't want him feeling pressured. He has to want to do it. That's why he has been married twice, pressure. I know he would if I asked him, but he's got to want to do it for himself. You can take her, if you really want to. I don't want anyone feeling pressured."

"I want to." She smiled at him. "I really want to help."

"I love you, Cherish Murray." Darius hugged her, caressing her soft body with his hands. He eased her nightshirt off her body and tossed it on the floor.

"I love you, too. And I really love this caring family, Darius Crawford. I think it's great."

Darbi lay in bed nestled comfortably under the covers. Curry sat in the chair next to the bed. "How do you feel?" He rubbed her flat tummy with gentle, caring strokes.

Darbi's hand rested on top of his, stilling his motion. "Pretty good," she whispered. "What are you doing here?"

"I had to see you." He couldn't keep the desperation out of his voice.

She laced her fingers with his, making a vanilla-chocolate swirl. "Curry, we talked about this in the hospital. You're not ready for marriage. I'm okay with it, really. I won't force you to do something that you aren't ready for."

"Actually, Darbi, I wasn't consulted about it," Curry reminded her. "You decided that I couldn't handle being a father or a husband. You decided one of the most important decisions in our life without me. I was married to Julie over twenty years ago. People change. I know you aren't the same woman who married Amos. How dare you limit my qualifications?"

"I know I've made a lot of mistakes concerning the baby. I should have told you and Darius the minute I found out, but I was scared." Darbi ran her fingers through his curly hair. "I'm sorry, Curry. I did what I thought was right at the time. I didn't mean to hurt you, Curry, or anyone else. I didn't mean for any of this to happen."

"I know, sweetie. But now it has. So the stakes have changed. I still love you and want to be with you." He paused, not wanting to pressure her. "Why don't we just continue dating for a little while and see where we stand?" He knew she was just as afraid of marriage as he was.

Darbi smiled. "That sounds good."

Curry kissed her gently on the mouth, trying to hold back his desire. "Do you need anything?" He kissed her again.

"Could you help me up or call Darius or Cherish?" She pushed back the covers and struggled to sit up.

"What is it?" He caressed her face.

"I have to go to the bathroom," she whispered.

"I can take you." He kissed her, then scooped her up in his strong arms and took her to the toilet.

CHAPTER TWENTY-THREE

Over the next month, Curry and Darbi "dated." Usually their "dates" entailed him coming to Darius's and watching a movie with her, since she was still on modified bed rest.

Curry slowly showed her how much he'd changed. He no longer drank in front of her, since the mere smell of alcohol sent Darbi running to the bathroom and running was not an option. He usually spent the night, but slept in the guest room down the hall. That impressed everyone, especially Otis. Darius usually made himself scarce on Fridays, knowing the couple needed some quiet time together.

This Friday night was no different from any other. Darbi snuggled against Curry, awakening a fire in his loins that he desperately tried to control. He closed his eyes in a silent prayer, took a deep breath, and caressed her face gently. He wondered when she would start noticeably showing. "Will you marry me?" He counted the seconds as he waited for her customary refusal.

"After," she murmured, rubbing her body against his, knowing she was driving him over the edge. "You know, you can sleep in here, Curry. It's okay. Daddy's not going to barge in with his shotgun, demanding you do right by me," she teased. "He was kidding when he said that."

Curry wasn't concerned about Otis. His mind was on her half answer. "What do you mean, after?" Curry sat up and faced her.

"I mean after I have the baby." Darbi rubbed her tummy and yawned, closing her eyes.

"What?"

She did not answer him; she was asleep.

Curry left Darbi sleeping and went to the guest room. He smiled as he opened the door. Mrs. Collins had already pulled back the covers on the bed for him. As he slipped on his pajamas he decided to wait for Darius in the morning. Curry had won half the battle; maybe Darius could help him finish the job.

The next morning Darius stared at Curry in disbelief. "What do you mean she said after the baby's born?" Darius poured coffee into the oversized coffee mug. He didn't want to laugh at Curry's serious expression but it was pretty hard not to. Darius was still amazed that Darbi had finally said yes, at least sort of.

"She said *after*, man." Curry took a deep breath. "I just can't understand why she wants to wait. I just feel like I'm not connecting with her. I don't know what's going on inside her head." Curry banged his head against the wall in frustration.

Although Curry was visibly upset, Darius smiled. Curry the free spirit was ready for a huge commitment. "I'll see what's going on. She can be stubborn, you know. Don't worry, Curry. How did your parents take the news?"

"Pretty well, considering. Mom was upset that we weren't already married." Curry picked up his bag and prepared to leave the kitchen. "Let me know what you find out, okay?"

"You know I will." Darius walked him to the front door. As he watched his friend of eight years drive away, he took a deep breath and headed upstairs to talk to his pregnant, headstrong sister.

When he walked into Darbi's room she wasn't in bed where he thought she should be. Darius's heart leapt to his throat; he feared the absolute worst. "Darbi?"

Darbi walked slowly out of her bathroom, tying her robe, shocked to see her brother standing in the middle of her room. She hastily wiped her eyes, avoiding her brother's observant gaze. "Darius, what are you doing in here?"

"What's wrong with you?" He'd noticed her tears. "Did Curry upset you last night?"

"No, Darius."

"What is it?" He helped her to sit on the bed. "I can take a lot, but this cryin' stuff is too much!"

Darbi smiled through her tears. "Darius, I'm pregnant. My hormones are going up and down on an hourly basis." She stood. "This is the reason I'm crying." She untied her robe.

Darius smiled as he saw a protruding stomach under her Fort Worth University shirt. While it wasn't very protruding, he could tell her stomach was no longer flat. "Darbi, it's okay." He fought the urge to touch it. "You look beautiful. You're twelve weeks along, you had to start showing sometime."

Darbi rubbed her belly, reveling in the feel of the life inside of her. "I know. But last night my stomach was flat, well, somewhat flat. How could so much happen overnight?"

Darius shook his head. "I don't know, Darbi. I think it's one of those mysteries of the body. Otherwise, how do you feel?"

"Pretty good. I didn't throw up this morning."

Darius glanced at his sister. "Why did you tell Curry you would marry him after the baby was born?"

Darbi lowered her head. "It's a woman thing, Darius."

He looked at his sister in confusion. She was fast becoming more challenging than the Senator's campaign. "What?"

"I want a wedding. You know, the wedding dress, Dad escorting me down the aisle, a church."

"Why? You didn't have one the first time." She'd run off with that loser without as much as a goodbye, he remembered.

"My first marriage," Darbi explained, "I made a lot of mistakes. Darius, this is the last time, hopefully, I'm getting married. I want it done right." She walked to her closet.

"You can have a wedding now. I'm sure you won't be the first, and surely not the last, woman to walk down the aisle already pregnant."

"I know, Darius. I'm just not sure that's what Curry wants. I don't want to seem selfish and Curry might not want a wedding since this would be his third time around." She picked out a blouse and shorts.

"Curry wants what you want, I'm sure." He smiled. His father was right. It would all work out after all. "Have you had breakfast yet?"

Darbi shook her head. "You know, I think Mrs. Collins must have some kind of radar. Usually the second I'm dressed, that woman is at my door with a tray of food." She took a deep breath and went into her bathroom.

Darius waited patiently as his sister changed clothes. A wedding was all she wanted. He would talk to Cherish later and see what could be done. When a loud curse came from behind the bathroom door, he immediately burst into the bathroom, afraid he'd see a puddle of blood and Darbi passed out on the floor. He relaxed with his sister's words.

"I can't button my shorts!" Darbi's teary eyes met her brother's smile. "What's so funny? I don't have any clothes to fit my body! I'll have to start wearing tent dresses," she cried.

Darius had a hysterical woman on his hands. "Darbi, it's okay." He exited her room and immediately returned with a gift-wrapped box Curry had given him over a month ago. He sat it on the bed next to his crying sister. "A gift from Curry."

Darbi wiped her eyes with the sash of her terry-cloth bathrobe. It was a very large box with blue wrapping paper and a big pink bow. She touched the box timidly, as if it might snap at her. With shaky hands, she opened it. Clothes. Curry had bought her maternity clothes, enough for the entire pregnancy, Darius thought. No wonder the darn thing was so heavy.

She took out a shorts ensemble and began laughing immediately as she read the lettering on the shirt. She turned the shirt around so he could see it. It read: *I rode the Fitzgerald Express!*

At first Darius didn't understand the private joke between his sister and his best friend. Slowly the fog cleared and Darius chuckled to himself. Same old Curry.

After Darbi dressed, Mrs. Collins arrived, as if on cue, with a breakfast tray. Darius assured her that he'd return the tray to the kitchen. With a nod, Mrs. Collins left.

Darius watched his sister shovel down the better portion of breakfast before he broached the subject of her going to lunch with Cherish.

"Are you sure you feel well enough to go out? You know you guys can have lunch here. I know Shelby said you could go out once in a while, but you guys can have girl talk here. I promise to stay in my office," he said.

Darbi drank half a glass of milk before she answered. "Darius, I haven't been out of the house since I came home from the hospital. It's just lunch and I feel good."

"I know, but we almost lost you. I don't want anything to happen to you. I'll take your temp before you leave."

Darbi laughed, wiping her mouth on the linen napkin. "Darius, I promise to be good. Shelby said it was okay as long as I didn't overexert myself. Cherish is driving, and I'll come back and take a nap."

"I'm hovering, aren't I?" He stood and reached for the tray. "It's hard, this uncle stuff."

Darbi reached for his hand and patted it. "I'm glad you're hovering, Darius. It tells me you care."

He nodded. "You know I would do anything to keep you healthy, and I do mean anything." He smiled at her. "I'm going to eat. Why don't you relax until Cherish gets here?" He left the room, closing the door.

~~~~~~

Later, Cherish arrived at the Crawford house. As customary, Mrs. Collins answered the door, smiling. "Good afternoon, Ms. Murray. I'll tell Mr. Crawford you're here. He's upstairs taking Ms. Crawford's temperature." She motioned Cherish inside.

Cherish snickered. "Please tell me you're kidding."

Mrs. Collins shook her head. "No, since this is Ms. Crawford's first official outing that doesn't involve a doctor's visit, he's taking no chances."

Now that sounded like Darius. "Thank you, Mrs. Collins. I'll go on up. You don't have to announce me."

"Of course, Ms. Murray."

Cherish walked upstairs trying to school her features into a serious face so Darius or Darbi wouldn't know she was laughing. She reached Darbi's room, took a deep breath and knocked. After Darius invited her inside, she entered the room. The scene was comical. Darbi dressed in shorts and a maternity t-shirt was sitting on the bed with a thermometer in her mouth and looking very irritated.

"Hey guys." She walked to Darius and kissed him quickly. For all his strict unbendable rules, Darius was a caregiver. Cherish knew if Darbi had a temp there was no way in hell Darius would let her out of his sight.

"Hey Cherish." Darius smiled at her. The thermometer beeped and Darius's attention returned to his sister. He took the gauge out of her mouth and read it. "Okay Darbi, you're normal. You can go to lunch."

After Darius's blessing, they went to lunch. Cherish watched Darbi consume a pasta dish, a seafood dish, and dessert. She laughed. "I have to ask. What is the Fitzgerald Express? Does it mean what I think it means?"

A knowing smile crossed Darbi's face as she drank her tea.

"It's nice to know Curry hasn't lost his sense of humor," Cherish said between bouts of laughter.

Darbi sat back in her chair and rubbed her stomach. "Can you believe I'm showing already? My shorts wouldn't fit this morning."

"I know. You really don't look bigger, though. You look very contented and happy."

"I feel bloated and I'm constantly starving."

"I have a surprise for you in the truck."

"Cherish, you've done more than enough for me. You and Darius are back together, that's enough."

Cherish sighed. She and Darbi had endured so many trials together in such a short span of time. She felt closer to Darbi than to the cousins she grew up with. "Darius told me that you wanted a wedding. I've been working on a dress for just such an occasion, for someone in your situation."

"It has room for my huge stomach?" Darbi patted the offending body part.

"Darbi, you aren't big. Shelby says you are right on track." Cherish smiled. Everything was going to work out after all.

∼ꝰ

"She wants a wedding? That was the reason?" Curry couldn't believe it was something so small. "Can I talk to her?" One simple phone call from Darius had relieved so many of Curry's fears.

"She's having lunch with Cherish. You know, girl talk. They claimed they couldn't do that here. Oh yeah, she's showing, so be careful what you say to her. I can only handle so many tears in a day," Darius warned his friend.

"She's showing! I'll come over this evening." Curry couldn't wait to see her.

"I'll have Mrs. Collins make something and we can talk about the plans."

"Sounds great." The men ended their call.

∼ꝰ

After their lunch and much girl talk, Cherish parked her Blazer in Darius's driveway and gazed worriedly at her companion. Darbi was fast asleep, had been since leaving the restaurant. One hand gently lay atop the bulge under her shirt. Cherish took a deep breath, eased out of the truck and walked to the front door and rang the doorbell. After she explained the situation to Darius, he walked to Cherish's truck, picked up his sleeping sister, and carried her into the house. Cherish's heart swelled as she watched Darius settle Darbi on the couch.

After he put some cover over his sister, he led Cherish into the kitchen. "What did you guys do? I thought it was just lunch and talking. I knew she would overdo it."

"Darius," Cherish said, exasperated, "we ate and I showed her my vision for her dress. Darbi said she hasn't been sleeping well the last few nights. She said between the bathroom and leg cramps, it's been hard to sleep. I think those sleepless nights are catching up to her."

Darius noted the odd look on Cherish's face. "You're excited about the baby, aren't you?" He laughed. "I guess I am, too."

"Yes. I'm happy she gets to be a mom. I hate that it's at such a high price."

Darius noticed Darbi's contented look as she slept, her hand resting on her stomach where a new life was growing. Quietly, he and Cherish walked hand in hand to his office.

Cherish was shocked at the sight of bride magazines atop Darius's massive desk.

"I-I went out and got them while you guys were out. After all they've been through, I want them to have the best. We'll probably have to plan most of it, since she needs to take it easy."

"I thought so. I have a few ideas. Is Curry coming over anytime soon?" Cherish began looking through the magazines.

"Yes, he's coming over later tonight. Why?"

"We'll have to iron out some of the details with him, like the date, for one."

"Oh, yeah, that's right." He walked over to Cherish and kissed her. "Thanks for all your help. We couldn't do any of this without you."

Cherish smiled and kissed him in return. "Even if I didn't love you to pieces, I would still help."

Darius smiled. He wished he had the nerve to propose right now, when he felt so much love for Cherish. The chicken in him knew it wasn't possible. He watched as Cherish described the design of the dress and how long it would take her to make it.

"It will probably take me a week of intense concentration, if they chose a close date. But let's see what the bride wants. Then I can give a more accurate timetable." She smiled at him, raising his blood pressure a couple of notches.

Darius looked at Cherish's eyes; they sparkled with challenge. She looked as she did at the fashion shows, excited and ready to get to the task. He knew the next few weeks were going to be hectic and time-consuming.

The doorbell rang a few hours later. Darius opened his eyes and immediately smiled. It seemed to him that since his and Cherish's reconciliation, they couldn't get enough of each other, literally. Like now, as Cherish lay on top of him sleeping. Thank goodness they'd had the foresight to lock his office door. Impromptu lovemaking was not in his repertoire. Unplanned, spontaneous bouts of passion caused too many other problems. But it was great when it was happening.

His mind flashed back a few hours. As they were making plans for Darbi's wedding, before they knew it, their clothes were flying in the air and Darius landed in the loveseat with Cherish on top of him.

After he woke Cherish, they began to get dressed hastily. He hurried out of the office to ward off Curry, giving Cherish a few extra minutes. He made it to the door just as Mrs. Collins was letting Curry inside the house. Darius looked at his friend in amusement. "Need any help?"

Curry juggled three very large boxes. The stack almost covered his face. "No, thanks, I got it." He walked toward the living room and suddenly stopped as if the image of Darbi asleep on the couch was the most beautiful sight he could behold. He set the boxes down on the floor. "Presents from Mom," was all he said.

Darius whispered to his friend. "Let's go into the kitchen."

Curry silently nodded to his friend and followed him. Darius offered Curry a beer, but he shook his head. "It makes her sick, remember."

Darius nodded. He'd forgotten. Every time Darbi came near the smell of alcohol, she became very ill and it took her at least a day to recover. "I forgot. Man, lately so much upsets her stomach. But somehow she makes up for it." Darius laughed as he remembered his sister's growing appetite.

"I know. I don't know where it goes." Curry smiled at his near brother-in-law. "Hey, what do you think about this?" Curry pulled a small black velvet box from his pocket and opened it.

Darius smiled. "I think she will love it. How did you figure out the size?"

"I just took the average size and added one for good measure. If it's too large, I can get it re-sized later. Why is she sleeping?"

"The girls went out for lunch. Cherish said Darbi hasn't been sleeping well lately."

Curry smiled at his friend. "You and Cherish have been keeping her awake with all that noise!" They walked out of the kitchen. Curry lingered where Darbi was sleeping until Darius nudged him. Darius knocked on his office door, hoping Cherish took the hint.

She did, answering the door fully clothed and smiling. A floral scent filled the air. She gave Curry a big hug. "Congratulations, Curry."

Curry looked down at her, winking his eye, letting her know he knew what had just transpired in the room. "Thank you, Cherish."

Cherish showed the men all the preliminary plans she had made. They were impressed with her eye for detail. "I'll check with Darbi, of course. What would you like, Curry? Any special ideas?"

"Whatever Darbi wants," he said simply. "I know the wedding shouldn't be too taxing on her. Where do you guys think she would like to go for a honeymoon? Mom mentioned going to Ireland; she's hung up on this family history thing."

Both Cherish and Darius looked to each other for guidance. Darius's eyes pleaded with her to tell Curry.

Cherish's eyes did the same with Darius. He won. Cherish spoke first.

"Curry," she began slowly, "with Darbi's condition she can't fly right now, especially a plane trip that would be over fourteen hours long. I would suggest something locally."

Curry couldn't hide his disappointment. "I wanted to take her somewhere nice. You know, special."

Cherish smiled. "There's a ritzy bed and breakfast on Lake Arlington. You could take her there. I know Shelby would kill me if I let her go out of town."

"Shelby?"

"Her doctor. She's a friend of mine. Okay, guys, we have a wedding to plan."

"What about me?" Darbi stood at the door, rubbing her stomach gently.

All three rushed to her and ushered her to the nearest chair. Darbi tried to get comfortable in the leather chair, with no luck. "Why don't we do this in the living room? Darius, could you help Darbi back to the couch?" Cherish asked.

Before Darius could answer, Curry was at Darbi's side. "I'll do it, Dare." He wrapped his arm around Darbi and helped her out of the room.

Darius followed Cherish into the living room with an armful of catalogs and bridal brochures. Darbi snuggled on the couch under the covers, resting her feet on Curry's lap. Darius and Cherish sat on the floor in front of the couch, so Darbi could participate in the planning.

Curry stared at the slight mound under Darbi's cover. He longed to feel the life he had put there, but he thought the others might think him strange. Deciding this was the time and the place, he reached in his pocket for the ring box. The people he loved were there for emotional support. He cleared his throat and shifted his position. Three sets of eyes stared at him as he fidgeted. "Darbi, I have something for you." His eyes met hers as he placed the box in her hands.

Darbi bit her tongue as she opened the box. Tears sprang to her eyes as she saw the three-carat princess cut diamond. The ring winked at her, promising happiness for years to come. Curry nervously slipped the ring on her finger. It fit perfectly. He immediately looked in Darius and Cherish's direction.

They had become seriously quiet as they witnessed the interaction between the two people on the couch. Darbi sat up slowly, and moved to sit in Curry's lap. She kissed him deeply. "You think you're so smart, don't you, Curry?" she said when finally their lips parted.

"What?" Curry asked between ragged breaths.

"You are exactly what I've been waiting for all my life."

Curry was not expecting that answer. He kissed her and hugged her tight. He had been waiting a lifetime to fall in love, too.

CHAPTER TWENTY-FOUR

A month later, Darbi peeked out of the dressing room door of the church, watching the guests slowly making their way to their seats. She actually had begun to think the wedding would have to be called off. Bad luck had plagued the wedding plans from the very beginning.

Darbi's blood pressure became elevated and it landed her in the hospital for a few days. Curry got snowed under at work and couldn't help with the details. For an earth-shattering moment it looked like they were not going to be able to take a honeymoon. Otis had had a bad reaction to one of his new medicines, and was hospitalized. Darius had begun to work long hours as well.

But everything worked out. Otis was fine and still able to walk his daughter down the aisle. Not only was Curry able to take off for the honeymoon but also he got an extra week off, a gift from Mr. Sloane.

As Darbi entered the very busy dressing room, Cherish was chasing her young cousins around the room. If it weren't for Cherish, Darbi wouldn't have a ring bearer or a flower girl.

"How are you doing, Darbi?" Cherish patted Darbi's tummy. "You might want to snack on something before you walk down the aisle, so your stomach won't get upset." She nodded to the tray of cheese, crackers, and a glass of milk.

"Cherish, you are too much!" Darbi immediately walked over to the table and promptly stuffed a cracker topped with cheese in her mouth. "This is good. I didn't realize I was hungry." She quickly disposed of the food on the tray.

Cherish smiled. "Well, we didn't have breakfast, remember?"

Darbi had spent the night with Cherish so they could get a jump on the morning's activities. Darbi had been too nervous to eat breakfast. "I know. Sometimes I feel like a pig, eating so much." She patted her stomach. "But when your godchild wants to eat, it wants to eat now." She laughed as she relaxed in a chair.

Later as Cherish adjusted Darbi's veil, she smiled at all her hard work. "Darbi, you look like a vision. Curry will attack you on sight."

"I wish," Darbi pouted. "He really hasn't touched me in months. The most passionate he's been lately was the night he gave me the ring, and that was a month ago! It's like he thinks I'll break or something." Darbi's eyes searched Cherish's face for support. She saw none. Cherish was laughing.

"Darbi, in case you have forgotten, you were in the hospital and he didn't even know you were pregnant. Of course he's scared to touch you. Give him some time and you'll be taking another ride on the Fitzgerald Express."

"He'd better hurry. I might have to start demanding my wifely rights and we haven't even said I do yet." Darbi ran her hand over the fabric of the dress. "Cherish, I would like to thank you for all you've done, especially making this terrific dress. I especially like not looking like I have a bun in the oven, as Dad says."

~~~~~

Waiting alone in the groom's dressing room, Curry thought his tie was going to choke him alive if the wedding didn't start soon. It was hard to believe this was his third marriage, considering the bullets he was sweating. He paced the short length of the room. He could really use a drink right now to calm down. Darius, the best man, had left Curry's side to check on Otis.

A knock interrupted his anxiety. He walked to the door, wondering why Darius was knocking instead of just entering. He opened the door and found his answer. "Mom! What are you doing here?" Curry's heart danced with joy as he took in the sight of his parents, his siblings, their spouses and kids. Tears ran down his face as he hugged his mother. "I'm so happy to see you! I didn't think you were coming."

"Well, Curran, you told me the date and the time." Sarah gave him her best innocent look. She gazed at the rest of the family and she issued a quiet command. "Why don't the rest of you go find your seats? Your father and I will stay with Curran."

The rest of the group nodded and left. She followed Curry into the small room, took a seat beside her husband and said, "Well, since we missed your first two courthouse weddings, we thought we should be here for this one, since it's at a church."

Curry nodded in approval, as if his mother were making perfect sense, and smiled at his parents.

Sarah reached into her purse and pulled out a small white linen pouch and handed it to her son. Having been raised in a traditional Irish household, Curry knew exactly what the small pouch held. He reached inside and pulled out a small bottle of Irish whiskey. He smiled. "Just exactly what I need, but I can't."

"Why not? It's part of an Irish tradition. This is part of your heritage," his mother pointed out.

"I can't because I have to kiss Darbi. And if I kiss her with whiskey on my breath she's going to get sick."

Sarah was puzzled. "Why?"

Curry looked at his mother as he dried his face with a towel. "The scent of alcohol makes her sick."

Sarah nodded in understanding. "Why didn't you say so? How's Darbi?"

Curry smiled proudly. "She's been doing great. The doctor says she is right on schedule, but she's been having a little trouble sleeping."

"You aren't living together, are you?" his mother asked in her usual accusatory tone.

Curry smiled. "No, Mom. Her father feels the same way as you do about premarital cohabitation. She told me so. Besides, she's always tired." Curry paused. "I'm very happy you were able to make it." His eyes twinkled at his mother.

"Me, too. We'd better go take our seats." She stood and hugged her son, as did Thomas, before they left the room.

Darius walked into the room a few minutes later. He noted Curry had calmed down immensely. "Do you know there are about forty people from your family out there?" Darius smiled broadly. For two weeks, he had kept secret the fact that Curry's family was coming.

"Yes, my family. Our family," Curry corrected himself. "They really surprised me. I didn't think they would come. You know, with this being the third time around and Darbi being in the family way and all."

Darius smiled, feeling the same force of the day as his friend. Two very different families were about to become one. "I know. Sarah called me two weeks ago. She wanted to show you that you had her blessing, even under these circumstances."

~~~

Darbi heard the organ music as it filled the air, signaling the beginning of the ceremony. Cherish pushed her tiny cousins out of the room. They were a little skittish about walking down the aisle and being gawked at by strangers, but after Cherish promised them a trip to the toy store afterwards, they scampered down the aisle.

The wedding was intended to be a small, intimate affair. But after both Curry and Darius invited their respective clients, the wedding was neither. With a candidate for the most watched Senate race in the nation also in attendance, the press, both local and national, were also present. Whether Darbi wanted it or not, her nuptials were going to be on the local evening news and probably CNN.

As Darbi watched Cherish walked down the aisle, Otis snapped her out of her daydreaming. It was her time. She took a deep breath and let her father escort down the aisle.

"You look like your mother the day I married her," Otis said as his baby girl glided down the aisle on his arm.

"Thank you, Dad. You look very handsome. If you start feeling tired, you just let me know."

Otis smiled. "I'm so proud of you. You have come so far in the last year. Now in five months, you'll be a mother." Tears ran down his face as he walked. "You just take care of my grandbaby." He smiled through his tears. "Don't you ever be afraid to come home, honey. No one will think any less of you."

Darbi wouldn't have thought a simple walk down the aisle would bring tears to her father's eyes as well as her own. "I won't, Dad. Thank you for everything, especially for not being mad at me for getting pregnant." She smiled as she noticed Curry and her brother standing next to the minister, waiting for her.

"I love you, baby girl. Don't you ever think otherwise." He kissed her on the cheek and handed her over to Curry, then walked the necessary steps to the bench and sat by the nurse.

As Darbi stood next to Curry, her stomach felt nervous. But when Curry took her hand, her stomach finally settled down. She tried to concentrate on the words being said by the minister but her mind kept floating to all the obstacles she had faced in the last two years. Now she was where she was supposed to be. Teardrops fell to her hand.

"Miss Crawford?" The minister broke into her thoughts. He winked at her.

Darbi returned his look, thoroughly confused. Curry slightly tugged her hand.

"Oh, sorry! I do." The audience roared with laughter, including Curry. After the laughter died down, Curry said his I do, and they exchanged rings.

"You may kiss your wife," the minister announced.

Curry turned and faced Darbi with tears in his eyes. As he lifted her veil, Darbi tried to blink her tears away, but it was no use, they were just coming too fast. He took a deep breath and leaned forward to kiss her gently on the lips. "I love you, Mrs. Fitzgerald."

More tears fell as she heard her new last name for the first time. *Mrs. Fitzgerald.* "I love you, Curry."

Darbi and Curry enjoyed the solitude of the limo ride to the reception that was being held at the Klondike Hotel in Fort Worth. Darbi's brown hand was entwined with Curry's larger pale one. She glanced down at their hands. Their gold bands shone bright with hope and love. A few months ago, she wouldn't have thought this day would be in her future.

"How are you holding up?" Curry kissed her forehead and rubbed her stomach. "I can't even tell you're pregnant today."

Darbi leaned against him. "I definitely feel pregnant, but you're right. Cherish is a fabulous designer. It seems weird the baby picked today to start wiggling around."

"If this is too much for you, just say the word. I've booked a room for us tonight, so we don't have to go home. Maybe we can sneak upstairs later and take a nap." He nuzzled against his wife's neck.

Darbi giggled, knowing sleep was the last thing on Curry Fitzgerald's mind.

As the reception progressed, Darius watched the interaction between his sister and Curry's ex-flames, who were also co-workers. Eight women of varying hair colors circled Darbi as if doing some kind of warrior dance and she was the prey, while the Senator and the press had Curry cornered across the room.

Darius had expected some trouble at work when Curry announced he was getting married to Darbi, but most of the women just wanted to know how she *got* him. Darius felt the women had viewed Curry as a prized animal needing to be caught.

Curry looked around for his wife. Spotting the women from work surrounding her, Curry excused himself from the Senator and walked to her. After what had to be the world's shortest conversation, the women dispersed quickly. Darius wondered what Curry could have said to them to make them leave Darbi so suddenly.

The newlyweds looked so happy today. However, both wore tired smiles. All the trouble the foursome had endured was worth the end result. Darbi and Curry were husband and wife. Seeing Curry help Darbi to a nearby chair and fearing the worst, Darius rushed to the couple's side immediately.

"What's wrong?" He sat by his sister, wiping her forehead with his handkerchief. "Do you need to go to the hospital? I knew this was going to be too much today."

Darbi placed a warm hand on her brother's hand to stop him from going into a full-blown tirade. She took a deep breath. "I'm just a little tired and the room started spinning around."

Curry sat beside Darbi, letting her head rest on his shoulder. He kissed her forehead. "I think she just needs to rest. I'll take her to our room."

Darius looked around the room for Cherish, but she was dancing with Otis. The nurse was also occupied. Darius agreed with Curry's thoughts. Darbi looked like she needed some rest. Darius was sure her unhealthy pallor would go away as soon as she was rested. "Why don't you go take a nap? I'm sure it will be okay." He looked around the room. There had to be at least two hundred people milling about. He was sure no one would miss the bride for a little while. He'd rather chance the guests questioning the bride's absence than a trip to the emergency room. Nothing mattered but Darbi's well-being.

～～～

Curry helped Darbi to the room and into bed. At her insistence, he went back downstairs. He sat at a table, sipping sparkling juice in his champagne flute, missing his wife and wanting to join her. His eyes were fixed on

Darius and Cherish as they danced to a slow number. They acted more like the bride and groom, sharing stolen kisses, being congratulated by clients, co-workers and friends.

"Where's Darbi?" Sarah Fitzgerald sat next to her son. "I haven't seen her in some time. Is she alright?"

Curry glanced at his mother. "I took her upstairs for a nap. I think all this might have been a little too much for her today." But she'd wanted a wedding and he'd wanted to give her what she wanted. He just hoped she didn't have to pay a price too high.

"Curran, go check on your wife," his mother insisted.

"I can't, Mom. What about my clients?" He'd been fighting the urge to join Darbi in bed. But business sense had prevailed.

Sarah shook her head. "They're having a good time. They probably won't even notice." She pointed to the exit door leading to the elevators.

"Okay, Mom. I'll just check on her and be right back down," Curry lied, knowing the minute he entered the bridal suite he wasn't coming back to the reception.

As Curry entered the room his heartbeat accelerated. In the semi-darkness, he made out the shape of his wife in bed asleep.

He heard Darbi's steady breathing as she slept. Quietly, he walked over to the bed where she slept. She was wearing only her bra and panties. Earlier, he was so focused on making sure she was all right, he hadn't focused on her body. Now he had the time to get a good look at his new wife. He stared at her growing stomach, then sat down beside her and gently caressed her stomach. It felt hot to his touch. He hoped and prayed nothing was wrong. He didn't want to spend their wedding night in the emergency room. Then he felt some movement under his hand. Smiling, he realized it was the baby.

"What are you doing?" Darbi's hand rested on top of his. "How long have I been asleep?" She struggled to sit up.

Curry helped her upright. He couldn't stop looking at her. She was so beautiful, a sexy pregnant siren. "An hour or so." Curry stood and started taking off his tuxedo jacket. "I thought we could nap together." He took off the rest of his clothes and slipped in bed with his wife.

Darbi snuggled next to him, waking his tired body. "Won't they miss us downstairs? You know, for the rice throwing and stuff?"

"No," he kissed her forehead, "Darius is taking care of that. Mom, Dad, and the rest of the family want us to join them for breakfast. I hope you don't mind." He kissed her as his hands caressed her body.

"No, I don't mind. Where are they staying tonight?"

"Here at this hotel." He rubbed her stomach, amazed at the roundness and hardness of it. "Sorry."

"What is it, Curry?" Darbi asked in a frightened voice.

Curry saw the look of fear on her face. He dared not tell her his thoughts.

"Am I bleeding?" Not waiting for Curry's answer, Darbi pulled back the bedsheet and then relaxed. "You scared the crap out of me," she laughed. "I thought I was bleeding."

"I didn't realize your tummy would be hard to my touch. I felt it earlier and it was just warm." He looked at her stomach, amazed. He could not believe that his son or daughter was inside her stomach. He couldn't wait to find out which one.

She pulled the sheet up and smiled. "My stomach is firm because I have been up all day. My body is used to resting during the day. That's probably why I feel so tired."

"Too tired for a gentle ride on the Fitzgerald express?" He unsnapped her bra.

"A gentle ride would be nice." Darbi laughed as he helped her out of her undies, barely giving her time to answer.

He was out of his silk boxers in record time. He hopped back in bed and kissed her, rolling her over so that she was on top of him. He gently caressed the out-line of her body. "Are you sure?"

"Yes, I'm sure." Darbi leaned down and kissed him deeply.

Curry guided her onto him gently. He was so afraid of hurting her, he barely entered her body.

"This is no way to start a marriage, Curry." Their eyes locked as she took control and took him deep inside her body. Then they took a ride to end all rides.

Curry wanted to be gentle, but had been denied her touch for too long. He was on fire, but he had to hold back or at least try. "Wow, baby. Slow down," Curry panted between breaths.

But they couldn't. Passion overtook every other emo-tion. Soon Darbi collapsed on his chest and they fell asleep. It was only seven in the evening, yet they already had had a full day.

An hour later the phone rang. Darbi moaned, and moved closer to him, easing her leg between his in her sleep. Curry didn't know which was more torture: the sounds of her moans and her squirming around trying to find a comfortable position, or him trying to answer the phone before she woke.

He finally reached the phone.

"Hey, Dare," Curry breathed into the phone, knowing only one person had their room number.

Darius laughed. "I didn't want to call, but people are beginning to ask about the bride and groom, especially the Senator and his wife and some of your other clients. Are you guys coming back downstairs? Or are you in for the night?"

Curry looked at the woman lying beside him. If she didn't find a comfortable sleeping position soon, he would have to wake her for another ride on the Fitzgerald Express. "I think we're in for the night. I know you can hear her moaning, she can't get comfortable."

"Yes, I can hear her. You want me to bring some food up? Later, of course." Darius tried to suppress his laughter as he heard Curry moan in pain.

"That would be great. She didn't eat at the reception, so I know she'll be hungry later." Curry ended the call and woke his wife.

Darius put his cell phone back in his suit pocket, laughing at his best friend.

"What's wrong?" Cherish asked, returning his smile. "Is Darbi okay? I guess so, if you're wearing that goofy smile, huh?" She laced her fingers with his and hugged him. "How are the newlyweds?"

"They're fine. Tired."

Cherish winked at him. "Sounds like the Fitzgerald Express is up and running again." She burst into a fit of giggles.

Cherish quieted, then kissed him gently on the lips. Darius knew the woman in his arms was more than a blessing to his entire family. She'd befriended Darbi and helped solve the mystery about Darbi that had plagued the family since her return. He wished he could find the courage to propose marriage to the only woman he could ever love.

"Darius?" Cherish pulled him out on the dance floor again. "Since the newlyweds are resting, we might as well make use of this band."

He nodded and pulled her tight against his body. "I know I'm not the most romantic person. I actually think my father is more of a romantic than I am, but I am trying."

"I know, Darius, and I appreciate it." Cherish rested her head against his chest. "I love you."

Darius kissed her forehead. He was one lucky man.

The next morning, Sarah watched as her son and daughter-in-law approached the large table and sat down.

They were both dressed casually in shorts and a t-shirt, and holding hands. Under Darbi's shirt stating something about a train and bearing the family's name, Sarah could see the beginning stages of pregnancy. For some strange reason, Sarah wanted to pat Darbi's stomach. She had seen all of her other children go through the many stages of pregnancy, either as daughters or sons, but this was different. Curran was going to be a father and had an entirely different persona. This woman had changed him and had won the approval of the entire family. They were all happy to see Curran grounded and smiling.

Sarah had also invited the Crawfords and Cherish to breakfast. She smiled as Darius, Otis and Cherish walked into the restaurant, surprising Darbi. Cherish sat next to Darbi, Darius sat beside Curry and Otis took a seat between Sarah and Thomas.

"It was a lovely wedding, Otis. They look very happy this morning," Sarah observed as she watched the couple at the other end of the table.

"Yes, baby girl was a beautiful bride," Otis said, pride evident in his voice. "You do know about the bundle coming?"

Sarah choked on her coffee. Curry had warned them that Otis did not mince his words. "Yes, he told us. We're very happy. This is what he needed to settle down. I have never seen him so accommodating to another human being."

After breakfast was over, Sarah watched as Curry helped Darbi up. She smiled. The Fitzgerald clan had just changed drastically. She had always imagined keeping the

Irish bloodline true to the Emerald Isle, but as she watched Darbi hold Curry's hand, she realized fate had had a different plan in mind. Even she couldn't disrupt the path of true love.

She stood and approached her daughter-in-law. "Darbi, you looked very pretty last night and you're absolutely glowing this morning. May I?" She gestured toward Darbi's stomach.

When Darbi nodded, Sarah reached out and gently caressed her stomach. "You take care of my grandchild. If you have any questions about pregnancy, feel free to call me. If my son gets out of line, I'm sure Darius can handle him." She winked at Curry. "But just in case he can't, you just call me."

"Thank you, Mrs. Fitzgerald," Darbi said quietly.

"I believe that's your name now," Sarah reminded her. "Please call me Mom."

Later, Darius and Cherish enjoyed a nice quiet evening at home. They snuggled on the couch, both letting the exhaustion of the last few weeks exit their bodies.

Now it was too quiet. Darbi was no longer upstairs. She was with Curry. Darius smiled at the memories of the last week. Every time he'd seen Darbi, she'd had some kind of food in her mouth. The baby was slowly making its presence known.

"You think they're okay?" Cherish let out a content moan.

"Yes, they're fine. I can't believe Sarah told Darbi to call her Mom. That almost blew me away. But I knew if Sarah got to know Darbi, she would like her." Darius stood and held out his hand, wanting some quality time with Cherish.

Cherish allowed herself to be led to his bedroom. The wedding had taken its toll on everyone. "Darius, I've decided what I want to do with my life." She sat on the bed.

Darius sat on the bed beside her. "What?" Was she going to leave him now? How could he survive without her? Now that things were settling down and back to normal, he had hoped to expand their relationship.

"Well," she started, unbuttoning his shirt, "I really enjoyed making the wedding plans. I thought about starting my own business."

"What kind of business?"

"As a wedding designer or consultant. You know, I could meet the bride-to-be and design a dress especially for her. Help them plan the entire wedding. I know Darbi's case was special, but I feel like I was meant to do that."

Darius released the pins that held her hairdo. He ran his fingers through her soft, luxurious hair. "Sounds great. If you need an investor, I'd be happy to invest." It would almost be as good as a marriage proposal, he thought.

Cherish shook her head. "I have some money saved, Darius. I don't need your money. I just want your support."

He knew Cherish didn't *need* his financial help, but he wanted to help her. "Cherish, I want to. You'll have start up costs. Let me help you. You helped Darbi so many times, let me do this for you."

"I don't know. I'll have to sleep on it." She smiled at him coyly.

Darius returned her smile. The plans he had for her had nothing to do with sleeping.

CHAPTER TWENTY-FIVE

Five glorious days later, Curry parked the BMW beside Darbi's Explorer in the garage. Darbi sat beside him in the passenger seat. She had not moved since they had started their journey home almost an hour ago. During their honeymoon they had been pampered to the highest degree. They'd had massages every morning, whirlpools in the afternoon, and sat in the jacuzzi every night.

He'd tried very hard to stay within Shelby's gentle lovemaking range, but his wife had been otherwise determined. They were both so happily exhausted they would probably sleep the entire next week. Reluctantly, he woke her. Her eyes fluttered opened and she glanced in his direction, smiling.

"We're home already?" Darbi yawned, releasing the seatbelt.

Curry nodded. "Sit tight, honey. I'll help you out of the car." He opened his car door, but Darbi's voice halted his actions.

"Curry, I'm not helpless," Darbi complained. "I just can't drive."

"I know." He eased out of the car and walked to the passenger side to help her out. "Why don't you take a nap and I'll get the bags out of the car?"

Darbi nodded, yawned, and stretched, revealing her growing abdomen. "I feel exhausted. Someone really tired me out last week!" She kissed him deeply.

Curry had to think fast or he was going to forget about the luggage and the fact that his pregnant wife was indeed pregnant. He pulled away from her. "No, you need your rest. Go take a nap. I'll join you when I'm done."

Darbi smiled seductively at him. "I'll be waiting." She walked inside the house.

As Darius drove into his garage, he yawned. He was tired. Since Curry was still on his honeymoon, he had been working on the Senator's project single-handedly. Darius thought he would feel a marked change once Curry legally became his brother-in-law, but he didn't. Everything felt the same. The only thing that was different was Curry wasn't at work, and everyone had congratulated Darius on the wedding.

Curry had called him earlier, as well as Cherish, and they'd had serious talks about Darbi. Everyone wanted to make sure she would be okay once Curry returned to work. Now as Darius walked into the house, Otis sat at the kitchen table, sipping on a cup of coffee and apparently waiting for him.

"Hey, Dad. Is everything okay?"

"Yes, I wanted to talk to you. Let's go to my room." Otis didn't wait for a reply. He was already out of the kitchen and walking down the hall to his room.

Otis Crawford was a man of few words. If he wanted to talk, it was serious. Darius silently followed Otis to his room, sitting in a nearby chair as Otis sat on the bed. A few minutes ticked by before Otis spoke.

"You know Curry goes back to work next week. I'm worried about baby girl. What will she do while he's at work?"

Darius smiled. His father had referred to Curry by his name instead of *that boy*. Curry had been *that boy* ever since he and Darbi started dating. Something Darius had thought was a part of Alzheimer's was just Otis Crawford being Otis Crawford.

"I know, Dad. Cherish, Curry, and I came up with a plan, one that wouldn't rob Darbi of the independence she fought for and yet enable her to get help if she needs it. Curry will bring her over here every day and she can help Cherish get her business going. You know, making phone calls, something not too taxing. She can still feel useful and she can eat healthy."

Otis nodded. He was proud that his stiff, rigid son had some thoughts about it. "I'm happy to see this side of you. They could eat dinner here. That way, if he has to work late or something, she would already be here. If that's okay with you."

"Yes, Dad, that sounds fine. That's a great idea. They're coming over tonight for dinner, so that we can break the news to her."

Darius and his father exchanged glances; they both knew Darbi wouldn't take it sitting down.

~~~~~

Darbi felt the four sets of eyes staring at her signaled an intervention, not a family dinner. After she and Curry arrived, Cherish soon followed. She should have known something was up. Now as they sat in the living room, Darius had dropped the bomb.

He, Curry, Cherish, and Otis, had assembled a schedule for her to follow. Curry would drop her off at Darius's each morning. Cherish would come over so she and Darbi could work on getting her new business started. Darbi knew it was because she was still not allowed to drive and Curry would be returning to work. She also knew how limited her cooking skills were, but still objected.

"No. I can stay at home by myself," Darbi said, daring anyone to object.

"What happens if you get sick? What happens if you start bleeding? How are you getting to the hospital?" Darius asked, acting over-protective as usual.

"I can call Shelby. I am an adult. I've been married before. I know how to use a telephone," Darbi countered.

"Darbi," Cherish spoke softly, "no one said you couldn't do for yourself. We just want you to have a healthy pregnancy."

"I feel fine. I don't need a babysitter!" Darbi rubbed her stomach; the baby was getting hungry and it had been a whole two hours since she ate last. *I'm going to be as big as a house by the time the baby gets here.* "I know I can't cook much, but I can always order something in." She looked toward Curry for a little support, but she didn't get any. She crossed her arms in front of her chest, as best she could. "I know I'm only your wife and the mother of your child, but you could say something on my behalf, Mr. Fitzgerald!"

Otis intervened before Curry could formulate an answer. "Not order in every day! Now, baby girl, you know that's not healthy. I don't want my grandbaby coming into this world addicted to take-out! No, ma'am. You and Curry are having dinner here. You also need to be taken care of, so if you want to be mad, be mad!" He folded his arms in front of his chest as well, showing his daughter how childishly she was behaving.

A few minutes of deafening silence passed before Darbi spoke. "Thank you all for caring so much," Darbi mumbled in an unsteady voice. She'd originally thought she was going through this pregnancy alone, but her family had been with her for every pound she had gained. Which in the last week had been more than normal. "I'll try to be more cooperative. I won't like it, but I'll try."

Otis hugged his daughter. "That's my baby. You'll see, the next few months will fly by and it will be worth it once you hold that baby in your arms. Come on, let's eat." Otis stood and then helped Darbi up. He looked at her with fatherly pride as the t-shirt molded to her stomach. "That bun is growing!"

A month later, Cherish was ready for business. She found office space in a building ten minutes from

Darius's house. She had initially thought about running the business out of her home, but Darius had talked her into getting office space.

Cherish began to feel a part of the Crawford family. Darius was her chief investor, Curry set up her computers, and Darbi was acting as receptionist. Cherish was overwhelmed at all the love and support they showed her.

The large office held two desks, a lounge area for Darbi when she needed to relax, and ample modeling room. The front desk, which Darbi occupied, was used as a reception area. The second more cluttered desk was Cherish's.

Cherish felt as if she'd been entrusted with something sacred in making sure Darbi was okay. She also kept Darbi too busy to worry about what kind of mother she would be.

"This is the first time in years that I haven't had a real job and didn't need one. This seems weird to me," Darbi said one afternoon after her daily call from Curry.

"You do have a real job," Cherish replied, "helping me." She saw Mrs. Collins park in front of the office. Every day since Cherish had moved her business into the building, Mrs. Collins brought the women lunch. Cherish knew Otis sent her. "Ready for lunch?"

"Yes, this kid is always hungry. It has to be a boy. No girl would eat this much." Darbi stood and stretched. "You know, Curry's parents want to come visit next month. I'm a little scared about that. I'm worrying about having Sarah underfoot. I can just imagine that tiny woman telling me I'm not taking good enough care of Curry or something," Darbi said.

"What does Curry think about it?" Cherish asked, walking to the door to greet the nurse.

"He thinks it's wonderful, of course. He promised to take some time off when they visit. I don't know how he could with that Senator's campaign being in full swing." Darbi paused, her eyes alight. "Hello, Mrs. Collins." Darbi peeked into the basket. "Smells good, and I'm starving."

Mrs. Collins smiled at Darbi. "Your father says he will see you tonight. I made you turkey and ham sandwiches, fruit and salad. What you smell is the freshly baked chocolate cake. I know you've been craving chocolate lately. Dr. Allen said you could have a little." She winked at Darbi as she set the basket down on the table.

Darbi hugged the nurse, grateful for the food and for the fact that someone listened to her when she talked about her cravings. "Thank you so much." She immediately sat down and began eating.

Both Cherish and Mrs. Collins laughed at Darbi's ever increasing appetite.

~~~~~

After the nurse left, Cherish sat at the computer fiddling with her Virtual Brides program. "I still can't believe Curry wrote this program. I'm very impressed. He's always full of surprises," Cherish commented. "I think I'm ready to open for business. What do you think?"

Darbi surveyed the small office. Several wedding gowns adorned the wall, and numerous veils sat on her desk. "I think you're ready, Cherish."

With the busy wedding season gone, Cherish wasn't expecting many bites. She wanted to use this time to get all the kinks out of her system, so it would run perfectly in season. Also, when Darius invested his money he told her he wasn't in any hurry to get an immediate return.

A Cherished Wedding was open a week before Cherish got her first nibble. Since the only calls usually received were from Darius, Curry and occasionally, Otis, Darbi was quite surprised to hear a female voice was at the other end of the phone. She almost dropped the phone, and then almost forgot to get the caller's name before ending the call.

Cherish was excited as well. She and Darbi watched the clock until appointment time. They both half-expected the caller to be a no-show and were stunned when a small, waifish blonde woman walked inside the small office. Cherish wiped her hands on her pants leg and rushed to meet her client. "Welcome to A Cherished Wedding. I'm Cherish Murray, this is Darbi Fitzgerald." She pointed to the pregnant woman sitting behind the desk.

The petite woman extended her hand to Cherish. "I'm Sunshine Brady. My father is Alfred Brady."

Cherish shook the tiny woman's hand. She had heard of the business magnate. This was his only daughter, his only child. Dollar signs and the sounds of a cash register ringing immediately filled Cherish's mind.

After about two hours of hearing Cherish's ideas and thoughts, Sunshine hired her on the spot. She planned a Valentine's Day wedding.

Cherish broached the price carefully, not wanting to lose her first client. But Sunshine had to know the price. "Flowers will be expensive that time of the year."

"That's okay. Daddy says whatever I want, price is no object."

"Valentine's Day it is. First marriage?" Cherish guessed, trying to keep the green-eyed monster at bay.

"Fourth," Sunshine admitted.

Cherish held back her retort. Slowly, she realized her first client was ten years younger and on her fourth marriage. Cherish had not even gotten her first marriage proposal!

———

Over the next month, Cherish began to wonder if Darius would ever propose to her. They dated, when their schedules permitted. He stayed overnight at her house and she at his. Still, the question hung in the air like an impending cloud. She couldn't really blame him for not thinking about it.

Darbi's high-risk pregnancy had become so family involved, it was easy for other things to be put on the back burner. Slowly, she expected it less and less. Cherish herself continued to be closely involved in Darbi's pregnancy.

Darbi was incredibly upbeat about her weight gain. The doctor, though, still said she was a little small for being twenty-four weeks along. Both Darbi and Curry looked extremely happy. Cherish thought it was because the visit from Curry's parents wasn't as long as they had originally planned.

"Cherish," Darbi called softly.

"Oh, sorry. I was daydreaming." She watched as Darbi slowly left the front desk and walked toward her. "Are you okay?" The gold band on Darbi's hand seemed to mock her.

Darbi smiled. "You know, I hear that phrase more than I hear my own name. But to answer you, I'm fine. Shelby says I'm doing great. My next sonogram is in a few weeks. What about you? How are things going with you and Darius?"

"Things are fine," Cherish sighed.

"Cherish, this is me. We've been through a pregnancy test together, remember?" Darbi stared at her. "Come on, spill it!"

Cherish gazed at Darbi's contented face and something in her resolve slipped. The outburst she had been holding back for so long found an outlet. "I don't think Darius will ever propose. Each day when I take you to his house, I see how happy you and Curry are. Sometimes it makes me sick with envy! I know Darius loves me. Why can't he make the commitment?" She burst into tears.

Darbi was shocked at Cherish's statement. "Because," she cooed softly, "he's afraid you will say no."

Cherish wiped her eyes. "W-why, h-how could he think something so stupid? We spend all our free time together. He's even met my aunt and passed her test. He adores my little cousins; he even helped me finish clearing out my mother's room and redecorate it." She grabbed a Kleenex from the box and blew her nose.

"He's too afraid. Give him some time. Curry told me that when he showed Darius my ring, he asked how he figured the size. So maybe he's thinking about it. He's gone through a lot of emotional changes these last few months." She patted her stomach. "Not only with me but also Dad as well. So just give him a little more time."

"I know, Darbi. I'm trying to understand, really. I'm not some cold-hearted woman who doesn't understand family responsibility and is demanding a ring. It seems every time I think he's getting close to proposing, some-thing happens and he loses his direction." Cherish inhaled deeply and sighed. "Thank you, Darbi. I know he's worried about both you and Otis. I'll just have to wait for a sign that he's ready, although I have no clue as to what that sign would be."

Darbi nodded as she rubbed her stomach. "I've got to go to the bathroom. Just you wait, Cherish, you'll soon be planning your own wedding."

Cherish smiled as she watched Darbi hoist herself up and walk slowly to the restroom in the rear of the shop. After she heard Darbi close the door, Cherish walked into the lounge. The lounge had been created especially for Darbi, so she could rest during the day, but she didn't. It held a comfortable couch, a TV/DVD combo and a small refrigerator.

Cherish walked to the sofa and lay down. Why couldn't her relationship with Darius be like Darbi and

Curry's? She wouldn't mind a few of the bumps Darbi and Curry had endured, like Curry's mother. But even she had come around. Initially, she hadn't much liked Darbi simply because she was black. Now, however, she treated Darbi like a daughter. Since their visit, Sarah called every week, sometimes not even speaking to her son.

"Cherish," Darbi whispered.

Cherish opened her eyes. Darbi stood at the doorway of the lounge, rubbing her stomach. She had a strange look on her face, alarming Cherish automatically. "What is it, Darbi?" She immediately sat up.

Darbi whispered, her voice trembling, "I'm sure it's nothing. Could you take me to Shelby's office? I'm bleeding."

She said it so calmly, Cherish thought. No hint that danger was around the corner. Her heartbeat sped up. "Where?"

"I noticed it in the toilet. I'm not sure where it's coming from." She leaned against the door for support.

Cherish rushed to Darbi's side and helped her to the couch, then hurried to the desk and called Shelby.

"I'm sure it's nothing, Cherish," Shelby reassured Cherish. "But just to make sure, I'd like to check her out. How soon can you get her to the hospital?"

"Fifteen minutes." Cherish hung up the phone. She locked the front door and returned to the lounge. Darbi's eyes were closed and she was lying down. Cherish helped Darbi to her car parked in the back. A thought occurred to her as she headed to the hospital.

Who should she call first? If she called Curry first, Darius might think she was hiding something from him again. On the other hand, Darbi was Curry's wife and carrying his child. She called Curry on the way to the hospital.

CHAPTER TWENTY-SIX

"Mr. Fitzgerald, Ms. Murray on line two," Mica announced in a very calm voice.

Both Curry and Darius's laughter ceased. There would be only one reason Cherish was calling Curry instead of Darius. Something was wrong with Darbi. Curry's shaky hand reached for the telephone.

"W-what is it, Cherish?" Curry choked the words out, hoping against hope.

"We're on our way to the hospital," Cherish reported in her soothing voice. "Darbi's bleeding and Shelby wants to check it out. You want me to call you when we find out what's going on?"

"Hell, no! I'm on my way," Curry said as he rose, patting his pocket for his car keys. "I'll meet you there." Curry slammed the phone down. He looked straight into Darius's questioning face and said, "Cherish is taking Darbi to the hospital." He walked out of his office with Darius right on his heels.

"Curry, I'll drive you."

"No, Dare. I'll be fine." He knew he had to be emotionally strong, but all he wanted to do was scream how unfair it was to his new wife. He had known it would be a difficult pregnancy for Darbi, but had hoped they wouldn't have to face problems so soon.

Darius grabbed Curry's arm, making his brother-in-law look him in the face. "Look, man, you're trembling already. The last thing we need is for you to be in a car accident." Darius stared at him as tears rolled down Curry's face. "Come on, Curry. It's probably nothing," Darius said, trying to ease the pain Curry was feeling.

Curry knew that wasn't so.

~~~

By the time Cherish arrived at the hospital, Darbi was semi-conscious in the passenger seat. The bottom part of her maternity blouse was now stained with blood. Cherish reached over, grabbing Darbi's hand, silently willing her friend to hold on to life.

The attendants immediately took Darbi inside the hospital. One of the transporters told Cherish to wait in the maternity waiting room on the third floor. She opened her mouth to object, but the transporters were already gone. Cherish was forced to wait alone.

Time ticked by slowly. Cherish sat quietly in the uncomfortable chair waiting for Shelby to appear and tell her it was nothing and Darbi could go home. But over an hour passed and Shelby still did not appear. Neither had Curry or Darius. Cherish felt alone and scared, much like the day her mother died.

Her mind casually floated to that morning's conversation. Darius not proposing didn't seem so important now. All that really mattered was that Darbi was okay and she had not miscarried.

"Cherish?" A husky voice interrupted her feelings of guilt.

Cherish's eyes found the source of the masculine voice. A young man stood at the entrance to the waiting room. "Yes?" This was not going to be good!

"Please follow me." The tall attendant began walking toward the elevators. "Dr. Allen will meet you on the third floor, room 317." He punched the elevator button for her as she stepped inside.

"What's wrong with my friend?" Cherish wanted information.

"I'm sure Dr. Allen will have all the answers you need, ma'am." The elevator door closed.

Cherish did not like the answer she had gotten. This was the classic the-doctor-should-tell-you news. Darbi had been admitted and had a room in the hospital. It could only get worse. She took a deep breath and tried to slow her heartbeat. *Be strong, Cherish.* Darbi was only six months along, too soon to give birth to a healthy baby. Cherish composed herself to look like a ray of sunshine, so she could face Darbi. Losing it emotionally was not an option.

She walked into the room and breathed a sigh of relief. Darbi was lying in bed asleep. The monitors beeped quietly. Cherish laughed as she saw the baby moving around on the screen. She noticed Shelby sitting in a chair making notes in Darbi's chart. "Shelby?"

"Hi, Cherish." Shelby stood and walked to her friend.

"What's wrong?" Cherish hoped her friend didn't distort the truth for her benefit. "The real story."

"Okay, Cherish, this is the story. This is very active baby. So needless to say, it moves around a lot. When the baby does rest, it is resting in the one place it shouldn't."

Cherish knew exactly which area Shelby meant. Darbi complained every time the baby got near that incision. "What can be done? You can't control where the baby turns, can you?"

"Up to a point, yes." Shelby smiled, attempting to soften the blow. "If it gets worse, I can slow the baby's movements down. But that would be a last resort. I don't know if Curry could handle that. I need to talk to him as soon as he gets here."

Curry walked into the room, followed by Darius. "Why do you need to talk to me? What's wrong?" He walked over to his sleeping wife. Concern for Darbi blocked out every other sound in the room, including Shelby's voice.

Darbi looked so helpless attached to monitors, wires, and IVs. He just wanted her to be safe. Who knew something that started out as a phenomenal mistake would make him love her more each minute?

Shelby walked over to him, gently touching his arm. "Curry, this should really be discussed with just you and Darbi."

"You can discuss it here." Curry glanced around the room. "We're family."

Shelby glanced from the sleeping woman to Curry, to Darius and finally to Cherish. "Okay, here's what's wrong." She described the movements of the baby and how those movements were affecting Darbi. "There are some options."

"Such as?" Darius asked, not liking the doctor's cold, clinical tone.

"Well," Shelby began, "she'll need to be on bed rest for a few weeks. I mean strict. That means no unnecessary walking, and definitely no driving. I want her in bed as much as possible. If she does walk anywhere, she'll need to wear a support belt. This belt will take some of the pressure off the wound and won't make her sick. Hopefully, that will keep her out of the hospital until delivery time." Shelby's dark brown eyes stared directly at Curry as she said the next sentence. "Sexual relations will need to cease until after the birth."

"Of course, I wouldn't do anything to jeopardize…" Curry sputtered, feeling that he was being accused of some horrible deed before a Senate committee.

"I know, Curry. I'm not saying that is the problem; I just want to take every precaution possible to keep her well. I'm sure we all would like her to deliver as close to term as possible. Agreed?"

Three heads nodded in agreement.

"Good. She'll be in here a few days. Her temperature is a little high right now but the bleeding has stopped. Luckily this time was not like the first time." Shelby walked toward the door, then turned and faced the men. "Cherish reacted very quickly and accurately. She probably saved her from a long hospital stay." She left the room.

Cherish sat in the chair and took a deep breath. *I'll be an emotional wreck by the time that kid gets here.* She felt Darius walking toward her. He tried to comfort her, but she shrank away from his touch. "Don't touch me!" She tried to compose herself.

Darius stared at Cherish as she wiped her eyes. "What?"

"Oh, nothing, Darius. I'm sorry." She caressed his arm softly. "I was very frightened earlier." Her eyes went to Curry as he stood by the bed holding Darbi's hand. Why did she feel jealous at the sight of him caring for his wife? *Stop it, Cherish! Darbi's health is in jeopardy and you're pouting!*

Curry absentmindedly caressed his wife's tummy, feeling his son or daughter kicking his hand. He took a deep breath and took out his organizer.

Darius knew Curry's dilemma. He had a solution that would help everyone involved, but didn't want Curry to think he was trying to take over his role of husband and provider.

Darius looked to Cherish for some support, but she seemed to be battling something of her own. "Curry, what are you doing?"

"Seeing what I can rearrange so that I can be here with Darbi." Curry tapped the small display screen, muttering to himself.

"Any luck?" Darius knew Curry had several important meetings next week. They both did. The Senate campaign was in full swing. Time off was a luxury that neither man could afford at that moment.

"No. I've got a meeting Friday and it can't be cancelled. They postponed it for me once and it wouldn't look good for me to cancel again. It's the Board of Directors, and it's about the advertising budget for next year."

"I think I have a solution," Darius started cautiously.

Curry looked at his friend. "I've thought about hiring a nurse or a maid. Where did you find Mrs. Collins?"

Darius shook his head. "It took weeks and countless interviews to find Mrs. Collins," Darius stated in his no-nonsense voice. "You don't have weeks. Why don't you guys just stay at the house until she gets off bed rest? Mrs. Collins could take care of her during the day, so you can concentrate on the Senate campaign."

Curry shook his head. "I don't know about that, Dare."

Darius pleaded his case to his friend. "It will be fine. The nurse can take care of her and Dad will be there. You have some really big meetings coming up, and you can't afford to be distracted worrying about Darbi. And I can't be distracted being worried about you. We both need to be focused on the campaign. This way we won't be worried about her care."

"Darius, I don't think it's fair to you. You have given up so much in the last year. Plus, we'd be cluttering up your house."

"Curry, you're my best friend and that's my sister. I want her to be well. I also want my niece or nephew to get here as healthy as possible. So you can live with me for a few weeks."

"I'll see what Darbi says. Although it seems the best solution, I'll still need to clear it with her. She's been a little touchy lately."

Darius laughed. Curry had indeed changed.

Hours later, Darbi opened her eyes and focused on the overhead lights. The beeping noise beside her attracted her attention. She rubbed her stomach, smiling at the sensation of kicking. The baby was going to be just fine, she mused.

Curry slept slumped in the chair. He looked like an angel. An angel who desperately needed a shave. The door opened and Darius and Cherish walked in. Darbi put her finger against her mouth, signaling them to be quiet. But it was too late; Curry had already opened his eyes.

Curry stood and stretched. "Hey, you're up. How do you feel?" His eyes glanced at the monitors. As if on cue, he watched his son or daughter turn over and then turn again.

"Dizzy," she whispered, trying to focus on her husband. His face kept going in and out of focus. She decided to watch the lights above him to steady herself and gripped the bedrails for support.

"Shelby says you lost some blood and you have a fever." Curry held her hand, caressing it gently.

Darius walked to his sister's bed and looked at the monitor before he spoke. "Shelby wants you on restricted bed rest. So I suggested to Curry you guys could live with me for a while. Before you say no, just think about it. Mrs. Collins could look after you while we're at work. So, what do you think?"

Darbi caressed her tummy with her free hand. "That sounds fine."

Darius and Curry exchanged shocked glances. Darbi had agreed too fast.

"What gives?" Darius asked as he noticed beads of perspiration across her forehead.

Darbi smiled feebly. The room had tilted. She wondered why Darius and Curry were standing on their heads. Everything looked darker. "Well, when you're bleeding, dizzy and threatening a miscarriage, independence doesn't seem so important anymore. I want a healthy baby."

Darius smiled and rubbed Darbi's hand. "You're hot!" He automatically felt her cheeks. "You're burning up! I'll get the nurse." He was out the door before Darbi could stop him.

Cherish shook her head in disbelief. Darius was going to be a nervous wreck by the time that kid got there. She turned her attention to Curry and Darbi and watched enviously as Curry helped Darbi drink a glass of water. Cherish marveled at how much Curry had changed in the last few months. She only hoped that Darius's change was coming.

Soon Darius returned with the nurse. She took Darbi's temperature and shook her head. "Okay, Mrs. Fitzgerald, your fever has increased. Dr. Allen wants you to take this. It's mild, it won't hurt the baby and it will help break your fever." She injected the medicine into the IV.

Darbi reacted to the medicine and was soon asleep. Cherish wondered how close to the due date Darbi would deliver. Curry sat by the bed watching Darbi sleep. Cherish stood and walked toward him. "Curry, why don't you and Darius go home? I'll stay with her tonight."

"No, Cherish. You've done more than your share. I'll stay."

"Curry, go home. I know you have a meeting coming up. I'll call you if anything changes."

Curry didn't move from his chair. Cherish stared at Darius until he made eye contact with her. Darius took the unspoken hint. "Come on, Curry. You won't do her any good if you are too tired."

Reluctantly, Curry agreed. After the men left, Cherish settled in the chair and watched her friend sleep. She thought of Darius; his not proposing didn't seem so important now. Her friend lying in the hospital bed was what was more important. Cherish fell asleep to the quiet hum of the machines.

Later that night, Cherish heard the door open. She assumed it was the night nurse making her rounds, but it was Darius. He walked into the room dressed in sweats and tennis shoes. She just couldn't get used to this relaxed Darius. "What are you doing here this late? It's after three in the morning." Cherish whispered so as not to wake Darbi.

Darius sat down in a chair across the room. "I couldn't sleep, so I thought I would come up here and relieve you for a little while."

"That's okay, Darius. I don't mind staying with her. She's my friend and I want to help."

"No, Cherish. Go home." He glanced at the machines. "I never realized how those machines keep track of her every breath. Amazing," Darius said, purely in awe of medical science.

"Darius, I have a flexible schedule, you don't. Curry doesn't. I'm working on Sunshine's dress and I can do that here. I don't mind."

Darius stood and walked over to Cherish. "Okay, Cherish," he agreed, seeing that he had a stubborn woman on his hands. "We can both stay. I'll just leave early enough to change clothes for work."

Cherish nodded, enjoying the company. Her shoulders felt lighter with Darius there to share the burden of watching his sister. "Okay. How's Curry?"

"Confused. He knows he has some really important meetings coming up and he wants to be here twenty-four hours a day. He knows he can't do both." Darius walked back to the chair he had vacated, and then moved it closer to Cherish. As he sat down, he noticed one of those monitors started beeping faster. A few minutes later it slowed down. He caressed Cherish's soft hand and then held it, closing his eyes and falling asleep.

～⌒つ

The next morning, Cherish woke with a smile on her face. She'd snuggled against Darius's strong chest during the night and felt safe. Glancing at her watch, she woke Darius. He had just enough time to go home, shower, dress and drive to work.

"I enjoyed last night, Cherish." He kissed her and prepared to leave.

After he left, Cherish watched Darbi sleep. She stood and leaned over the bed to get a better look at her godchild on the computer screen. She rubbed Darbi's arm, noticing she was still quite warm. The opening of the door alerted Cherish to an incoming nurse. But as she turned toward the door, she smiled as Shelby instead walked into the room.

"Hi, Cherish. How did our patient do last night? Where is her husband?" Shelby grabbed Darbi's chart and began making notes.

"She did pretty well. One of those machines sped up, then it slowed back down. I sent Curry home last night. I wanted to stay with her."

Shelby looked at the machines and pushed the button for the nurse. "Do you remember which one? She still feels a bit warm. Did she wake up last night?"

"No, she never did. She tossed and turned a little, but that's it. Why does she still have a fever?"

"Because the medicine I prescribed is very mild. I have to break her fever in stages. But it appears to have increased since last night. It's nearing the 103 mark. I'll have to increase the dosage so I can break her fever. She'll make it, Cherish. Don't worry. Why don't you go home and get some rest?"

Cherish shook her head. "I promised Curry that I would stay. He has a big presentation today."

Shelby opened her mouth, but nothing came out. The nurse walked in. "Yes, Dr. Allen?" The nurse stood waiting for instructions.

"Increase Mrs. Fitzgerald's dosage by 25 cc, per four hours, until her fever breaks. Could you get one of the transporters to find Ms. Murray a bed to sleep in? She will be staying with her friend. Make sure that she is not bothered by the other staff. If anyone has a problem with it they can come and see me."

"Yes, Dr. Allen. Right away." The nurse backed out of the room.

"Wow, Shelby. I'm impressed."

"Well, when you get the rep of a ball buster, you get results. I think most of the male doctors fear me. It's actually kind of funny."

"Thanks, Shelby, for everything you've done for her. I know it was beyond the call of being her doctor."

"Cherish, you're my friend. And I have come to think of Darbi as a friend as well."

CHAPTER TWENTY-SEVEN

A week after Darbi was released from the hospital, Darius thought he and Cherish deserved a night out. He loved his sister and brother-in-law dearly, but everyone needed a break. Darbi's stubborn streak was wearing him down fast. Not only did he have to remind his sister the rules were for her own good, he had to remind Curry.

At dinner, Darius sat across from Cherish at a crowded restaurant. He had played the scene over in his head a million times that day, had even rehearsed it with Curry. Why couldn't he choke out a simple marriage proposal? Four simple words.

He watched her as she perused the menu. She was gorgeous. Her shoulder length hair was up in a French roll, showing off the graceful column of her slender neck. Diamond earrings dangled from her delicate ears. She gave him a seductive smile, as if she didn't know she was turning him on in a room full of people. He was about to speak when they were interrupted.

"Hi, Cherish."

"Hello, Sunshine. How are you? This is my friend, Darius Crawford. Darius, this is Sunshine Brady, a client." Cherish smiled with pride.

Darius stood and shook her hand. "Please to meet you, Ms. Brady." So this is Sunshine, he thought. She lived up to her name. The petite blonde seemed to brighten up the room with that million-watt smile.

"It's nice to meet you as well," Sunshine said as Darius took his seat. "I'm meeting Preston here for dinner to discuss the honeymoon plans. You know men, you have to make them decide on these things or they would never get done. I guess I'll see you next Wednesday, Cherish. How's Darbi?"

"She's much better. Thanks for asking."

"She's nice. She should be a poster woman for pregnancy. She looks so radiant and that gorgeous husband of hers dotes on her like crazy. Preston better treat me like that when we start our family. Well, see you Wednesday." Sunshine walked away from the table.

Darius watched the small woman leave the table, wondering when Curry had met Sunshine and why he hadn't mentioned it. Darius instantly knew why. Since falling in love with Darbi, other women had ceased to exist in his eyes. "How are the plans coming?"

"Pretty good. She's finally approved my sketches for her wedding dress. This is her fourth, you know."

"Wow, that's amazing. How can anyone be married that many times?" He watched as a funny look crossed Cherish's face. Was she sick?

"I don't know, Darius. Excuse me," Cherish murmured as she placed her napkin on the table.

Darius watched Cherish walk hurriedly to the ladies' room, minutes from an emotional outburst. Something was wrong. Why couldn't women just say what was bothering them? He wondered if she was worried about

Darbi. A few minutes later she returned. Darius spoke, hoping to ease her worry. "I'm sure Darbi is fine."

"I know." She smiled stiffly at him. "I'm starving. Where's our food?" Luckily the waiter appeared with a rolling tray.

After the waiter distributed the food, he left the table and conversation resumed.

"How is Otis? I know he seems ready for the baby to get here. You think a baby will affect his illness in any way?" Cherish picked at her food.

"I'm hoping it keeps him active. He asked me if Darbi was going to stay at home with the baby or return to school. I know Curry doesn't want her to work or go to school, so he's pushing for her to stay home. But I can't see her doing that." Darius knew his sister wanted her college degree, even if she would never use it.

Cherish had thought about that too. "If she does return to college, I would love to baby-sit. I love kids and I don't live that far from the college."

"You could always come to the house to baby-sit. That way Dad would see the baby all the time."

Cherish ordered a crème brulee for dessert. When it arrived, she picked up her spoon and cracked the top caramel layer with just a little too much enthusiasm, attracting the attention of the other patrons as well as Darius.

"Cherish, are you okay?" Darius hoped Cherish wasn't having some sort of fit.

"Yes, Darius. I'm fine now." She ate the custard and savored every bite.

~~~~

When they entered Darius's house, it was so quiet Cherish asked, "Should we check on them? It's after ten."

Darius nodded. Hand in hand they walked to Darbi's closed door. Light spilled into the hallway from under the door. "They're still up," Cherish whispered, leaning against the door to listen for noise. All she heard was a passionate moan from Darbi. Surely they weren't having sex, she thought. She knocked on the door, determined to protect her godchild. She waited a few moments, and then opened the door.

They were on top of the bed covers, dressed in pajamas and lying spoon fashion. Curry stopped caressing Darbi's stomach at the sight of Darius and Cherish in the doorway. "What is it?"

Cherish blushed. When Curry didn't remove his hands from under Darbi's nightshirt, Cherish averted her gaze, noticing their feet. They were entwined and rubbing against each other. The pose did nothing for Cherish's libido. "Nothing. Just checking on you guys, goodnight." She hurriedly closed the door. Why couldn't Darius be just a little like that?

Darius led her down the hall to his bedroom. Once inside, he sat on the bed, watching her every move as she prepared for bed. "What's wrong, Cherish? You've been in an odd mood for the last few weeks. Is it because we haven't made love in three weeks? You know we have both been very busy."

Cherish shook her head. Men! How blind, dumb, and thick could one man be? "No, Darius. I hadn't even thought about it. I guess I was thinking about Darbi and Curry. They look so happy together. Their gold bands always seemed to shine at me. Sometimes I wonder if they had this last year to do over if they would have still met and gotten together."

Darius nodded. "Probably. It was weird that they hadn't met before that class. Just like us. It was meant to be." Darius slid from the bed and headed for the shower.

A ringing phone woke Darius early Saturday morning. He answered by the third ring and sat up as he recognized the caller's voice.

"Darius, this is Sarah Fitzgerald, Curran's mother. I was wondering if Curran and Darbi are out of town? I thought she couldn't travel anywhere. Is everything all right? I've been having an awful feeing lately. I've called the house several times with no luck. I even called the shop and got no answer."

"They're staying here, Mrs. Fitzgerald. Is Mr. Fitzgerald all right?" Darius asked, remembering about Curry's father's heart condition.

Sarah giggled. "You're as bad as Curran. I can call with something other than bad news. Thomas is fine. I was just calling to see how Darbi is. I got worried when I didn't get an answer at the house or at Cherish's shop."

"They've been here a week. Darbi was in the hospital for a few days last week and is on bed rest. Curry wasn't going to have time to hire a nurse to take care of Darbi while he was at work, so they came here," Darius explained.

"Why didn't he call us? We're family, too!" Sarah's voice rose slightly. "We could have flown down there with no problem and taken care of her. That's our grand-child, too," she whispered in a small voice. "All he had to do was call."

Darius was stumped. Sarah sounded hurt that they hadn't called her. He didn't know what to tell Curry's mother. "It was not intentional, Mrs. Fitzgerald." Darius pleaded Curry's case, knowing there would be hell to pay with this woman.

"I'm sure it wasn't. Could I speak to my son, please?"

Darius looked at his phone as if it had just bit him. "Sure, Mrs. Fitzgerald." That woman was pissed. Darius took the cordless phone down the hall to Curry.

He opened the door to their room, and smiled. Curry and Darbi were sound asleep. Even in their sleep, they held each other closely. Reluctantly, he tapped Curry's shoulder. He moaned, snuggling closer to Darbi. Darius repeated the action. Curry finally opened his eyes. "What is it, Dare?"

"It's your mom."

Those three words woke Curry completely. He eased out of Darbi's embrace and got out of bed. He took the phone out of the room and into the hall. Darius followed him, closing the door. Curry took a deep breath, looked at Darius, and whispered into the phone, "Hi, Mom."

"Curran, you could have called us. We are also your family."

"I know, Mom. Everything just happened so fast."

"Well, how is she doing?"

"She's better. She just has to stay in bed for the next few weeks. We'll know more at the next sonogram. The doctor says the baby will be likely a month early."

"You could have just called us. We would have been happy to help. In fact, we still will. I'll call you with our flight information." Sarah ended the call before he could say anything else.

Curry looked at the phone as it hummed at him. He turned the phone off and leaned against the wall for support, closing his eyes.

"What is it?" Darius asked, hoping there wasn't another crisis around the corner.

Curry opened his eyes and faced his friend, shrugging his shoulders. "Not much, my parents are coming here to take care of Darbi."

"You're kidding. Your mother? Sarah Fitzgerald? Just when did hell freeze over?"

Curry nodded. "I know, but she says I should have called her. I just can't figure Mom out anymore. She calls sometimes and never speaks to me." He opened the door to the room and told Darbi the latest.

When Darius returned to his room, Cherish was still asleep. He smiled as he watched her feel his side of the bed for him. Immediately, she sat up and looked around the room for him, smiling as she noticed him in the doorway.

He walked back to the bed and got in. She welcomed him into her embrace and snuggled against his strong chest. "Is Darbi okay?"

Darius kissed her forehead. "I don't know. She was asleep." Slowly he pulled her on top of him. "Curry's mom called and I went to give him the phone." Darius kissed her deeply as his hands roamed freely over her naked body.

Cherish spoke when he finally ended the kiss. "Maybe you should put a phone in their room." Cherish handed Darius a gold packet.

Darius slid the condom on in record time, instantly reaching for Cherish. She gasped as he entered her in one smooth move.

"Actually, his parents are coming to take care of them. So they'll be going home soon." Darius moaned. "We can either talk about them or we can continue this activity. Which shall it be, Cherish?"

"Since you put it like that, I guess the latter." She kissed him loudly on the mouth and wiggled her hips. He had just rolled her over so that he was top when there was a knock at the bedroom door. He looked at Cherish and whispered, "See, you were too loud. What?" he yelled.

A discreet cough was his answer. "Mr. Crawford, I was just wondering when you want breakfast served."

"Give us about thirty minutes," he said through gritted teeth.

"Yes, Mr. Crawford."

It was more than thirty minutes before Darius dragged out of bed. After he had coaxed Cherish into another lovemaking session, they took a shower, dressed, and went downstairs. Cherish's small hand warmed his entire body as he held it going downstairs.

They took a seat at the table and Mrs. Collins soon brought their plates. They ate breakfast in silence until Curry joined them. The nurse put a plate in front of him almost as soon as he sat down.

"I see you and Darbi are doing fine, huh?" Cherish giggled.

"Yes, we are." Curry glanced at Cherish. She had a smirk on her face.

Darius coughed. "What Cherish is referring to is that hickey the size of a nickel on your neck. I trust there was no sex involved." He also knew Curry hadn't had it earlier.

Curry quickly rose from the table and walked to the downstairs bathroom. He returned, muttering to himself. "I don't remember that, pity. It must have been after that massage." He smiled to himself as he resumed eating.

As she refilled the coffee cups at the table, Mrs. Collins asked, "Mr. Fitzgerald, would you like me to carry Mrs. Fitzgerald's breakfast to her?"

"No, Mrs. Collins, she's still asleep. I'll take it up to her later." He smiled at the nurse and thanked her.

"I'll leave it on the stove for you." She exited the dining room quickly.

Darius couldn't believe the changes in Curry in the last few months. He was no longer the hollow man that love eluded but a man deeply in love. He was content and happy and it showed, making Darius envious. "It's nice to know that you aren't neglecting my sister, but remember, she's twenty-six weeks. Be careful."

"We are careful. She attacked me while I was asleep. Mom's phone call really freaked me out this morning, but when I told Darbi, she was all calm about it. I so hope that kid is a boy. I just can't seem to figure women out any more."

Cherish giggled as the men continued talking as if she weren't there. "Curry, you aren't supposed to figure us out. That's what makes it fun."

Curry shook his head. "Mom sounded really upset that we didn't think to call her. I know a lecture about the responsibility to family will accompany this visit."

"I think it's sweet that your mom is coming. It shows she really accepts Darbi and wants to help," Cherish offered as she sipped her coffee.

"See, Dare. This is what I mean." He pointed at Cherish as she giggled uncontrollably.

CHAPTER TWENTY-EIGHT

A week later, Otis sat across the breakfast table from Darius and Cherish. Darbi and Curry had left the week before and the house didn't seem the same. Otis talked to his daughter every day, but he hadn't seen her since Curry's parents came to town. Although he wanted to see his baby girl, something else claimed his attention now.

He studied the couple across from him. Darius had a strange look in his eyes. Was it longing? Otis wondered if Darius would ever get around to proposing to Cherish. He watched as Cherish rose and kissed Darius on the cheek.

She then came to Otis. "Otis, I'll see you later." She kissed the wise old man on his weathered cheek.

"Where are you going, girl?"

"I need to get started on Sunshine's wedding dress. The wedding's only four months away. I just can't seem to concentrate when I'm here." She gazed in Darius's direction.

"I understand." Otis smiled at his son. Beneath that chocolate brown skin, Otis knew Darius was blushing.

After Cherish left, Otis decided a little father-son talk was in order. "When are you going to propose to her?"

Darius dropped his fork.

Otis laughed. "Well, at least you're thinking about it, but are you ever going to ask her?"

One afternoon a few days later, Cherish sat in her office, the stereo blaring her favorite old school mix. She was desperately trying to lighten her mood, but it seemed a lost cause. She'd finished the final details of Sunshine's wedding dress. It was perfect. The white gown was laced with pearls and hugged her waist. Yet there was not a lot of satisfaction as she finalized most of the details of the wedding.

She missed her friend. She needed a shoulder to lean on. Since Curry's parents had arrived, Darbi was being looked after but Sarah was quite strict, not allowing Darbi to have visitors at lunch. Suddenly realizing it was past Darbi's lunchtime, Cherish closed the shop and headed for Darbi's house.

Sarah answered the door and Cherish greeted her with a smile. "Hi, Mrs. Fitzgerald, is Darbi awake?"

"She was sleeping earlier. I'll go check on her. Thomas is in the living room."

Cherish took the hint and walked into the living room. Thomas sat in a chair reading the newspaper. He stood as Cherish entered. "Hello, Mr. Fitzgerald. How are you feeling?"

He smiled at Cherish. "Pretty good. Just waiting on my grandson to get here. It feels like our first grandchild instead of our sixteenth. I think it's because it's Curry's.

We thought he would never settle down." Thomas sat back down.

Sarah entered the living room. "Okay, Cherish, she's awake."

"Is she okay?"

"She's had a little fever today. My grandson is being very active."

Cherish smiled as she walked up the stairs. *If that kid knows best, it had better be a boy.* She walked into the room and greeted Darbi as she sat up in bed.

"Cherish, are you okay? You look like you've been crying." Darbi patted the space beside her.

Cherish sat in the space offered. She smiled at Darbi's concern for her. "I guess I just wanted to talk."

"What is it, Cherish?"

She took a deep breath and began. "Well, I was working on Sunshine's wedding dress and I just got to thinking about everything. Darius won't or can't propose. Sunshine is on her fourth husband and is barely thirty years old. Today, I turned 40."

"Cherish, I'm sorry that I didn't realize it was your birthday." Darbi gently caressed Cherish's arm in sympathy.

"I know. Anyway, I'm not really into celebrating birthdays anymore. I told Darius a few months ago, but that was pre-pregnancy so maybe he forgot."

"I'm sorry, Cherish," Darbi said. "Hey, we could order pizza and celebrate here. I don't think the Sarah Gestapo will let me have any, but we can still celebrate. You can eat my share. Plus, Curry is out with Darius, doing some male bonding. We could have a girls' night in."

Cherish smiled at Darbi's attempt to make her feel better. It was just what she needed. "Pizza sounds great. I wish you could have some. But just think, in a little while you will be holding a baby in your arms." She tried to keep the envy out of her voice.

Darbi rubbed her stomach and grinned widely. "The first thing I'm doing is drinking the biggest glass of Coke you have ever seen!"

After they informed Sarah of the pizza delivery, the women decided to watch some movies. At first, Cherish felt odd, lying on Curry's side of the king-sized bed. Darbi eased her nerves.

"Mom changes the sheets every day." She winked at Cherish. "Anyway, the most we do in bed is cuddle."

Cherish relaxed in the bed beside Darbi and they were engrossed in the movie by the time the pizza arrived.

After pigging out on pizza, Cherish felt better. She was spending her birthday with her best friend. "I think I'm going to tell Darius we should see other people."

"Why?" Darbi asked as she ate her smoked turkey sandwich and drank her milk, though she wanted the thick crust pepperoni.

Cherish sighed and picked up another piece of pizza. "I feel like we're going nowhere and I'll just feel more and more anger toward him for not asking." She took a bite. "I don't want to be one of those women who wastes her life waiting for the man who never asks."

"Cherish, just give him some time. He's slow emotionally."

"I know. I had to wait for him to ask me out, for us to make love, and for him to say 'I love you.' But I'm tired of waiting. Maybe I just need a breather. Who knows, maybe I don't want to be married. Plus, I don't want to be the one with the balls in the family."

Darbi laughed at Cherish's choice of words. "Cherish, I do know he's trying to work through some issues right now."

"Why couldn't we work on those issues together? That's what couples are supposed to do. They help each other through the troubled times, not shut the other out. Am I supposed to just wait around until he works this out?" She shook her head. Darbi nodded. "Just think before you talk to him."

"Okay, promise."

~~~

Curry walked into Darius's office Monday morning expecting to see his friend smiling. He was supposed to have proposed to Cherish Sunday night. The grim look on his face told Curry that something hadn't gone as planned. Curry took a deep breath and sat down. "Dare?"

Darius's brown eyes gazed into space; he didn't answer.

"What happened? Is it Otis? Why didn't you call?"

Darius finally looked in Curry's direction. "I went to Cherish's last night, ready to propose."

Curry nodded. "Okay, go on."

Darius stood, walked to the doorway and closed the door, something he rarely did. He stalked back to his chair and plopped down, letting out a tired breath. "Well, we were sitting on her couch and she starts talking again about Sunshine's wedding. You know, stuff like this was her fourth wedding, and the guy's third, and they're acting like it was their first. Then she says she's making all these networking contacts due to Sunshine and already has four high profile weddings lined up for between Valentine's and Easter!"

"Yeah." Curry nervously tapped his finger on the armrest of the chair, waiting for the bad news. "Darius, spit it out!"

"Then she starts spouting some gibberish about needing space and I kind of over-reacted," he said.

"What did you do?" Curry asked.

"I screwed up and said some things I shouldn't have," Darius admitted. "I don't know how to fix it."

"Dare, I'm sure this is fixable. You are going to have to give her the space she's asking for. She's just having a moment. She turned 40 Friday, so maybe she's feeling that clock thing," Curry reassured his friend.

"Oh, man." Darius held his head in hands. "I forgot her birthday, too!"

"I thought you knew," Curry said, regretting having made the situation worse than it already was. "When I got home Friday night, Cherish was over. She ended up spending the night and sleeping in my bed with my wife!" Curry smiled at the memory of seeing the two women asleep in bed.

Darius shook his head. "How will I ever get out of this mess? Changing the subject, when is Darbi's sonogram?"

"In two days, why?"

"I want to be there," Darius said.

"I thought seeing her lying on the table like that made you sick." Curry remembered the one and only sonogram Darius had attended a few months ago. He got sick and threw up on the doctor.

"I still want to be there."

Curry shrugged his shoulders, dropping the subject. "It's Wednesday at eleven. Mom is convinced it's a boy and it will be early."

Darius smiled. If Sarah Fitzgerald said it, then it was true. "I'm going to take the rest of the day off, and probably tomorrow, too. Can you handle the campaign by yourself?"

"Yes, it's just overseeing those last final commercials. Hopefully no scandal will surface between now and the election. Go make up with Cherish."

Darius smiled and left his office, intending to do just that.

CHAPTER TWENTY-NINE

"Darius, what on earth?" Cherish opened her front door and let him inside. Discreetly, she wiped her eyes and faked a smile.

"H-how are you, Cherish?" The sight of her swollen eyes was almost too much for him to handle.

"Fine," came her short reply. "Why are you here, Darius? My new lover will be over in just a minute," she added sarcastically.

Darius sat on the couch and lowered his head in shame. "I'm sorry, Cherish. I've really been on edge lately. I know that's not an excuse. I shouldn't have accused you of those things."

Cherish walked to the couch, but remained standing. "Darius, I suggested we see other people not to break up or whatever this is. I just want to exercise all my options. I don't want to end up some bitter woman because I waited for you."

"I don't want to date anyone else. I want you! Can't you see that? Why are you being so difficult?"

"Because, Darius Andrew Crawford, I have no commitment from you." She sat by him. "Think of it this way. You think you have just landed a huge contract, but you don't have confirmation. I need confirmation, Darius. I need to know that I'm what you think about when we aren't together. I want to know that we connect spiritually as well as physically."

"Cherish, we do connect. I can talk to you for hours. I always ask your opinions. I think you are smart and beautiful."

She stared into space. "I just feel like we'll be at this stage forever." She stood. "I need some space. Give me a few days." She walked to the door and opened it. "Good-bye, Darius."

He closed the door and pulled her to the couch. "I'm not giving you space, Cherish."

"Darius, what the hell?"

He kneeled in front of her, taking her smaller hands in his large ones. "I love you, Cherish. You're the main reason I haven't gone over the edge emotionally. You keep me grounded. You make me want this so much, I can't wait."

"W-wait for what?"

His eyes told her everything that was in his heart. "I wanted to wait until I had the perfect speech, the perfect place and the perfect ring. But I have the perfect woman, so this is good enough for me. Will you marry me?" Cherish was shocked. The answer was on the tip of her tongue, but she couldn't push the words out of her mouth.

"Cherish," Darius said. "Did you hear me?"

She nodded.

"Well?" He smiled at her. "Can I get an answer?" He kissed her softly.

She nodded.

"What's your answer?" He kissed her again.

Her face split into a wide grin. "Yes, Darius, I will marry you." She wrapped her arms around him and hugged the stuffing out of him.

Darius wasn't quite prepared for that. He landed on the floor, flat on his back with Cherish on top of him. "Thank you, Cherish. I will love you with my last breath."

She kissed him. "Oh, just shut up and kiss me."

"Happily."

~~~

"You think Darbi and Curry will be surprised?" Cherish asked, stepping out of the shower. She and Darius had just finished celebrating their engagement.

Darius looked at her naked body as he wrapped a towel around his waist. "Probably, I'm still in shock myself. I hadn't planned on proposing today, but I'm very glad I did. When do you want to get married?"

Cherish wasn't expecting that question so soon. She'd expected Darius to drag his heels as he had during the course of their relationship. She decided to see what Darius Crawford was made of. "How about New Year's? It's about three months away."

Darius stared at her, smiling. "I think it sounds great. And we could honeymoon in Hawaii." He walked toward her. "A New Year's Day wedding would mark the start of our new life together. Our separate lives will become one."

Cherish tied the sash on her bathrobe. "You're a romantic, aren't you." She stepped closer to him. "You're a closet romantic."

Darius smiled shyly. "That has to stay our secret. Darbi would never let me live it down." He reached for her and she went into his arms. "I thought we were going to go tell Darbi and Curry the good news, but I can't think about getting dressed with you looking all sexy like that."

Cherish stepped back, untied her robe and let it fall to the floor. She stood before her fiancé without a stitch of clothing on and basked in his approval of her body. "Tomorrow. We can tell them tomorrow at the sonogram."

Darius let his towel drop to the floor. He picked Cherish up and carried her back to the bedroom, deposited her on the bed, and lay beside her. He kissed her slowly and thoroughly. "Tomorrow sounds good."

The next day as Darbi lay on the examination table, she didn't feel well. Her head ached and she was begin-ning to feel dizzy. As she held Curry's hand, she felt her grip weakening. Instead of the usual nurse, it was the physician's assistant, Max, who would be helping Shelby. Now he was conversing with Shelby; something wasn't right.

"I'm sure everything is fine, honey," Curry tried to reassure Darbi. "Try to calm down." He kissed her forehead.

"I wish I could be sure, Curry." Darbi smiled through her teary eyes as she noticed both Darius and Cherish entering the room holding hands and grinning.

Darbi sighed. Her brother had proposed. No one had to tell her; she knew from the larger-than-life smiles they both wore. Nevertheless, she was thrilled to see the three-carat diamond ring on Cherish's left hand. "Darius?"

He laughed and kissed Cherish on the mouth. "Yes, Darbi, we're officially engaged."

"I knew it would happen," Curry said, grinning. "Congratulations, guys. When's the big day?"

"New Year's Day." Darius and Cherish answered together.

"That's wonderful, Cherish. Now we'll really be sisters. And I can help you plan your wedding, just like you did for me."

Shelby and Max rejoined the foursome, halting all the wedding talk. She raised Darbi's hospital gown and put the cold gel on her stomach. "Well, Darbi, are you ready?" Shelby smiled at her patient.

Darbi smiled as she released Curry's hand. "Yes. Can you tell me the sex of the baby?"

"Weren't you the one saying you wanted to be surprised?" Curry asked as he caressed his wife's forehead.

"I changed my mind." Darbi tried to display an air of confidence. She had the feeling something bad might happen and that had compelled her to ask the question.

Shelby laughed at the interaction between the family members and began the sonogram. "Darbi, you feel warm. Any pain or discomfort, more than usual?" Her hand hovered over Darbi's enlarged abdomen.

"This morning. It felt like indigestion or something."

"I'll check your temp after this." Shelby continued moving the wand over her stomach. She smiled. "It's a boy!" She pointed to the obvious body part on the computer screen.

Curry sobbed uncontrollably as he watched his son on the screen. When the baby gave his mom a good strong kick, he said, "I told you he would be a soccer player!" He kissed his wife and wiped some of her tears away. "I love you, Darbi."

As Shelby continued the sonogram, moving her cold hands over Darbi's stomach, Darbi felt a sharp, piercing pain. "Ow!" Darbi's high-pitched yell silenced the previous moment's joy.

"What is it?" Shelby asked, putting the wand away. "Where is the pain?"

Darbi's shortness of breath made Darius's heart race with fear. After an eternity, she said, "It feels like my side. Like someone is poking my left side."

Shelby examined the lower part of Darbi's stomach. Blood. She signaled her assistant while speaking to Darbi. "Your wound is opening. We're going to have to act fast." She looked in Curry's direction as she spoke.

"Darbi will be in surgery a few hours. I'm sorry, Curry, you can't come in for the birth as we planned originally. You'll have to wait with Darius and Cherish. Remember, no news is good news," she told him and walked out of the room hurriedly.

The transporters came and took Darbi away. The three walked to the waiting room and took a seat. Darius used his cell phone to call his father to let him know his grandson was on his way. Then he called Thomas and Sarah and handed the phone to Curry so he could tell his parents. Curry opened his mouth to speak, but no words came out, only deep, heart-wrenching sobs. He handed the phone back to Darius to break the news to the Fitzgeralds.

"Darius, do you want us to come?" Sarah asked, her voice choked with tears.

Reluctantly, Darius took charge of the situation. He thought it would be best if Curry's parents stayed home. Sarah wasn't exactly doctor friendly. "No, Mrs. Fitzgerald. If anything changes, I'll call you." He pushed the end button on his cell phone. He then called work and explained the situation to their boss.

After all the calls were taken care of, Darius had the task of comforting his brother-in-law. "Now, Curry, we both know Shelby is an excellent doctor, and Darbi is a survivor, she'll make it."

"At what cost?" Curry rubbed his face nervously. "I have never been so near to having everything I want in my life. I'm scared I'll lose it all, Darius." He lowered his head.

Darius didn't have any comforting words for Curry as he felt the same way about his sister. Darbi had been through so much and just when it looked as if happiness was hers, there was another disaster.

He looked at Cherish, silently asking for help. She stood and Darius moved so she could sit next to Curry. She gently caressed his tanned hand. "I don't want to lose my friend either."

Five hours later, Shelby appeared at the waiting room entrance. Curry stood immediately, bracing himself for the worst possible scenario. He tried to take a deep breath but it came out as a sob. Shelby took off her face mask and walked toward him, her face expressionless.

"She did fine, Curry. I stitched up the wound and she shouldn't have any more problems. Usually, a C-section takes a month to recover. Since surgery was also performed it will be closer to three months' recovery time."

Curry nodded, taking in what she said. Shelby hadn't mentioned the baby. What about the baby? He didn't know if he wanted to hear the answer to his question. "H-how about the baby?" He forced the question out of his mouth.

Shelby took a deep breath and spoke slowly. "Your son is in critical condition. Because he was born over two months early, his lungs aren't fully developed yet. He's in NICU, Neo-natal Intensive Care. He'll be in an incubator for the first few weeks, but I'm confident he will be fine. Both he and Darbi will be in the hospital for at least three to four weeks. Otherwise, things look good. I think it was due to all the care and love she received during her pregnancy. Things could have been much worse."

All this medical mumbo jumbo was fine and all, but now Curry wanted to see his wife. He wanted to touch her, hold her, and tell her that he loved her. "Can I see Darbi?"

"I could say no, but I know it will be useless against you guys." She glanced at Cherish and Darius as well. "Give her a couple of hours to get back to the room.

Right now, she's in recovery and I want to watch her for a while for any post-surgery complications."

Curry nodded. He was so overcome with emotion he pulled Shelby into his arms and hugged her. "Thank you, Shelby." The words didn't seem enough for saving the woman he loved and his child.

Shelby, being a doctor, was used to a new father's uncontrollable runaway emotions, and hugged him back. Gently, she eased out of the embrace, straightening her lab jacket. "You can see your son now. You won't be able to hold him, but you can see him."

Shelby looked directly at him, her brown eyes unwavering. "He weighs about two pounds and is very susceptible to germs at this time. Preemies should be handled as little as possible. Be patient, in a week or two he will be out of the danger zone and you will be able to hold him," she said, patting him on the shoulder.

A misty-eyed Curry nodded. When Shelby left the room, he sat down in the nearest chair and closed his eyes, giving thanks to the Almighty.

Darius wasn't quite sure as to what to do. This wasn't the Curry he had known over the years. This was a man thankful for the blessing of life he had just received. His wife and son were going to be fine. Darius saw tears escaping from behind Curry's closed lids.

"I'm glad things went so well," Cherish said to no one in particular. "Curry, if your parents need to get back to Seattle, I would be more than willing to come and help with Darbi and the baby."

Curry smiled. "Thanks, Cherish. I appreciate it."

Darius joined the conversation. "If your parents need to go back, you guys are coming back to the house," Darius said matter-of-factly.

Curry stared at his best friend, who had become his brother-in-law, and began to smile. "Thanks, Dare, but somehow I don't think you could make Mom leave now. But how could we have ever made it without you?"

A few hours later, Cherish softly stepped into Darbi's room. Shelby had pulled a few strings so Darbi could have a private room. The room was dark and quiet and Darbi slept soundly. No longer were there machines keeping track of her every move. Cherish was grateful for the quiet. She had coaxed Darius into making Curry leave long enough to eat something. They had been at the hospital practically all day and night.

She sat in the chair nearest the bed and surveyed the bouquets, balloons, and cookie grams. She stood and walked over to read some of the cards. To her surprise, the gifts were from Curry's family in Seattle, Curry's boss, Darbi's ex-supervisor, Sunshine, and the greatest surprise of them all, DeMarcus.

"Cherish, what are you doing here?" Darbi asked in a whisper.

She immediately walked back to the bed. "I was waiting for my best friend to wake up." She sat down in the chair, carefully watching Darbi for any signs of discomfort. "How do you feel?"

"Sick. Did the baby make it? Where's Curry?" Darbi moaned in pain as she attempted to turn to face Cherish.

"Yes, he made it. He's in an incubator right now; his lungs weren't fully developed. Shelby says he'll have to be there a while. He's beautiful. He's got a head of curly hair and hazel eyes like his father. Curry and Darius went to get something to eat. Curry hadn't eaten all day."

"I'm glad you made them go eat and I'm glad you're here," Darbi whispered, reaching for Cherish's hand. "I'm so glad you're my friend."

Darius and Curry returned to the room and saw Cherish holding Darbi's hand as they talked. Curry smiled at his wife. Nothing in his life could compare to the happiness he felt. He had a wife he loved with all his heart and a new son. His best friend had proposed to a woman he truly deserved. "Cherish, you were supposed to call me," he admonished as Cherish vacated the chair next to the bed.

"Sorry, Curry. We started talking and . . ."

"I know, you forgot all about me." He laughed as he sat on the hospital bed, eschewing the chair. "How do you feel?" He caressed Darbi's hand.

"I feel warm and tired. You know, like after one of your marathons." She smiled as she kissed his hand.

Shelby walked into the room, shaking her head. "I thought the nurses were kidding. You are up! I know you probably feel like crap right now. You'll feel that way for a few days. I fixed your wound and stitched it properly. But . . ." She paused. "I hate to be the bearer of bad news." Shelby bit her lip.

The room was suddenly quiet. "What is it?" Darbi asked.

"This should be your first and only birth. I—"

Darbi laughed. "Don't worry, he'll be an only child. Do you actually think I would go through this again?"

Shelby laughed. "Well, I like to let my patients know everything up front."

"I appreciate that, Shelby. But this factory is closed. I was blessed once and that will be enough."

Shelby left the room. Curry leaned over the bed to give his wife the kind of kiss she had been requesting for the last month. Darius interrupted them.

"Hey guys, slow down." Darius laughed as they ignored him and continued kissing.

Finally, they stopped. "Now, that is a kiss," Darbi said. Then she and Curry laughed; Darius and Cherish were kissing like teenagers in heat.

Curry winked at his wife and mother of his child. "We can't let them outdo us, can we?"

"No, we can't." She pulled his head toward hers for another heart-stopping kiss.

EPILOGUE

ONE YEAR LATER

Cherish watched Darbi chase her year-old son around the living room with a disposable diaper in her hand. Christian Crawford Fitzgerald was a ball of energy and had just mastered walking.

He giggled as his mother finally caught up with him. His little chubby honey-beige cheeks were red from the chase. Darbi quickly changed his diaper and dressed him in his birthday outfit. The minute she fastened the last button on his baby Gap shirt, he took off again.

Darbi let out a tired breath and plopped on the sofa. "Just wait, Cherish. You'll soon be doing this too. Chris wasn't this active before Curry and I left for Ireland. Now it's like he wants me to chase him all over the house."

Cherish rubbed her stomach. At 41, she was finally going to be a mother. She'd married Darius ten months earlier on New Year's Day and she was eight weeks pregnant. She and Darius had had a dose of instant parenting for the two weeks Darbi and Curry were in Ireland.

"Darbi, I swear, he wasn't like this when you guys were gone. It was like he knew that I wouldn't play with him like that. He was quite a handful, though. I don't think he went to bed on time once, thanks to Darius."

She smiled at the memory of Darius falling asleep with Christian lying on top of him.

Otis walked into the room, dressed in a sweatshirt and sweat pants, with the nurse discreetly behind. He sat on the couch, by his daughter. "Darbi, why is Christian beating on your back door?"

Darbi rose, walking toward the kitchen. "He's waiting for Curry to come back. He and Darius went to the store to get Chris's cake."

Cherish laughed, watching her sister-in-law disappear to the back of the house. "I still can't believe that Darbi is back to her pre-pregnancy weight. I hope I have the same luck."

Otis laughed. "If your baby's anything like Chris, you'll have no problem. That boy never stops moving."

Cherish reflected over the last year after Chris made his entrance into the world two months early. Darbi and Curry had blossomed under the new addition to their family and were more in love now than ever.

Darius and Curry had both received promotions at work. Darius was now a full partner and Curry had Darius's old job as marketing vice-president. Darbi was getting ready to return to college after her stint as a stay-at-home mom. Cherish had offered to baby sit while she was in class. And though he'd had occasional lapses, all in all Otis was doing reasonably well. Being surrounded by happy people seemed to be a magical elixir.

"How many times have I told you not to hit the door?" Darbi entered the room with her son on her hip.

She smothered his chubby face with kisses. "You are as stubborn as your father."

Christian smiled as his mother scolded him, grabbing her earring. "Oh no, you don't." Darbi tapped his little hand.

She heard the back door open and Chris scrambled to get down. Darbi let him down and he took off again for the kitchen.

"I see what you mean, Dad." Cherish laughed, rising to meet Darius as he and Curry came in with the cake.

She met him as they entered the dining room. Her hormones had been giving her fits the last few days. Today was no exception. She kissed him as he placed the cake on the table.

"What's that for?" He put his arm around her, guiding her to the living room.

"I just missed you."

"Hey, you gave me a workout last night. Not that I mind, but I'm worried about you." He kissed her. "I want you to rest and do nothing, okay? You're carrying a Crawford, you must be careful." He kissed her again.

Cherish sighed. Knowing that Darius, Curry, and Darbi wouldn't let her help with anything, she sat on the couch beside Otis.

"Dad, are you sure you feel okay?"

Otis smiled. "Yes, Cherish, I feel good. It's my grandson's first birthday, I got another grandbaby on the way and my children are here with me today. The world never looked brighter. Baby girl looks like she's in seventh heaven with Curry doting on her all the time. She deserves that. Not to mention I gained another daughter when Darius married you."

Cherish couldn't help the tears that sprang to her eyes as she hugged Otis. After losing her mother, after all the dark days of grief and guilt, she'd been welcomed into this wonderful, loving family. She glanced over Otis's shoulder to see Darius smiling at her, his eyes aglow with love for her. As always, her heart skipped a beat. The arrival of their child would complete everything she'd ever wanted. She wished her mother could know all this. Even as the wish came, she sensed that maybe she did.

ABOUT THE AUTHOR

Celya Bowers was born and raised in a small Central Texas town. After attending Sam Houston State University in Huntsville, Texas, she relocated to Arlington, Texas. Her hobbies include reading, writing, listening to audio books and keeping in touch with good friends.

Her love of books started at a very young age and she's been an avid reader ever since. Being a die-hard romantic, she enjoys writing about falling in love, no matter the cost. Quirky plots are her favorites, but true love is worth it all.

Celya is a member of Romance Writers of America, Dallas Area Romance Authors, and Kiss of Death. She is also currently a member of the Sizzling Sisterhood Critique Group.

Please visit her website at *www.celyabowers.net.*

**Coming in January 2008 from Genesis Press—an
exciting debut novel by Maryam Diaab.**

1

WHAT'S GOIN' ON?

Alexis rolled over on her crisp white Ralph Lauren
sheets, an uncharacteristic splurge, and looked over at the
pillow next to her. Kevin was gone. The man who had
been there last night and gave her so much pleasure had
disappeared—as usual. Her memories of their lovemaking vanished in an instant. She ran her manicured
hand over the pillow, trying to gauge how long she had
been sleeping alone. The cool pillow suggested she had
probably been alone minutes after she had fallen asleep.

This disappearing act was an ongoing sore point
between Kevin and Alexis in the six months they had
been together. They would have amazing dates, followed
by amazing nights together. Afterward they would talk
about their hopes and dreams until they fell asleep in
each other's arms. Alexis would wake up smiling until she
saw and touched that cool pillow. She had questioned
Kevin about it numerous times, and he always had what

seemed to be a perfectly plausible excuse: He had to be at work really early in the morning or he had to chauffeur his mother to the doctor. It was always something, and she always ended up frustrated and disappointed.

Alexis rolled out of bed, tugging at her white Victoria's Secret silk gown, which had bunched up around her waist, crossing the carpeted bedroom to her beautifully decorated living room. Beige couches, matching chaise lounge, and antique walnut cocktail table, all purchased at estate sales and bargain warehouses, lent a warm and luxurious feel to the room. The walls had been recently changed from basic "apartment" white to a gorgeous shade of camel accented with midnight-blue trim, reflecting Alexis' tastes and underlining her refusal to live in an apartment that was a clone of a hundred others. On the walls were black and white framed photos dating back to the late 1800s. The pictures had been passed down through her family for generations, and they explained her mixed heritage of African-American, Irish, and Spanish. That and her clear, caramel-hued skin, dark eyes, narrow nose and silky, naturally curly hair that when blown straight, reached to the middle of her back.

In the kitchen Alexis noticed an expensive pair of gold hoop earrings lying on the breakfast bar and picked them up. She knew that Kevin had left them for her to soften the blow of waking up alone again. She gently slid each earring through her pierced lobes, and thought of the man who had left them. Kevin was always doing sweet and thoughtful things like this, leaving little notes or gifts for her to find upon waking up. Alexis enjoyed such things, but she knew they were just attempts to mollify her mounting frustration. She would have much preferred to wake up in Kevin's arms instead of next to an empty pillow.

Kevin was everything that Alexis had always thought she wanted in a man. She had been instantly attracted to him when they met in of all places, the grocery store. She clearly remembered the moment she saw the smooth skinned, chocolate-brown man with the chiseled features, clean-shaven face and hazel eyes reading the back of a box of dryer sheets. He had taken her breath away, and she had nearly crashed her cart into the laundry-detergent display. After getting to know him, Alexis found that, aside from being the most beautiful man she had ever seen, he was caring, sensitive, funny, an attentive lover and was a successful businessman as well. As the head of his own public-relations firm, he represented many of Detroit's most prominent figures and earned six figures a year. In addition, he was free to make his own work schedule. He wanted kids and even expected to be married some day. On paper, he sounded like the type of strong, independent and focused man that her mother, Dana, had always hoped and prayed her daughter would find. But in reality and in the cold light of day, there were problems with their relationship. Kevin's frequent disappearing acts were just the tip of the iceberg. They rarely went out and spent most of their time together eating takeout and watching DVDs in Alexis' apartment. When they did go out on a real date, it was somewhere so far outside of the city it was like being in another world. Kevin had never taken her to his home or to meet his parents, nor had he ever offered to.

Alexis knew all the signs were there, but she just didn't want to face them. She liked Kevin too much to believe, a la *Sex and the City*, that he "just wasn't that into her". Everything pointed to the obvious, but she believed the good outweighed the bad. He called daily, sent flowers often and when they were together it was as if they were the only two people on planet Earth.

Alexis sighed, flopped down on the couch and clutched a midnight-blue and camel silk pillow to her stomach. Her conscious was trying to tell her that Kevin wasn't right for her, but her heart refused to listen. As always she wanted it to work and she wanted it to work right now. Ever since she was a little girl, she had wanted to have a lifelong love like that of her parents. Married thirty years, Dana and Isaiah Hunter met during their senior year of high school and had been together ever since. Their life had its ups and downs, its laughter and tears, but it was full and complete as long as they had each other. That's what Alexis yearned for, but thus far she had failed to make it happen.

Her history with men was not very encouraging, to say the least. It seemed as if the wrong men were drawn to her and Alexis to them. She had dated the drug dealers, the women beaters; the ones with baby-mama dramas and the ones who couldn't, or wouldn't, keep their dicks in their pants. She had been used and abused so many times that when Kevin came along with all the right credentials and goals, she refused to see the problems that were so apparent to everyone else. After all, of the three children her mother and father shared, she was the only one who wasn't seriously attached. Her brother, Aaron, had married two weeks after she graduated from college and her sister Alicia, though only a college sophomore, was planning her wedding for just a month and a half away.

The ringing phone jerked Alexis back to reality. She lifted the receiver off its base and reading the caller ID smiled when she recognized the coming call from her longtime best friend and confidant.

"What do you want?" Alexis asked Claire jokingly.

"Someone's in a funky mood this morning. Houdini must have pulled another one of his little magic tricks," Claire laughed.

Alexis threw the pillow to the side, and climbed off the couch. Returning to the kitchen, she poured herself a glass of orange juice. "Ha, ha, aren't you a regular Dave Chappelle today. Are they giving you a show on *Comedy Central* or will you stick to holding your sign off I-96? Will Tell Jokes For Food."

"Yeah, your attitude really is nasty today, so I know I must be right."

"Look, I haven't got time to play your little games, so let's cut this short. What did you call my house this early in the morning for?" Finishing the orange juice, Alexis rinsed the glass and placed it in the dishwasher.

"I called to tell you that everything is set for the trip. We will be leaving on Thursday and the first concert starts the next day. We reserved a room at the Ramada Plaza right on Bourbon Street. We're not going—"

"What do you mean one room?" Alexis asked loudly, cutting Claire off. "Three people are coming right? And I know how you can be. I am not going to have to sleep in the lobby when you bring some local back to the room. No, I don't think so. I want my own room where I can have some rest and relaxation! I'm sure Morgan feels the same way with her overly-in-love ass." By now Alexis was checking herself in the bathroom mirror to make sure Kevin hadn't left any marks on her body as he had done the last time. She had made it a point of telling him that she was not a child and that if he wanted to mark his territory, he would have to do it by making a commitment, not by leaving tacky marks on her neck in the middle of summer.

"You're one to talk. Always making excuses for Kevin. Anyway, Ms. High and Mighty, all the hotel rooms are booked for that weekend, and if you can find something else in that area and for that price, *please* be my guest. Don't you think I would rather have my own room? All your granny-acting ass is going to do is cramp my style, anyway. Talking about getting some rest and relaxation in New Orleans! There is something seriously wrong with you. We are going to Crescent City, the Big Easy. We are not going to sleep; we are going to party and if you are going down there for any other reason than that, then you should stay home and knit."

Alexis laughed and remembered why Claire was her best friend. She had the balls to tell not just Alexis but everyone how she saw it and didn't care what someone thought afterward. She was honest, blunt and straight to the point. Alexis thought that every woman needed a Claire in her life.

"Anyway," Claire continued, "we are going down there to celebrate your birthday, so *you* of all people should be planning to have the time of your life. And again, *you* of all people should be trying to find a local to have a little fling with, considering what you have—Or rather don't have at home."

In that moment Alexis regretted ever telling Claire anything about Kevin and his highly suspect behavior. Claire reminded her of the fact that though Kevin had the means, he was oftentimes less than attentive, and she was of the mind that he either had someone on the side or was on the downlow. Alexis personally thought Claire had been watching entirely too much *Oprah*.

"Okay, well, whatever you think is irrelevant to me right now. I am not that kind of girl, and I am going down to New Orleans to hear some great music, go sightseeing, eat some awesome food and shop. Notice how I didn't include boning the first Southern guy that crosses my path on my itinerary," Alexis said a matter-of-factly as she searched through her closet for her favorite fuchsia-and-white yoga outfit.

"Alexis, you are so stuck up that it's disgusting. Anyway, as I was saying before I was so rudely interrupted, we are not going to all the concerts because some of them aren't that great, unless you're a baby boomer. Friday on they have Destiny's Child and Floetry on the main stage. Then they have Alicia Keys and John Legend. Sunday, Kanye West and Common will be performing. Since you are off work the entire summer we figured that we would stay an extra day and leave Tuesday morning. "

That was what Alexis loved about teaching—all the time off. She looked forward to summer vacation and always used that time to do the things she hadn't the time to do during the school year. Traveling was one of those things. Thinking about the upcoming trip, Alexis couldn't help but smile. Leave it up to her girls, Claire and Morgan, to plan the trip to end all trips. She had always wanted to go back to New Orleans, and had fond memories of the time the three traveled down to the Big Easy for Mardi Gras during their junior year of college. That had been a trip they would never forget. The wild things that had happened there always put smiles on their faces but would have to remain there. *What happens in New Orleans stays in New Orleans.*

"Claire, this trip is going to be great. Thank you so much for planning it," Alexis said sincerely.

"No problem; that's what best friends are for. Just remember to keep your ass out of that hotel room and in the streets with Morgan and me and you will be fine." With that, Claire slammed down the phone in Alexis's ear, praying that her friend wouldn't ruin the trip she'd so painstakingly planned.

Returning home from the gym, Alexis felt relaxed and rejuvenated; yoga usually did that for her. Not only was it a good workout that kept her 5'6-125-pound frame toned, it also helped her to clear her mind and make her more focused. She needed this degree of focus to deal with Kevin, having decided to call him and find out what plans he had for the evening. She wanted to spend as much time with him as possible in the two and a half days before leaving for New Orleans, but more importantly, she wanted to find out what excuse he had for leaving her bed this time.

Alexis threw her gym bag onto the navy, camel and white checkered duvet cover and picked up the cordless phone from the glass end table next to her bed. She dialed Kevin's cell number, and he picked up after the fourth ring.

"Kevin Washington," Kevin's deep baritone voice did things to her body that no one else's had ever come close to. Just hearing it made her tingle and she was instantly aroused.

"Hi, baby. How are you?" Alexis asked, trying to match the sexy timbre of his voice.

"I'm good. Busy. I'm sorry about this morning, but I had an early meeting and I didn't bring my suit over to your place last night. You know how my memory is."

"I know, I know. But it would be nice if we could spend just one *full* night together every once in a while." Alexis inserted a pout into her voice and hoped he heard the disappointment.

"It's coming, baby, I promise. But work has been so hectic these past few months. Trying to land this new account has left me little to no free time. As soon as all this madness is over, I'll take you anywhere you want to go. Paris, Spain, sky's the limit," Kevin said trying to pacify Alexis yet again.

"I don't need all that, Kevin. I will be completely satisfied if you would just stay the entire night with me. I mean, we have been pretty serious for six months now and every time we make love, you take off like a thief in the night. I'm beginning to think that something is going on."

"Alexis, I can assure you that nothing is going on. As I said before, I'm just really swamped at work. Anyway, on a more pleasant note, I'll be over tonight around seven with your birthday present."

"Kevin, how many times do I have to tell you not to get me anything?" she asked firmly, even though she was already excited about the promised gift. Maybe it would match the earrings he'd left that morning.

"I can't help it. You are so wonderful, and it's the least I can do. I love to see you smile. I'll see you soon."

Alexis hit the end button on her phone and sighed. Kevin always knew exactly what to say to make her forget her anger and disappointment. But none of that really mattered because the right words or not, she still had that nagging feeling in the pit of her stomach that something was not quite right with their relationship.

2007 Publication Schedule

January

Corporate Seduction
A.C. Arthur
ISBN-13: 978-1-58571-238-0
ISBN-10: 1-58571-238-8
$9.95

A Taste of Temptation
Reneé Alexis
ISBN-13: 978-1-58571-207-6
ISBN-10: 1-58571-207-8
$9.95

February

The Perfect Frame
Beverly Clark
ISBN-13: 978-1-58571-240-3
ISBN-10: 1-58571-240-X
$9.95

Ebony Angel
Deatri King-Bey
ISBN-13: 978-1-58571-239-7
ISBN-10: 1-58571-239-6
$9.95

March

Sweet Sensations
Gwendolyn Bolton
ISBN-13: 978-1-58571-206-9
ISBN-10: 1-58571-206-X
$9.95

Crush
Crystal Hubbard
ISBN-13: 978-1-58571-243-4
ISBN-10: 1-58571-243-4
$9.95

April

Secret Thunder
Annetta P. Lee
ISBN-13: 978-1-58571-204-5
ISBN-10: 1-58571-204-3
$9.95

Blood Seduction
J.M. Jeffries
ISBN-13: 978-1-58571-237-3
ISBN-10: 1-58571-237-X
$9.95

May

Lies Too Long
Pamela Ridley
ISBN-13: 978-1-58571-246-5
ISBN-10: 1-58571-246-9
$13.95

Two Sides to Every Story
Dyanne Davis
ISBN-13: 978-1-58571-248-9
ISBN-10: 1-58571-248-5
$9.95

June

One of These Days
Michele Sudler
ISBN-13: 978-1-58571-249-6
ISBN-10: 1-58571-249-3
$9.95

Who's That Lady?
Andrea Jackson
ISBN-13: 978-1-58571-190-1
ISBN-10: 1-58571-190-X
$9.95

2007 Publication Schedule (continued)

July

Heart of the Phoenix
A.C. Arthur
ISBN-13: 978-1-58571-242-7
ISBN-10: 1-58571-242-6
$9.95

Do Over
Celya Bowers
ISBN-13: 978-1-58571-241-0
ISBN-10: 1-58571-241-8
$9.95

It's Not Over Yet
J.J. Michael
ISBN-13: 978-1-58571-245-8
ISBN-10: 1-58571-245-0
$9.95

August

The Fires Within
Beverly Clark
ISBN-13: 978-1-58571-244-1
ISBN-10: 1-58571-244-2
$9.95

Stolen Kisses
Dominiqua Douglas
ISBN-13: 978-1-58571-247-2
ISBN-10: 1-58571-247-7
$9.95

September

Small Whispers
Annetta P. Lee
ISBN-13: 978-158571-251-9
ISBN-10: 1-58571-251-5
$6.99

Always You
Crystal Hubbard
ISBN-13: 978-158571-252-6
ISBN-10: 1-58571-252-3
$6.99

October

Not His Type
Chamein Canton
ISBN-13: 978-158571-253-3
ISBN-10: 1-58571-253-1
$6.99

Many Shades of Gray
Dyanne Davis
ISBN-13: 978-158571-254-0
ISBN-10: 1-58571-254-X
$6.99

November

When I'm With You
LaConnie Taylor-Jones
ISBN-13: 978-158571-250-2
ISBN-10: 1-58571-250-7
$6.99

The Mission
Pamela Leigh Starr
ISBN-13: 978-158571-255-7
ISBN-10: 1-58571-255-8
$6.99

December

One in A Million
Barbara Keaton
ISBN-13: 978-158571-257-1
ISBN-10: 1-58571-257-4
$6.99

The Foursome
Celya Bowers
ISBN-13: 978-158571-256-4
ISBN-10: 1-58571-256-6
$6.99

Other Genesis Press, Inc. Titles (continued)

Echoes of Yesterday	Beverly Clark	$9.95
Eden's Garden	Elizabeth Rose	$8.95
Enchanted Desire	Wanda Y. Thomas	$9.95
Everlastin' Love	Gay G. Gunn	$8.95
Everlasting Moments	Dorothy Elizabeth Love	$8.95
Everything and More	Sinclair Lebeau	$8.95
Everything but Love	Natalie Dunbar	$8.95
Eve's Prescription	Edwina Martin Arnold	$8.95
Falling	Natalie Dunbar	$9.95
Fate	Pamela Leigh Starr	$8.95
Finding Isabella	A.J. Garrotto	$8.95
Forbidden Quest	Dar Tomlinson	$10.95
Forever Love	Wanda Thomas	$8.95
From the Ashes	Kathleen Suzanne	$8.95
	Jeanne Sumerix	
Gentle Yearning	Rochelle Alers	$10.95
Glory of Love	Sinclair LeBeau	$10.95
Go Gentle into that Good Night	Malcom Boyd	$12.95
Goldengroove	Mary Beth Craft	$16.95
Groove, Bang, and Jive	Steve Cannon	$8.99
Hand in Glove	Andrea Jackson	$9.95
Hard to Love	Kimberley White	$9.95
Hart & Soul	Angie Daniels	$8.95
Havana Sunrise	Kymberly Hunt	$9.95
Heartbeat	Stephanie Bedwell-Grime	$8.95
Hearts Remember	M. Loui Quezada	$8.95
Hidden Memories	Robin Allen	$10.95
Higher Ground	Leah Latimer	$19.95
Hitler, the War, and the Pope	Ronald Rychiak	$26.95
How to Write a Romance	Kathryn Falk	$18.95
I Married a Reclining Chair	Lisa M. Fuhs	$8.95
I'm Gonna Make You Love Me	Gwyneth Bolton	$9.95
Indigo After Dark Vol. I	Nia Dixon/Angelique	$10.95

Other Genesis Press, Inc. Titles (continued)

Other Genesis Press, Inc. Titles (continued)

Matters of Life and Death	Lesego Malepe, Ph.D.	$15.95
Meant to Be	Jeanne Sumerix	$8.95
Midnight Clear (Anthology)	Leslie Esdaile	$10.95
	Gwynne Forster	
	Carmen Green	
	Monica Jackson	
Midnight Magic	Gwynne Forster	$8.95
Midnight Peril	Vicki Andrews	$10.95
Misconceptions	Pamela Leigh Starr	$9.95
Misty Blue	Dyanne Davis	$9.95
Montgomery's Children	Richard Perry	$14.95
My Buffalo Soldier	Barbara B. K. Reeves	$8.95
Naked Soul	Gwynne Forster	$8.95
Next to Last Chance	Louisa Dixon	$24.95
Nights Over Egypt	Barbara Keaton	$9.95
No Apologies	Seressia Glass	$8.95
No Commitment Required	Seressia Glass	$8.95
No Ordinary Love	Angela Weaver	$9.95
No Regrets	Mildred E. Riley	$8.95
Notes When Summer Ends	Beverly Lauderdale	$12.95
Nowhere to Run	Gay G. Gunn	$10.95
O Bed! O Breakfast!	Rob Kuehnle	$14.95
Object of His Desire	A. C. Arthur	$8.95
Office Policy	A. C. Arthur	$9.95
Once in a Blue Moon	Dorianne Cole	$9.95
One Day at a Time	Bella McFarland	$8.95
Only You	Crystal Hubbard	$9.95
Outside Chance	Louisa Dixon	$24.95
Passion	T.T. Henderson	$10.95
Passion's Blood	Cherif Fortin	$22.95
Passion's Journey	Wanda Thomas	$8.95
Past Promises	Jahmel West	$8.95
Path of Fire	T.T. Henderson	$8.95

Other Genesis Press, Inc. Titles (continued)

Other Genesis Press, Inc. Titles (continued)

THE FOURSOME

Order Form

Mail to: Genesis Press, Inc.
P.O. Box 101
Columbus, MS 39703

Name _____
Address _____
City/State _____ Zip _____
Telephone _____

Ship to (if different from above)
Name _____
Address _____
City/State _____ Zip _____
Telephone _____

Credit Card Information
Credit Card # _____ ☐Visa   ☐Mastercard
Expiration Date (mm/yy) _____ ☐AmEx   ☐Discover

Qty.	Author	Title	Price	Total

Use this order form, or call 1-888-INDIGO-1	Total for books _____
	Shipping and handling:
	$5 first two books,
	$1 each additional book _____
	Total S & H _____
	Total amount enclosed _____
	Mississippi residents add 7% sales tax